Praise for the
#1 *New York Times* bestselling author
Debbie Macomber

"It's easy to see why Macomber is a perennial favorite: she writes great books."
—RomanceJunkies.com

"There are a few things I know when I settle into my favorite chair to read one of Debbie Macomber's books: sleep is overrated, popcorn is considered a dinner delicacy in some circles and finally, this book's gonna be great."
—ArmchairInterviews.com

"Debbie Macomber writes characters who are as warm and funny as your best friends."
—New York Times bestselling author Susan Wiggs

"Macomber's assured storytelling and affirming narrative are as welcoming as your favorite easy chair."
—Publishers Weekly on *Twenty Wishes*

"[Debbie Macomber] demonstrates her impressive skills with characterization and her flair for humor."
—RT Book Reviews

"Debbie Macomber is one of the most reliable, versatile romance authors around. Whether she's writing light-hearted romps or more serious relationship books, her novels are always engaging stories that accurately capture the foibles of real-life men and women with warmth and humor."
—Milwaukee Journal Sentinel

"Popular romance author Debbie Macomber has a gift for evoking the emotions that are at the heart of the genre's popularity."
—Publishers Weekly

February 2015

Dear Friends,

Years ago, back in the mid-1980s, I wrote three books that were modern-day versions of classic fairy tales. The first two were republished a few years ago in a volume called *Fairy Tale Weddings*. The third story, *Almost Paradise*, is the retelling of Snow White. However, in this instance, the little people aren't dwarves. Instead they're young girls, and Snow White (Sherry, in my version of the famous tale) is a counselor at a summer camp. Oh, there's a prince involved, all right, although he doesn't appear to be one in the beginning... I won't tell you any more. It's tempting to tell you the entire plot, but I'll restrain myself. The rest of the story is for you to discover!

The other book in this volume is a classic love story of love gone wrong—with a bit of a twist. Boy meets girl, boy marries girl, boy leaves girl. Girl is frustrated and angry, boy returns... Oops, I'm doing it again, outlining the whole plot. So once again, you'll have no option but to read the story.

You can reach me at my website, debbiemacomber.com, or on Facebook, or write me at PO Box 1458, Port Orchard, WA 98366. And yes, I read every single letter and guest-book post. Your feedback is important to me!

I hope you enjoy *The Reluctant Groom*.

Warmest regards,

Debbie Macomber

DEBBIE MACOMBER

The Reluctant Groom

MIRA®

MIRA

ISBN-13: 978-0-7783-1741-8

Recycling programs for this product may not exist in your area.

The Reluctant Groom

Copyright © 2015 by Harlequin Books S.A.

The publisher acknowledges the copyright holder of the individual works as follows:

All Things Considered
Copyright © 1987 by Debbie Macomber

Almost Paradise
Copyright © 1988 by Debbie Macomber

For Lisa Jackson and Nancy Bush,
friends through the years from the '80s and together still.

Also by Debbie Macomber

Blossom Street Books

The Shop on Blossom Street
A Good Yarn
Susannah's Garden
Back on Blossom Street
Twenty Wishes
Summer on Blossom Street
Hannah's List
The Knitting Diaries
 "The Twenty-First Wish"
A Turn in the Road

Cedar Cove Books

16 Lighthouse Road
204 Rosewood Lane
311 Pelican Court
44 Cranberry Point
50 Harbor Street
6 Rainier Drive
74 Seaside Avenue
8 Sandpiper Way
92 Pacific Boulevard
1022 Evergreen Place
Christmas in Cedar Cove
 (*5-B Poppy Lane* and
 A Cedar Cove Christmas)
1105 Yakima Street
1225 Christmas Tree Lane

Dakota Series

Dakota Born
Dakota Home
Always Dakota
Buffalo Valley

The Manning Family

The Manning Sisters
The Manning Brides
The Manning Grooms

Christmas Books

A Gift to Last
On a Snowy Night
Home for the Holidays
Glad Tidings
Christmas Wishes
Small Town Christmas
When Christmas Comes
 (now retitled *Trading*
 Christmas)
There's Something About
 Christmas
Christmas Letters
Where Angels Go
The Perfect Christmas
Choir of Angels
 (*Shirley, Goodness and Mercy*,
 Those Christmas Angels and
 Where Angels Go)
Call Me Mrs. Miracle

Heart of Texas Series

VOLUME 1
 (*Lonesome Cowboy* and
 Texas Two-Step)
VOLUME 2
 (*Caroline's Child* and
 Dr. Texas)
VOLUME 3
 (*Nell's Cowboy* and
 Lone Star Baby)
Promise, Texas
Return to Promise

CONTENTS

ALL THINGS CONSIDERED

One

Lanni Matthiessen dropped a quarter into the machine and waited for the thick black coffee to pour into the wax-coated cup. It would be another late night at John L. Benton Realty and the coffee would have to hold her until she had time to squeeze in dinner. A frown compressed her brow. This would be the third evening this week that she wouldn't be eating with Jenny, her four-year-old daughter.

Carrying the steaming cup of coffee back to her desk, she sat and reached for her phone, punching out the number with practiced ease.

Her sister answered on the second ring. "Jade here."

"Lanni here." She smiled absently. Her sister was oftentimes as fun-loving as her four-year-old daughter. Jade picked up Jenny from the day-care center and then stayed with her until Lanni arrived home.

"Don't tell me you're going to be late again," Jade groaned.

Lanni's frustration echoed her younger sister's. "I just got a call from the Baileys. They want to come in and put down earnest money on the Rudicelli house."

"But, Lanni, this is the third night this week that you've been working late."

"I know. I'm sorry."

"If this gets any worse I might as well move in with you."

"You know I'd like it if you did." If Jade were there, the nights wouldn't be so lonely and she wouldn't have to listen to her own thoughts rummaging around in her troubled mind.

"No way, José," Jade argued. "This girl is on her own. I like my freedom."

Looping the thick swatch of honey-colored hair around the back of her ear, Lanni released a tired sigh. "I shouldn't be too late. An hour, maybe two. Tell Jenny I'll read her favorite bedtime story to her when I get home."

"Do you want to talk to her? She's swinging in the backyard."

"No," Lanni shook her head as she spoke. "Let her play. But be sure to tell her how much I love her."

"I will. Just don't be too late. If you leave me around here long, I'll start daydreaming about food and before I know what's come over me, I'll be eating."

Lanni's sister continually struggled with her excess weight. She claimed there wasn't a diet around that she hadn't tried. Lanni had watched her sister count calories, carbohydrates, grams and chocolate chips all to no avail. She wished she could lose those extra fifteen pounds for Jade. Her problem was just the opposite—too many missed meals and too little appetite left her as slender as a reed. She preferred to think of herself as svelte, but even Lanni admitted that she'd look better carrying a few extra pounds. When Judd had lived with them, she'd had plenty of reason to cook decent meals....

Momentarily she closed her eyes as the rush of remembered pain washed over her. Two years had passed and she still couldn't think of Judd without reliving the hurt and regrets of his departure. With no more reason than he felt it was time to move on, Judd had expected her to uproot their lives and follow him to only God knew where. Even Judd didn't know where he was headed. Lanni had refused—one of them had to behave like an adult. She wouldn't leave her family and everything she held dear to traipse around the world with Judd as though life were some wild adventure and the whole world lay waiting to be explored. Judd had responsibilities, too, although he refused to own up to them.

In the end he'd given her no option but to file for a divorce and yet when she did, he hadn't bothered to sign the papers. Lanni hadn't pursued the issue, which only went to prove that the emotional bond that linked her to Judd was as strong as when he'd left. She recognized deep within her heart that her marriage was dead, only she hadn't fully accepted their failure. She had no intention of remarrying. Some people fit nicely into married life, Lanni just wasn't one of them. Marriage to another man was out of the question. The thought of suffering through that kind of emotional warfare again was beyond consideration. She'd been married once and it was enough to cure her for a lifetime. She had Jenny, and her daughter was the most important person in her life.

The intercom on her desk buzzed and the receptionist's voice announced, "The Baileys are here."

"Thank you, Joan. Could you send them in?"

Lanni took the first sip of her coffee and her long,

curling lashes brushed her cheek as she attempted to push the memories to the back of her mind. She wished she could hate Judd and cast him from her thoughts as effectively as he'd walked out on her and Jenny. But part of him remained with her every day as a constant reminder of her life's one colossal failure…her marriage.

Setting aside the cup, she stood and forced a smile as she prepared to meet her clients.

By the time Lanni pulled into her driveway in Burien, a suburb of south Seattle, it was after seven. Everything had gone smoothly with the Baileys and Lanni experienced a sensation of pride and accomplishment. The Bailey family had specific needs in a new home and Lanni had worked with them for several weeks in an effort to find the house that would fulfill their unusual requirements.

Now she prepared herself to meet Jenny's needs. A four-year-old had the right to expect her mother's undivided attention at the end of the day. Unfortunately Lanni wanted to do nothing more than relax and take a nice hot soak in the bathtub. She would, but not until after she'd read to Jenny as she'd promised and tucked her daughter in for the night.

A note on the kitchen counter informed her that Jade had taken the little girl for a walk. No sooner had Lanni finished reading the message when the screen door swung open and her young daughter came roaring into the kitchen. Chocolate ice cream was smeared across her face and Jenny broke into an eager grin as she hurried toward her mother.

"How's my girl?" Lanni asked, lifting the child into her arms and having trouble finding a place on the plump cheek that wasn't smudged with chocolate.

"Auntie Jade took me out for an ice-cream cone."

"So I see."

Jade followed on her heels, her face red from the exertion of chasing after a lively four-year-old. "I thought the exercise would do me good. Unfortunately some internal homing device led me to a Baskin & Robbins."

"Jade!"

"I couldn't help it," she pleaded, her hazel-green eyes rounding. "After eating tofu on a rye crisp for dinner, I felt I deserved a reward."

In spite of her effort not to, Lanni laughed. "The ice cream isn't going to help your diet."

"Sure it is. Jenny and I walked a good mile. According to my calculations, I could have had a double-decker for the energy expended in the walk."

"You *did* eat a double-decker, Aunt Jade."

Placing her hand on her hip, Jade looked at the little girl and shook her head. "Tattletale."

"Oops." Jenny placed her small hand over her chocolate-covered mouth. "I wasn't supposed to tell, was I?"

"I'll forgive you this time," Jade said seriously, but her eyes sparkled with laughter.

Taking out a fresh cloth, Lanni wet it under warm water from the kitchen faucet and proceeded to wipe off Jenny's face. She squirmed uncomfortably until Lanni completed the task. "Isn't it time for your bath, young lady?"

Lanni found it a little unusual that Jade lingered through Jenny's bath and story time, but was grateful for the company and didn't comment. She found her sister in the kitchen after Jenny was in bed.

"Did you have a chance to eat?" Jade asked, staring into the open refrigerator.

"Not yet. I'll scramble some eggs later."

"Sure you will." Jade closed the refrigerator and took a seat at the kitchen table, reaching for a soda cracker. She stared at the intricate holes, then set the cracker aside.

"You know," Lanni commented, hiding a smile. "It suddenly dawned on me. For all your dieting, you should be thin enough to dangle from a charm bracelet."

"Should be," Jade grumbled. As if to make up for lost time, she popped the soda cracker into her mouth.

Lanni laughed outright, and reached for the box, tucking it back inside the cupboard to remove temptation. Without bothering to ask, she poured her sister a cup of spiced tea and delivered it to the table.

"Jenny asked about Judd again," her sister stated with little preamble.

"Again?" Lanni felt her stomach tighten with dread.

"She talks about him all the time. Surely you've noticed."

Lanni had. She'd answered her daughter's questions with saintly patience, hoping to satisfy her curiosity. In the beginning Jenny's questions had been innocent enough. She wanted to know her father's name and where he lived. Lanni had shown the little girl a map of the world and pointed to both the state of Alaska and lush oil fields of the Middle East. The last she'd heard, Judd was somewhere over there. No doubt he'd collected his own harem of adoring females by now. Lanni winced, angry with herself that the thought of Judd with another woman still had the power to hurt so painfully.

The following week Jenny had wanted a picture of Judd to keep on her nightstand. Reluctantly Lanni gave her daughter a small five-by-seven photograph. The image captured was of Lanni and Judd standing on the front lawn near the blooming flowerbeds. Jenny was only a few months old at the time the picture was taken, and Judd held her, smiling proudly into the camera. It nipped at Lanni's heart every time she looked at the photo with their smiling, innocent faces. Their happiness had been short-lived at best.

For a time the picture had satisfied Jenny's inquisitiveness, but apparently it wasn't enough. Jenny wanted more, and Lanni doubted that she could give it to her.

She hadn't really known Judd. It wasn't until after they'd married that Lanni realized that she was head-over-heels in love with a stranger. The details of his past were sketchy. She knew little of his life other than the few tidbits he let drop now and then. His mother had died when he was young and he'd been raised on a ranch in Montana. His father had never remarried....

"Her teacher told me Jenny's been bragging to the other children that Judd's an astronaut."

"Oh no." With all the pressure of being a single parent weighing heavily upon her shoulders, Lanni claimed the seat opposite her sister and slumped forward, holding up her forehead with the heel of her hand. "She knows that's not true."

"Of course she does. The poor kid sees her friends' fathers pick them up every night. It's only natural she'd make up an excuse why her own doesn't."

"Lying isn't natural." Depressed, Lanni released a heartfelt sigh. "I'll have another talk with her in the morning."

"What are you going to tell her?"

"I don't know."

Jade's brows drew together in a frown. "The truth?"

"No." She couldn't. The naked facts would hurt too much. She was a mature adult, but the day Judd left them had devastated her. She refused to inflict that kind of pain on her own daughter.

The real problem was that Lanni didn't know how to explain the events that had led up to the separation. Judd found Seattle stifling and claimed it didn't offer him the challenges he needed. He'd built his reputation as a pipefitter in Alaska and the Middle East and he wanted to return there. When she wouldn't go with him, Judd left on his own, emotionally deserting Lanni and Jenny.

Lanni couldn't tell Jenny that her father had walked out on them. For a long time after Judd had gone, Lanni wanted to hate him—but she couldn't. Not when she continued to love him.

"Do you know what the truth is anymore, Lanni? There are two sides to everything."

Lanni was shocked. Next to Judd, Jade was probably the only other person who knew everything that had happened in her marriage. Even her parents weren't aware of all the details. Now her sister seemed to be implying that there was something more. "Of course I do." Her eyes fell to the round table. But sometimes the truth had a way of coming back to haunt a person, she reflected. It was times like these—when Lanni learned that her daughter had lied about Judd—that she wondered if she'd made the right decision. Her thoughts spun ahead and returned filled with self-recriminations. Judd had loved her, Lanni couldn't doubt that. For months after he'd left, he'd written her; each letter filled with enthusiasm for Alaska, requesting her to bring Jenny and join him. His declarations of love for her and their daughter had ripped at Lanni's heart.

Her decision had been made, she wasn't leaving Seattle and no matter what she said or did, Judd refused to accept the fact. After a while Lanni couldn't bear to read his letters anymore and had returned them un-opened.

Standing, Jade brought her untouched tea to the counter. "I can see you've got lots to think about. I'll see you tomorrow, but call me if you need anything."

Joining her sister, Lanni gave her a small hug. "I will. Thanks, Jade." She followed her sister to the front room.

"Anytime."

The door made a clicking sound as it closed after Jade. Both her sister and her daughter had brought Judd to the forefront of her thoughts. She stood alone in the middle of the darkened living room as a numb sensation worked its way down her arms, stopping at her finger-tips. The tingling produced a chill that cut all the way through her bones.

She wasn't going to think about Judd. She refused to remember his exquisite touch and the velvet-smooth sensations he wrapped around her every time they made love. She could have died from the ecstasy she discov-ered in his arms, but the price had been far too precious. He demanded her pride and everything she held dear. She couldn't leave her family and friends and every-thing that was comfortable and familiar.

The pain was as fresh that moment as it had been the day he walked out. Trapped in the memory, Lanni swal-lowed convulsively. Tightening her hands into small fists, she breathed out slowly, turned and moved into the cozy bathroom to fill the tub with steaming hot water. She'd soak Judd out of her system, erase his indelible mark from her skin and do her best to forget.

Only it didn't work that way. She eased her lithe frame into the bubbly hot water and scooted down into its inviting warmth. Leaning her head against the back of the tub, Lanni closed her eyes. Almost immediately depression swamped her.

Unbidden, the memories returned. In vivid detail Lanni remembered the day Jenny was born and the tears that had filled Judd's eyes when the nurse placed his newborn daughter in his arms. Judd had looked down upon the wrinkled pink face with such tenderness that she hadn't been able to take her eyes from the awe expressed in his face. Later, after she'd been wheeled into her hospital room, Judd had joined her.

To this day Lanni remembered the look of intense pride as he pulled out the chair and reached for her hand.

"You're sure you're all right?"

She'd smiled tenderly. "I feel wonderful. Oh, Judd, she's so beautiful."

Love and tenderness glowed from his warm, brown eyes. "I don't think I've seen anything so small."

"She'll grow," Lanni promised.

"I don't mind telling you that for a few minutes there I was terrified." His gaze darkened with remembered doubts so uncharacteristic of the man who buried his feelings. "It seemed like a miracle when the nurse handed her to me." His smile was warm. Once again, he appeared shaken by the enormity of the emotion that shook him. "But, Lanni, I'll never make you suffer like that again. I love you too much."

She'd endured hours of hard labor and had been absorbed so deeply in her own pain that she hadn't considered what torment Judd had endured. "Darling, every woman goes through this in childbirth. It's a natural part of life. I didn't mind."

Standing, he leaned over her and very gently kissed her brow. "I love you, Lanni."

"I know." The moment was poignant, but Lanni

couldn't stifle a yawn. She felt wonderful, but exhausted. Despite her efforts to stay awake and talk to her husband, her eyelids felt as though they had weights tugging them closed. "I'm sorry, Judd…" she paused to yawn again, covering her mouth with the back of her hand "…but I can't seem to stay awake."

"Sleep, little mother," he whispered close to her ear. "Sleep."

Lanni did, for hours and hours. When she stirred, the first thing she noticed was Judd sprawled in the chair by the window. He had slouched down in what appeared to be an unlikely position for anyone to sleep comfortably. His head lolled to one side and a thick latch of dark hair fell across his wide brow. His arm hung loosely at his side; his knuckles brushed the floor.

Lanni smiled at the long form draped so haphazardly in the visitor's chair. His strong features were softened now in sleep. Lovingly, she watched the man who had come to be her world and was astonished at the swell of emotion that went through her at the memory of the new life their love had created.

Lanni blinked back her own tears. "Judd," she whispered, afraid if he slept in that position much longer he'd get a crick in his neck.

Dazed, Judd looked up and straightened. Their eyes met and as long as she lived, Lanni would remember the love that radiated from his warm, dark eyes.

The lukewarm bathwater lapped at her skin and Lanni pulled herself from thoughts of the past and into the reality that was her life now. How sad it was that a love so beautiful and pure should ever have gone so wrong.

Lanni rose from the water and reached for the thick

terry-cloth towel. Judd had been gone two years—
and in reality longer than that. The last months before
their final separation, he had been home infrequently.
He started traveling to help pay the mounting medical expenses following Jenny's birth. The money in
Alaska was good and there were even better wages,
Judd claimed, in the Middle East. Lanni had been forced
to admit that they had enough pressing bills to warrant
his taking a job elsewhere.

Dressing in her shimmery housecoat and fuzzy slippers, she crept quietly into Jenny's bedroom. The little
girl was sound asleep, curled on her side with her doll,
Betsy, tucked under her arm. Gently, Lanni brushed
the thin wisps of hair from her angelic face. Jenny was
everything that had ever been good between her and
Judd. She would always be grateful that she had this
child. She couldn't have Judd, but Jenny was all hers.

The phone pealed impatiently in the distance and
Lanni rushed from the room, not wanting the loud ring
to wake her daughter.

"Hello," she said, somewhat breathlessly.

"Hi there. It's Steve. I heard you sold the Rudicelli
house." His low voice revealed his pride in her accomplishment.

Steve Delaney was an agent in the same office as
Lanni. They'd worked together for the last year and
had become good friends, often teaming up for Bro-
ker Opens and Open Houses. Lanni wasn't interested
in becoming emotionally involved with any of her co-
workers, and she'd avoided any formal dates with Steve.
They'd gone on picnics, to a baseball game when the
office handed out free tickets, and even a couple of
lunches at a restaurant close to the office. Steve knew
Lanni was still married, but after he'd questioned her

about Judd, the Realtor seemed satisfied that the marriage was over in every way but legally.

They'd continued to see each other over the last three months and though Lanni enjoyed Steve's companionship, she wasn't interested in a deeper relationship.

Recently, however, Steve had been urging Lanni to do what she could to get the divorce business settled. He felt that she would never be able to face the future until she settled the past. Although he hadn't told her he was falling in love with her, Lanni could see it in his eyes. He wanted her marriage to Judd over so he could pursue her himself.

"I took the earnest money this afternoon," Lanni said.

"Great. It looks like I may have a buyer for the Bailey place," he said, then added thoughtfully, "Have you noticed what a good team we make?"

Lanni decided the best answer was to pretend she hadn't heard the question.

"The Baileys will be pleased." They'd made their offer on the Rudicelli house contingent on the sale of their own two-storey Colonial. Now it looked like everything was going to work out perfectly.

"I think we should celebrate."

Lanni hesitated. Lately he found more and more excuses for them to be together, so not only did they share the same office during the day, but they were seeing each other in the evenings as well. He was patient with Jenny and the two appeared to get along well.

"Don't you think it's a bit premature to celebrate?" she asked. Steve knew it was common for house deals to fall through for any number of reasons.

"Maybe, but we deserve it; just you and me, Lanni."

His voice dipped slightly. "I'll cook dinner for you at my place."

Still she hesitated. She liked Steve, but she wasn't ready for an emotional commitment and an intimate dinner together could cause problems. "Let me think on it."

"Come on, Lanni, loosen up a bit. Enjoy life."

Steve was a fun guy; she hated to disappoint him. "I don't know—we've been seeing a lot of each other recently."

Lanni could feel him weigh his words. "I haven't made any secret of how I feel about you. I'm not going to rush you into anything you don't want. I'm a patient man; you've been hurt and the last thing in the world I want to do is cause you any more pain. I enjoy your company, and I promise I'm not going to put any pressure on you. Let me pamper you the way you deserve; champagne, a candlelight dinner, music."

"Oh, Steve, I don't know." Lanni understood what made him the top salesperson for the firm. He was smooth and sincere and persuasive. And frankly, she was tempted.

"Jade could watch Jenny for one night," he coaxed. "What if I promise to have you home before midnight?"

"I'm not Cinderella."

"To me you are."

His voice was so warm and enticing that for a moment Lanni wavered. Everything she'd avoided in the last two years was facing her, demanding that she make a decision. She couldn't spend the rest of her life cooped up, afraid to trust and love again. She worked hard being the best mother and Realtor possible that it seemed her life was void of any real fun and laughter.

"Come on, Lanni," he cajoled.

Lanni squeezed her eyes shut. She thought of Jenny making up stories about her father to impress the other children. The girl needed male influence. Lanni's father was wonderful with the child, but Jenny seemed to require someone more than a grandfather.

"Do this for yourself," Steve prodded gently.

"I'll check with my sister and see if she can babysit," Lanni murmured, succumbing.

"That's my girl," Steve murmured, obviously pleased.

They spoke for only a few minutes longer, but by the time Lanni replaced the receiver she was convinced she'd done the wrong thing to accept Steve's invitation. The problem with Jenny lying at the preschool had made Lanni vulnerable.

The following day, Lanni regretted her impulsive acceptance, but not to the point that she was willing to cancel the date. It put everything between her and Steve in a new light. It frightened Lanni, but at the same time she realized she couldn't torture herself with thoughts of Judd forever.

But if Lanni was amazed at herself for her willingness to trudge ahead in her relationship with Steve, she was shocked by Jade's reaction.

"Are you sure this is what you want?" Jade asked that evening when Lanni mentioned the dinner with Steve.

"I think so." Lanni was nothing if not honest.

"Why now after two long years?"

Lanni was confused herself. "Because it's time." She had come a long way this week in sorting through her feelings for Steve and she wasn't about to step back because her sister disapproved. It was true that Steve didn't inspire passion within her, but she'd had that once and now she considered it highly overrated.

Jade made a rueful sound.

"What was that all about?"

"Nothing," Jade answered with a distracted look.

Lanni's green eyes darkened. "You don't like Steve, do you?"

"He's all right." For emphasis, Jade shrugged one shoulder. "I'm just wondering what Judd would say if he knew you were romantically interested in another man."

Lanni's mouth went dry. "He probably wouldn't care. I haven't heard a word from Judd in well over a year."

"That doesn't mean he's stopped caring. He's got his pride, too. How long did you expect him to continue reaching out to you only to have you reject every attempt?"

Color blossomed in Lanni's cheeks. "He should never have left us the way he did. Believe me, I'm well aware of what Judd thinks and feels."

"How can you be so sure?"

"I just am." In an effort to disguise her dismay, Lanni stood and walked to the sliding glass door that opened onto the patio and small yard. Jenny was in her sandbox playing contentedly with her toys. "I sometimes wonder if he even thinks about Jenny and me."

"Oh, Lanni, I'm sure he does."

Folding her arms around her waist, Lanni shook her head absently. "I somehow doubt it."

"But he sends you support every month—"

"Money!" The word escaped on the tail end of a long sigh. "I'll admit he's been generous. He always was—to a fault."

"Lanni, listen." Jade nodded annoyingly and joined her sister. "I'm convinced you're wrong. Judd thinks about you all the time. He must."

"He doesn't." She dropped her hands and moved

away. "It's been two years, Jade. Two years. Time says it all. I'm having dinner with Steve; I deserve an evening out. If you won't stay with Jenny then I'll find someone else who will."

Jade's shoulders sagged in defeat. "Of course I'll sit with her."

Almost immediately, Lanni felt guilty for having snapped at her younger sister. Since Judd had left, Jade had been a godsend; Lanni would never be able to work as many hours as she did without her sister's help. "I didn't mean to be so sharp with you."

Jade's smile was instantaneous. "I only want what's best for you and Jenny." Making an effort to lighten the mood, Jade reached for a sack with a prominent department store's name boldly written across the side. "Hey, did I tell you I signed up for an aerobics class?"

"Not again." Lanni wasn't surprised at her sister's latest effort to lose weight. The last time Jade had signed up for a dance class, she'd convinced Lanni to join her. When her eyebrows started to sweat, Lanni knew it was time to quit.

"Get this," Jade added, laughing. "The lady on the phone told me to wear loose clothes. Good heavens, if I had any loose clothes I wouldn't be taking the class in the first place!"

"So what's in the sack?"

"Bodysuit, leotards, leg warmers, and a disgustingly expensive nylon jacket. The whole bit. I figure that since I spent my monthly food allowance on this outfit, everything will be loose by the time I take the first class."

"Honestly, Jade…"

Jade stopped her by holding up the palm of her hand. "This time I mean it."

Lanni had heard it all before, but nodded as seriously as possible, somehow managing not to laugh. "I know you can do it."

"Of course I can. Exercise is the answer. I'm going to stop worrying about what I eat and concentrate on the basic elements of burning calories and expending the proper amount of energy in relation to the amount of food consumed. Sounds good. Right?"

"Right."

"You don't believe me?" Jade challenged.

"I already told you I know you can do it."

"So says the woman who can live three weeks on a compliment."

"You're exaggerating."

"All right, two weeks."

"Now don't insult me by saying that if I caught a chest cold there wouldn't be any place to put it."

"In addition to no boobs, you're much too thin."

Lanni couldn't argue. "I'm working on it."

"You know what I think?"

Lanni was beginning to doubt the wisdom of asking. "What?"

"I think you and Judd should get back together. When you were pregnant with Jenny, you looked wonderful. I've never seen you happier."

The instant sorrow that engulfed her was so strong that for a moment Lanni couldn't breathe. What Jade said was true, but that happiness had been so fleeting, so fragile that it had lasted only a few months. She dropped her gaze and sadly shook her head. "It wouldn't work again. There's been too much water under the bridge, as they say. Judd's not coming back. After all this time, we'd be strangers." Probably even more so now.

"How can you be so sure?" Jade questioned softly.

"Listen," she mumbled, "do you mind if we don't talk about Judd anymore?"

"But it could help you—"

"Jade, I mean it. Enough. With Jenny bringing up his name every day and you hounding me with questions about him—it's just too much. I'm about to go crazy. We were married and we failed. I've got a fantastic little girl to remember him by, but my husband is gone. It's over and I've got a life to live."

Jade became strangely quiet and left soon after the conversation ended.

As the days progressed, Lanni's conscience didn't ease about the dinner date with Steve. A couple of times it was on the tip of her tongue to cancel, but whenever she approached him, Steve would smile and tell her how much he was looking forward to their evening together. His eyes grew tender and Lanni refused to give in to her doubts. Perhaps if she hadn't made such a big issue of it with Jade, she might have found a way to gracefully extract herself.

Thursday evening, the night of their arranged dinner, Lanni felt as nervous as a teenager on prom night. Her heart pounded with a hundred questions. By the time she was dressed, half her closet had been draped over the top of her bed. Clothes said so much and the silk dress was meant to tell Steve that she was not optimistic about this dinner and their relationship.

"What do you think?" she asked her sister, feeling painfully inadequate.

"Hey, you look great," Jade murmured, stepping back to examine Lanni.

"This isn't a time to tease. I feel terrible. A hornet's nest has taken up residence in my stomach. I can't do a thing with my hair." For years she'd worn it in the same style, parted in the middle in a smooth even line. Her honey-gold hair hung loosely, framing her oval face, and tucked in naturally just above the line of her shoulder. Judd had once told her that her hair color resembled moonbeams on a starlit night. What a terrible time to remember something like that.

"What's wrong?" Jade gave her an odd look. "You've gone pale."

Gripping the back of the kitchen chair, Lanni offered her sister a feeble smile. "I don't know that I'm doing the right thing."

"It's not too late to call it off."

The doorbell chimed.

"It's too late," Lanni said evenly. Almost two years too late.

"I'll get it." Jenny rushed past Lanni toward the front door.

Lanni cast a panicked glance in that direction. "My makeup isn't on too heavy, is it?" Her eyes begged Jade to tell her that everything was perfect.

Jade, however, appeared more interested in adding sunflower seeds to her yogurt and stirring in fresh fruit.

"Jade?" she pleaded again.

"I already told you, you look great."

"Yes, but you didn't say it with any real conviction."

Dramatically Jade placed her hand over her heart. "You look absolutely marvelous, darling."

"Mommy, Mommy—" Jenny came racing back into the kitchen. "There's a man at the door who says he's my daddy."

Two

Jenny's words hit Lanni with all the force of a wrecking ball slamming against the side of a brick building. Frantically her gaze flew to her sister as though asking Jade to tell her it wasn't true. Jade's expression was as shocked as Lanni's.

"Is he, Mommy? Is he really my daddy?" Jenny began to jump up and down all over the small kitchen. She grabbed Lanni's hand and literally dragged her into the living room.

No time was allowed for Lanni to compose herself, or collect her thoughts. Her lungs felt void of oxygen, her eyes were wide with shock. Distraught, she could find nothing to say.

"Hello, Lanni." Judd stood just inside the door, more compelling than she dared remember.

"Judd." He hadn't changed. The range of emotions that seared through her were the same as the first time she'd seen him. He was tall, and as lean as an Arctic fox. His shoulders were wide and his hips narrow. Every inch of him almost shouted of strength, stamina, and experience. There wasn't a place he hadn't been or an experience he'd bypassed along the way—including marriage.

Long hours in the sun had bronzed the angular planes of his face, creasing permanent lines on his forehead. His eyes were dark and bold, glinting with a touch of irony that told her he wouldn't be easily fooled. He knew the effect he had on her and would use it to his advantage.

Judd Matthiessen was strong-willed and had complete confidence in himself and his abilities.

In those brief seconds, Lanni knew nothing had changed about him. Nothing. He was the most devastating male she'd ever known and every prayer she'd uttered over the last two years had been for naught. She didn't want to love this man who had ripped her heart from her breast. But she had no option—she would always love him.

Only she couldn't allow him back into her life. He'd leave again and she refused to let him drag her and Jenny with him. She wasn't a camp follower. Seattle was their home; it was where they belonged—all three of them.

"Why are you here?" she demanded, her voice tight with shock.

"My father's dying."

Lanni felt her legs go weak. From what Judd had told her, the father and son had never been close. By the time Judd was eighteen he was on his own, supporting himself.

Lanni had met Judd's father when she was only a few months' pregnant with Jenny. Stuart had come to dinner at their home in Seattle. The meeting had been strained and uncomfortable; the older Matthiessen had left early. The entire evening had been spent listening to Stuart tell Judd that the time to make something of his life was now—when he had a wife and a family. He offered to support them if Judd decided to go to college. Instead of being grateful for his father's generous offer, Judd looked furious. He'd gone pale and quietly asked Stuart if he'd ever learn to accept him as he was.

After they'd separated, Lanni had written Judd's father and received a brief note in return, stating his disappointment that the marriage had failed. Conscientiously, Lanni had sent him birthday pictures of Jenny, but had never heard back from the elder Matthiessen. As far as Jenny knew, her only grandfather was Lanni's father.

"I—I'm sorry to hear about Stuart," Lanni murmured, saddened.

"I didn't think you knew him well enough to feel any sadness," Judd retorted.

Lanni stared at him, biting back angry words. For his own part, Judd's returning stare contained no emotion. He revealed no sympathy at Stuart's illness nor did he appear to feel any great sense of loss.

"Your father's illness doesn't explain why you're here," she said again, her voice gaining strength and conviction.

"Dad's never seen Jennifer."

Automatically, Lanni's arm closed around the little girl's shoulders, pressing the child closer to her side. "What has that got to do with anything? I—I've sent him pictures."

Judd's mouth thinned. "He wants to see her."

"I suppose he can come—"

"I told you he's dying. I'm taking Jennifer to him."

"No." The word wobbled out on a note of disbelief. She wouldn't let Judd take her daughter halfway across the country. Both Judd and his father were strangers to the child.

Before either of them could say anything more, the doorbell chimed again.

Jenny shot free of Lanni's grip and hurried across the room to open the front door. Steve, holding a small bouquet of pink rosebuds, stepped inside. His broad smile quickly faded as he spied the small group standing there awkwardly. Everyone's attention focused on Steve.

"Hello," he greeted cordially, and shot Lanni a questioning glance.

"Judd Matthiessen," Judd announced, stepping forward and extending his hand. "I'm Lanni's husband. Who are you?"

From the way Steve's jaw clenched, Lanni could tell that he was experiencing the same shock she'd suffered earlier. In an effort to rescue them all from further embarrassment, she accepted his flowers and smiled appreciatively. "Steve's a good friend."

"How good?" he demanded. Judd's gaze painfully pinned her to the wall, accusing her with his eyes until Lanni felt the anger swell up inside.

"That's none of your business," Lanni shot back hotly.

"Lanni and Steve were going out to dinner," Jade inserted quickly, placing a calming arm around her sister's shoulders.

"*Were* going out," Judd commented, placing heavy emphasis on the past tense. "We need to talk."

"Maybe it would be better if we arranged our dinner another night," Steve said thoughtfully. The understanding look he shared with Lanni lent her confidence. She was furious with Judd.

"Steve and I are going out," she stated with a determination few would question. "I'm ready, as you can see. Judd stopped by unannounced, so there's no reason for us to cancel our evening."

"Let me help you put the flowers in water," Steve suggested, nodding toward the kitchen.

Lanni looked blankly at the flowers in her hand, then caught a glimpse of the direction of his gaze.

"She doesn't need any help," Judd announced.

"As a matter of fact, I do," Lanni countered quietly. Steve's hand at her elbow guided her into the kitchen.

"Steve, I'm so sorry," Lanni murmured, embarrassed and miserable.

"Don't be. It isn't your fault." Steve shot a look over his shoulder before he cupped her shoulder with his hands. His dark eyes delved into hers and without a word spoken, his gaze revealed the depth of his affection. "If the truth be known, I'm glad he's here."

"But how could you when…"

"I know it's a strain on you," he said softly, encouragingly, "but now you can get those divorce papers signed and go about your life."

"I…should, shouldn't I?" Divorce was such an ugly word—Lanni hated it, but the action was necessary. She would never be emotionally free of Judd until their marriage had been legally dissolved.

"Yes, you most definitely should." He paused to kiss her forehead. "I'll leave and we can talk in the morning."

"You're a wonderful friend," Lanni told him.

Disappointment flared briefly in his eyes, but he quickly disguised it. "I want to be a whole lot more than your friend, Lanni."

"I know." She dropped her gaze, uncertain about everything at the moment.

When they returned to the living room, Judd's look was angry enough to sear a hole through them both. Steve made his excuses and left. It took all of Lanni's restraint not to whirl on Judd and ask him to leave, but that would solve nothing.

The screen door closed with hardly a sound and Jade moved into the center of the room, rubbing the palms of her hands together. "Since I'm not needed here, I'll head on over to my aerobics class."

"It was good to see you again, Jade," Judd said casually. "You're looking good."

Jade's soft chuckle filled the stark silence that enveloped the small room. "You always were my favorite brother-in-law."

"Jade!" Lanni was horrified by her own sister's lack of tact.

For the first time since his arrival Judd grinned. Lanni couldn't term it a real smile. Only one corner of his mouth edged upward, as though smiling went against his nature and he didn't do it often.

"I'm off," Jade said, walking toward the door. "I'll give you a call tomorrow."

"Goodbye, Aunt Jade." Jenny ran to the living room window and waved eagerly to her aunt.

Judd's gaze rested on the child and softened perceptively. "You've done a good job with her."

"Thank you." Her gaze flew to Jenny and she experienced anew the fierce tug of the maternal bond between mother and child.

Seeming to feel her parents' eyes, Jenny turned around. "Are you really my daddy? Mommy never said."

"I'm your daddy."

"I've been waiting to meet you."

Judd went down on one knee in front of the little girl. "And I've been waiting to see you, too."

"You don't look like your picture."

Suddenly, Lanni realized she still had the flowers in her hand. Shaking her head, she carried them into the kitchen and haphazardly placed them in a vase. After filling it with water, she set it in the middle of the kitchen table and returned to the living room.

Jenny was sitting in her father's lap and rubbing her small hands over the five o'clock shadow that covered Judd's face.

"What's this?"

"Whiskers."

"How come I don't have any?"

Judd gave another of his almost smiles. "Girls don't. Your skin will be as soft as your mother's."

"Do you have a daddy, too?"

Leave it to her astute daughter to have picked up on their earlier conversation.

"Yes." As always, whenever Judd mentioned his father, it was done briefly. For a moment Lanni thought she recognized something in those hard, dark eyes. Perhaps regret, or maybe even doubt, but she quickly dismissed the notion.

"Is your daddy sick?"

"He's dying."

Lanni wished Judd had been a bit more subtle.

"I had a goldfish who died once. We prayed over him and Mommy flushed him down the toilet."

Momentarily, Judd's gaze met Lanni's. She smiled weakly and gestured with her hand, letting him know she hadn't known what else to do.

"If your daddy dies will you get a new one, like I

got a new goldfish?" Jenny's eyes, so like her father's, stared intently at Judd's.

"No, I'm afraid not. I only have one father and you only have one father."

"You."

"That's right, Jennifer."

Lanni took a step in their direction. "I call her Jenny." Judd had no right to step into their lives like this and make demands. She regretted that Stuart was dying, but it was unreasonable for Judd to believe that she would just hand over her daughter.

"I like it when he calls me Jennifer," Jenny said, contradicting her mother.

"Right." Lanni sat on the armrest of the sofa, glaring at Judd. She was the one who was raising their child. He had a lot of nerve to waltz in without notice and start changing the way she did things.

"What took you so long to get here?" Jenny asked.

Judd's gaze fell to his daughter and softened. Although Lanni was confused by the question, Judd appeared to understand. "I was working far, far away."

"Mommy showed me on a map." She scooted off Judd's lap and raced across the room and down the hallway to her tiny bedroom. Returning a minute later, Jenny fell to her knees on the worn carpet and flipped through the pages of the atlas until she found the pages Lanni had tabbed. The little girl glanced up proudly. "Here." She pointed to the Middle Eastern country Lanni had outlined in red.

"No, I was in Mexico."

Lanni felt a wave of fresh pain. The last letter she'd received had a foreign postmark showing Saudi Arabia. "You might have let me know." She couldn't swallow down the note of bitterness that cut deep into her words.

"And have you return my letter unopened?" He hurled the angry words at her with all the force of his dominating personality. "Besides, Jade knew."

"Jade?"

"You may not have had the decency to read my letters, but Jade kept in contact with me so I knew what was happening with you and Jenny."

"You…Jade?" Lanni was stunned, utterly and completely shocked.

"You and I didn't exactly part on the best of terms," Judd murmured, his tone grim. "And you didn't seem willing to work toward a reconciliation."

"I wasn't willing to drag my daughter to some hovel while you chased rainbows. If that makes me unreasonable, then fine, I accept it—I'm unreasonable."

He recognized the hurt in her eyes and knew that nothing had changed. Several times over the last two years he'd exchanged letters with Jade, hungry for word of his wife and daughter. He couldn't be what Lanni wanted, or Stuart either, for that matter, but it didn't mean he'd stopped caring about them. Without a moment's hesitation he would have come had he been needed. Stuart wanted him now and he was on his way to his father.

Judd watched Lanni as she nervously paced around the room. Jade had sent him long letters every four months or so, but Lanni's sister had never mentioned this Steve character so Judd assumed the relationship was fairly recent.

Equal doses of betrayal and outrage burned through Lanni. Her own sister, whom she adored, had turned on her. Lanni couldn't believe that Jade would do anything so underhanded.

Lanni watched Jenny sitting on her father's lap and her heart constricted. He wanted his daughter with him now, but he hadn't been around when the child needed him most. From birth, Jenny had been a sickly infant. She suffered from ear infections and frequent bouts of asthmatic bronchitis. Lanni spent more nights in Jenny's bedroom than her own.

Soon Judd was traveling, coming home sporadically. The space between his visits lengthened and the time spent with his family become shorter and shorter.

Finally Lanni couldn't take it anymore. There was plenty of work in Seattle for a skilled pipefitter. Judd didn't need to travel—they could find a way to meet expenses as long as he was home and they were together.

The next time Judd came home, waving the exorbitant paycheck he'd received for working in the Middle East, Lanni was waiting for him. She decided to put everything on the line—their love, their marriage, and their daughter. In her anger and frustration, she'd hurled accusations at him. Lanni burned with humiliation every time she remembered the terrible things she'd said to him. A thousand times since, she'd wished she could have swallowed back every word.

On that one horrible night, Lanni forced Judd to choose. Either he stay in Seattle with them, or everything was over. Judd had walked to the door, turned and asked her to come with him. He wanted her to travel with him—he felt suffocated in Seattle. She had no choice but to refuse. Judd left, and ten days later, Lanni filed for divorce.

"Where's Mexico?" Jenny asked, unaware of the undercurrents flowing through the room.

Judd flipped through the pages and turned the atlas upside-down in an effort to find what he wanted.

"Here." He knelt beside her and turned to the appropriate page.

"Can I go there someday, too?"

"If you want."

"What about Mommy?"

Briefly Judd's eyes sought Lanni's. "She'd love the sun and the beach. You would, too, sweetheart."

"I want to go. Can we, Mommy?"

Still numb from his announcement that Jade had been involved in any subterfuge, Lanni didn't hear the question.

"Can we go, Mommy? Can we?"

The childishly eager voice forced Lanni into the present. "Go where, darling?"

"To Mexico with Daddy."

"No," she cried, flashing Judd a look that threatened bodily harm. If he was going to use Jenny against her, she'd throw him out the door. Her eyes told him as much. "There wouldn't be any place for us to stay." Silently she dared Judd to contradict her.

"Is that still your excuse, Lanni?" The words were issued in a low hiss that was barely audible.

"What's yours, Judd?" she flared. "You're the one who walked out on us. Remember? How have you salved your conscience?" She hadn't meant to accuse him and hated herself for resorting to angry words. It always turned out like this. They couldn't be civil to each other for more than a few minutes before the bitterness erupted like an open, festering wound.

He stood, moving close to her. The anger drained from him and he lifted a thick strand of golden hair from the side of her face. When Lanni flinched and stepped away, Judd's spirits plummeted. He'd tried so hard to reach her and had utterly failed. He had walked out, but only when there wasn't any other option. He hadn't wanted to leave, but he couldn't stay. There were plenty of things he regretted in his life, but hurting Lanni would haunt him to his grave.

It had been a mistake to have married her, he silently reflected, but he couldn't help himself. He'd wanted her so badly that nothing on earth would have stopped him. She was perfect. Lovely and delicate. Her home and family had radiated more warmth and love than anything he'd ever known.

Judd knew from the beginning that Lanni was special. With her, he could offer nothing less than marriage. He'd done so gladly, latching onto the elusive promise of happiness for the first time in his life.

He liked to think that their first year together had been ordained by God. He'd never known what it meant to be part of a family.

Lanni had flinched when Judd's hand lifted her hair. She feared his touch. Despite all the hurt and bitterness that was between them, she could vividly remember the feel of his smooth skin beneath her fingers and the way her long nails had dug into his powerful muscles when they made love. They may have had their differences, but they were never apparent in bed. Judd had always been a fantastic lover.

Dragging her eyes away from him, she turned to Jenny, lifting the small girl into her arms. Jenny was like a protective barrier against Judd.

The glint of knowledge that lurked in his smiling eyes told her that he recognized her ploy.

"I'm leaving in the morning," he told her as Jenny squirmed in her arms.

Unwilling to fight her daughter, Lanni set the child back on the carpet. "What do you mean?"

"I told you I'm taking Jenny."

"Judd, no." Her voice wobbled with regret. He couldn't come in and expect her to willingly hand over her daughter. Her eyes sparked in his direction. She'd fight him with everything she had.

"Listen." Frustrated, Judd raked his fingers through his hair. "I'll do everything possible to ensure her safety. I'm her father, for heaven's sake. Don't suffocate her the way you did me."

For a second Lanni was too shocked and hurt to speak. She refused to address his accusation. "Jenny's only a child. You can't uproot her like this—separate her from me and the only home she knows."

"Dad may not last much longer."

"Jenny's in preschool." The excuse was lame, but Lanni was desperate.

Inserting the tips of his fingers in the high pockets of his well-worn jeans, Judd strolled to the other side of the room. She wasn't fooled by his casual stance. There was a coiled alertness to every movement Judd made. "All right, we can work around those things."

"How?"

"Come with us." He turned, his gaze pinning her to the wall.

Lanni couldn't hold back an abrupt, short laugh. "I can't take time off work at a minute's notice. There are people who depend on me."

"Like Steve." He said the name as if it didn't feel right on his tongue.

"Yes…like Steve. And others, plenty of others. I've done well for myself without you. I can't—and I won't—allow you to charge into my life this way."

"Lanni, Stuart's dying. Surely you aren't going to deny him this final request."

For the first time Lanni saw the pain in Judd's eyes. He may not have gotten along with his father, but he cared. Judd honestly cared. Probably against his flint-hard will, he was concerned.

"I'm sorry, really sorry, but I can't." Tears formed, stinging the back of her eyes.

"Jenny has a right to meet her grandfather."

"I wrote… I sent pictures. What about my rights? What about Jenny's rights?"

Reaching out, he gripped both her wrists and pressed them against her breast. "You hate me, fine. I may deserve all the bitterness you've got stored up against me. But you aren't any Mother Teresa yourself and I refuse to let you punish an old dying man for my sins."

"I'm not punishing Stuart," she cried, and shook her head from side to side. "All I want is for you to leave Jenny and me alone."

Abruptly Judd dropped her hands and Lanni rubbed them together nervously. "I won't be bullied into this. My…decision is made."

"Okay, fine, but take a night and sleep on it. Once you've had time to think things through, I'm confident you'll realize we don't have any choice."

"Mommy, are you and Daddy fighting?"

"Of course not, sweetheart," Lanni said instantly.

The young face was tight with concern. "Is Daddy going away again?"

"Yes," Judd answered, then added, "but I'll be back tomorrow and we can talk again." His eyes held Lanni's. "I'll see you first thing in the morning."

It was all she could do to nod.

Judd felt Lanni's round, frightened eyes follow him

as he walked out the front door. He hadn't expected her to deny him this request. He'd never asked for anything from her, not even visitation rights to his daughter. Jade had frequently mailed him pictures of the little girl. He kept them in his wallet along with the photo he carried of Lanni. But he rarely looked at them. It hurt too much. Stuart's letter had changed all that.

As Judd walked out to his car, thoughts of his father produced a heavy frown. By the time the envelope had reached him, it had three different addresses penned across the surface. In all his years of working for the big oil companies, Judd could remember only a handful of times that he'd heard from his father. This letter had caught Judd by surprise. The old man was dying and Stuart Samuel Matthiessen wanted to mend his fences. Stuart had asked to see Jenny before he died and Judd wouldn't deny him this last request.

Seeing Lanni again was difficult, Judd mused with a sigh. He couldn't look at her and not remember. Briefly he closed his eyes as a wave of whispered desire from the past swept over him, then he climbed into the car and headed toward the motel. Lanni was as breathtakingly lovely now as the day he'd left her and Jenny. Perhaps even more so. Her beauty had ripened. One look told him the cost of her struggle to gain that maturity. He was proud of her, and in the same moment experienced an overwhelming guilt that it had been him who had brought the shadow to her eyes.

In the beginning, his intentions had been impeccable. He hadn't expected the restlessness to return. For a year it hadn't.

At first the only symptoms of his discontent had been a few sleepless nights. He'd go to bed with Lanni and after making love and holding her in his arms, Lanni would cling to him. She worried when he was late and fussed over him until he wanted to throw up his arms and ask her to give him some peace. The family he'd wanted so much to become a part of disillusioned him. Lanni's parents were wonderful people, but they wanted to control their lives, and worse, Lanni couldn't seem to get dressed in the morning without first checking with her mother. Judd felt the walls close in around him. The baby had helped give Lanni some independence, but not enough.

The day Jennifer Lydia Matthiessen was born would long be counted as the most important of his life. There was nothing in this world that could duplicate the feelings of pride and love when the nurse handed him his newborn daughter. When she became ill, Judd was sick with worry. The doctor bills destroyed their budget and he couldn't think of any option but to travel to the high-risk jobs that abounded for a man with his experience. And so he'd taken a job in the oil-rich fields of the Middle East. The money had been good, and the challenge was there. He didn't try to fool himself by thinking that he didn't miss Lanni and the baby—he did.

On the trips home, Judd could see how unhappy Lanni was, but she'd only bury her face in his shoulder and beg him not to leave her again. They never talked, at least not the way they should. They were both caught up in acting out a role, pretending there were no problems. So he'd stayed on the oil fields, coming back to Seattle less and less often, avoiding the inevitable. Lanni didn't understand the reason he'd stayed away, and Judd hadn't the heart to tell her.

Judd sighed and pulled the car into the motel parking lot. Turning off the ignition, he thought of the dark night ahead of him.

* * *

Lanni waited until Jenny was in bed, sound asleep, before she called her sister's number.

"Jade, it's Lanni."

"I'm so glad you phoned," Jade said with an eager sigh. "I'm dying to find out what happened. What did Judd say about Steve?"

"You wrote to him." The words conveyed all the feelings of betrayal Lanni had harbored over the last two hours.

Jade's voice instantly lost its vivaciousness. "Yes, I wrote, but only because you wouldn't."

At least she didn't try to lie about it. Lanni was grateful for that. "Why didn't you say anything?"

"A hundred times I tried to talk about Judd, but you wouldn't listen."

"I can't believe that."

"I did, Lanni," she cried. "Remember last weekend while we were at the mall? I asked you then if you were curious about Judd. I asked you if you had a chance to know where he was, and what he was doing, if you'd want to know. Don't you remember what you said?"

Vaguely, Lanni recalled that the conversation had taken place, but the details of it eluded her. "No."

"You told me that for all you cared Judd could be rotting in hell."

"I wasn't serious!"

"At the time it sounded very much like you were. And last Christmas, do you remember how I tried to talk you into making some effort to contact him?"

That Lanni remembered; she and Jade had exchanged heated words in that disagreement. But Christmases without Judd were always the worst. They'd met during the most festive season of the year. She'd been working part-time at the cosmetics counter of a department store and attending night school, still uncertain about what she wanted to do with her life. Then Judd had swept so unexpectedly into her existence. She'd been so naive and so easily captivated by his worldliness. They were together every day until…

"Lanni."

Jade's concerned voice broke through the fog of memories.

"Yes, yes, I'm here. I was just trying to remember…"

"Judd only wrote a handful of times. I couldn't refuse him. He loves you and Jenny, and wanted to know how you were—that's only natural. You wouldn't write to him, so I had to."

The anger dissipated. Lanni hadn't meant to be cruel when she'd returned Judd's letters. She couldn't read his words and keep her mental health at the same time. She wanted him to stop telling her that he loved her and wanted her with him. She didn't want to read about the exciting places he was living, where the sun was always shining and the white beaches sounded like paradise. He'd left her, walked out on her, and she couldn't—wouldn't—forgive him for that.

"I'm sorry, Lanni. A thousand times I wanted to tell you. Especially when Jenny started asking questions about Judd. If you'd given me a hint that you were interested in contacting him, I would have given you his address."

"No." Slowly Lanni shook her head. "You're right, I wouldn't have wanted to know. You did the right thing not to tell me."

"Then why do I feel so terrible?" Jade asked.

"Probably because I came at you like a charging bull. I apologize."

"Don't. I'm relieved that he's here. Have you decided what you're going to do about letting him take Jenny?"

"No," Lanni answered honestly. Every passing minute made the problem of Judd's dying father more complex. Judd was right to want to take Jenny. And her apprehensions about the trip were equally strong.

Lanni spoke with her sister a couple of minutes more, then replaced the telephone receiver.

That night when she climbed between the sheets, memories of their first Christmas together crowded the edges of her mind.

She'd been so much in love with Judd. He'd arrived in Seattle on his way to a job assignment in Alaska and decided to stay a few extra days in order to explore the city. Those days had quickly turned to weeks. They'd met on his second day in town, where Lanni was working in a downtown department store for the holidays.

Lanni had helped Judd pick out a gift for his boss's wife and he'd casually asked her out to dinner in appreciation for the help she'd given him. Lanni had been forced to decline, although her impulse had been to accept his invitation. She was meeting her family that evening for an annual outing of Christmas caroling. As it turned out, Judd joined her and met her family, adding his deep baritone voice with her father and uncles.

From that first meeting, other dates had followed until they spent every available minute together. Each night it became more and more difficult to send him away.

Lanni remembered. Oh, sweet heaven, she remembered the night they hadn't stopped with kissing and touching....

* * *

"Lanni, no more." Judd had pushed himself away from her, leaning back against the sofa in her apartment and inhaling deep breaths in an effort to control his desire.

In vivid detail Lanni recalled the pain she saw on his face. "I love you," she whispered urgently. "Oh, Judd, I love you so much, I could die with it."

"Lanni," he begged, "don't tell me that. Please don't tell me that."

She'd been crushed at his harsh words. She wasn't a fickle teenager who fell in and out of love at will, but a woman with a woman's heart and she was filled with desire for this man.

"Oh, my sweet Lanni, don't you know how much I love you?"

"But…"

His callused hands had cupped her face and tenderly he'd kissed her face, drawing closer and closer to her mouth. Unable to bear this any longer, she removed her sweater, peeling it over her head. Judd had looked stunned. "What are you doing?"

She'd grinned coyly and kissed the corner of his mouth. "What does it look like?"

"Lanni!" His eyes were everywhere but on her. "You can't do that."

"Sure I can."

Judd got up and stalked to the other side of the room. "This isn't right."

"We love each other," she countered. This was a night to be remembered. When he discovered that she was a virgin, he'd know how much she treasured what they shared.

"I do love you," he moaned, seemingly at odds with

himself. "But I won't do this. Making love with you now isn't right."

"And it would be with another woman?"

"Yes."

Lanni supposed she should be shocked and offended, but she wasn't. "Are you saying that you won't make love to me?"

"Yes," he fairly shouted.

Smiling, Lanni eliminated the space that separated them and gently placed her hands on his shoulders. Standing on the tips of her toes, she brushed her mouth over his. Judd went rigid and groaned.

"You didn't believe me when I said I loved you. I only want to prove to you how much," she challenged softly.

"Lanni," he begged, his voice so low it was barely audible. "Not like this."

"I've been waiting for you all my life," she whispered. They had such little time. He was scheduled to fly into Anchorage the day after Christmas. "Can't you see that what we share is rare and beautiful?"

Judd tilted his head back and closed his eyes. "Oh, Lanni, you're making this difficult."

"I love you, Judd. Love you, love you, love you. I'm giving you something I've never offered another man. What do I have to do to make you accept my gift?"

He opened his eyes then and lowered his gaze to hers. Passion burned in their dark depths, consuming her with his need. "I'll take your gift on one condition," he'd said.

"Anything."

"Marry me, Lanni. Tonight. This minute. I can't wait for you any longer."

Three

"Marry you," Lanni replied softly. "But, Judd, why?"

From the way he tossed his head back, Lanni suspected he'd dislocated several vertebrae. "The proper response to the question is yes. You're not supposed to squabble with me. This isn't the great debate."

"But what about your job?"

"I'll find one in Seattle. Don't argue with me, Lanni. We're in love and people in love get married."

Lanni was enjoying this immeasurably. "People in love do other things." She cozied up to him, reveling in the feel of her torso rubbing against his firm body.

"No, they don't. At least we don't—won't—until it's right." Before she knew what was happening, he took her sweater from the sofa and pulled it over her head, leaving the knit arms dangling at her sides. "I'm not touching you again until we're married. And I don't want to hear any arguments about it, either." With all the purpose of a federal court judge, he marched to the chair and reached for his jacket. He stuffed his arms inside as though he couldn't get away from her fast enough. "Well, hurry up," he barked when he noticed she hadn't moved.

"Where…are we going?"

"To see your parents to talk to about our wedding."

"But…"

"You aren't going to argue with me, are you?"

Lanni had the distinct feeling that he wouldn't hesitate to bite her head off if she did. "No."

He waved his index finger in her direction. "You better comb your hair for heaven's sake. One look at you and your family will know what we've been doing."

A quick glance in the bathroom mirror confirmed that what he'd said was true. Her hair was mussed, her lips swollen and dewy from his kisses. Her face was flushed, but it beamed with happiness. Her eyes revealed an inner glow that came from loving Judd and being loved by him.

By the time she rejoined him, he'd taken her coat from the hall closet and held it open for her. "I'd prefer a nice quiet ceremony, but if you want the whole she-bang then that's fine, too."

"I…haven't given it much thought."

"Well, the time is now. You'd better decide."

"Judd," she said, then hesitated, not knowing how to voice her thoughts. She wasn't even sure she should be saying anything. She wanted to be Judd's wife. "You… you don't seem very happy about this."

"I'm ecstatic."

"I can tell." She folded her arms across her breasts and proudly shook her head. "I told you before, we don't need to get married. I'm willing to…"

"But I'm not." His brow arched over frowning eyes. His scowling glare defied argument. "Who should I talk to first? Your father?"

"I…guess."

"Well? What are you waiting for?"

"You mean you want to talk to him now?" She checked her watch. "It's almost eleven o'clock."

"Feeling the way I do now, he'll be pleased that I've come to him instead of being here alone with you."

"Oh, Judd, am I tempting you?" She placed her hand on his shoulder and gazed lovingly into his dark eyes. "It's the most heady feeling in the world to know you want me so much."

He broke the contact and his index finger flew at her again. "I'm not in any mood for your funny business."

"Right." She swallowed down a giggle, but her gaze sobered when she noticed how serious Judd had become. "I do love you, you know."

"I don't know why, but I'm not going to question it. I want everything you have for me, Lanni—a home, a family—love. I need it all."

Lanni needed it, too, although she hadn't felt it was necessary until that moment.

Together, braving the cold wind and the uncertainties that faced them, they drove to Lanni's parents' home near Tacoma.

The late-night visit with her family was little short of hilarious. Her mother brought out Christmas cake and coffee, all the while dressed in an old terry-cloth housecoat that was cinched at the waist. When Judd explained the reason for their unexpected appearance, Lanni noticed a silent tear slip from her mother's eyes.

Her father, on the other hand, sat on the sofa with his legs crossed, nodding now and again, and seemed to have been struck speechless. Eighteen-year-old Jade hid on the top stair outside her bedroom door, not wanting to come down because she had an apricot mask on her face.

After leaving her parents' place, Judd and Lanni located an all-night diner and sat drinking mugs of spiced hot cider.

"Are you sure you still want to go through with this?" she asked, half-expecting Judd to have decided otherwise.

"I want it now more than ever." His hand gripped hers as though the simple action linked them together for all time.

"Then I've made a decision."

"Okay, let's hear it."

"I want to be married on the first weekend of the new year," she stated decisively.

"I don't want a formal wedding. No bridesmaids, just Jade as my maid-of-honor and no organ music. I'm not even sure I want the long flowing gown and veil."

He nodded, agreeing with her.

"At dusk I think, just before the sun sets, when the sky is golden and the stars are outlined in the heavens."

"Sundown sounds nice."

"Our love is so unexpected and special that I don't want to be bound by the chains of tradition."

"I agree," he murmured, and smiled softly.

"I want to be married in a hundred-year-old church on Vashon Island. I'm afraid it may be closed down so we'll need to see about having it opened for the wedding." She paused to hear his reaction, but like her father only minutes before, Judd was speechless. "It's near the beach," she elaborated. "My grandmother attended services there nearly all her life. I always loved that old church. I want us to be married there."

"Anything else?" He looked skeptical.

"I don't think so."

"A hundred-year-old church that may be closed down?"

"Right."

Judd looked doubtful.

"Well, what do you think?" She knew it sounded impractical, but she was in love for the first time in her life and everything had to be perfect. She only planned to be married once.

His expression softened as he raised her fingertips to his mouth and lovingly pressed his lips against them. "All these weeks we've been seeing each other, I've wondered what it was about you that attracted me so strongly. I've known beautiful women in the past, but I've never wanted to marry any of them. Listening to your appreciation of the past and your love of beauty helps me to understand why I find you so extraordinary."

And so they were married in a tiny church close to a windswept shore as the sun set in the background. The sound of the waves slapping against the pebble beach echoed in the distance as a handful of family and friends formed a half circle around them. Outside, sea gulls soared, their calls merging with the sounds of the water. When Judd slipped the ring on Lanni's finger, their eyes met and held and Lanni knew then that she would never know a happiness greater than that moment…

A tear slipped from the corner of Lanni's eye and rolled down the side of her face, wetting her pillowcase. Somehow things had gone very wrong. Maybe she'd gotten pregnant too soon, she didn't know. Judd had changed jobs twice within the first year they were married. He seemed to become bored with routine. Then, after Jenny was born, everything had gone wrong.

She recalled the night Jenny was sick with an ear infection and cried incessantly. Helpless to know how to comfort the three-month-old baby, Lanni had walked the bedroom floor gently holding the baby against her shoulder and patting her tiny back. But nothing she did seemed to quiet her.

Judd had staggered into the room. "I can't sleep with you in here. Let me walk her while you try to sleep."

"I couldn't sleep," she said, and continued pacing. Trying to lighten the mood, she told him something her mother had recently claimed. "We should enjoy these days. It's said that they're supposed to be the best times of our lives."

Judd had chuckled. "You mean it gets worse?"

For them it had. Much, much worse.

Her pillowcase was damp before Lanni reached for a tissue from her nightstand and wiped her face. She'd assumed all her tears over Judd had been shed. The power he held to dredge up the past and hurt her was frightening. She couldn't allow that to continue. Severing the relationship was vital for her emotional well-being. Since he'd been gone, her life had been in limbo. She lived a solitary lifestyle and yet she was bound by invisible chains. Having lived with Judd those first years, she was well aware of his hearty sexual appetite. She couldn't believe that he had been faithful to her.

The instant flash of pain that shot through her was so fierce and so sudden that Lanni bolted upright. She had to get away from Judd no matter what the price.

The following morning, Jenny woke and came into Lanni's room. Her eager fingers tugged at the pillow. "Mommy, are you awake?"

One eyelid reluctantly opened. "Nope."

"I'm hungry."

It had been almost morning before Lanni had finally drifted off to sleep. When the alarm had rung, she rolled over and turned it off. Going to the office would be completely unproductive. Her head hurt and her eyes ached from hours of restless tossing.

"What time is it?" she asked Jenny, unwilling to open her eyes to read the clock.

Jenny climbed off the bed and raced into the kitchen. In an effort to escape the inevitable, Lanni buried her head under the plump pillow.

Within seconds Jenny was back. "The big hand is on the eleven and the little hand on the eight."

"Okay," Lanni mumbled. It was nearly eight. Normally Jenny would have been fed and dressed before now and ready for the day-care center. "I'll get up in a couple of minutes."

"Can I have Captain Crunch cereal?"

"Yes," she mumbled, "but I'll pour the milk."

"When will Daddy be here? He said he was coming back, didn't he?"

This time Lanni forced her eyes open. "I don't know."

"But he said…"

"Then he'll be here."

Lanni had spent a sleepless night, trapped in indecision. Judd wanted to take Jenny. She couldn't let him. The best thing to do would be to hold her ground. It was unreasonable of him to arrive unannounced and ask to take their daughter. And yet, Lanni understood. Judd's father was dying.

As the early light of dawn dappled the horizon, before Lanni slept, the questions had become more tangled, the answers more elusive and the doubts overwhelming.

Now, sitting upright in the bed, she tossed the blankets aside and stood, glancing at her daughter. "You know what I want to do?"

"What?" From the way Jenny answered her, Lanni could tell all that interested her daughter at the moment was eating her sugar-coated cereal.

"Let's go to the beach," she suggested, knowing that Jenny loved it as much as she did. "I'll call the office and tell them I'm not coming in and we'll escape for the day."

"Can I have breakfast first?"

As Lanni had expected, Jenny was more concerned with her stomach. Lanni followed her into the kitchen and poured the cold milk over her cereal. While Jenny ate, she dressed in faded jeans and a pale pink sweatshirt.

After making the necessary phone calls and sticking Jenny's breakfast dishes in the dishwasher, they packed a small lunch.

Seahurst Park on the shores of Puget Sound was only a short distance from the house. Had she felt more chipper, Lanni could have peddled her bike to the park, placing Jenny in the child's seat attached to the rear of the ten-speed. But her eyes burned from her sleepless night and she had no desire to expend unnecessary energy.

They found a parking place in the large lot and carried their lunch down to the pebble beach. The waters of the Sound were much too cold for swimming during any season of the year so they spent the first hour exploring the beach, locating small treasures.

As her father had done with her as a child, Lanni had given Jenny a love and appreciation for the sea. Barefoot, they walked along the shore. The swelling waves broke against the sand, leaving a creamy trail in their wake. Lanni paused to breathe in the fresh salt-laden air.

The four-year-old discovered a small seashell to add to her growing collection. Soon a variety of valuables were stored in the plastic bucket. A smooth, shiny rock, a dried piece of kelp and a broken sand dollar were the rare finds of the morning's outing.

"I want to show this to my daddy," Jenny told her proudly, holding a tiny seashell in her palm.

Lanni managed to disguise her distress. Jenny had a right to know and love her father, but at what price? Judd would take her for a week or two and then drift out of their lives again. Only heaven knew if he'd ever show up again.

As an adult, Lanni had trouble dealing emotionally with Judd's disappearances. If he hurt her, she could just imagine what he would do to Jenny. As Jenny's mother, she couldn't allow Judd to hurt their daughter.

When they returned from the lazy stroll, Lanni noticed a tall male figure silhouetted against the bulkhead watching them. It didn't take her long to recognize the man as Judd.

"I thought I'd find you here," he murmured, joining her. His footsteps joined hers.

"How'd you know where I'd go?"

A light but sad smile curved one corner of his mouth. "Whenever anything was wrong between us, you'd go to the beach."

"It's beautiful here. I needed time to think."

"Have you decided?"

Lanni understood his urgency, but this decision was too important to rush. They were talking about the future of their daughter's life and the memories she would store in her young mind about her father and grandfather.

"Look what I found!" Jenny's tightly clenched hand opened to reveal the small pinkish shell in her palm.

"Did you find it by yourself?"

Jenny looked up at her mother. "Mommy helped. And see what else." She lifted the yellow bucket filled with her priceless finds.

With unexpected patience Judd sorted through Jenny's small treasures, commenting on each one. The little girl beamed with pride at the words of praise and soon ran off to play on the swing set.

Wordlessly Lanni followed, sitting on a park bench within easy sight of the playground toys.

Judd claimed the seat, settling his lanky build beside her. "You look like hell."

"Thanks." Her eyes narrowed into slits and she bit back a more caustic reply. He was probably right. She hadn't bothered to do anything more than run a brush through her hair.

"When was the last time you had anything to eat?"

She shrugged and added, her tone waspish, "I had a dinner date last night, but unfortunately that was interrupted." She could feel Judd grow tense and experienced a small sense of triumph. But almost immediately she felt guilty for baiting him. They were playing the games they always did after one of his long absences.

"I didn't mean that to sound the way it did," she whispered.

"Sure you did, Lanni, but don't worry. I don't plan to stick around long enough to interfere with any more of your dates."

"I didn't imagine you would."

"All I want is my daughter, and then I'll be on my way."

She was silent for a long moment. When she spoke, her voice was soft and strained. "I didn't sleep much last night," she admitted. "Memories kept me awake, forcing me to face how I felt. I haven't wanted to do that these last couple of years."

"Lanni—"

"No, please, let me finish," she whispered. "I loved you, Judd, really loved you. I don't know what went wrong. A thousand times I've gone over our marriage and…"

"Nothing went wrong."

Her teeth bit unmercifully into the skin on the inside of her cheek. "You left me and Jenny, walked out the door without so much as a backward glance. Something was very wrong. You said yesterday that I suffocated you. I didn't know that…I honestly never knew that."

"It was wrong in the beginning."

"It wasn't," she contradicted. "You can't have forgotten how good it was with us. That first year was—"

"The happiest of my life."

"Then Jenny was born and—" She stopped abruptly in midsentence, her eyes widening. "You didn't want the baby?" She'd had a miserable pregnancy, but Judd had been marvelous. He'd taken the Lamaze classes with her and had been loving and supportive the entire nine months. Maybe it was because he had been so caring and gentle with her that Lanni had been unable to recognize the root of their problems. Not once had she suspected that Jenny was the beginning of their troubles.

"I wanted children." His eyes burned into hers, defying her to deny it. "You can't doubt that."

Remembering the day Jenny was born and the emotion she'd witnessed on Judd's proud face, she realized he couldn't be lying. "Those first months after she was born weren't easy on you."

"They weren't easy on either of us," he returned gruffly. "I didn't know one baby could cry so much."

"She was colicky."

"I know. I was there."

Lanni dropped her gaze. "But only part of the time."

Jenny was less than six months old when Judd left the first time. Lanni had felt like a zombie by the time he returned. Day in and day out she was alone with the baby, cut off from the world. If it hadn't been for her parents, Lanni was convinced she would have gone crazy. She and Judd were new to the neighborhood and Lanni hadn't met any of the other mothers. The only adult contact she had during those long, miserable weeks had been her parents and Jade.

"Right," Judd echoed. "I was only there part of the time."

The silence stretched between them, heavy and oppressive. Her heart pounded wildly in her ears and she stared at him for several long seconds before she was able to continue. "All night I thought about when you left. I…I drove you away, didn't I? I never let you know what I was feeling, holding it all inside until…until…"

"Lanni, no." His hand took hers, squeezing her fingers so hard that they ached. "Stop trying to blame yourself. It's me who was wrong. I should never have asked you to share my life. Not when I knew all along that I was all wrong for you."

"You told me once you found the walls closing in around you. You tried to tell me, but I didn't understand."

"Stop blaming yourself." Judd's response was instantaneous and sharp. "It was both of us. We were young and immature."

She held her chin at a regal angle, refusing to reveal the doubts and agonies she'd endured. "But you left anyway."

His eyes revealed the struggle he waged within himself. "I saw you hold back the tears and I hated what I was doing to you and the baby. I never wanted anything to work more than my life with you. I tried, Lanni, you know I tried."

"We've been through all this before," she whispered, hardly able to find her voice. "It doesn't do any good to drag it up again. At least for us it doesn't. The arguments have already been said."

"Mommy, Daddy, look," Jenny shouted, her shrill voice filled with glee. An older child stood behind the little girl, pushing the swing. Jenny's short legs eagerly pumped in and out. She leaned back as far as her hands would allow and pointed her toes at the sky, straining to reach higher and higher.

"Jenny," Lanni said, coming to her feet. "That's enough."

"I want to go real high."

"Jenny no…" Terror rose in her throat, strangling off her reply as the swing rose steadily until the chain buckled, swerved and tossed the little girl to the ground.

"Oh, no." For a paralyzing second Lanni couldn't move.

"Jenny." Judd's own voice revealed his silent terror.

The child lay prone on the sand, holding her stomach and kicking her stubby legs.

Judd moved first, reaching Jenny before Lanni. He bent over the child, his face devoid of color. "She's had the wind knocked out of her."

"Do something," Lanni pleaded. "She can't breathe."

"She will in a minute."

But Judd's assurances didn't ease Lanni's fear. Her fingers bit into his shoulder until Jenny sucked in a gulp of air and let out a horrifying cry. Judd picked Jenny up and handed her to Lanni. Sitting in the sand, she held the child to her shoulder and gently rocked back and forth, trying to comfort her. Lanni was trembling so hard that she felt faint for a moment.

"She'll be all right."

Judd's words barely registered above Jenny's frantic cries, which gained volume with every breath she inhaled. Gradually her cries subsided into giant hiccuping sobs.

Carefully coming to a stand, Lanni carried her over to the park bench where she'd been sitting. With the little girl in her lap, she brushed the hair from her small temple, searching for evidence of any further injuries. "Tell me where it hurts."

The child shook her head, not wanting to talk.

Standing above them, Judd's face was pinched into a tight frown.

"This is all your fault," she cried, barely recognizing how unreasonable she sounded. It didn't matter. None of it did. Jenny was her daughter. Judd was the one who left them. "Go away." Her voice was high and scratchy.

"Lanni—"

"Just go away," she cried. "I don't want you here."

Judd was as shaken as Lanni. He'd seen Jenny go toppling off the swing and his heart had stopped. Pausing, he raked his fingers through his hair. "Listen, I'll go down by the beach." She may be acting unreasonably, but he understood. Lanni had her face buried near

Jenny's shoulder and refused to look at him. "I'll be on the beach," he repeated.

Still she didn't answer. Reluctantly he walked away. He wanted to slam his fist against the rock wall and welcome the release of pain.

Sand filled his shoes, but he continued walking. If Lanni claimed she'd been up half the night remembering, it didn't surprise him. He'd been up most of the night as well. That final horrible scene when he'd left two years ago had played back in his mind again and again.

Lanni had delivered her ultimatum: either he stay in Seattle or they were through. Judd recognized at the time he had no choice. He loved her, wanted her with him, and she'd refused. He'd walked out the door. He remembered the pain etched so deeply in her soft features. For nearly eighteen months she'd clung to him, begged him not to leave her again. This time she hadn't. With a calm he hardly recognized in his wife, Lanni had told him to choose. The most difficult thing he'd done in his life was walk away from her that day. The sounds of laughter filled the park as Lanni watched Judd walk away from her. Jenny's painful cries faded to a mere whimper and Lanni regained control of her fragile emotions. She continued to hold her daughter, but her gaze followed Judd's dejected figure as he meandered along the shore, his hands stuffed inside the pockets of his jeans. A brisk wind buffeted against him, plastering his shirt to his torso.

Lanni had been completely unreasonable to shout at him. It was no more his fault than hers. The frustration of the moment had gotten to her and she'd lashed out at Judd, wanting to blame him for the troubles of the world. That was the crux of the problem with their relationship. They each struck out at the other, hurting each other.

"How do you feel?" she asked Jenny.

She squirmed off her lap. "I want Daddy."

Lanni let her go and sat motionless as the small child climbed over the bulkhead and down onto the sandy beach. Her small arms swung at her sides as she rushed to join her father. Judd apparently didn't see her coming and hesitated when her hand reached for his. He went down on one knee and wrapped both arms around the child. Lanni felt the strings on her heart yanked in two different directions. Her throat muscles were so tight she felt as if she were being strangled.

Tilting her head toward the sun, she closed her eyes. She prayed for wisdom; she didn't know what to do. In all the time she'd raised Jenny, alone with only her parents and her sister for help, she'd never faced a more difficult dilemma.

When she straightened, she noticed Judd and Jenny walking toward her. Jenny's hand was linked with her father's.

"Feel better?" he asked Lanni softly.

After watching Judd with their daughter, she whispered her apology. "I'm sorry. You weren't to blame for what happened any more than I was. Accidents happen."

Judd sat down beside her. "I understand. You were angry for all the other times Jenny's been hurt and I haven't been here."

She nodded, accepting his explanation. She hadn't realized it herself.

"We need to talk about Jenny." He forced the subject that she'd been avoiding from the moment he'd discovered her at the park.

"I…know."

"Have you decided?" Pride stiffened her shoulders. He wouldn't take Jenny without her permission. Nor would he plead with her. This was the only request he'd made of her since leaving.

"I can't let you take Jenny alone."

"Then come with me." He offered the only other solution.

"I'll only do that on one condition."

"Name it."

Boldly her eyes met his. "I want you to sign the divorce papers."

Four

"What's a divorce?" Jenny wanted to know, glancing from one parent to another.

"An agreement," Judd answered patiently, his gaze lowering briefly to his daughter's before rising to pin Lanni's. He supposed he shouldn't be surprised. He'd carried the papers with him for two years. He hadn't wanted a divorce, but she'd given him no option. He supposed he should have prepared himself for the inevitable. Yet he was amazed at the fierce regret that ravaged him.

Divorce.

How final that ugly word sounded. His inclination was to agree and be done with it if that was what she sincerely wanted. But he'd seen that milquetoast agent she'd been dating and had disliked him instantly. Steve Delaney wasn't near man enough for a woman like Lanni.

"Well?" she prodded.

"Fine, I'll sign the papers."

At the sound of his words, Lanni felt almost as if a weight had settled on her shoulders. Surprised, she wondered why she was reacting so negatively. She should be glad that it was nearly over. At last she could cut herself free of the invisible bonds that tied her to Judd and make a new life for herself and Jenny.

It was apparent that if it wasn't for his father, Judd wouldn't be here now. He hadn't intended to come back. He hadn't returned because he wanted to be with her and Jenny. Basically nothing had changed between them. He hadn't given her an argument when she demanded he sign the divorce papers. He'd revealed no hesitation. From his reaction, Lanni could only assume that he wanted the divorce as much as she did.

Judd reached down and lifted Jenny into his arms. The little girl looped hers around his neck and smiled. "I'm glad you're my daddy."

"So am I, sweetheart."

"We're going on a long trip," Judd was saying to Jenny.

"To see your daddy?"

Judd's thick brows darted upward to show mild surprise.

"That's right."

"Where does your daddy live?"

"In Montana."

"Mon-tan-a," Jenny repeated carefully. "Does he have whiskers, too?"

Judd threw back his head and laughed. "Yes."

Jenny grinned. "Is Mommy coming?"

Judd responded with a sharp nod. "She'll be with us."

"Good," Jenny proclaimed, and lowered her head to Judd's shoulder. "I'm glad you're here," she murmured on the tail end of a long yawn.

"It's almost her nap time," Lanni said softly. "I'll take her home and make the necessary arrangements while she's asleep. When do you want to leave?"

"First thing tomorrow morning." His hand gently patted Jenny's back.

"I may need more time than that." Her mind scanned the calendar on her desk. Summers were the busiest time for real estate agents. Most families preferred to make a move during the vacation months of June, July and August to avoid uprooting children during the school year.

"We leave tomorrow."

Judd's words broke into her thoughts and she bristled. He must realize she had responsibilities. She couldn't just walk away from everything because he was in an all-fired rush.

Resentment simmered within Lanni. As he had all his life, Judd expected her to walk away from her responsibilities. "I said, I'll do my best to be ready by tomorrow. But I can't and won't make any promises."

"Listen, Lanni, I don't know what Stuart's condition is, but he wouldn't have written if he wasn't bad. I haven't got time to waste sitting around here while you rearrange your dating schedule."

Dating schedule. Lanni fumed as they marched to the parking lot. Judd had some perverse notion that she'd been playing the role of a swinging single since he'd been gone. Well, fine, she'd let him think exactly that. In two years the only man she'd ever dated was Steve and that had been only within the last three months.

Judd followed her to her car, slipping a droopy-eyed Jenny inside the child's protective car seat while Lanni waited silently. The little girl's head rolled to one side as she was strapped into place. If she wasn't already asleep, she would be soon. As silently as possible, Judd closed the car door.

Then, defying everything she'd told herself on the long hike to the car, Lanni turned to him, her hands braced against her hips. "I'll have you know that the only man I've dated since the minute you walked out the door is Steve Delaney and I resent your implying otherwise."

Despite the outrage flashing from her cool, dark eyes, Judd grinned. He'd always known Lanni had spunk. He hadn't meant to suggest anything and realized how offended she was. "I know. I didn't mean anything," he said, and sighed. "I'm worried about Stuart."

Lanni's indignation vanished as quickly as it came. "I'll do everything I can to be ready so we can leave on schedule."

"I'm counting on it." He hedged, needing to say something more and not sure how to do it without the words getting in the way. "I appreciate this, Lanni. I'll sign those papers you want and we can both go about our lives in peace. I'm sorry it turned out like this. I never was the right man for you."

"It was my fault," she whispered, the emotion blocking her throat. "I was the wrong type of woman for you."

"It's over, so let's quit blaming ourselves."

"All right," she agreed, her eyes burning bright with unshed tears. Part of her had hoped Judd didn't want to make their separation final and that he'd suggest they wait and give themselves another chance. She'd asked for the divorce, demanded that he sign the papers, but deep down, Lanni had held onto the belief that he loved her enough to change and make everything right between them again. What a romantic fool she was.

"I'll pick you and Jenny up around six tomorrow morning, unless I hear otherwise."

"We'll be ready," Lanni told him, climbing inside the driver's seat of the car. Judd remained standing in the parking lot. Lanni watched from her rearview mirror, his figure growing smaller and smaller.

Once home, and with Jenny securely tucked in bed for her nap, Lanni sat at the kitchen table, her hands cupping a mug of hot coffee. So it would soon be over.

Lanni knew her parents would be relieved for her sake. They liked Judd, but had been witnesses to the turmoil he had brought into all their lives. After Judd left, they'd been wonderfully supportive. Lanni was grateful, but she was concerned that her problems caused her parents to worry. As luck would have it, they were vacationing in California this month and they need never know about Lanni and Jenny leaving with Judd.

With a determined effort, Lanni forced herself to deal with the necessities of this trip. She reached for a pen and paper to make a list of people she needed to contact and appointments that would need to be re-scheduled. The house was silent, almost eerie. She paused and set the pencil aside. Her heart ached. She felt as if she were dying on the inside—never had she been more lonely.

Her hand was on her phone before she could stop herself from contacting Jade.

"Mr. Boynton's office," came Jade's efficient-sounding voice.

"I need to talk to you," Lanni announced starkly, her voice tight with emotion.

"Lanni? What's wrong?"

"I'm…leaving with Judd and Jenny in the morning to visit his father."

"But that's nothing to be upset about," Jade offered enthusiastically. "In fact, it just might be that all you two need is some time together. I've tried to stay out of it, but honestly, Lanni, I'm just not any good at biting my tongue. You love Judd, you always have—"

"We're going through with the divorce," Lanni cut in sharply, biting into the corner of her bottom lip.

"What?" For once Jade was nearly speechless.

"It's what we both want."

"It isn't what either of you want—even I can see that and I know zilch about love. Lanni, for heaven's sake, don't do something you'll regret the rest of your life," she pleaded.

"Jade, please, I only phoned to let you know that I'm leaving with Judd. Jenny and I shouldn't be gone any longer than two weeks. Can you pick up my mail and water the houseplants once or twice?"

"Of course, but…" Jade hesitated, "can you hold on a minute?"

"Sure."

"Lanni," she said when she came back on the phone, "listen, I've got to go. I'll stop by on my way home from work and we can talk this out."

Almost immediately the line was disconnected. From past experience Lanni knew how much Jade's boss frowned upon his employees using the office phone for personal calls.

While Jenny slept, Lanni used the time to make the necessary arrangements for this trip with Judd. When she contacted the office, Steve was unavailable, but she left a message for him, asking that he phone her when convenient. She wasn't sure Steve would be pleased when she told him she was going with Judd. From experience, Lanni realized her fellow worker could be persuasive when he wanted to be.

The washer and dryer were both in full operation,

and suitcases brought up from the basement by the time Jade arrived late that afternoon. Jenny was playing at the neighbor's.

"Hi," Jade said, entering the kitchen. "You aren't really going through with this, are you?"

Lanni glanced up from inside the refrigerator. Perishables lined the countertop. "Through with what? Traveling with Judd, or the divorce?"

"The divorce."

Lanni set a head of cabbage on the counter. "It's not open for discussion."

"It's just that I feel so strongly that you're doing the wrong thing."

"Jade," Lanni said fiercely. "I don't want to hear it. It's done. We've agreed and that's all there is to it."

Suspiciously Jade eyed the eggs, leftover spaghetti and a loaf of bread on the counter. "Fine, but either you've just recently discovered food or that's one disasterous omelette you're cooking."

"This is for you."

"Me?" Jade slapped her hand against her chest. "Hey, I know you're upset, but that isn't any reason to sabotage my diet."

"I'm not," Lanni said, smiling despite herself. "These will only spoil while we're gone, so I'm sending them home with you."

Jade reached for a pickle, munching on the end of it. "I am pleased about one thing, however. You need this time with Judd."

"It isn't exactly a vacation, you know."

"I do, but I've always thought that all you two needed…"

"Jade! Stop it! I'm going with Judd for one reason and one reason only."

"Sure you are," Jade said, batting her long lashes provocatively. "But if things happen between you two while you're away, I won't be surprised. Not me. Not one little bit."

Deciding the best thing she could do was ignore her sister's antics, Lanni set a package of luncheon meat on the counter. "Wrong again. Nothing's going to happen, because I won't let it."

Her phone rang and Lanni reached for it, hoping it was Steve. It took her a couple of minutes to inform the caller that she wasn't interested in having her carpet cleaned.

"I haven't talked to Steve," Lanni said, disconnecting.

"Don't," Jade said sharply.

"What do you mean by that?"

"It's none of his business, Lanni. He's good looking and smooth and as stable as the Rock of Gibraltar, but he isn't for you. Judd is."

"Get your head out of the clouds," Lanni barked, snapping at her sister. "My marriage was over a long time ago. Nothing's left but a thin shell." And shattered illusions, she added silently. "Judd may love me in his own way, but it isn't enough to repair the damage to our marriage. We're both adult enough to realize that."

"But…"

"There aren't any buts about it. We both want out of this farce of a marriage and as soon as possible."

"But you're leaving with him."

"Yes."

"That has to mean something," Jade argued.

"It means nothing. Nothing," she repeated, more for her own benefit than Jade's.

* * *

The following morning, at 6:00 a.m., Judd parked the midsize SUV in front of the house. He dreaded this trip, every mile of it. He didn't know what to expect once he arrived in Twin Deer. For all he knew, Stuart could already be dead. But confronting his father was the least of his worries. Little could alter the problems in that relationship. His real concern was this time with Lanni and Jenny. It wouldn't be easy being close to them. Having them constantly at his side was bound to make him yearn for the way things used to be. How easy it would be to hold Lanni in his arms again. But it wouldn't be right—she wanted this divorce. For that matter, he should have done something to give her her freedom long before now.

Judd climbed out of the vehicle and walked around the back, opening the tailgate to make room for Lanni's and Jenny's luggage. When he finished shuffling his gear, he glanced up to discover Lanni standing on the front porch, watching him.

"Are you ready?"

She nodded, seeming to feel some of the heaviness that weighted his heart.

"I brought the divorce papers with me. Do you want me to sign them now?" he asked.

Lanni hedged, then remembered the times Steve had told her that the divorce was necessary for the emotional healing to take place. More than any other time since Judd left, Lanni yearned to be whole again. "Maybe you'd better," she murmured sadly.

Judd followed her into the house. "Have you got a pen?"

"Don't you want to read it first?"

He shook his head. "I can't see the point. Whatever you want is fine."

"But…"

"I told you I'd sign them. Arguing over the finer points now isn't going to change anything."

Reluctantly Lanni handed him the ballpoint pen.

Leaning over the desk, Judd flipped the pages until he located the necessary place for his signature. He signed his name on the dotted line. "There," he said, handing her both the document and the pen. "What next?"

"I…I don't know," Lanni admitted. "I'll deal with it once we get back. Is that all right with you?"

"Whatever you want." He didn't sound concerned either way. He'd kept his part of the bargain, just as she was keeping hers.

Jenny wandered out from the hallway, her small hands fumbling with the buttons of her printed cotton coveralls. "I need help."

"I'll get them," Lanni offered, grateful for an excuse to move away from Judd and break the awkwardness of the moment.

"I already had breakfast," Jenny announced to her father. "Captain Crunch cereal is my favorite, but Mommy only lets me have that sometimes. I ate Captain Crunch today."

Judd grinned, his gaze skipping from Jenny to Lanni. "Dressed and already eaten breakfast. You always were well organized."

"I try to be," she said, striving for a light tone.

"Then let's hit the road." He lifted the two large suitcases from the living room floor.

"I'll lock up."

By the time she'd reached the station wagon, Judd

had taken Jenny's car seat from Lanni's car and positioned it in the back seat of his. Jenny had climbed aboard and was strapped into place. With the morning paper tucked under one arm, a thermos filled with coffee in the other, plus her purse and a small traveling bag, Lanni joined them.

Judd sat in the front seat, his hands on the wheel. "Ready?"

"Ready," she concurred, snapping her seatbelt into place. As ready as she would ever be.

Judd started the car and pulled onto the street. A road map rested on the seat between them. This trip wasn't going to be easy, Lanni mused. Deafening silence filled the car. Jenny played quietly with Betsy, her doll, content for the moment.

Lanni's mind flirted with some way of starting a conversation. They couldn't discuss the past. That was filled with too many regrets. They had no future. The divorce papers were signed and as soon as they returned, she'd take the necessary steps to terminate their marriage. The only suitable topic for discussion was the present and that, too, presented problems.

"I told the office I wouldn't be gone more than a couple of weeks."

"That should be more than enough time," Judd said, concentrating on the freeway stretched out in front of him. They hadn't been on the road ten minutes and already Lanni was making it sound like she couldn't wait to get back. His mouth tightened with impatience. He hadn't asked her about Steve Delaney, and wondered how much her relationship with the other man had prompted her to press the issue of the divorce.

Lanni saw the way Judd's lips thinned and tried to explain. "I simply can't stay any longer. As it is I'm having another agent fill in for me, which doubles her work-load. I don't like doing that and wouldn't if it wasn't necessary. I mean…" She paused, realizing she was rambling.

"It's all right, Lanni. I understand."

But she wondered if he really did.

For the first hour Jenny's excited chatter filled the silence. She asked a hundred questions, her curious mind working double time. Lanni was astonished at the patience Judd revealed. He answered each question thoroughly and in terms young Jenny could easily understand.

Lanni gleaned information as well. The trip would take the better part of three days, which meant they'd spend two nights on the road. Sleeping arrangements would need to be discussed soon. Not a thrilling subject, but one they'd face at his father's house as well. Surely Judd realized she had no intention of sharing his bed. Not for appearance's sake, convenience or any other reason. Her face grew warm at the realization that she feared her reactions to Judd should he try to make love to her. Heaven knew they'd never had any problems in bed. If anything… She shook her head sharply, causing Judd to look at her.

"Are you too warm?"

"I'm fine, thanks."

They stopped for a break on the top of Snoqualmie Pass. Jenny claimed she was hungry again and since Judd hadn't eaten breakfast, they found a restaurant. Lanni rarely ate anything in the morning, but Judd talked her into tasting something. Rather than argue, she ordered eggs, convinced it was a waste of good food. But to her surprise she was hungry and cleaned her plate.

Judd noticed and shared a warm smile with her. "Jade thinks a strong wind is going to blow you away."

"Did she suggest you fatten me up?" That sounded like something Jade would say.

"As a matter of fact, she did." One side of his mouth twitched upward. "But not with food."

Lanni's cheeks filled with hot color. She had never realized what an interfering troublemaker her younger sister could be. She still couldn't believe the gall of such a remark. "When did you two talk?" After she'd learned about Jade and Judd's communications, little would surprise her.

"Last night. I took her to dinner."

A tiny pain pricked her heart. Jealous over her own sister. Ridiculous. Insane. Childish.

"She wanted to talk to me about Steve," Judd explained.

"Steve Delaney is none of your business," Lanni returned tartly, furious with Jade and even more so with Judd.

"We're married; I'd say your relationship with him concerns me."

"*Were* married," Lanni whispered fiercely. "Those divorce papers are signed."

"Signed yes, but not filed."

"They will be the minute I get back to Seattle."

"Then so be it, but until they are you'd do well to remember you're my wife and Jenny will always be my daughter."

With trembling fingers, Lanni wiped the corners of her mouth with a napkin and reached for her coffee, lowering her gaze. She'd promised herself that she would do anything to avoid arguing with Judd, yet here they were, not fifty miles from home and already going for each other's throats. "I imagine Steve wasn't the only thing my sister wanted to discuss," she said, striving for a lighter tone.

Judd hesitated, but figured Lanni knew her sister as well as he. "She thinks we should get back together again." His eyes studied her, watching for a sign, anything that would tell him her feelings. Years ago Lanni's eyes had been as readable as a first-grade primer. No longer. She'd learned to school her emotions well. He found her expression blank, and experienced a sense of regret. Her eyes weren't the only thing that had changed. The picture he'd carried in his mind did her little justice. Maturity had perfected her beauty. It astonished him that it had taken another man this long to discover her. On the tail end of that thought came another: Lanni wouldn't have encouraged a relationship. He was convinced she'd shunned male interest; Jade had confirmed that. But not because Lanni carried any great hope he'd be back, Judd realized, but because she wasn't free to do so. He believed her when she claimed Steve was the first man she'd dated in two years.

"A reconciliation isn't what either of us wants," she said slowly, raising the coffee cup to her lips.

"Right," he agreed. "It didn't work once. It won't work again." No one knew this better than Judd. But being with Lanni and Jenny was seductive. He'd spent less than half a day in their company and already his mind was devising methods of remaining close to them. He loved his daughter—she was a delight.

Just being with Jenny made him realize how much he was missing. The thought produced another: he couldn't be close to Jenny without being near Lanni. Seeing her with Steve was something he'd never be able to tolerate. Lanni deserved her freedom and the right to find happiness. When this business with Stuart was over, he'd head back to Mexico or Alaska or maybe the Middle East again. The farther away he was, the better it would be for everyone involved.

Jenny slept after breakfast, long enough not to require her usual nap. But by the middle of the afternoon, she was whiny and bored. Lanni did her best to keep the little girl occupied, reading to her and inventing games. Judd did what he could by making frequent stops, granting the child the opportunity to stretch her legs. By dinnertime all three were exhausted.

"I don't think I've ever realized what a handful one little girl could be," Judd commented, pulling into a parking spot in front of a restaurant outside of Coeur d'Alene, Idaho. It was only mid-afternoon but they were all exhausted and ready to call it a day.

"I've tried not to spoil her," Lanni said somewhat defensively.

Judd's hand compressed around the steering wheel. "I didn't mean to suggest that."

"Judd, listen—"

"Lanni—"

They spoke simultaneously, paused, then laughed thinly.

"I think we're as tired as Jenny. I've been up since before five," Lanni admitted.

"Me, too." A gentle smile tugged at his mouth. "Let's get something to eat and find a motel."

"That sounds like an excellent idea."

Lanni felt much better after a meal, although they'd made three stops previously for munchies. She took Jenny into the ladies' room while Judd paid the bill, joining him at the car.

"The cashier suggested a motel a couple of miles

from here." Her eyes avoided his as he opened her car door. Doubts grew in Lanni's mind as Judd placed Jenny in her car seat, then joined her in the front of the car before starting the engine. She should say something about their sleeping arrangements, but she didn't want to seem like a prude. Nor did she wish to make an issue over the subject. Judd wasn't dense. He knew the score.

Lakeside Motel was situated on the sandy shores of Lake Coeur d'Alene and, as the cashier had said, was only a few miles from the restaurant. A paved walkway led down to the water's edge. Lanni got Jenny out of the car and walked down to the lake while Judd was in the motel office, booking their room. He joined her a few minutes later.

"I got us a room with two double beds?" He made the statement into a question.

"That'll be fine. I'll sleep with Jenny." Lanni wanted to bite back the words the minute they'd slid from her mouth. Naturally she'd sleep with Jenny. To cover her embarrassment, she stood and followed Judd back to the motel.

Instantly Jenny spied the crystal clear waters of the motel pool. "Can we go swimming?"

"We'll see," Lanni told her daughter. The comment was a mother's standby.

The room was clean and cool. Two freshly made double beds dominated the interior. Judd carried in their luggage, and Jenny automatically dug through hers, searching for her swimsuit. Lanni felt as if she had less energy than a rag doll, but she helped Jenny change clothes.

"I'll take her to the pool," Judd offered. "You look like you're about to collapse."

"We'll both go," Lanni compromised. "I can lounge

on one of the chairs. All I ask is that you wear her out, otherwise no one's going to get any sleep tonight." From past experience Lanni knew that once Jenny became this hyperactive, she wouldn't fall asleep easily. All afternoon, the little girl had been acting like a coiled spring. Now she was beyond the stage of being tired.

Father and daughter splashed gleefully in the cool waters of the kidney-shaped pool. Jenny swam like a fish. She'd taken lessons since she was two years old and had no fear of water. Judd was amazed at her ability and, encouraged by his enthusiasm, Jenny outdid herself, diving from the side of the pool into his arms and swimming underwater like a miniature dolphin.

The sun was setting by the time the two finished romping in the water. The evening was glorious, the limitless pink sky was filled with the promise of another glorious day. A gentle, sweet-smelling breeze blew off the lake.

"I'll want to get an early start in the morning," Judd said, drying his face with the thick towel. Lanni purposely avoided looking at his lean, muscular body.

She nodded her agreement. "You don't need to worry about me. I'm tired enough to sleep now."

"I don't want to go to bed," Jenny said, yawning.

Judd picked her up and carried her back to their room. "You're so tired now you can barely keep your eyes open," he told her softly.

"I'm not sleepy," Jenny argued.

"But your mommy is so can you lie still and be real quiet for her?"

Reluctantly Jenny nodded.

Lanni gave Jenny a bath, and tucked her into the bed, lying beside her on top of the bedspread until she was convinced the little girl was asleep. It took only a matter of minutes. Relieved, she momentarily closed her eyes. Judd was using the bathroom. She'd have a turn when he was finished. But the next thing she knew he was shaking her gently awake, suggesting she climb under the covers.

Bolting upright, Lanni was shocked to find that it was hours later. "Why didn't you wake me?" she asked him lightly. He sat in the middle of the other bed, leaning against the headboard. His long legs were crossed at the ankles. It took her a moment to realize he wore pajama bottoms, the top half of his torso was bare. Pajamas were a concession on his part and one for which she was grateful.

"You'll note that I did wake you."

"Right." She paused to rub the sleep from her eyes. "I think I'll take a bath," she said to no one in particular.

Judd had assumed, after his shower, that he'd fall directly asleep just as Lanni and Jenny had done. He'd been quiet when he came back into the room and smiled gently at the two sleeping figures. He'd even covered Lanni with a blanket. But he hadn't slept. He couldn't. Just watching the two of them had occupied his eyes and his mind. For the first time in years, he'd experienced a craving for a cigarette. He'd quit smoking five years ago.

Lanni slept on her side, the folds of her blouse edging up and revealing a patch of her smooth stomach. The pulling buttons left a gap open in the front of her blouse so that he could see the edges of her bra. He diverted his gaze to the blank television screen. Until Jenny was born she'd worried that her breasts were too small. Then she'd nursed the baby and had been thrilled with their increased size. Judd had never been overly concerned. Her breasts were simply a part of this woman he loved. A wonderful, erotic part of her. Now he'd caught a glimpse of her bra and discovered it had the power to arouse him. It was a shock. If this was the way he was going to react, then it was a good thing she hadn't gone swimming. Heaven only knew what would happen when he caught sight of her in a bathing suit.

Expelling his breath, he bunched up the pillow and slammed his head against it. He'd ignore her and go to sleep. Instead a vision of Lanni sitting in the tub of warm water formed in his mind. His throat grew dry as he remembered how readily she responded to his touch. Judd groaned inwardly. Drums pounded in his head. He was a disciplined man. All he needed to do was find something else on which to center his thoughts. The dryness in his throat extended to his mouth and his lips.

"Judd," Lanni called softly.

He bolted upright. "Yes?"

"I can't seem to find a towel."

Five

"No towel," Judd repeated. The drums in his head pounded stronger and louder.

"It was silly of me not to have noticed." Lanni had stood for several minutes assessing her situation before saying anything, and now she was shivering with cold.

Judd paused, glancing around him. "There's probably something around here." For a panicked second, he actually considered ripping the bedspread off the bed and handing her that. Anything that would keep that scrumptious body of hers from his gaze. He was having enough trouble taming his imagination as it was. When his frantic thoughts finally jelled, he patiently searched the room and discovered a fresh supply of towels on the vanity outside the bathroom.

The door opened a crack. "Any luck?"

Judd's gaze was everywhere but on Lanni. "Here." He stretched out his arm and gave her the towel.

Gratefully, Lanni accepted it. "Thank you."

"In the future, *think*," he snapped. Being with her the next couple of weeks was going to be bad enough without her creating situations like this. He stalked into the other room and reached for his pants. He had to get out of the motel room. Already the need for a cigarette had multiplied a hundredfold. There were only so many temptations a man could be expected to handle at one time. Lanni, dressed in a nightgown, was one more than he had the strength to deal with now.

He'd just finished tucking his shirt inside his waistband when she appeared.

"Are…are you going someplace?" she asked in a small voice. She made busywork of stroking the brush through her hair, unable to disguise her surprised dismay.

"What does it look like?" Deliberately he refused to turn around and face her. "I'll be back in a while. Don't wait up for me."

Feigning a complete lack of concern, Lanni pulled back the bedspread and climbed between the clean sheets. "Don't worry, I won't," she murmured testily, furious at her inability to cloak her disheartenment. "I wouldn't dream of wasting my time on such a futile effort."

An argument was brewing. Judd could feel the static electricity in the air. The sooner he left, the better it would be for both of them. He opened the door and stalked outside. The night air felt cool against his heated face. He slipped his hands inside the pockets of his weather-worn jeans, walking purposely forward, unsure of his destination. His only thought was that he had to get away from Lanni before he did something they'd both regret.

A thin seam of sunlight poured into the room from a crack between the drapes. Wishing to avoid the light, Judd rolled onto his side, taking the sheet with him. His mouth felt like the bottom of a toxic waste dump, and his head pounded. So much for the theory that good whiskey doesn't cause hangovers. He sat up and rotated his head to work the stiffness from the muscles of his shoulders. He stopped abruptly when he noted that the double bed beside his own was empty. He was more surprised than alarmed, but hadn't the time to ponder Lanni and Jenny's absence before the little girl flew into the room.

"Morning, Daddy," she said, vaulting into his open arms.

"Hello, sweetheart." She smelled fresh and sweet and he wrapped his arms around her and hugged her close.

"I didn't think you were ever going to wake up. Mommy and me already had breakfast. I had pancakes with little yummy fruity things."

"Blueberries," Lanni inserted, entering the room carrying a Styrofoam cup. "I hope she didn't get you out of bed."

"No." Judd couldn't take his eyes from her. Today Lanni wore white shorts and a striped red T-shirt. Her blond hair was tied back at her neck with a bright ribbon the same ruby shade as the one that held Jenny's pigtails in place. Lanni looked about sixteen. A breathtaking sixteen. "She didn't wake me." He spoke only when he realized she was waiting for a response.

Lanni handed him the cup of black coffee and walked over to the bed and started fumbling with her bags. Jenny climbed onto the mattress beside her and reached for her doll. "I…I didn't know if I should get up," Lanni said. "You said something about an early start yesterday afternoon and—"

"What time is it?"

"Nine-thirty."

That late! "If it happens again, wake me."

"All right."

Judd pried the plastic lid from the coffee cup and took the first sip. "Give me ten minutes and I'll be ready."

"Fine. Jenny and I'll wait for you by the lake."

"Lanni." His voice stopped her. "Thanks."

Her nod was curt. Wordlessly she left him and led Jenny down the pathway that led to the shore of Lake Coeur d'Alene. She didn't know what had happened last night, but this morning everything was different. Judd hardly looked at her. In fact he seemed to avoid doing so. That wasn't like him. The faint scent in the room this morning had distracted her as well, and seemed to come from Judd. It took her a moment to identify it as the cloying fragrance of cheap cologne mingled with cigarette smoke.

Lanni stopped, a sudden attack of nausea clenching her stomach so violently she thought she might be ill. Locating a park bench, she quickly sat down until the pain subsided. Jenny joined her, and rhythmically swung her short legs while humming a sweet lullaby to Betsy.

The first flash of pain faded, only to be replaced by a dull ache. Lanni knew. In an instant, she knew. Judd had left her last night and found another woman. She hadn't heard him come in, but it must have been late for him to sleep until midmorning. Her lungs expanded with the need to breathe and she released a pain-filled sigh. The ink on their divorce papers wasn't even dry and already he'd found his way to another woman.

Organizing her thoughts, Lanni's heavy heart gave way to anger and simmering resentment. She shouldn't care; it shouldn't hurt this much. The fact that it did only went to prove how far she had to go to reconcile herself to the loss of this man and their marriage.

"The car's packed." Judd's rich voice came from behind her.

Instinctively Lanni stiffened. She didn't want to face him yet. She needed time to paint on a carefree facade until they could speak privately. The thought of riding beside him drained her already depleted strength and she felt incredibly weak.

"Lanni?"

"I…heard. I was just admiring the view."

"Are you ready, Cupcake?" Judd asked, effortlessly lifting Jenny into his arms.

"Do I get to see my grandpa soon?" the little girl asked eagerly.

Already Lanni could see that traveling with her daughter today was going to be difficult. Jenny had slept restlessly, tossing and turning most of the night. Being cooped up in a car with her for another eight to ten hours would be torture for them all.

"We won't see grandpa today," Judd answered, "but we should sometime tomorrow."

"Betsy wants to see Grandpa, too."

"Betsy?"

"My baby." Jenny lifted the doll for him to see.

"Right," Judd murmured and shot a quick smile in Lanni's direction, disregarding her sober look.

She ignored his smile and rose to her feet. "I don't imagine we'll get far today after this late start."

"We should do fine," Judd contradicted, eyeing her suspiciously. He didn't know what was troubling her all of a sudden, and was mystified at the unexpected change in her mood. Only a few minutes earlier she'd brought him a fresh cup of coffee and greeted him with a warm smile. Now she sat as stiff as plywood, hardly looking at him. Apparently he'd committed some ill deed to have gained her disfavor. But he hadn't an inkling of the terrible deed he'd done.

The three walked silently to the car. Within ten minutes they were back on Interstate 90, heading east. The tension in the car was so thick Judd could taste it. Even Jenny seemed affected. They hadn't gone fifteen miles before she started to whine. Judd left Lanni to deal with her. When that didn't help, Judd invented a game and involved Jenny. Her interest in that lasted a total of five uneasy minutes. Lanni sang silly songs with her daughter and that seemed to entertain her for a few minutes.

It seemed they stopped every twenty miles. Jenny wanted something to drink, Jenny was hungry. Without questioning any of his daughter's whims, Judd gave in to her. Discipline would have to come from Lanni, and again he was puzzled by his wife's surly mood. Jenny wasn't spoiled and yet Lanni seemed to give in to the child's every demand. It was a relief when Jenny finally fell asleep.

Exhausted, Lanni sighed as she tucked a blanket in the side window to keep the sun from Jenny's face. The little girl had worn herself out and was able to rest, but in the process, she'd drained Lanni of every ounce of patience. Feeling guilty, she realized Jenny's ill-temper was a reflection of her own unsettled mood. Although no cross words had been spoken, Jenny had known something was wrong between Lanni and Judd. Rather than argue with her daughter, Lanni had continually given in to her irrational demands.

Settling into her own seat beside Judd, Lanni resecured the seatbelt and leaned her head against the headrest, closing her eyes. She was a better mother than this.

But she hadn't the strength to discipline Jenny. Not now. Not when her emotions were churning so violently inside her. She'd attempted to hide what she suspected, wrapping the pain around herself, struggling to deal with it alone, but it hadn't worked out that way. Jenny had been affected.

The silence was bliss and Judd relaxed, increasing the speed of the car. He wanted to make good time while he could. He attempted conversation a couple of times. Lanni's one-word replies ended that. It didn't take long for him to realize that it was far more pleasant to deal with Jenny's whining than the stony silence that hung between him and Lanni.

Determined to ignore her unreasonable, foul mood, he concentrated on driving, but his attention was drawn again and again to Lanni and the wounded look in her eyes. When he couldn't take it any longer, he asked, "All right, something's bothering you. What is it?"

"Nothing."

"Come on, Lanni, don't give me that."

She crossed her arms and stiffened. Her eyes narrowed slightly. It was a look Judd recognized well.

"I'd think you'd know."

Judd felt the internal pressure mount. It had always been like this. She'd be hurt and unhappy about something, but far be it from her to bring anything into the open. Oh no. He was supposed to pry it out of her a word at a time and be grateful when she saw fit to inform him of the grievous crime he'd committed. In two years, nothing had changed.

"Obviously I don't know, so maybe you should tell me."

Lanni glanced over her shoulder at her sleeping

daughter. Jenny was stirring restlessly and Lanni wanted to avoid waking her. "Not now."

"When?" he demanded.

"When I'm good and ready," she told him between clenched teeth.

"You're angry because I left you last night," he said, his patience gone. "That's it, isn't it? You always had to know where I was and how long I'd be, as if you staked a claim to my soul. I'd thought you'd matured, but I was wrong."

"I could care less about where you go or how long you want to stay," she hissed. "The only thing I'm concerned about is who you were with."

"When?"

"Last night," she told him, despising him for this charade.

"I wasn't with anyone."

Lanni snickered, crossed her arms and glared out the side window.

"While we're on the subject of who I was with—what did you do last night? Pine away for Steve?"

"At least he's kind and sincere."

"Sure he is," Judd countered angrily. "You can lead him around by the nose. If that's the kind of man you want, he'll suit you fine."

"I prefer any man who isn't like you."

Judd's jaw knotted at her tight-lipped response. Fine. If that was the way she wanted it. He'd done what he could. She'd tell him what was really troubling her once she'd punished him enough. From experience, Judd realized it was bound to come in the form of tears or an angry tirade. And then, only then, would he discover what had caused this most recent bout of angry silence.

The pattern was well set, and the separation had done nothing to change it.

Jenny slept for two hours and they stopped for something to eat when she woke. He noted that Lanni did little more than nibble at her meal. For that matter, he hadn't much of an appetite either.

Following their break they traveled another two hundred miles to Bozeman, Montana, before Judd called it quits for the day. They hadn't gotten as far as he'd hoped, but driving farther was intolerable. Jenny was fussy and unhappy; Lanni, cool and taciturn.

When Judd announced that they'd traveled enough for one day, Lanni heaved an inward sigh of relief. With every mile it became more and more impossible to hide her pain and her pride.

Time and again she recalled the look Judd had given her when he learned she'd been dating Steve. The nerve of the man was astonishing. But it hurt too much to think about it now. Tomorrow would be better. She'd have had the opportunity to speak to him without the worry of Jenny listening in on the conversation.

The motel they checked into in Bozeman was neat and clean and that was all Lanni required. A rodeo was in town and people crowded the streets. Jenny didn't eat much dinner and fell asleep watching television. Lanni gently kissed her daughter's brow and tucked the covers around her. Silently she readied for bed, determined to try to talk to Judd. But when she returned, he'd stepped out of the room. Instead of waiting up for him, she slipped into bed beside Jenny. For a long time after the light was out, Lanni lay awake. Her bed was only a few feet from Judd's, but seldom had they been separated by a greater distance. Judd had been closer to her while working in the Middle East. Infinitely closer in Alaska. For a time, far too brief, nothing had been able to come between them. The agony of the realization burned through Lanni. The pain of their failed marriage ached like a throbbing bruise.

Close to midnight, Lanni slipped into a light slumber. Before she fell asleep, she promised herself that she'd make a point of talking to Judd in the morning.

Lanni didn't know what time it was when Jenny woke crying.

"Mommy, I don't feel good," she groaned, sitting up in bed. "I think I'm going to be sick."

Waking from a drugged sleep, Lanni heard Jenny, but the words didn't penetrate the cloud of fatigue until it was too late.

Throwing back the sheets, Lanni reacted instinctively, reaching for the light. "Oh, baby," she cooed, lifting her daughter into her arms and carrying her into the bathroom.

"Is she all right? Should I get a doctor?" Concerned, Judd staggered into the bathroom after them.

"I don't feel very good," Jenny groaned again as Lanni washed her face.

Jenny's head felt cool. At least she didn't have a fever. "I think she'll be fine now. It was only a bad tummy ache."

"Is there anything I can do?" Judd felt the overwhelming urge to help. This was his child who was ill. The feeling of helplessness that he'd experienced when he'd seen her fall in Seahurst Park returned.

Lanni understood the plea in his voice. "Would you get her a fresh set of clothes?" she asked softly.

"Sure. Anything."

He was gone only a few minutes. "I called the office. They're sending someone over to clean the bed."

He handed Lanni a fresh pair of pajamas, then paced the area outside the bathroom until a light knock sounded against their door.

Several minutes passed before Jenny's stomach was settled enough to leave the bathroom. For a time, Lanni held her in her lap, rocking gently to and fro while she tenderly smoothed the curls from the little girl's brow. When she returned to the room, Judd glanced up.

"How is she?"

Lanni mouthed the word *asleep.* The bed on which they'd been sleeping was stripped bare of the sheets.

"The lady from the office said it was best to air the mattress."

Lanni nodded, understanding the reasoning.

"They brought in a cot for Jenny."

Gently Lanni placed the sleeping child onto the thin mattress. Lovingly she spread the blanket over her shoulders. It wasn't until she'd straightened that she realized there was only one suitable bed in the room: Judd's.

Judd read the aggravation in her eyes.

"I didn't plan this."

"I'm not going to sleep with you." Hell would freeze over before she shared a bed with Judd Matthiessen ever again.

"What do you suggest then?"

"I don't know. But I'm not sleeping with you."

"Fine." He pulled the bedspread from the top of the bed and headed toward the bathroom.

"Where are you going?"

"Where does it look like?" he whispered furiously.

"Don't be ridiculous. You can't sleep in there." The thought of Judd trying to sleep in the bathtub was ludicrous. If anyone slept there it should be her. "I'll move in there. I'm the one…"

"This is crazy." He dragged his hand over his face, struggling for control. "I'm not going to attack you, we're married. Can't you trust me enough to believe I wouldn't do anything?"

"But…"

"Never mind. I'll get another room."

"No." Lanni swallowed her pride. With the rodeo in town, they'd been fortunate to obtain a room in this hotel. Judd was right. She was overreacting. They were married, and if he said he wouldn't touch her, then he wouldn't. She believed him. "All right."

"All right what?"

"We can sleep here."

"Thank you," he muttered sarcastically. He tossed the bedspread on top of the double bed. He didn't know what was troubling Lanni, but he couldn't remember her ever being this unreasonable. She looked confused and unsure; not unlike young Jenny. Judd longed to re-assure her, comfort her. But he knew she wasn't in the mood for either.

He waited until she was settled in bed, ridiculously close to the edge, before reaching for the lamp and turning out the light. Confident there wasn't any possibility of touching her, he slipped inside the sheets and lay on his back, staring at the moon shadows playing across the ceiling. After ten minutes, he forced his eyes closed, convinced the effort to sleep wouldn't do any good.

He couldn't with Lanni like this. He'd never been able to deal with her when she was in a dark mood. Maybe if he knew what he'd done that was so terribly wrong, he could say something that would ease her doubts. He'd given up trying to understand her long ago.

Lanni lay on her back as well, holding the percale sheet over her breasts. Pain tightened her chest, making breathing difficult. She took several shallow breaths and forced her body to relax. Falling asleep the first time had been difficult, but now, with Judd at her side, it was impossible. From his breathing patterns, Lanni knew he was awake as well.

"Judd?" Her fingers gripped the sheet, twisting the material so tightly that her fingers ached. "Why'd you do it?"

"Do what?"

"Why did you go to *her* last night?" Despite her effort to sound calm and collected, Lanni's voice trembled, threatening to crack.

"Her? Who the hell are you talking about?"

"That woman."

"What woman?"

"The one you were with last night."

"Last night?" He vaulted to a sitting position. "Are you crazy? I told you once I wasn't with anyone!"

Lanni's eyes dropped closed as she struggled to maintain her composure. "Please, don't lie to me. I know differently." The pressure to give in to tears was so strong that it felt as if someone were sitting on top of Lanni's chest.

"I went to a tavern last night. Sure there were women there, but I didn't so much as look at one of them." He couldn't—not when all he could think about was Lanni. One woman had been particularly insistent, leaning over him in an effort to catch his attention, but she'd gotten the message soon enough. He wasn't interested. How could he be when his thoughts had centered around the times he'd come home late to find Lanni in bed asleep? In living Technicolor he recalled how he'd stripped off his clothes and slipped between the sheets beside her. Lanni would nestle her sleepy, warm body against him and sigh. Man and woman as God had intended them from the beginning of time.

And Lanni honestly believed he'd gone to another woman. Instead he'd been in torment, drinking in an effort to dispel the image of those days when their love had been purer and stronger than anything he'd ever experienced. Alcohol had done little to diminish the memory and he'd returned to the hotel more confused than when he'd left. A lot of things had changed over the years, but Judd doubted that their lovemaking ever could. They had been magnificent together. But anything physical between them would be wrong now. He recognized and accepted that, but the knowledge did little to eat away his desire.

"I'm not lying," he told her, shaking his head as a weariness of heart and soul settled over him. So this was the reason she'd been so taciturn all day, wreaking payment for imagined wrongs. He swung his legs off the bed and sat on the edge of the mattress. Lanni had such little faith in him. So little faith—so little trust. The pain-filled anger within him mounted with each heartbeat.

"So that's why you've been treating me like I had the plague all day. What kind of man do you think I am?" Twisting around, he gripped her shoulders and anchored her against the mattress. His eyes resembled those of a wild animal caught in a trap. Stricken. Intense. Dangerous.

"I thought—"

"I know what you thought." He glared down at her with an anger that would have panicked a lesser woman.

Startled, Lanni struggled to break free, flattening

her hands against his hard chest and pushing with all her strength. The weight of his anger held her firm. He was crushed against her, his tight features above hers pinning her more effectively than the strong hold of his arms.

"Don't try and tell me you weren't with some woman last night." Her voice became a strangled whisper in an effort to keep from waking Jenny. "I smelled her perfume."

"I wasn't with anyone," he answered, just as furious. He stared down at her, silently challenging her to contradict him a second time.

Their panting breaths echoed as Lanni defiantly met the fury in his gaze.

"I know you, Judd, I know how virile you are…"

"Me?" He said it with a short, humorless laugh. "You were the one who was always so hot. How have you survived the last two years? I suppose you sought a substitute in Steve."

"That's ridiculous!"

"How far did you go with that milquetoast?"

"Judd, stop—"

"Did he kiss you?"

"Judd," she cried. "Please…"

Their gazes held for a moment longer while Judd struggled to subdue his temper. Fearing his grip would hurt her, he released her voluntarily. Moving away, he raked his fingers through his hair and stared sightlessly into the distance. "Never mind. Don't answer because I don't want to know."

"I… You wouldn't look at me this morning. Like you were guilty of something. And then I could smell cheap cologne on you."

"I'd gotten drunk. If you want the truth, there was

a woman who approached me. I sent her away. I'm not proud of what I did—leaving you in the hotel while I drowned my problems. It's not the type of thing a man likes to do when his wife and daughter are with him."

"You felt bad because you had a drink?"

He nodded, unwilling to look at her.

"That's it?"

He stood and walked to the other side of the room, pushing back the drape. A wide ribbon of moonlight flooded the room. His fist bunched up the thick material as he gazed sightlessly into the night.

The numbness gradually left Lanni and she raised herself onto her elbows. Judd stood at the window, the moonlight silhouetting his profile against the opposite wall. His head drooped as if the weight of holding it upright was too much for him. His shoulders were slouched; his hand gripped the drape as though he wanted to rip it from the rod.

"I don't know what to say," she whispered, confused. She hadn't meant to unjustly accuse him. She hadn't meant for any of this to happen. He'd left her and Jenny in that hotel room the way he had always walked out on them and she hadn't been able to deal with the rejection. Not again. Not now.

Judd heard her but didn't turn around. Lanni left the bed and started to pace the area behind him. "I was wrong to accuse you," she admitted.

He acknowledged her with a curt nod. "We all make mistakes. Don't worry about it." He forced his voice to sound light, unconcerned. "Go back to bed. At least one of us should sleep." He turned away from the window and reached for his clothes.

He was leaving her again. For two nights running, he had walked out on her. Lanni couldn't bear it.

"Don't go," she whispered desperately, holding her hand out to him. "Please, not again." She couldn't handle it. She needed him with her. Tomorrow they'd be in Twin Deer. The problems awaiting them in Judd's hometown were overwhelming. They needed to secure a peace between them and if Judd left tonight they would solve nothing.

Judd hesitated. The desperation in Lanni's voice tugged at his heart.

"Please." Her heart pounded. She had so much pride. They both did. Judd knew what it had cost her to ask him to stay—she'd sworn never to do it again.

His features were difficult to make out in the dark. Lanni didn't know what he was thinking; she no longer cared.

Judd dropped his clothes and without thought Lanni walked into his arms. His crushing grip on her made breathing difficult. She whimpered softly, holding onto him with all her strength. Judd buried his face along the curve of her neck and exhaled forcefully.

"I believe you," she whispered again. The chaos and tension inside Lanni gradually subsided. The chill left her bones. She could feel Judd's breath whisper against her hair and smell the masculine scent of his body.

"Not once in all those months was I unfaithful," he told her forcefully. "Not even once."

A huge sob slid from Lanni's throat as her heart swelled, making her giddy with relief. She didn't doubt him. Not after what she'd seen in him tonight. All these months, he'd kept their vows pure. She wasn't so naive to believe that there hadn't been temptations. She knew better. There'd been plenty of those. Lots of eager women. Months of loneliness.

Laughter blended with the tears as she gripped the

side of his face and rained kisses across his brow. Her lips found his eyes, his nose, his cheek.

"Lanni." He raised his hand to stop her and discovered he couldn't. She was like a child who'd been granted an unexpected surprise. It felt too good to hold her in his arms to put an end to it so quickly.

When her mouth inadvertently brushed against the corner of his, Lanni paused and Judd softly caught his breath. Time skidded to a standstill as they stared at each other in the dark. He needed to taste her. Desperately wanted her. Unable to stop himself, Judd's mouth claimed hers, hungry with two years of pent-up need and desire. Her lips parted in welcome.

Lanni sagged against him, weak and trembling.

Hot sensation raced through him. She was like a flower. Petal soft. Silky. Lovely.

"I thought…" Lanni felt the need to explain.

"I know. I swear to you there was no one."

"I believe you." She propped her forehead against his chin. "Things will be better once we're in Twin Deer."

"Right." But he knew differently. He dropped his arms, releasing her. "I didn't mean for that to happen."

"It was my fault. I was the one—"

"Must it always be someone's fault?"

"No. Of course not."

The tender moment was over. They stepped away from each other, struggling to put their relationship back into the proper perspective.

Six

"I feel all better."

Reluctantly Lanni opened one eye to discover her daughter standing above her. Betsy, Jenny's beloved doll, was securely clenched under one arm. The plastic pacifier in the doll's mouth loomed over Lanni's face.

"I'm not sick anymore."

"I'm glad, sweetheart." Five more minutes. All she needed was a few more minutes to clear her befuddled head.

"Can I get in bed with you and Daddy?"

Jenny's request propelled Lanni into action. She climbed out of bed and headed for her suitcase. "Not now. We're going to see your grandpa today. Remember?" She took a fresh change of clothes and brought Jenny into the bathroom with her. By the time she returned, Judd was up and dressed as well. Either by design or accident, their gazes just managed to avoid meeting. They'd slept in the same bed, but had gone to lengths to keep from touching. Lanni hadn't thought she'd be able to sleep, but surprisingly, she'd drifted off easily. She didn't know about Judd.

"Morning," he said when they appeared and he offered them a good-natured smile. He stood on the other side of the room, bright-eyed and refreshed, looking as though he'd risen with the sun after a restful night of slumber.

"I'm not sick anymore, Daddy."

"What about Betsy?" he asked, glancing at the doll.

"She's all better, too!" Jenny exclaimed proudly. "Am I really going to see my grandpa today?"

"Sometime this afternoon if everything goes well."

"I'm going to be real good," Jenny promised. "And Betsy, too."

True to her word, the four-year-old was a model traveling companion. She played quietly in the back seat of the car for a good portion of the morning. When she grew bored, she sang songs she'd learned in nursery school. Soon Lanni's voice blended with her daughter's. At familiar childhood ditties, Judd's deep baritone joined theirs. Jenny loved to hear Judd sing and clapped her small hands to show her delight.

The miles sped past. Judd was the quiet one this day, Lanni noted. But the silence wasn't a strained one. From the way his brow was creased, she knew his thoughts were dark and heavy introspective. Lanni realized that his mind was on the approaching meeting with his father and not their disagreements.

They had a truce of sorts—more of an understanding. Their marriage was over; they both had accepted the truth of that. It had been damaged beyond repair two years before. Even longer, but Lanni had refused to acknowledge the failure before Judd left her and Jenny. Their vows had continued to bind them to each other, but it was long past the time to get on with their lives.

They stopped for lunch at a small café outside Billings. Jenny fell asleep in the back seat of the SUV soon after. The traffic on the freeway was light and Lanni noted that for the first time Judd was driving faster than the speed limit. She found it curious that he would do so now. It was as though an urgency drove him, pushing him harder and faster as he neared the town of Twin Deer.

He hadn't told her much about Stuart's condition, other than the fact his father was dying. Lanni believed that Judd probably didn't know much more himself.

Resting her head against the headrest, Lanni allowed her lids to drift closed. She knew so little about Judd's childhood. He had mentioned his youth only in passing and usually in the briefest of terms, as if the subject were best left undisturbed. From what she had been able to glean, his younger years had been unhappy. There'd been no Christmases. No tree, no presents, no stocking by the fireplace. That much she knew. And probably no Easters or any other holidays, either.

For a time after they were first together, Lanni had suspected that Judd had married her because of her strong family ties. She was close to her parents and sister. After they'd married, Lanni's parents warmly welcomed Judd into their lives. He was accepted by her extended family of aunts, uncles and a multitude of cousins as well. It astonished her how well he blended in, as if he'd always been a part of them. It wasn't until after Jenny was born that Lanni noticed Judd withdrawing from her family. He objected when her mother and father offered solutions to their financial problems. He didn't like her dad "putting a good word in for him" with a local contractor. Nor did he appreciate the unexpected visits her parents paid them without notice.

"Another hour," Judd said. When Lanni opened her

eyes and glanced at him, he realized he'd spoken aloud. He hadn't meant to.

Lanni straightened.

"Sorry," he murmured, "I didn't mean to wake you."

"You didn't. I was just resting my eyes."

Judd concentrated on the road. He'd been awake most of the night, thinking about the ranch and mentally preparing himself for this so-called homecoming. He didn't expect it to be pleasant. He'd been away from the ranch for nearly eighteen years. Not once in all that time had he looked back. When he'd left, he'd told Stuart he wouldn't return—not unless he was asked. It'd taken all these years for Stuart to send for him. And now, only because he was dying. Judd wanted to curse his father's stubborn pride, but recognized that his own was equally unreasonable.

He dragged in a breath of clean air. The scent of wildflowers brought a brief smile. Now as he neared the ranch, he realized how much he had missed Montana.

Jim Peterman, his father's foreman, had once told him that Montana was good for the soul. Funny that he'd remember that after all these years. Another quirk in his memory was that Twin Deer was only a few miles from Custer Battlefield where Lt. Col. George Custer had made his last stand against the Sioux and Cheyenne warriors. As a boy Judd had wandered over the bluffs of the battle-scarred ground. He'd even discovered a few tarnished arrowheads. At twelve he'd considered them priceless treasures, and now fleetingly wondered what had happened to them. Knowing Stuart, he'd probably tossed them in the garbage just to be ornery.

Sadness permeated Judd's spirit at the thought of his father. The realization that the old man was dying produced a heaviness that felt like concrete blocks weighing down his heart. There was no love lost between them—never had been. Nonetheless Judd hated the thought of Stuart suffering.

"You're awfully quiet," Lanni said.

"Just thinking."

"About what?"

"The Circle M."

Lanni's brows arched. "What's that?"

"The ranch." Judd was astonished that he'd never told her the name. "It's also our brand."

"You mean they still brand cattle?"

Despite his efforts not to, Judd chuckled. "At least they did when I was last home." The word "home" seemed to echo in the close confines of the station wagon. The Circle M was home, no matter how much he tried to deny it. He was going home. Home with all its memories—with all its lures.

"Did you raise cows?"

A suggestion of a smile touched his eyes as he glanced at Lanni. "Steers."

Feeling a bit chagrined, Lanni said, "Right."

"Do you have horseys?" The eager voice from the back seat surprised them both. Lanni hadn't realized Jenny was awake.

"When I was a little boy, I had a pony."

The information was news to Lanni. "What was his name?"

"Trigger."

Lanni smiled. "You weren't very original, were you?"

"Sure I was. At the time my name was Roy Rogers."

"I'll be your Dale Evans anytime." The words came without thought. Color crept up Lanni's neck in a flush of hot pink. She didn't know what had gotten into her to make such a suggestion. "That isn't exactly what I meant to say."

"Don't worry. I know what you meant."

Lanni was pleased he did, since she hadn't the foggiest notion where the words had come from. Certainly not her head—her heart, perhaps. This time with Judd was going to be far worse than she'd imagined. Last night she'd wanted him to make love to her. Sensation after sensation had shot through her—ones Lanni had assumed long dead and conveniently buried. Thirty seconds of sexual awareness had momentarily wiped out two years of bitterness. She wouldn't allow it to happen again, and she wouldn't, Lanni vowed.

Color tinged her cheeks at the realization of what could have happened, but then Judd had always been able to do that to her. There'd never been another man she'd wanted half as much. Little had changed from the time when they'd first met all those years ago. Lanni had feared that Judd would think her brazen. At the time, her behavior had been little short of audacious. He'd been so worldly, so traveled. She'd strived to seem sophisticated, but none of it had mattered to Judd. He'd wanted her then just as he had in the motel last night and she'd nearly succumbed to his lovemaking. In the cruel light of day, Lanni thanked God that Judd had had the common sense to put an end to the kissing. All things considered, allowing their kissing to get out of hand now would be disastrous to them both.

"We're on Circle M land now," Judd announced solemnly.

"Will I get to see Grandpa soon?" Jenny's voice rang clear, light and excited.

"Real soon." The muscles of Judd's abdomen tightened with nervous anticipation. The letter from Stuart had been brief. Stark. Judd had no conception of what awaited him.

"Is that the house?" Lanni pointed ahead to the two-storey structure. The faded brown structure melted in with the surroundings so completely that they had already turned into the long driveway before she realized that the dilapidated building must be Judd's home. The house looked like something out of the nineteenth century with a wide front porch. Four pillars supported the second-storey balcony. One leaned dangerously to the side so that the upper structure tilted off-center. Shutters lined the large rectangular windows. Several were missing and the remaining few hung precariously. The house was badly in need of paint. The once white exterior had faded with weather and time to a dull shade of earthtone. Once, Lanni could tell, the house had been a source of pride and care. No longer. Like Stuart Matthiessen, the house was dying.

"That's it," Judd confirmed in a low voice.

"What about the other buildings?" Another smaller home was close to the large barn, separated by only a few hundred feet from the larger house.

"The Petermans live there."

"Neighbors?" It didn't make sense to have all this land and then allow someone to build in your own backyard.

"Dad's foreman." The shortness of Judd's response revealed how distracted he was. The house was a shock. It had never been much of a showplace, but Stuart had his pride. The house had always been kept clean and in good repair, painted white every few years. Betty Peterman had been housekeeper and Jim Peterman had been a jack of all trades. The couple had lived in the small house for as long as Judd could remember. Whenever

Judd thought about the Circle M, his mind automatically included the Petermans.

Stuart's letter had briefly mentioned that the Petermans were gone, leaving Stuart to himself. Compassion filled Judd. Not only was Stuart sick, but now he was alone and friendless.

Judd followed the driveway and parked at the back of the house in the half circle that arced toward the main house. As Lanni opened the car door, she noted the gallant attempt of a rosebush as it struggled to poke its head through the underbrush that knotted what must have once been flowerbeds a long time past. One velvety red blossom stuck its head through the thick patch of weeds and aimed for the sky, valiant and determined.

Lanni's attention abruptly rotated from the brave flower to the screen door as it swung open and Stuart Matthiessen moved onto the porch. He held onto the door as though he needed the support. And from the look of him, he required something to help him remain upright.

Judd saw his father and was so shocked by the change in his appearance the words froze in his throat.

"I see you made it." Stuart spoke first.

He was dangerously underweight, to the point of being gaunt. His thinness sharpened his features to such an extent that Judd suspected Jenny would be frightened.

"You asked me to come." Judd straightened and closed the car door. Lanni climbed out and moved to the back of the car in order to help Jenny out of the car seat.

"I notice that you took your own sweet time," Stuart accused him. The intense eyes narrowed on Judd. "I suppose you thought if you waited long enough, I'd be dead."

Judd opened his mouth to deny the accusation and quickly closed it, determined not to fall victim to verbal battles with his father. Let him assume what he would; it made little difference to Judd.

"I see you don't bother to deny it. Well, I fooled you this time. You thought I'd be dead and you'd sashay in here and claim the ranch." His laugh was rusty and sharp. "I fooled you again, boy."

"I don't need a thousand acres of headaches."

"Good, because you're not getting it." The words were hurled at Judd like acid. The sight of his father and the bitter words hit Judd in the chest and for an instant, he couldn't breathe evenly. He thought he was prepared for this meeting and realized that little could have readied him for this. The man had been waiting eighteen years to have his say and wouldn't be cheated out of it now.

"I suppose you think that because you've been all over the world that the Circle M isn't good enough for you."

Judd responded with a sharp shake of his head. He had traveled thousands of miles to be insulted? He should have his head examined.

The tone of Stuart's voice paralyzed Lanni. She paused, uncertain of what to do. Her gaze skidded from Judd's father back to her husband. She marveled at Judd's control. The insults washed off his back like rainwater on an oil-slickened street. He gave no outward indication that the anger and resentment affected him in any way. But Lanni knew differently. The words to defend Judd burned on her lips. Stuart had no right to talk to her husband like this. He'd come at Stuart's request. If there'd been any delay it had been her fault, not Judd's.

"Mommy, I want to see my grandpa," Jenny called from inside the car. "Let me out. Mommy, let me out."

Reluctantly Lanni unbuckled Jenny from the car seat. The minute Jenny was free of the confining straps, she bolted from the car and up to the porch steps where her grandfather was standing.

"Are you my grandpa?"

The transformation in Stuart's face was almost unbelievable. The thick frown softened and the tired, aged eyes brightened. "She looks like Lydia," he murmured to no one in particular. "Yes, I'm your grandpa," he said softly. "I've been waiting for you to come." Gently he took Jenny's hand to lead her into the house.

"We came a long, long ways. Daddy drove and drove and drove. I saw a cow. Daddy says he had a pony when he was a little boy. Can I have a pony?"

Left standing alone by the car, Lanni looked to Judd. "He didn't mean what he said."

Judd pretended not to hear as he retrieved the largest suitcase from the back end of the station wagon. "He meant it. Every word."

Lanni longed to erase some of the pain she knew Judd was experiencing. While she searched, Judd picked up two of the largest suitcases and headed for the house.

Carrying Jenny's doll and a few odds and ends, Lanni followed him. If the outside of the house was in disrepair it was nothing compared to the confusion that greeted her on the inside. Dirty dishes filled the huge porcelain kitchen sink. The table was littered with an open jar of peanut butter, jelly, instant coffee and a sugar bowl. The door off the kitchen led to the bathroom and a glance revealed dirty clothes in every conceivable space.

"Where are the Petermans?" Judd demanded of Stuart, setting down the suitcases.

"Gone."

"What do you mean gone?"

The anger in Judd's tone brought Lanni up short. Judd was furious and was doing a poor job of disguising it.

"They left about a month ago," Stuart elaborated briefly.

About the time he'd mailed the letter, Judd assumed. It didn't make sense to him. The Petermans had lived most of their married lives on the Circle M. They wouldn't have left without just cause. "Why would they go after all these years?"

Stuart grunted. "You'll have to ask them that."

"I plan on it."

Stuart snorted a second time and raised an arthritic finger, pointing it at Judd's chest. "I won't have you interfering in my business. You hear me?"

Judd ignored his father's words and stepped past him to the stairway, hauling the suitcases with him. Lanni claimed Jenny's small hand and followed. Two weeks. They were committed to two weeks minimum of this terrible tension. Lanni doubted that she'd last a second longer. She yearned to cover Jenny's ears.

"It doesn't look like any of the beds have been made up," Judd said apologetically, glancing in turn in the three doorways.

"That's no problem," Lanni said quickly, grateful to have something to do. "I'll get them ready."

"I didn't bring you along to do housework." The fierce intensity of his gaze pressed her to the wall.

"I don't mind. Honestly. What do you expect me to do for the next couple of weeks?"

"Not dirty dishes!"

"Can I sleep in this room?" Jenny peeked into the room located at the farthest end of the long narrow hallway. "I like it in here."

Judd's harsh countenance relaxed. "That used to be my bedroom."

"Any treasures hidden in there?" Lanni questioned, wanting to steer him away from a bad mood. She followed him to the bedroom.

Judd shrugged his shoulders. "Treasures? I don't know." It was the truth. He'd left nearly everything behind, taking only the bare essentials with him. The parting, like the reunion, had been bitter. Judd didn't know what Stuart had done with the contents of the room and was mildly surprised to find it was exactly as he'd left it. Except for the stripped bed, it didn't look as though Stuart had once come upstairs in all the years Judd had been away. His old football helmet rested on the top of the bureau, along with a picture of his mother, holding him in her arms. He'd been only a year old at the time. The narrow triangular shaped banner from his high school team remained on the wall, along with a paint-by-number picture of two horses he'd patiently painted the year he was in the sixth grade.

Lanni's eye caught the photograph of Judd and his mother first and was amazed at how accurate Stuart's statement had been. Jenny did have the same startling blue eyes as Judd's mother. Lydia was lovely. Petite. Delicate. Refined. Lanni couldn't imagine such a gentle woman married to Stuart Matthiessen. They were as different as silk and burlap.

"There may be a few old love letters lying around," Judd teased, watching Lanni. Her gaze rested on the photo of his mother, and he wanted to distract her from the questions that burned in her eyes. They were ones he'd asked himself often enough over the years.

"Love letters? No doubt," she replied with a fair amount of feigned indignation. Purposefully she crossed her arms, boldly meeting the mischief in his eyes.

"I was known to turn a head or two in my day."

"I don't doubt that, either." He was still capable of garnering attention from the female population. After all that had passed between them, Lanni still found him devastating. She always had. Sitting beside Jenny on the bare mattress, Lanni pulled the little girl onto her lap. "Do you want to help Mommy put sheets on the bed?"

The four-year-old nodded, eager to assist.

"I told you I don't want you doing housework!"

"I've been doing it for a lot of years, Judd Matthiessen. What's different now?" Her own voice contained a sharp edge. He had to know that she didn't make enough income selling real estate to hire a live-in housekeeper. To his credit, the checks he sent every month were generous enough to afford one, but Lanni hadn't once entertained the notion of such an extravagance. A large portion of each check went into a savings account for Jenny.

"I won't let Stuart use you," Judd continued, his temper gaining momentum.

"Use me? Judd, you're overreacting."

"I won't argue about it. You take care of Jenny and I'll make up the beds."

"You're being ridiculous."

"I'm not going to stand here and argue with you, Lanni." He stalked out of the bedroom and down the narrow hallway to the first bedroom. With only a bed and dresser, this was the smallest of the three bedrooms located upstairs. The ornate four-poster bedframe had to be a hundred-year-old antique. Lanni paused in the doorway to admire the simple elegance of the piece, mildly surprised to find something of beauty in this neglected house.

"It's lovely."

"Right," Judd grumbled, pulling open the bottom dresser drawer and taking out a set of sheets. Lanni moved inside the room to help him. He ignored her as much as possible, unfolding the bottom sheet and spreading it across the bed. It lay haphazardly on the padded mattress. Lanni reached for the same corner as Judd, their hands bumping into each other's in an effort to secure the sheet.

"Lanni," he muttered.

"Yes?"

"Don't. Please."

Frustrated, she threw up her hands, releasing the smoothed edge of the cotton sheet. "All right, all right." She left the room, and immediately located the middle bedroom. This one was equally small; there was hardly room for the double bed and dresser. Again the furniture was heavy, sturdy mahogany from yesteryear. She found the sheets and blankets in the bottom drawer of the dresser. Working silently, she efficiently spread out the sheets and blanket.

"Lanni!" Judd growled from inside the doorway a couple of minutes later.

The sheer volume of his voice frightened her half out of her wits. Her hand flew to her heart. "Don't do that," she gasped in a husky whisper.

"Sorry." But he didn't look apologetic. He moved into the room, dominating what little space there was. In an effort to scoot past Lanni, his torso brushed hers grazing his chest. The contact paralyzed him for an in-

stant. His heart began to pound almost painfully. Lanni
was the sexiest, most alluring woman he'd ever known
and she didn't even know it. She had yet to guess the
overwhelming effect she had on him.

"Judd," she asked innocently, "what's wrong?"

"Nothing."

"Then why are you standing like that?"

"This is why," he said with a groan. He turned to her,
pulling her toward him by the shoulders. The back of
her knees met the side of the mattress.

Lanni's eyes widened as her gaze flew to his. It
shocked her to find how good Judd's body felt pressing against her softness. Her own body reacted instinctively to his, shaping, molding, yielding to his hardness.
His splayed hands spread wide across her back, arching
her closer, craving the taste and scent of her softness.
He moaned as her body yielded to meet his.

Sensation seared a path through Judd. Slowly, deliberately, he lowered his mouth to hers, starving for the
taste of her. She was honey and wine. Champagne. Or-
chids. Love. Acceptance. All that had ever been good
in his life. And all that had been denied.

The pressure of his hold had Lanni nearly bent in
half. When she could endure it no longer, she fell backward, taking him with her as they tumbled onto the
mattress. The force of his weight over hers knocked the
breath from her lungs and she gave a small cry of fright.

"What's wrong? Are you hurt?" His forearms framed
her face as his wide gaze studied her.

She shook her head. Unable to resist, she raised her
hand and touched the frowning lines that fanned out
from the corner of his eyes. Character lines.

His torso pressed her deep within the soft mattress.
His body felt incredibly good over hers. He paused,

half-expecting Lanni to stop him, and when she didn't, he kissed her with a thoroughness that rocked her very being.

Lanni shut her eyes, longing to lose herself in the passion of the moment, yearning to forget all that had gone before them and savor these priceless moments of contentment.

"Lanni, Lanni," he groaned, kissing her as though he couldn't bear to let her go, even to breathe. "No. No. This is wrong. I promised you… I *promised* you…" Even as he spoke, his mouth came down on hers.

Lanni was shocked into numbness. Judd had always been extraordinarily gentle with her. This urgency was so unlike him that she didn't know how to react. At first she did nothing, letting him kiss her greedily as though she were an unwilling participant. Her lack of response lasted less than a moment. Judd's mouth gentled and Lanni was lost. Frantically she combed her fingers through his hair and pressed closer to him.

"Mommy. Daddy." Jenny's soft voice calling to them permeated the fog of passion that cloaked Judd's mind.

"Yes, sweetheart." Lanni recovered first.

"I made my bed all by myself."

Lanni pushed against Judd, wanting him to release her, but he held her fast and she doubted that he felt the pressure of her hands.

"Are you proud of me, Daddy?"

"Very proud." His voice was little more than a whisper. He rolled onto his back, freeing Lanni. His hand covered his eyes. "And very relieved." Sweat broke out across his upper lip as the shivers raced down his arms and legs. He'd come so close. Too close. He didn't know what was the matter with him. His word. He'd given Lanni his word. He'd committed his share of sins in his life, but he'd promised Lanni and himself that he wouldn't touch her. When they returned to Seattle she would be free of him.

Lanni struggled into a sitting position, her heart pounding at how dangerously close she'd been to tossing aside everything that was important for a few minutes of pleasure.

"I'm on my way, Cupcake," Lanni said, her voice incredibly weak. "Let me see your bed."

Seven

Betty Peterman's work-gnarled hands surrounded the steaming coffee mug. She looked out of place in the tiny apartment kitchen two blocks off Main Street in Twin Deer. Her husband, Jim, sat next to her and Judd was across the table from them both.

"He asked us to leave. Gave no reason," Jim stated, his eyes revealing the shock of the request. "After nearly forty years, I don't mind telling you it came as a jolt."

"But why?" Judd couldn't begin to understand what had driven his father to such drastic measures.

"He didn't give us any reason."

"Money?" Judd voiced the only plausible explanation. As far as he knew the ranch had always been financially sound. The only possible reasoning was that his father had fallen onto hard times. Judd wasn't ignorant of the problems ranchers faced—low beef prices had brought foreclosure to many of their neighbors.

"He gave us a settlement," Betty said. She smiled at him, but the effort to show any pleasure was negated by the hurt disbelief in her eyes. Judd was aware of how much the two had aged. Jim had always been tall, wiry, and bowlegged from so many years in a saddle.

His hair was completely white now and his shoulders hunched forward. But his firm handshake proved that he was still as rough as a bronco and as tough as shoe leather. Twenty years had only changed the outward appearance. As few things are in life, Jim Peterman was constant.

Betty was round and motherly. More round than Judd remembered, which caused him to grin. She was the only female influence he'd had in his youth and she'd been able to give him only a minimum of attention since Stuart had claimed he didn't want Judd growing up to be a sissy. Nonetheless Betty had faced her employer's wrath on many occasions to take Judd's part. She'd been the one to urge him to leave as a young high-school graduate, although he'd seen the sheen of tears in her eyes when she told him it would be better if he left the Circle M and Stuart.

Judd had already accepted that he would never be able to get along with his father. Having Betty and Jim recognize the fact and advise him to leave had been the encouragement he'd needed to pack his bags and head out. Over the years he'd sent both the Petermans money for their birthdays and Christmas. Not once had he ever imagined them away from the ranch. They were as much a part of the Circle M as the land itself. His father must have lost something mentally to send the Petermans away so callously.

"So it isn't money?" Judd continued.

"Not from what we can see," Jim answered with a soft snort. "In fact we got the best beef prices in years."

"Then why?"

"Don't rightly know." Jim paused and took a sip from the side of the mug, making a light slurping sound. "He had me sell off the best part of the herd. Fences are down all over, but he said he didn't want me to do any repairs. From talk in town he'd got himself a temporary ranch hand, but from what I can see, he's not doing much good."

"He hasn't been himself for months," Betty added, her gaze drifting down. "He hasn't eaten much the last few months either, although I tried to tempt him with his favorite meals."

"He's been ill, but he didn't tell me much about it," Judd told them, looking for some confirmation in their gazes. He'd come for more than one reason. He wanted to learn what the Petermans could tell him about Stuart's health. Although his father was thin and frail looking, he looked in better shape than Judd had expected.

"Is that why you've come?" Jim asked.

"He wrote and asked me to bring Jenny."

Jim and Betty's gazes shot toward each other. Forty years of marriage made words unnecessary. A small smile brought dimples into Betty's round cheeks and Jim nodded knowingly.

"Have you talked to his doctor?" Betty asked, looking concerned now.

"Not yet." But Judd had already called the small medical center in town and planned on stopping by there when he'd finished with Jim and Betty. He wanted to talk to Doc Simpson, who had been the family physician for as long as Judd could remember.

"He didn't say anything to us about any medical problem, but he hasn't been himself for months," Jim said.

Judd took a drink of coffee. "How soon can you two move back?" Seeing the Circle M in such a run-down condition had affected him nearly as much as seeing his father leaning against the railing on the porch, looking fragile and sickly. "In addition to some fences, we're going to rebuild the herd."

"Hot dog!" Jim slapped his hand against his jean-clad thigh and grinned like a twenty-year-old.

"Jim doesn't hanker much for city life," Betty said, her brown eyes alight. "Can't say that I do, either."

"My wife and daughter are at the house now."

"I'll be pleased to meet them." Both of the Petermans looked as if they'd dropped ten years in the fifteen-minute visit. "I suppose the house was a disaster."

"Worse." Judd thought of the spotless kitchen Betty had always insisted upon and knew the housekeeper would have cringed at the sight of week-old dishes piled high in the sink. Knowing Lanni, she'd never be able to sit idle. He'd bet a month's wages that she'd torn into the kitchen the instant he was out the door. If there'd been any sensible way to stop her, he would have.

"You staying?"

Judd hesitated. "For now." What Stuart's doctor had to say would determine the length of his visit. For the first time in his life, Stuart needed his son. A weak voice in the back of his head urged Judd to do what he could to make his father comfortable, and then move on. But he couldn't. Judd knew in his heart that no matter how wide the rift between him and Stuart, he wouldn't desert his father now. He'd stick by Stuart until the end. Lanni would go and take Jenny with her. He couldn't hold them for any more than two weeks. Lanni had another life in Seattle now. He didn't like to think about her and Jenny leaving, but recognized that eventually he'd need to let them go. He couldn't ask anything more of Lanni than what he had already.

* * *

Humming softly as she worked, Lanni ran water into the kitchen sink. She was grateful Judd had left. He would have been furious had he seen her working so hard in the kitchen. Fine. She'd do it when he wasn't around to stop her. He didn't honestly expect her to sit down and thumb through a magazine when so much needed to be done? The house was a disaster and an unhealthy environment for a man in ill health.

A large roast was cooking in the oven and the smell of simmering meat, potatoes and onions permeated the large kitchen.

Jenny was in the living room, sitting on her grandfather's lap while he read to her from a children's book. The sight of the two of them warmed Lanni's heart. Stuart was so loving and patient with the child. The last time she'd checked on them, she'd discovered Jenny asleep, cuddled in his arms, and Stuart snoring softly.

Washing the last of the lunch dishes, Lanni paused to look around. Like everything else in the house, the kitchen was grossly outdated. The linoleum was cracked and peeling up at the corners as was the dull red countertop. The stove had a cantankerous streak and the oven was another matter entirely. Lanni had viewed the kitchen as a challenge and after working only one afternoon in it, she was ready to surrender. What she wouldn't have given for a microwave! She could deal with escrow loans, mortgage companies and feisty appraisers, but not this nineteenth-century kitchen.

The back door swung open as Judd stepped inside, giving her a knowing look. For a moment it seemed as though he wanted to argue with her, but changed his mind. He knew her well enough to realize she couldn't leave the place in such a mess.

"Hi." She smiled at him and pressed her finger to her lips, indicating that he should be quiet. She pointed in the direction of Jenny and Stuart in the other room. "They're asleep." She hoped that the need for quiet would quell his objection to her streak of domestic integrity.

If the clean kitchen hadn't been a surprise, then viewing his daughter in Stuart's arms was. His father's gaunt face was relaxed in sleep. Peaceful. Serene. Judd couldn't ever recall seeing his father so tranquil—he'd run on nervous energy most of his life, demanding more of himself than he did from others.

Judd pulled out a kitchen chair and Lanni brought him a bowl of hot tomato soup and a thick turkey sandwich she'd made earlier.

He was a little amazed at her thoughtfulness, although he realized that he shouldn't be. "I saw the Petermans."

"Good."

"They're moving back tomorrow."

"Won't your father be upset?"

"I don't see why. I'm paying their wages."

Lanni nodded and hid a grin. Over the years, Judd must have learned how to get around his father, sometimes to his own detriment. "What did the doctor have to say?"

Judd's expression changed to a dark scowl as he slowly shook his head. He lowered the sandwich to the plate. "Not much."

"What do you mean?"

"Dad's been in a couple of times with stomach ailments. But as far as Doc Simpson knows, Stuart isn't anywhere close to dying."

"He could have gone to another doctor."

"Maybe, but that's doubtful. The nearest medical

facility of any worth is in Miles City, and that's more than a hundred miles. It's unlikely that Dad would go that far."

"It's obvious that he's been ill." Just looking at Stuart was proof enough. "It has to be more than stomach ailments."

"Apparently he has an ulcer."

"An ulcer?"

"Other than that, Doc claims Dad's in perfect health."

Lanni pulled out the chair across from Judd and sat. She didn't know what to think. Stuart had claimed to be dying, but from the sounds of what Judd had just learned, he was a fair distance from the grave.

"Why do you think he sent for you?"

"Not me," Judd corrected, remembering the bitterness in his father's greeting. "If you recall, he asked to see Jenny."

"He wanted you to bring her."

Judd took another bite of the turkey sandwich, chewing thoughtfully before speaking. He'd been a sentimental fool to believe Stuart wanted him home. From birth, his father had had little use for him. "I have the feeling this is all an elaborate charade."

"I can't believe that." Lanni hadn't meant to take Stuart's side, but she honestly felt that something must be terribly wrong with Judd's father for him to have sent for Judd and Jenny.

"Stuart may *believe* he's dying, but he's not," Judd murmured.

"Maybe the doctor made it sound less serious than it actually is."

Judd leaned back in the high-backed chair and shook his head. "I can't believe Doc Simpson would do that. No," he stated emphatically. "Doc said that Dad needed to watch his diet, but with the medication he gave him and a few dietary restrictions, Dad should be feeling great." He pushed the lunch plate aside. "I think the problem may be psychological. Dad hasn't been sick a day in his life. He can't tolerate it in others, let alone himself. Doc seems to believe that with his stomach causing him a fair amount of pain, Dad might believe that his number is coming up."

Lanni watched as Judd frowned thoughtfully. "What are you going to do?" The strain of being around his father was already exacting its toll on Judd. It seemed that every time Stuart opened his mouth, he made some comment about Judd's lack of ambition. Lanni disagreed—Judd had plenty of drive; she'd never known a man who worked harder than Judd. From what he'd told her, Stuart had always wanted Judd to be an attorney or a doctor. Something more than the rancher he was, and from Judd's teens, Stuart had pushed his son toward college and a professional career. It hadn't worked, and Judd had left home soon after graduating from high school. Twice since they'd arrived, Lanni had to stop herself from defending Judd to his father. She didn't like being put in that position and had remained silent. In some ways she felt Stuart was waiting for her to intervene, but she refused to get caught in the battle between father and son.

Judd stood, carrying his plate and bowl to the sink and dumping his leftovers into the compost pile. "Don't wait dinner for me."

An icy chill shivered up her back and her hand knotted into a tight fist as dread filled her. So often when he left, Judd didn't bother to tell her where he was going or when he'd return. In light of the comment he'd made about her suffocating him, Lanni refused to ask him now. He knew her feelings and chose to ignore them.

Judd watched the anger play across her features and recognized what was troubling her. He hesitated before adding, "Jim claims there's a lot of fence down. I want to check it out."

Lanni's gaze shot to his, knowing he was making an effort. "Will you be riding a horse?"

The smile curving his lips was evidence of his poorly disguised amusement. "I'm taking the pickup; there's a lot of range out there. The Ford's parked on the other side of the barn." The Petermans' house was between the huge shed and the main house and blocked her view.

Lanni was pleased that the elderly couple were returning, but she wondered how Stuart would react to the news. It would be up to Judd to tell him, not Lanni. With other things on her mind, that was one topic she didn't want to wade into with Judd's father. As it was, their conversations were stilted and often one-sided. Lanni did the best she could to carry any dialogue, but Stuart made it nearly impossible, answering in clipped one-word sentences.

The only subject that he became animated on was Jenny. From the moment he'd seen the child, something had come over him. His harsh features had smoothed into an almost smile and his eyes had brightened. The unconcealed love he felt for Jenny transformed him into a different person.

Stuart couldn't seem to get enough of the child. He talked to her, read her stories and listened to her with all the attention of the doting grandfather he was. Lanni couldn't understand how he could be so hard on his only child and so loving to his granddaughter. Jenny's reaction to Stuart was one filled with the joy of discovery, while Stuart's love was returned a hundredfold and more. Lanni was astonished. For a man who had shown precious little patience in his life, he was a virtual saint with his granddaughter.

Their first night in the house proved to be eventful. Lanni woke around midnight when the house was peaceful and still. She rolled onto her back and pushed the hair off her forehead and stared sightlessly into the darkness. One minute she'd been asleep and the next she was wide awake. She blinked twice, and wondered at the reason for her sudden restlessness. The faint sound of the television drifted up from downstairs and, thinking Judd had returned and was unwinding with a late night talk show, Lanni threw off the covers and climbed out of bed.

She'd just finished tying the sash to her robe when she stepped off the bottom stair. She did an admirable job of disguising her disappointment when she discovered it wasn't Judd who was awake, but Stuart.

He glanced at her and then back at the television screen.

"Is Judd back yet?" she asked.

"He's home. I thought he was in bed with you." The blank face strayed momentarily from the television to Lanni.

"You know we're separated." Lanni sighed and moved into the kitchen, unwilling to discuss the subject further. Stuart flicked the television controller, stood and followed her. Doing her best to ignore him, Lanni took a carton of milk out of the refrigerator and turned, nearly colliding with the older man.

Reluctantly he stepped aside. "You'd know when Judd got home if you were sleeping with him the way a wife should. Seems to me it would solve a whole lot of problems if you two shared a bed again."

Lanni did her best to pretend she hadn't heard him.

"I bet you laid awake half the night waiting for Judd."

Purposely turning away from him, Lanni poured the milk into the glass and returned the carton to the refrigerator. "I appreciate what you're trying to do, Stuart, but it's two years too late. The marriage is over."

"I don't believe that," her father-in-law said, following her from one side of the kitchen to the next.

Lanni took a large swallow of the milk, refusing to discuss her private life with her father-in-law.

"I know Judd hasn't been a good husband to you in the past, but he'll change once he starts managing the ranch."

Lanni released a frustrated breath. "The minute we arrived, you told Judd he'd never get this land. Remember?"

Stuart chuckled. "Don't you recognize reverse psychology when you hear it, girl? Judd's been the same all his life. I say one thing and the blasted fool does just the opposite. I decided it was time I got smart. He wants the ranch now because I told him he could never have it. Only," he hesitated, studying Lanni hard, "he won't stay long unless you're here."

"I've got news for you," Lanni informed him sadly, her throat muscles constricting with the pain of reality. "If I'm here or not will make little difference with Judd."

"I don't believe that."

Lanni carried the empty milk glass to the sink. It wouldn't do any good to argue with Judd's father. It was obvious that the old man had hoped she and Judd would resolve their differences and remain on the ranch.

What a strange man Stuart Matthiessen was. He berated his son in one breath and sought to save his marriage in the other. "What's between Judd and me is none of your business."

"Maybe not, but you got a child to consider."

Lanni couldn't take any more. It was one thing to have the man treat Judd the way he did, but another for him to run interference in her life. "While we're on the subject of Judd, I want one thing understood."

Stuart's mouth snapped shut. "What?"

"Use all the reverse psychology you want, but if you utter one unkind, untruthful word about my husband in front of Jenny, the two of us will leave so fast it'll make your head spin. I mean that, Stuart. Judd is Jenny's father and I won't have you treat him disrespectfully when Jenny is around to witness it. Do you understand?"

Stuart blanched and cleared his throat. "Yes."

"Thank you for that." She brushed past him on her way out the door and marched up the stairs. When she reached the top, Lanni discovered that she was trembling. Her hands were bunched into tight fists as the anger fermented within her. She wanted to shake Judd's father for his stubborn pride. He honestly seemed to believe that if she and Jenny remained on the ranch, Judd would stay as well. Her love, their daughter, and the home she'd created hadn't been enough to hold him once. She had nothing else to offer him a second time.

"That was quite a little speech." Judd leaned against the doorjamb, his arms crossed over his bare chest, his eyes sparkling with amusement. "The next time I need a defender of truth and justice, can I call on you?"

"He infuriates me." Lanni still couldn't believe the gall of her father-in-law. He'd puzzled her the first time they'd met and even more so now.

"It's just his way, Lanni. I stopped letting him manipulate me years ago."

"I won't play his games, Judd. He wants you and me back together. He thinks you'll stay on the ranch if Jenny and I are here. But we both know differently, don't we?"

The barb struck its intended mark, nicking his heart. "I signed the divorce papers. I thought that was all you required."

"It is."

The pain in her eyes brought Judd up short and, expelling a broken sigh, he turned toward his bedroom. Regret expanded his chest, tightening his muscles until his heart and lungs ached. "Lanni." He moved toward her and paused. "I…"

"Don't." She raised both her hands and abruptly shook her head. "Don't say anything. It's better if we leave things as they are." She turned and quickly entered her room. The sound of the door closing echoed through the hallway like thunder, although she had shut it softly.

Rubbing his hand over his eyes, Judd turned back into his own room, drained both emotionally and physically.

Judd had already left the house by the time Lanni and Jenny were up and dressed. Stuart sat at the kitchen table, drinking coffee and staring absently into space with the morning newspaper propped in front of him.

"Morning." Lanni hoped to start the day on a cheerful note.

"Morning," came his gruff reply until he caught sight of Jenny, then he brightened and smiled. "Hello, Princess."

The little girl held out her arms and hugged his middle with an abundance of enthusiasm. "Hi, Grandpa. Is today the day I get to see the pony?"

"Soon," Stuart answered, looking displeased.

"What's this about a pony?" Lanni's eyes flew from one to the other.

"Oops," Jenny said and covered her mouth. "I wasn't suppose to tell, was I? It's a surprise, Mommy."

"You weren't supposed to tell me what?"

"That Grandpa's buying me a horsey."

"A horse?" Lanni exploded. "Stuart, this isn't true, is it? I told you before we only plan on being here a couple of weeks. I meant that. A horse for that amount of time would be extravagant."

He ignored her, downing the last of his coffee.

"Stuart?" Lanni demanded a second time. "What's this business about a horse?"

Jenny climbed onto the chair, clenching Betsy to her chest and looking uncomfortable. "Don't be mad, Mommy. I wasn't supposed to say anything like when Aunt Jade and I go have ice cream." Realizing that she'd done it again, the little girl looked thoroughly miserable.

"It's all right, honey, don't worry about it." Lanni decided it would be best to drop the subject for now and discuss it when Jenny was out of hearing distance.

Stuart leaned over and whispered something in the little girl's ear and Jenny instantly dissolved into happy giggles. Lanni hadn't a notion of what schemes the two were devising, but knew given time she'd find out.

When the breakfast dishes had been cleared from the table, Stuart announced that he was taking Jenny for a walk. He didn't ask Lanni to go with them. She wanted to suggest joining them, but Judd's father looked so excited at the prospect of going outside with his granddaughter that Lanni didn't want to risk destroying his mood.

"Where was Judd off to so early this morning?" she asked instead, doing her utmost to disguise her uneasiness.

The old man's eyes narrowed as the fun and laughter drained away. "He didn't say."

"Surely he must have given you some indication of when he'd be back."

"You should know him better than that." He opened his mouth as if to add more, but at her fiery glare, he changed his mind. Lanni had no doubt her look and their midnight conversation was responsible for his change of heart. "Knowing Judd, he'll be back when he's good and ready to come back and not before. He always was like that, you know. Going away for days without a word of explanation."

A glance out the kitchen window confirmed that the pickup was gone. He was probably on the range, checking fences and whatever else he did while away from the house for hours on end. Lanni hadn't a clue.

From her view out the same rectangular window, she kept close tabs on Stuart with Jenny. He took the little girl into the barn and returned with a feed bag. Together the two fed the chickens, much to Jenny's delight.

From there they walked to the edge of the fence and Stuart pointed to the rolling hills in the distance. Intently, Jenny stood at his side and nodded, as serious as the day was beautiful. After washing a couple of dishes, Lanni glanced outside a second time. Jenny was bending over a wildflower while Stuart smiled down on her. Bright rays of morning sun splashed the earth.

The little girl mentioned something to her grandfather and Judd's father threw back his head and laughed loudly. The sound of his mirth took Lanni by surprise. She'd never heard or seen Stuart be happy about anything. With the one exception of Jenny.

When the two ambled toward the Petermans' small home, Lanni removed her apron and followed them. She didn't want Jenny out of her sight for long.

The screen door slammed after her as she went down the sun-dried wooden steps. They creaked with age. Everywhere Lanni looked there were repairs to be made and work to be done. She imagined that with the ranch demanding so much attention, Jim Peterman had little time or energy to spare on the house. It could be, too, that Stuart didn't want anything fixed, but she couldn't imagine the reason why. He was a strange man and she understood him less than she did her own husband.

The door to the Petermans' house was left open and Lanni walked inside, amazed at how updated the home was in comparison to the main house. The kitchen was bright and cheerful, the room furnished with a dinette set and modern appliances. The white counter-tops gleamed.

Stuart's voice could be heard at the front of the house and Lanni went to join them.

"This will be your bedroom," Lanni heard Stuart tell Jenny as she turned the corner from the kitchen that led to the hallway.

"Your mommy and daddy will sleep in the bedroom next door," Stuart went on to explain.

Lanni was appalled. Apparently Stuart planned to move the three of them into this small house.

"Judd's and my room?" Lanni said, stepping into the room. "How interesting."

Eight

Stuart's head came up so fast that Lanni thought he might have dislocated his neck. It was apparent that she'd heard something he didn't want her to know about.

The dark eyes met hers unsteadily. The crease lines in his face became all the more pronounced as his gaze skidded past hers.

"I've already explained that Jenny and I will be leaving next week." Lanni wanted it understood from the beginning that she wanted no part of his crazy schemes.

Stuart went pale. "But...you belong here with Judd."

Jenny's eyes revealed her confusion and Lanni desperately wanted to shake some sense into the man. He couldn't possibly believe that she'd give up her life in Seattle, abandon her parents, her home and her career because of his half-baked belief that she and Jenny would bind Judd to the Circle M.

"He'll only stay if you do."

Lanni chose to ignore Stuart's plea. She took Jenny by the hand and led her out of the house. Stuart followed in her wake, mumbling under his breath along the way.

"I had them deliver a new stove just for you," he said loud enough for her to hear.

"I already told you what I think. Can't you under-stand that it isn't going to work?" she asked sternly, throwing the words over her shoulder.

"But I want to talk to you about it," Stuart pressed on, undeterred.

His eyes revealed the same stubbornness that Judd so often displayed and Lanni wanted to scream at them both for their foolish pride. "There's nothing to discuss."

Outside the small house, they were greeted with bright sunlight. A soft breeze carried the scent of apple blossoms from a nearby row of trees. In other circumstances Lanni would have paused and pointed out to Jenny the source of the sweet fragrance. But her thoughts were heavy and she barely noted the beauty surrounding her as she led Jenny back into the main house. She was so irritated, she discovered her hands were trembling.

She finished the breakfast dishes and Jenny, stand-ing at her side, dutifully helped dry them. With each dish, Lanni struggled to subdue her frustration. The Petermans were supposed to arrive anytime and she welcomed the thought of another woman at the ranch.

Lanni was filled with questions and the only one who could answer them was Betty Peterman. As much as Lanni was looking forward to meeting Betty, she didn't welcome the confrontation Stuart was bound to have with Judd over their return.

The clash came sooner than even Lanni expected. Judd came back to the house midmorning, bringing the Petermans with him. Jim and Betty walked into the kitchen where Lanni and Jenny were arranging wild-flowers, using a jar as a makeshift vase.

"Hello," Betty Peterman said, smiling shyly at the pair. Her eyes were round and kind and Lanni knew immediately that she would like this woman who knew Judd so well. Her troubled gaze flew from Betty Peterman to Judd in an attempt to warn him that Stuart was sitting in the other room.

"What's wrong?" Judd knew Lanni too well not to have noticed her distress. Something had happened this morning when he'd been away. That much was obvious. Lanni looked both angry and frustrated. Heaven knew Stuart was capable of driving man or woman to either emotion, and Judd felt guilty for leaving her to deal with his cantankerous father.

"What are they doing here?" Stuart demanded from the doorway leading to the kitchen. A scowl darkened his face, twisting his mouth downward.

"I hired them back," Judd informed his father.

"You can't do that."

"I'm paying their wages."

"I'm not dead yet. The Circle M still belongs to me and what I say goes!"

Jim shuffled his feet. Betty looked equally uncomfortable. Judd saw this and was all the more angry with his father for causing their old friends this additional embarrassment.

"If they go, I go," Judd told him calmly.

Stuart glowered at his son, but closed his mouth, swallowing any argument.

Jim Peterman removed his hat and rotated the large brim between his callused hands; his eyes studied the floor between his feet. "I can see we're not wanted here. The missus and me will move on."

"And I say you stay." Judd pointed to the wiry cowhand and emphatically shook his head. Slowly, methodically, he turned his attention back to his father. "This ranch is falling apart around you. The herd is depleted.

Fences are down in every section. The house is a disaster. What possible explanation could you have for not wanting the Petermans here?"

Stuart's brooding eyes clashed with Lanni's. Puzzled, Judd followed the exchange.

"Lanni," he asked, still perplexed, "do you know something I don't?"

"Your father apparently thinks you and I and Jenny will decide to live here permanently. He wanted the Petermans' house for us."

Stuart's pale face tightened as he moved into the kitchen. "The three of you belong here."

"You can't be serious?" Judd was incredulous.

"I'm afraid he is," Lanni said, coming forward so that she stood at Judd's side.

"The Petermans have lived in that house nearly as long as you've owned the Circle M," Judd countered sharply. "And they'll live there again."

For an instant it looked as if Stuart were going to argue. Stubborn insistence leapt from his eyes, challenging Judd.

Judd crossed his arms over his chest and the edges of his mouth curved up. The movement in no way resembled a smile. Wordlessly he accepted his father's challenge and tossed in one of his own. "Either the Petermans come back as employees of the Circle M or I take Lanni and Jenny home to Seattle."

Stuart looked shocked, as if this were the last argument in the world that he'd expected Judd to use against him.

"Well?" Judd pressed, staring at his father.

"Fine. They can stay," Stuart mumbled, turning. His walk was more of a shuffling of his feet; clearly it had cost him a great deal to concede the issue.

"So this is Jenny." Betty Peterman pulled out a kitchen chair and sat beside the four-year-old.

"Hi," Jenny returned, busy placing long-stemmed daisies into a jar. She gave the newcomer a bright smile, her chubby fingers bending a brittle stem. Lanni was grateful that Jenny couldn't understand all that was happening and was pleased that Betty was trying to smooth the rippling tension that filled the room.

"She resembles Lydia," Betty murmured under her breath, handing Jenny another yellow daisy to add to the vase. "It's in the eyes and the shape of her face. I suppose Stuart noticed it as well?" Betty glanced at Judd, seeking an answer. The resemblance offered a token explanation of Stuart's odd behavior.

"I'm sure he has noticed," Lanni answered for him, recalling all the pictures of Jenny she'd mailed Stuart over the years. He'd never given her any indication that he'd received the photographs.

"He loved Lydia, you know." Betty inclined her head toward the living room where Stuart sat watching a television game show with all the seriousness of a network war correspondent. "For a time after she died, Jim and I thought Stuart would never recover. He sat and stared at the walls for days."

Judd rubbed a weary hand over his face. "Sometimes I wonder if he's capable of loving anyone anymore." Judd had seen precious little evidence of his father's love. He thought he understood Stuart, but every day of this visit his father proved him wrong. They didn't know each other at all.

Jim helped himself to a cup of coffee from the stove, adding sugar to it before taking the first sip. "From what you said, I don't have time to stand around the kitchen."

"I'll go with you," Judd offered. "There's a problem with...." His voice trailed away as he went out the kitchen door with Jim. The back screen door slammed after them.

Lanni watched them leave. The two men stood in front of the pickup talking, and from the looks of it, the subject was a heavy one. Jim nodded abruptly, apparently agreeing with what Judd was saying.

"I've got a thousand things to do as well," Betty added, tacking a stray hair into the neatly coiled bun that graced the back of her head.

"Can Jenny and I help?" Lanni volunteered. She hoped to become friends with this motherly woman.

"No need." She gently patted Lanni's hand and glanced into the living room where Stuart was sitting. "I suspect he'll keep you hopping while I finish unpacking. Be patient with him. He isn't as bad as he seems."

For her part Lanni didn't want to be left alone with Stuart. "Are you sure?"

"Positive." She lightly shook her head. "He isn't normally this cantankerous. He loves Judd almost as much as he did Lydia. The problem is he has trouble showing it, just like he did with Lydia."

That had to be the understatement of the year. Before Lanni could question the housekeeper further, Betty was out the door.

At noon, Lanni cooked lunch and served it to Stuart on a television tray. He didn't comment when she delivered the meal and said nothing when she carried it back, untouched, to the kitchen. One look at his harsh features told her that Stuart was furious with both her and Judd.

Thankfully the afternoon was peaceful. Jenny took her nap in Judd's old room at the top of the stairs. While his granddaughter slept, Stuart appeared at loose ends and drifted outside. In order to kill time, Lanni cleaned out the kitchen drawers and washed cupboards. On the top shelf, she found a pre-World War II cookbook that must have belonged to Lydia. Flipping through the yellowed pages, Lanni discovered a storehouse of treasures. After a short debate, she decided to bake a cake listed as Stuart's favorite. A quick check of the shelf assured her that all the ingredients were available.

Humming as she worked, she whipped the eggs and butter together with a wire whisk. Dumping the measured flour into the frothy mix sent up a swirling cloud of the fine powder. Coughing, she tried to clear the front of her face by waving her hand.

"What are you making?" Judd asked, opening the back door that led to the kitchen. He paused, hands on his hips, surveying the tempting sight she made. An oversize apron that must have belonged to Betty was wrapped around her middle. The ties looped around her trim waist twice and were knotted in the front. Flour was smeared across her cheek and an antique cookbook was propped against the sugar canister on the countertop.

"Hi." She offered him a ready smile. "I'm baking a cake as a peace offering to Stuart. He hasn't spoken a word all afternoon."

Judd recalled how much she used to enjoy baking for him. In the first weeks after their marriage it was a miracle he hadn't gained twenty pounds. Every night she'd whipped up some special concoction for him to sample. Most of them proved to be scrumptious. Others proved less successful. It got to be that he'd rush home every night to see what confection she had planned next. Lanni had enjoyed his praise. Long ago, she claimed, her mother had told her that the way to a man's heart was through his stomach. Judd didn't bother to inform her otherwise. She'd owned his heart from their first fateful meeting.

He'd loved her then beyond anything he'd ever known and, he realized studying her now, he loved her still.

"Smells delicious." Without thought, he wrapped his arms around Lanni's waist and kissed the side of her neck. It was the most natural thing in the world to do. This was Lanni, his woman, his wife—no matter what those divorce papers said. She and she alone had filled the emptiness of his soul. Her love had helped him find peace within himself and had lessened the ache of bitterness and cynicism that had dictated his actions since he'd left the Circle M at age eighteen.

Lanni's heart leaped to her throat. Almost immediately she recognized the action as spontaneous—one Judd did without thought. For days he'd gone to lengths to avoid touching her and it felt incredibly right to have him hold her now. She wanted to comment to say something but feared any sound would shatter this spell. She yearned for his touch like a weak flower longs for the life-giving rays of the sun and the nourishment of cool water.

Heaven and earth couldn't have stopped Judd. He lowered his lips to hers, kissing her hungrily. He wondered if life could possibly be half so sweet as this moment with her.

Lanni felt his kiss throughout her body. It rocked her, leaving her yearning for more. Her heart swelled with remembered love. Her arms held him close, wanting to bind him to her for all time.

When he broke off the kiss his smile was filled with satisfaction. Lanni was velvet. Satin and silk. And he loved her. Dear sweet heaven, he loved her until there was nothing in all the world but her.

Releasing a huge sigh, he held her to him and closed his eyes. The need to hold and touch her was becoming as much a part of him as breathing. He was a man of his word, and it was increasingly difficult to keep his promise not to touch her. Already he'd broken it several times. The desire to lift her into his arms and carry her up the stairs to the bedroom was almost unbearable.

Lanni went still, savoring the welcome feel of his arms around her. She closed her eyes, wanting this moment to last, knowing it wouldn't. With everything that was in her, she battled down her weakness for Judd. There was something seductive with this ranch, this land and being with Judd. It almost made her believe there was nothing they couldn't overcome. Maybe it was Stuart, who was working so hard to fill her head with promises of a new life with Judd on the Circle M. She didn't know, but she couldn't give in to these sensations—she couldn't.

Awkwardly, Judd dropped his arms.

Still shaken by the encounter, Lanni turned back to the mixing bowl, focusing her attention on the cake once again. "Are you hungry?" The feeble sound of her own voice bounced off the empty kitchen walls.

"Starved." But Judd wasn't referring to food. He felt empty, with a physical ache that attacked with a ferocity that left him weak.

He walked over to the sink and turned on the tap.

"There's some leftovers from lunch," Lanni told him, striving to keep her voice even. On the off chance he'd be in later and hungry, Lanni had fixed a couple of extra sandwiches. She brought them to the table with a tall glass of milk and some cookies.

Drying his hands on a towel, Judd tossed it back onto the wire rack and joined her at the table. The sight of the meal produced an appreciative grin. "Is Jenny sleeping?" he asked, seeking protection in the subject of their daughter.

Seeing Lanni working in the kitchen was having a strange effect on him. It'd cost him a great deal to release her. Every male instinct demanded that he haul her into his arms and make love to her then and there. As much as possible, he ignored the powerful pull of his desire.

Lanni paused to check her wristwatch. "She'll be up anytime now." She hoped the information would cause Judd to linger a bit longer.

"Where's Stuart?"

"He left sometime after noon."

"Did he say where he was going?" Judd wolfed down another bite of the sandwich as he waited for her response.

She shook her head sadly. His plans for the Peterman house thwarted, Stuart had been uncommunicative from the moment Judd had left with the rehired foreman. Even Jenny had been unable to bring her grandfather out of his dark mood.

A worried frown knit Judd's brow as he pushed aside his plate. His mouth thinned with irritation. "I wonder what Stuart's up to now."

"I have no idea." Lanni braced her hands against the back of the chair, studying Judd. She knew he was concerned about his father, but nonetheless Judd looked happy. More alive than she could ever remember seeing him. Content.

"I spent most of the early afternoon on the range with Jim." He paused to swallow some milk. "The herd's depleted, but with care it can be built up again." His expression relaxed as he told her about a cattle sale coming up at the beginning of next week. "Jim seems to feel that with the purchase of a few head of cattle we could be back in business again by the end of next year."

"That soon?"

Between cookies, Judd nodded. "Maybe even sooner."

"Wonderful." She could hear the excitement and anticipation in his voice. Both caught her by surprise. Judd was speaking as if he planned to be around to see the task to completion.

"It's expensive, Lanni. Damned expensive."

She nodded as if she understood everything there was to know about stocking herd for a cattle ranch. Her expertise was limited to real estate transactions, and she knew little about ranching. For the first time since she'd known him, Judd was truly serene.

He stopped and gazed out the kitchen window. "This land was made for ranching. Look at it out there—those rolling hills are full of sweet grass."

"It is beautiful," Lanni agreed. To her surprise, she found she enjoyed the peace and solitude of the Circle M. Montana, with its wide blue sky, held an appeal that Lanni hadn't expected to feel.

"The whole state is like this." At least staring out the window helped him keep his eyes off her. He'd forgotten how beautiful she was. How enticing. How alluring. He felt good all the way to his soul. For the first time in years he was at peace with himself and the world. Working with Jim, riding side by side with the other man, had awakened in him his deep abiding love for the Circle M and Montana.

When he'd left all those years ago, Judd had closed his mind to the ranch. Now he was here and it seemed that everything was falling into place for the first time in a very long while.

* * *

Judd worked with Jim long past dinnertime. He'd told Lanni that with so much that needed to be done, she shouldn't hold up the evening meal for him. He felt guilty leaving her alone to deal with Jenny and Stuart, but the demands of the Circle M were equally urgent.

Wearily, Judd walked toward the house. The light beaming from the kitchen window gave him a comfortable feeling. He suspected Lanni would be waiting for him and the knowledge brought a sense of contentment. His body ached from the physical demand of ranching. It'd been years since he'd been on the back of a horse. His muscles protested the long hours in the saddle and as he sauntered toward the house, he rubbed the lower region of his back where a sharp pain had developed.

The kitchen was empty, and Judd was disappointed. In his mind he'd hoped to have a few tender moments alone with Lanni. He fought back the image of her asleep in bed and what would happen if he were to slip in beside her and turn her warm body into his arms. Judd groaned. The sudden physical ache of his body far surpassed any strain from riding a horse or mending fences.

The clock over the kitchen doorway told him it was far later than he'd thought. Lanni would be asleep by now and the way he was feeling tonight, it was probably for the best.

Upon further inspection, he found a plate covered with foil left warming in the oven. He smiled, grateful for her thoughtfulness, and wondered if she'd thought about him the way he'd been thinking about her all afternoon.

He ate slowly, savoring the fried-chicken dinner.

When he finished, he rinsed his plate and set it aside in the sink.

The house was quiet as Judd turned off the light and headed for the stairway that led to the upstairs bedroom.

"So you're home." The voice came out of the dark. It took Judd an instant to realize that his father was sitting alone in the moonlight waiting for him.

"Did you think I'd left?"

"It wouldn't be unheard of."

The blunt response briefly angered Judd. "Well I didn't."

"So I see. I suppose I should be grateful."

"I'm not leaving. Not until I know the reason you called me home."

"You know why. I want you here; it's where you belong, where you've always belonged," Stuart's raised voice returned with a sharp edge that invited an angry response.

Judd expelled a sigh. There was always tension between him and his father. They couldn't have a civil conversation without pride interfering and old wounds festering back to life. It was on the tip of Judd's tongue to argue with Stuart, to remind him that the letter he'd sent contained a different message. The stark words had asked him to bring Jenny to the ranch. Stuart hadn't asked to see him—only Jenny.

Judd sighed. One of them had to make the first move and Judd decided it would have to be him. He claimed an overstuffed chair and sat in the dark across from his father.

"She does resemble Mother, doesn't she?" There wasn't any need for Judd to mention who he was talking about.

"Lanni sent me pictures and each year I recognized it more and more."

His mother remained only a foggy memory in Judd's mind. He wasn't sure that he remembered her at all. Betty had told him about Lydia when he was younger and Judd wondered if he confused his memory with the information Betty had given him.

"Jenny belongs with me just as Lydia did."

"Jenny belongs with her mother," Judd said softly.

"If you'd patch things up with Lanni, then you could all stay. Fix it, boy, and hurry before you lose her to that city slicker."

"City slicker?" As far as Judd knew, Lanni had never left the ranch.

"That Delaney fellow. He phoned twice before you arrived and once since." Stuart's tone lowered with displeasure. "Lanni doesn't know, and I'm not telling her. You're going to lose her unless you do something and quick. I'm not going to be able to hold this fellow off much longer. Next time he calls, Lanni could answer the phone."

Judd felt the weight of the world settle over his shoulders. "It's too late for Lanni and me."

"You can't mean that. I've seen the way you look at each other. You're still in love with her and if both of you weren't so stubborn you'd see that she loves you as well."

The urgency in the old man's voice shook Judd.

"You're the only one who can convince them to stay."

Judd couldn't do that, but telling Stuart as much was a different matter. "I'll do what I can," he said after a long minute.

The words appeared to appease Stuart. "Good."

Judd relaxed in the chair, crossing his legs. This talk

wasn't much, but it was a beginning. "Jim and I were out on the back hundred this afternoon."

"That's a good place to start—been needing attention a couple of years now."

Judd welcomed the cover of darkness that cloaked the living room. So Steve had been trying to contact Lanni and he'd bet it didn't have anything to do with business matters either. Judd's fingers gripped the chair's thick arms as he concentrated on what his father was saying. "When did you stop caring about the ranch?"

Stuart snorted. "Last year sometime. I haven't the energy for it anymore."

From the run-down condition of the place, Judd knew his father was speaking the truth. "Jim and I are here now," Judd said. He knew his father expected a tirade, but for once he didn't want to argue with the old man. Tonight he yearned to pretend that they were like other fathers and sons who communicated freely about the things they loved most.

"I'm not overly pleased that you brought the Petermans back," Stuart added thoughtfully. "Now that you and Lanni are here, I don't need them anymore."

"Perhaps not, but they need you."

The truth silenced Stuart for a moment. "I wanted the house for the three of you."

"Dad," Judd said with a sigh, "listen to me. Lanni and Jenny aren't going to live here. The divorce papers are already signed. The only life Lanni knows is in the city."

"Divorce papers," he echoed, shaken. "You're divorced?"

"Not officially. Once she's back in Seattle, Lanni will need to file the papers before it's official."

"Then do something, boy. Do it now before it's too

late." The desperate appeal in Stuart's voice ripped at Judd's heart. "I lost Lydia because of my pride. Don't make the same mistake I did. You'll regret it, I swear you will; all your life it'll haunt you."

Judd came to his feet. "I can't change the past for you. Lanni asked for the divorce—not me. It's what she wants."

"I'd bet the Circle M that it was that city slicker who talked Lanni into this divorce thing."

Judd's fists knotted, but he held his tongue. "I'm going to bed," Judd said.

"But not to sleep, I'd wager."

Stuart's words followed Judd to the top of the stairs. Inside the darkness of his room, he sagged onto the bed, sitting on the edge of the mattress. He was tired, weary to the bone.

His father's words echoed around the chamber, taunting him. So Steve was phoning; Judd supposed the other man must be desperate for word from Lanni. He didn't like to even think about the other man. It angered him. Infuriated him.

He needed to move—anything to still the ramblings of his mind. Judd stood and paced the area in front of the bed. He remembered seeing Lanni in the kitchen that afternoon. The memory of their kiss caused him to groan. He gritted his teeth in an effort to drive the image from his mind. It didn't help. His reminiscences were costing him his sanity.

Jerking open a dresser drawer, he took out a fresh set of clothes. A cold shower would help. Afterward he'd leave and find a hotel in Miles City where he could spend the night. It was dangerous, too dangerous to be here with Lanni sleeping peacefully in the room across from his. If he stayed, he wouldn't be able to stop himself. He'd wake her and she'd turn into his arms and he'd make love to every inch of her until she cried for more.

As quietly as possible, Judd moved down the hall. But the cold shower did little to ease the ache in his body. He needed Lanni. But he'd promised; he'd given her his word. Within a few days she had every reason to pack her bags and walk away without a backward glance. He hadn't the right to stop her and he wouldn't. The thought of Steve Delaney holding her nearly crippled him.

The arguments echoed in his mind like demented voices flung back at him from a canyon wall. Unable to stop himself, he paused outside Lanni's bedroom door. Moonlight painted the room a soft shade of yellow. She lay on her back, her long flaxen hair splayed out on the pillow like liquid gold. Judd's chest tightened at the sight of her. She tossed her arm up and turned her head.

His breath froze in his lungs. He'd awakened her. For an instant he thought to hide, then realized the ridiculousness of such a plan. It took him another moment to note that she remained asleep.

He moved toward her, stopping at the edge of the bed. A cold sweat broke out across his upper lip. He loved her. Loved her more than anything in his life. More than the Circle M. More than anything he possessed.

His body trembled with emotion as he watched her sleep. He turned to leave and made it as far as the door. His hands braced against each side of the jamb, Judd paused. His fingers curved around the wood frame as he hung his head. His mind battled with his heart and his heart won.

He moved back into the room and stood once again beside the bed.

"Lanni," he whispered.

Lanni heard her name and knew it came from Judd. What she didn't recognize was the husky need. Her lashes fluttered open.

"Judd?" He was on the bed, kneeling over her.

"I need you," he whispered.

Nine

"Judd." Even in the dark, Lanni could see that his eyes were wild. "What is it?"

Urgently he slanted his mouth over hers, kissing her again and again as if he were dying of thirst and her lips were a clear, shimmering pool in the most arid region of the Sahara. "I need you," he repeated. "So much."

Lanni circled his neck with her arms. His weight pressed her into the mattress as the overwhelming desire to lose himself within her body dictated his actions. He needed her tonight more than at any other time because the reality of losing her was so strong. She would leave him and Steve was on the sidelines waiting.

"Judd, what is it? What's happened?"

He held her for a long minute, breathing deeply in an effort to control his desperate need. "Lanni, I can't lose you and Jenny. I want us to try again and throw away those damn divorce papers. I swear I'll never leave you. We'll build a new life together—we'll start over, here in Montana at the Circle M."

Instantly, tears began to burn the back of her eyes. It felt as if her heart was going to explode. After everything that had passed between them, the long months of heartache and loneliness, she shouldn't be this willing. But heaven help her, she didn't want the divorce any more than Judd did.

"It'll be as good as it was in the beginning," Judd coaxed, kissing her neck. "I swear, I won't let anything come between us again."

She swallowed down a sob and nodded sharply. "I love Montana." In her heart she acknowledged that she loved him. Always had. Always would. From the moment he'd shown up on her doorstep, she'd known that whatever passed between them, her love would never die. Tonight her hunger for him was as powerful as his was for her.

Again and again he kissed her, unable to get enough of her mouth. His lips sought the corners of her eyes, the high arch of her cheek, her neck—any place where her smooth skin was exposed. Then his mouth returned to hers, kissing her with raw, naked desire.

"Lanni," he whispered, breathless. "You're sure? After tonight, I'll never let you go."

She stared into his hard face, stamped with pride and love. Tenderly she brushed the dark hair from his brow, loving him more this moment than at any time in their lives.

"Lanni?" he repeated. "Are you sure?"

"I'm sure," she breathed.

He groaned. The instant his mouth claimed hers, all gentleness left him. Fierce desire commanded his movements.

Shocked by his need, Lanni clung to him, and her heady response drove some of the urgency from his mind. He must be crazy to come at her like this. A beast. A madman. But the knowledge did little to temper his actions. He was on fire and only her love would douse the flames.

"Lanni." Again and again he whispered her name, all the while kissing her. Her hands played over the velvet skin of his shoulders. Her lips felt swollen from his kisses and her body throbbed with need. She wanted to beg him to make love to her, but the words couldn't make it past the tightness that gripped her throat muscles. Nothing would stop him now, she was sure of it. In his own time, he'd claim her body. And she would welcome him, this man who was her husband.

Lanni was still trembling when Judd moved away. He lay on his side, facing her, and gathered her into his arms.

"I love you," he whispered without embellishment. Nothing more, no other words were needed.

She smiled contentedly and slid her hand over his hard ribs. Judd scooted closer, wrapping the sheets around them both. He paused to kiss the crown of her head. Secure in his love, and warm in his embrace, Lanni fell asleep almost instantly.

Sleep didn't come as easily for Judd. Although fatigue tugged at him from every direction, he found the escape elusive. He rolled onto his back, holding Lanni close to his side, and stared at the ceiling. He loved her and would thank God every day of his life that she had agreed to come back to him.

He'd meant what he'd said about them starting over. The moment they'd driven onto Circle M land, he'd felt that he was home. His traveling days were over. His heart belonged to Lanni and this thousand acres of land. His one regret was that he'd wanted their lovemaking to be slow and easy. Instead it had been a firestorm of craving and desire, but he doubted that he could have stopped to save his life.

Now that she'd agreed to be his wife again, Judd wanted to court her, give her all the assurances she needed and deserved. He vowed with everything that was in him that he'd never make her unhappy again.

Lanni woke early, feeling cozy and unbelievably warm. She pulled a blanket around her more securely and sighed contentedly. A small smile curved the corners of her mouth as she recalled the reason for her happiness. Judd had come to her in the night, loving her with such a fiery intensity that she was left trembling in its afterglow. They'd reconciled when Lanni had given up every hope of settling their differences. His traveling days were over. All Judd's bridges had been crossed and he was home and secure. And because Judd was content, she and Jenny were happy as well. Even now her skin tingled where he'd kissed and loved her.

Reaching out to touch him, her fingers encountered the sheet-covered mattress. She opened her eyes to find his side of the bed empty. The only evidence he had spent the night with her was the indentation on the pillow resting beside her own.

With a frown, Lanni sat up, tucking the sheet around her nakedness. She was disappointed. After their fierce lovemaking, she yearned to talk to Judd. Questions were churning in her mind.

She dressed quickly and hurried downstairs, hoping to find him there. As he had been the morning before, Stuart sat at the round kitchen table with the newspaper in one hand and a cup of coffee in the other.

"Morning," she greeted him. "Have you seen Judd around?"

"You look like you slept well. Judd, too, for that matter," Stuart muttered.

Lanni couldn't actually see him smile, but suspected he was. His gaze didn't waver from the newsprint.

"Then you've seen him?"

"He's in the barn."

"Thanks." Without waiting, Lanni rushed toward the back door. She saw Judd immediately. He stood beside the large chestnut horse close to Jim. She moved down a couple of stairs. "Judd," she called out and waved.

At the sound of her voice, Judd turned, his face breaking into a wide grin. He handed the reins of the horse to Jim and moved toward Lanni.

She met him halfway. "Morning."

"Morning." His gaze drank in the sight of her, and inside he felt a renewed sense of love and commitment to her and their marriage. "I didn't want to wake you."

"I wish you had."

He tugged the glove from his hand and lifted her hair from the side of her face, studying her. "You aren't sorry, are you?"

"No, but there's a lot we need to discuss."

"I know."

"Hey, Judd," Jim called out. "You going to stand there all morning saying goodbye to your missus? Kiss her and be done with it, will you? Those cattle aren't going to wait around forever, you know."

Judd tossed an irritated look over his shoulder. "Hold your horses, will you?"

"In case you haven't noticed, I'm holding yours as well as my own," Jim grumbled and then muttered something else that Lanni didn't quite hear.

"You better do as he says," she murmured, looking up at him. "Kiss me and be done with it."

Judd slipped his arms around her waist, bringing her to him as his mouth moved over hers. The kiss was deep, and greedy, and so thorough that Lanni was left weak and trembling. "I wish I could stay in bed with you all day," Judd groaned against the side of her neck. "We have a lot of time to make up for, woman."

"I wish we were in bed right now," she murmured, having difficulty finding her voice. He was lean, hard, masculine and strong. After everything they'd shared last night, Lanni couldn't believe that her passion could be so easily aroused. "Oh Judd, I love you so much."

"You must."

"You comin' or not?" Jim growled.

With a reluctance that thrilled her, Judd released her. He paused and reached up to touch her face. His eyes grew troubled. "I'll be back as soon as I can. If it's late, will you wait up for me?"

She nodded eagerly and watched as he marched across the yard and swung his lanky frame into the saddle. For a long minute after he'd ridden out, Lanni stood there, soaking up the early morning rays of the sun and remembering the feel of Judd's arms that had so recently held her.

She moved back into the house, but was reluctant to face Stuart. Judd's father had gotten exactly what he'd wanted and was feeling very clever at the moment.

Stuart was hauling a load of his dirty clothes to the washing machine when Lanni entered the kitchen. He paused, glanced at her and chuckled gleefully. Lanni ignored him and moved up the stairs.

Jenny was still asleep so Lanni quickly made her bed. By the time she'd finished, the little girl was awake and eager for breakfast. After picking out her own clothes and dressing, Jenny hurried down the stairs.

Stuart beamed at his granddaughter when she appeared, and hugged her gently. When Lanni moved toward the refrigerator, preparing to cook their breakfast, Stuart stopped her.

"I was in town," he said.

Lanni looked at him blankly, not understanding what that could possibly mean. When he brought out a large box of Captain Crunch cereal, understanding dawned on her. "Stuart, you're going to spoil her."

He grumbled something unintelligible and placed the box on the tabletop.

The phone pealed and he raised stricken eyes toward the wall. "I'll get it," he said, pushing his way past Lanni. "I…I've been waiting for a call. Business."

The phone rang a second time and Lanni glanced at it anxiously.

"I'll take it in the other room," Stuart said, nearly throwing Lanni off balance in his rush to move into the office.

Lanni thought his actions curious, but shook her head and brought a bowl and spoon to the table for Jenny's cold cereal.

When Jenny finished, Stuart suggested the two of them feed the chickens. As hot water filled the sink, Lanni watched them leave. The few dishes they'd dirtied for breakfast were clean within minutes. It could have been her imagination, but Stuart's eyes seemed to avoid her when he'd returned to the kitchen following the phone call. She'd half-expected him to make some teasing comment about her and Judd, but he hadn't. Instead he'd taken Jenny by the hand and rushed outside, saying the chickens must be starving by now. Yet it was an hour earlier than the time he'd fed them the day before. He was a strange man.

She wiped her hands dry and decided it was time to visit Betty Peterman.

"Hi, Mommy." Jenny raced to her mother's side when Lanni came out the back door. "Where are you going?"

"To visit Mrs. Peterman."

"Grandpa and me fed all the chickens. Can I come with you?" Her gaze flew to her grandfather who granted his permission with an abrupt shake of his head.

"If you like." Lanni wasn't all that sure she wanted her daughter with her. Her mind buzzed with questions about Judd and his youth. Questions only Betty Peterman could answer. This wasn't a conversation she wanted Jenny to listen in on, but given no other choice, she took the child with her.

Betty answered Lanni's knock with a warm smile of welcome.

"I hope I'm not disturbing you."

"Of course not." The older woman stepped aside so Lanni and Jenny could enter the kitchen.

Following Lanni's gaze around the room, Betty pursed her lips together and slowly shook her head. "Imagine Stuart buying a new stove for this place. The old one worked fine. I tell you, Lydia would be as angry as a wet wasp."

At Lanni's blank stare, Betty continued. "Lydia was after Stuart for years to buy her a new stove. He wouldn't do it. He claimed there was nothing wrong with the old one she had." Betty moved to the counter, took down a mug and poured some coffee for Lanni, delivering it to the table without asking. Next she opened a drawer and took out a small bag of colored dough. "Here you go, Jenny." She plopped it down on the counter with a miniature rolling pin. "You bake your little heart out."

Lanni tried to hide her surprise. She hadn't expected Betty to have anything to entertain a four-year-old.

"I've had a recipe for that play dough for years. Finally had an excuse to make it up." Betty smiled fondly at the little girl. "I still have trouble getting over how much she resembles Lydia."

At the mention of Judd's mother, Lanni straightened her outstretched arms, and cradled the steaming cup of coffee. She lowered her gaze, not wishing Betty to know how curious she was about Judd's mother. "What was she like?"

"Lydia?"

Lanni nodded.

"Gentle. Sweet. Delicate."

Those were the same qualities Lanni had seen in the photo in Judd's room. "What happened?"

Betty pulled out the chair opposite Lanni. "I don't really know. It was a shock to everyone in Miles City when Lydia married Stuart. They were as different as can be. I believe he honestly loved her and that she loved him. But she hated the isolation of the ranch. Every year I could see her wither up more. She was like a hot-house orchid out here in this desert heat. If pneumonia hadn't killed her, she would have eventually shriveled up and died from living here."

"How sad." It wasn't the first time Lanni had been touched by the unhappy story of Lydia Matthiessen's short life.

"When she was pregnant with Judd, she moved back into the city with her parents. Judd was only a couple of weeks old when Stuart brought her back to the ranch. Things changed between them from that point on, and not for the better I fear." A bleak light entered Betty's eyes. "Stuart loved her. I'm sure he did. But things weren't right between them. I'd see her out hanging diapers on the clothesline and her eyes would be red rimmed as though she'd been crying her heart out. She lost weight and got so thin that I fretted over her. Lydia told me I worried too much."

"Why didn't he let her visit her parents if she was so unhappy?" Lanni asked. Surely if he loved her, Stuart could see what life on the Circle M was doing to his wife. It seemed only natural that he'd do whatever possible to bring some happiness into Lydia's bleak existence.

"I can't rightly say why she never went back to see her family. Too proud, I suspect. Her parents had never been keen on Stuart, said she'd married beneath herself. Pride and stubbornness were qualities they both seemed to have in equal quantities. Lydia wanted Stuart to sell the ranch and move into the city. Stuart refused. This land has been in his family for two generations. His father nearly lost the ranch in the Great Depression, but through everything—drought, famine, disease—had managed to keep the Circle M and his family together. Stuart wasn't about to leave it all because his wife wanted a more active social life. After a while Lydia's eyes began to look hollow; she was so miserably unhappy, the poor dear."

"How did Stuart react toward Judd?"

Betty sighed. "It's hard to say. He was pleased he had a son; he held and bounced him on his knee, but all Judd did was cry. The baby was the only bright spot in Lydia's life and she spoiled him terribly. Judd clung to her."

"You say she died of pneumonia?"

Betty's mouth thinned with the memory. "This is the saddest part of all. One evening in late September, when it was cool enough to add an extra blanket on the bed at night, but warm enough in the daytime to keep a window open…" She paused and seemed to wait for Lanni to nod. Lanni did. "Well, my kitchen window was open and I heard Lydia crying. She had a bag packed and was carrying Judd on her hip. She told Stuart that she'd had enough of his stupid ranch. She was sick of the Circle M. Sick of his stinginess. Sick of his precious cows. She was leaving him if she had to walk all the way to Miles City."

"What did Stuart say?"

Sadly Betty shook her head. "He told her to go. He said that he didn't need her. All she cared about was spending money." Betty paused and waved her finger. "Now that was unfair. All Lydia ever asked for was a new stove. God knows she was right, but her pleas fell on deaf ears."

"It couldn't possibly be the same one that's at the house now?" Although the monstrosity was old, it wasn't an antique.

"Oh no. Now this is the funny part. About a month after Lydia died Stuart went out and bought that stove. Now isn't that nonsense? He was so crazed with grief that he bought her what she wanted after she was dead." Betty shook her head as though even now, thirty-odd years later, the action still confused her.

"You started to tell me how she died," Lanni prompted.

"Ah, yes. Well, Lydia left all right, with all the defiance of a princess. She lifted her bag and stalked out the driveway, taking Judd with her."

"And Stuart let her go?"

"He did. He'll regret it all his life, but he let her leave and shouted 'good riddance' after her."

"But Miles City is a hundred miles from here." At least that was what she remembered Judd telling her.

"Stuart seemed to think she'd come to her senses and come back on her own, especially when it started raining."

"She didn't?"

"No. An hour later he got in the pickup and drove out looking for her. She'd gotten only a few miles, but was soaked to the skin and shivering so bad her teeth chattered."

"Judd?"

"Oh, he was fine. She'd wrapped him up nice and warm and held him to her so he didn't catch cold."

"What happened next?"

"Lydia took sick. Pneumonia. Within a week she went to the hospital, and a few days after that she died."

Lanni felt tears well at the thought of such a senseless loss of life.

"Stuart blamed himself. I suppose that's only natural with him leaving her alone all that time in the rain. He was a loner before Lydia died, but after she was gone it was like he lost heart."

"The poor man." Lanni could understand how devastated he must have been. Shell-shocked by the loss of his wife and left with a young son who yearned for his mother. "But he had Judd."

"Yes, he had Judd." Betty purposely avoided meeting Lanni's eyes. "The problem was, Stuart felt he wasn't much of a husband to Lydia and that he was an even worse father to their child. As young as he was, Judd didn't want to have anything to do with his father. In the beginning Stuart tried everything, but he soon gave up. Perhaps if Judd had been a little bit older when Lydia died, he might have accepted his father easier. Every time he looked at his son, Stuart saw Lydia in him and the guilt nearly crippled him."

"If it was so painful then why didn't he send Judd to live with his grandparents?" Surely they would've take him no matter how they felt about Stuart.

"I wish he had, but apparently Lydia's parents blamed Stuart for her death and wanted nothing to do with Stuart. And from what I understand, his own were long dead."

"Then who took care of Judd?"

Betty smiled then for the first time. "I had him during the day, although I was a poor substitute for his mother. I took him in and gave him what love I could. Jim and I were never able to have children of our own, so having Judd here was real good for me. But each evening, Stuart came to the house to pick him up and take him to the main house with him. Every day Judd cried. It nearly broke my heart to see that baby cry. He didn't want to be with his father, but just as he did with Lydia, Stuart refused to let him go." Sharply, Betty tossed her head back, shaking free her troubled thoughts. "In a lot of ways, Judd and his father are alike. They both possess the same stubborn pride. They're both as arrogant as the sun is hot.

"From the time he was in school, Judd and his father locked horns. The two seemed to grate against each other. If Stuart said one thing, Judd did the opposite just to rile his father. Heaven knew it worked often enough."

"They're still at it."

"I hoped things would change," Betty murmured softly. "They're both so thickheaded that I sometimes feel it will be a miracle if they ever get along. Fools, the pair of them."

Lanni couldn't agree more, but she didn't know what she could do to help either of them.

"And now Stuart's trying to persuade Judd to stay on the ranch?"

"Yes."

"Do you think he will?" Betty looked a bit uncomfortable to be asking.

Lanni smiled into her coffee, remembering Judd's promises. "Yes…it looks like we'll all be staying."

"You and Jenny, too?" Betty looked both surprised and pleased.

"Yes, Judd's content here—happy. It's beautiful country, and although there will be plenty of adjusting for Jenny and me, we're willing. I know what you're thinking," Lanni said, watching Betty. "In some ways I may be a lot like Lydia, but I'm tougher than I look."

Betty shook her head. "You're beautiful the way Lydia was, but you're no orchid—not one bit. You're the type of woman who will blossom where there's plenty of love, and trust me, girl, Judd loves you. I saw it in his eyes when he mentioned you and Jenny were with him." She paused and laughed lightly, shaking her head. "I wonder what it is about the Matthiessen men that attracts the good lookers. From the time Judd was little more than a lad, the girls were chasing him."

Propping her elbow up on the table, Lanni looked at the older woman. "Tell me some more about his youth. Did he have girlfriends?"

Once again Betty laughed outright. "Lots of those. He was a real ladies' man in high school. It used to drive Stuart crazy the way the girls would come around here, wanting to see Judd."

"He played football?"

"Star quarterback. Jim and I attended every game.

He was a real good player; the pride of his school. In those days Judd and his father argued constantly. Stuart didn't want him playing football, said he could get hurt in that crazy sport. Judd ignored him and played anyway. Crazy part is, Stuart went to every game. Arrived late, thinking Judd wouldn't know he was there. But he did. As he'd run on the field, I could see Judd looking into the stands for Stuart. The one time Stuart wasn't there, Judd played terrible."

"He left home soon after graduation?" Lanni recalled Judd telling her that once.

The sad light reentered the older woman's eyes. "Two days later. By the time Judd was eighteen, he and his father were constantly at odds. They seemed to enjoy defying each other. Stuart wanted Judd in college—he had grand plans for the boy, but Judd wanted none of it. They battled night and day about the college issue. I don't think extra schooling would have hurt the boy, but Judd was opposed to the idea of becoming some hot-shot attorney to satisfy his father's whims. After a while the fighting got to be something fierce. Jim and I sat down with Judd and pleaded with him to appease Stuart. It didn't do any good.

"Finally Jim suggested that the best thing Judd could do was join the service. So Judd enlisted with the marines and was gone before Stuart could challenge it."

"But he kept in contact with his father."

"Stuart isn't much for letter writing, but I know that Judd wrote. Not often, I suspect, but a word now and then so Stuart would know where he was. From what I understand, Judd did take plenty of college classes, but they were the ones that interested him and not his father."

"He's been all over the world."

"I know." Betty pinched her lips together. "For the first eighteen years of his life, he was stuck on these Montana plains. When he walked out the door, he didn't look back. It's as if he needed to prove something to Stuart or to himself. I don't know which. He joined the marines and never came back to the Circle M. Not until he showed up with you and Jenny."

"Stuart came to see us once," Lanni spoke softly, remembering the miserable affair. "We'd been married less than a year."

"I remember. It was the first time either Jim or I could remember Stuart leaving the ranch for more than a few days. I suspect it was the first time he was on a plane."

"It...didn't go well."

Betty grunted. "You don't need to tell me that. It was obvious from the minute Stuart returned. He slammed around the ranch for days. There wasn't a civil word for man or beast."

"Even then Stuart wanted Judd to go back to college and become a lawyer," Lanni explained softly.

"Stuart's a strong-willed individual. He likes having his own way, especially when he believes he knows best. It's taken all this time for him to accept the fact that Judd is his own self. The last couple of years have been hard on him; he's feeling his age now.

"I don't think it's any problem figuring out why he sent for you and Jenny. He knew the time had come for him to swallow his pride. The pictures you sent him of Jenny helped. He sees Lydia in the little girl. It pained him at first, I know, but he kept her pictures by his bed stand and looked at them so often he nearly wore off the edges. He wanted Judd back, that's true enough, but he wanted you and Jenny with Judd. In his mind, I believe, Stuart longs to find some of the happiness he lost when Lydia died. It's too late for him now, but he wants it for Judd."

Judd belonged here. Within days, Lanni had witnessed an astonishing transformation in her husband. Judd was happy, truly happy here. This was his home; the one place in this world where he would be completely content.

With the insight came the realization that her place was at his side. He'd asked her to live on the Circle M and she'd agreed. Naturally there would be adjustments, major ones. But Lanni was willing to do everything within her power to be with Judd and build a good life for Jenny and any other children they might have.

When she was younger, newly married, she'd had trouble coming to terms with the thought of leaving Seattle. Judd seemed to want to travel and drag Lanni and Jenny in his wake. Lanni couldn't deal with that and longed for a reassurance Judd couldn't provide. How little they had known each other two years ago— Lanni thanked God they'd been given a second chance to make their marriage work. Now, if something were to happen and she did return to Seattle, her existence would be even more empty and alone than it had before coming to Montana.

"Grandpa's going to build us a house," Jenny announced casually. She'd rolled around bits of blue dough into perfectly shaped cookies and lined them neatly along the edge of the counter.

"What was that, honey?" Betty asked.

"Grandpa said now that you and Jim are back, he's going to build me, Mommy and Daddy a brand new house."

Lanni's and Betty's eyes met and Betty slowly shook

her head. "There he goes again, taking matters into his own hands."

When Lanni left Betty's house, she discovered that the main house was empty. Stuart hadn't let her know where he was going, but he often vanished without a word to her. Lanni accepted his absences without comment. He'd lived most his life without having to let anyone know where he was going. It wasn't her right to insist he start accounting for his whereabouts now.

Jenny went in for her nap without question. Lanni tucked her into the single bed with Betsy, her doll, and the little girl soon fell asleep. Feeling at loose ends, Lanni started straightening the mess in the living room. There were plenty of projects to occupy her if she'd felt comfortable doing them, but this was Stuart's house and he would rightly object to any redecorating.

Neat stacks of magazines lined the coffee table when Stuart came into the house.

Lanni glanced up from her dusting and greeted him with a shy grin, thinking he might object to her housecleaning the same way Judd did.

Stuart stood awkwardly in the doorway leading from the kitchen to the cozy living room. A small bag was clenched in his hand. "I was in town."

Lanni watched him expectantly, not knowing what to say.

"There's this jewelry shop there. A new place that opened up for business about five years ago."

Lanni successfully disguised a smile. A five-year-old business could hardly be considered new.

"Anyway…I saw this pretty bracelet there and I know how women are always wanting pretty things so I bought it for you." He walked across the room and gruffly shoved the sack toward her.

Lanni was too stunned to react and stared at the bag, not knowing what to do.

"It's gold," he said tersely. "Take it."

"But, Stuart, why?"

Ill-at-ease, the older man set the brightly colored sack on the tallest pile of ranching magazines. He stuffed his hands in his pant pockets. "As I said, women like having pretty things."

Lanni picked up the small package and found a long, narrow box inside. She flipped open the lid and caught her breath at the sight of the intricately woven gold bracelet.

"I wish you hadn't," she said gently, closing the lid. This was no ordinary piece of jewelry, but one that must have cost a lot of money. "Stuart, this is very expensive."

"You're darn tootin' it is, but I wanted you to have the best."

"But…"

"You deserve something pretty."

"Thank you, but…"

"Judd was humming this morning and you had a sheepish look as well. That's good, real good." For the first time since Lanni had met Stuart Matthiessen, he smiled.

Ten

As it set, the sun bathed the rolling hills of the Circle M in the richest of hues. The sweet scent of prairie grass and apple blossoms mingled with the breeze, drifting where it would, enticing the senses. Lanni sat on the front porch swing with Jenny on her lap, reading the tales of Mother Goose to her sleepy-eyed daughter.

The scene was tranquil, gentle. Lanni's heart was equally at peace. The beauty of what she'd shared with Judd had lingered through the day and into the evening. She longed for him to arrive home so she could tell him how important she felt saving their marriage was to her.

Jenny pressed her head against Lanni's breast and closed her eyes. The gentle swaying motion of the swing had lulled the preschooler to sleep. Gradually Lanni's voice trailed to a mere whisper until she'd finished the story. She closed the book and set it aside. Her eyes searched the hills, seeking Judd. Her stomach churned at the thought of how close they had come to destroying their lives. Already she knew what her husband would say, and he was right. She had suffocated him with her fears and lack of self-confidence. When they'd gotten married, she'd been immature and unsophisticated.

He'd been right, too, about her family. She had relied heavily upon them for emotional support. More than she should. Her greatest fear had always been that she would lose Judd and yet she had done the very things that had driven him from her.

Lanni sighed and rose from the swing. She carried Jenny upstairs and put her to bed, then moved to glance out the window. Jenny had been asleep only a matter of minutes when Lanni heard voices drifting in from the yard. From her position by the upstairs bedroom window, she overheard Judd tell Jim that he'd take care of the horses. Without argument, Jim murmured his thanks and limped toward his house. It looked as if the older man had twisted his ankle and it was apparent he was in pain.

Looking tired, but otherwise fit, Judd led the two horses toward the barn.

Lanni crept down the stairs to discover Stuart asleep in front of the television. She walked out the back door and to the barn.

The light was dim in the interior of the huge structure when Lanni cracked open the massive doors. Judd threw a glance over his shoulder at the unexpected sound and slowly straightened when he recognized Lanni.

"Hello there, cowpoke," she greeted warmly.

"Hello there, wife of a cowpoke." He walked toward her, but stopped abruptly and glanced down over his mud-caked jeans. "I'm filthy."

Lanni slipped her arms around his neck and shook her head. "I could care less," she said smiling up at him. "I've been waiting all day for you and I won't be cheated out of a warm welcome."

Chuckling, Judd bent his head low to capture her mouth. Their lips clung. Judd couldn't be denied her love and warmth another minute. All day he'd thought about her waiting back at the ranch house and he'd experienced such a rush of pleasure that it had been almost painful. The minute after he was home and had a chance to shower, he was taking her to bed and making slow, leisurely love to her.

"I thought it was all a dream," Lanni whispered. "I can't believe I'm in your arms like this."

"If this is a dream, I'll kill the one who wakes me," Judd said and groaned. He kissed her then with a wildness that stirred Lanni's heart. "Oh Lanni, love, I thought I'd die before I got home to you today. No day has ever been longer. I've been a horror to work with— just ask Jim. All I wanted was to get back to you."

Their mouths fused again and hot sensation swirled through her. When he released her mouth, Judd held her to him and breathed several deep, even breaths.

"Let me take care of the horses," he whispered.

Lanni moved provocatively against him. "Take care of me first," she said, nipping at his bottom lip with her teeth.

"Lanni…" He buried his face in her neck. She was cradled against him in a way that left little doubt as to his needs. "Not here."

"Yes here."

"Now?"

"Yes, please."

Judd kissed her again, his tongue outlining her bottom lip first and then her top lip. Lanni was so weakened by the sensuous attack that she thought she might faint.

With their mouths still fused, Judd lifted her into his arms. Without thought or direction he moved into a clean stall and laid her on the fresh bed of hay. Lying half on top of her, Judd kissed her again and again.

The loud snort from one of the horses brought up Judd's head. He released a broken, frustrated sigh. "Lanni."

"Hmm?" Her arms were stretched out around his neck, her wrists crossed.

Judd looked over his shoulder and groaned.

"The horses?" she asked.

"The horses," he repeated.

"All right," she murmured and smiled leisurely. "I suppose that as the wife of an old cowhand, I best get used to playing second fiddle to a horse."

Grinning, Judd got to his feet and helped her up, gently brushing the hay from her back. "Give me fifteen minutes to shower and shave and we'll see how second fiddle you feel." He patted the stallion on the flank, moved around to unfasten the cinch from the massive beast and then lifted the heavy saddle from the animal.

"Can I help?" Lanni wanted to know.

"If you'd like." He nodded to his right. "The pitchfork's over there. Go ahead and deliver some hay to these hungry boys."

Eager to help, Lanni did as he requested. "Aren't you going to ask me about my day?"

"Sure. Did anything exciting happen?"

"You mean other than Stuart going to town and buying me a thousand-dollar gold bracelet." She didn't know what he'd paid for the piece of jewelry, but hoped to capture Judd's undivided attention.

"What!"

She had it now. "You heard me right."

"Why would he do something like that?"

"I'm not exactly sure," Lanni replied. "But from what

I understand, although he was careful not to say as much, the bracelet is a gift because I've fallen so nicely into his schemes."

Judd scowled. "How'd he know?"

Lanni laughed and shook her head. "Didn't you talk to him this morning?"

"Not more than a couple of minutes. I told him where Jim and I were headed and what needed to be done. That was about it."

"Apparently that was enough."

"Enough for what?"

"Enough," Lanni said patiently, "for Stuart to know exactly what happened between us last night." To her amazement, Judd's eyes narrowed with disapproval. "You're angry?" she asked him, puzzled by his attitude.

"No," he denied, leading the horse by the reins into his stall.

"But you look furious. Is it because he gave me the bracelet?"

For a minute Judd didn't answer her. "Not exactly. However, I'm going to let my father know that if any man gives you gifts, it's going to be me." He returned to the second horse, his movements jerky, angry. So Stuart had been so confident that their little talk had reaped its rewards that he'd gone out and gotten Lanni that fancy bracelet. He was furious with the old man, and equally upset with himself for falling so readily into Stuart's schemes.

"Judd," Lanni said, placing her hand on his forearm to stop him. "Are you sorry about last night?"

"No."

"All of a sudden you're closing yourself off from me and I don't know why."

"It's nothing."

"I'm your wife," she cried, impatient now. "We were separated for two long, miserable years because we never talked to each other. I don't want to make the same mistakes we did before. For heaven's sake tell me why you're upset!"

"Stuart has no business involving himself in our affairs."

"Agreed. But you're not making sense. Why are you so mad at him—you already said it wasn't the bracelet."

Judd toyed with the thought of telling her about Steve's phone calls and rejected the idea. He couldn't risk having her suspect that pride alone had driven him to her bed. It was far from the truth and if she started to think that was his motive, she'd turn away from him. In reality, Judd had finally come to understand that if he were to lose Lanni now, life would have no meaning for him.

"I'm not angry," he said, forcing a smile. "Why don't you go fix me something to eat and I'll finish up here?"

"Judd...?" In her heart, Lanni knew something wasn't right, but this newfound peace was fragile and she didn't want to test it with something as flimsy as conjecture.

"You go into the house. I'll be there in a couple of minutes."

Bewildered, Lanni left the barn, not knowing what to think. Something was troubling Judd, but he obviously preferred to keep it to himself.

Judd exhaled slowly, watching Lanni turn and walk away. He was going to have a heart-to-heart talk with his father, and soon.

His dinner was on the table when Judd came into the house. He ate it silently as Lanni worked around the kitchen. They were both quiet, neither speaking. When he'd finished, Judd delivered his plate to the kitchen sink. "Lanni," he said. He took a step toward her, hesitated and frowned. "Is there a possibility you could get pregnant from last night?"

He looked so serious, so concerned, that Lanni's heart melted. "I don't think so."

"I'd like another baby. Would you mind?" Gently he lifted a thick strand of her hair from her face, twisting it around his finger. His eyes softened as he studied her. Somehow. Somewhere. A long time ago, he must have done something very right to deserve a woman as good as Lanni. "I love you so much," he whispered.

"I want another baby," she answered and nodded emphatically. "Anytime you say, cowboy."

Mindless of his dirty, sweaty clothes, Judd brought her into the loving circle of his arms and kissed her hungrily. Lanni slid her arms over his chest and linked them at the back of his neck. Her soft curves molded to his hardness and Judd deepened the kiss until their mouths forged. Lanni sighed, swaying against him, weak and clinging. Reluctantly he broke off the kiss, but continued to hold her, smiling tenderly down on her. "I'm a filthy mess."

Sighing with contentment, Lanni shook her head. "It didn't bother me in the barn; it doesn't bother me now."

She looked up at him and her eyes held such a lambent glow that it took all his restraint not to kiss her again. "Where's Stuart?"

"Asleep."

"I need to talk to him."

Lanni wasn't certain what Judd wanted to say, but she thought it would be best to clear the air. "He mentioned something to Jenny that you might want to ask him about as well."

"What's that?"

"He told her that since Jim and Betty Peterman are back, he's going to build us a house."

Judd could feel the frustration build in him. "We may have a battle on our hands, keeping our lives private; I'll say something to him about that while I'm at it. Any house building will be decided by you and me—not my father."

"I agree," Lanni said, studying Judd. He looked tired. "Are you sure you don't want to save this talk until morning?"

"I'm sure." There were more than a few items he needed to discuss with his father—some were about the ranch and others about Lanni and Jenny. He could make the decisions regarding the Circle M easily enough, but he sought Stuart's input. The ranch was one area on which they were in complete agreement. They both loved the Circle M. It was as much a part of their lives as the blood that channeled through their veins. And while he was with Stuart, he would tell his father exactly what he thought of him buying Lanni gifts and filling their daughter with tales of a new house. If they were going to live on the Circle M, Stuart was going to have to learn to keep his nose out of Judd's marriage and his family.

"It's going to take a lot of commitment to get this ranch operating properly," Judd told Lanni as she finished putting the leftovers back into the refrigerator. Commitment and funds. It would nearly wipe out eighteen years of savings and be the financial gamble of Judd's life.

"This is our home now." A wealth of understanding went into Lanni's statement.

"It is home," Judd concurred. He felt it all the way

through his soul. Montana. The Circle M. He loved it here. It was where he was meant to be. All these years he'd been searching for the elusive feeling that had returned the minute he'd pulled into the driveway leading to this beaten-down house.

"No more trips to Alaska?"

"Too cold!"

Lanni grinned, remembering Stuart telling her that it had registered forty below at the ranch only last winter.

"Saudi Arabia?"

"Too hot," Judd admitted with a chuckle.

Again Lanni tried to disguise a smile. Stuart had warned her that the summers could be as hot as a desert with temperatures ranging in the low hundreds.

"I'd better go have that talk with Stuart," Judd said reluctantly; he wasn't looking forward to this.

"I'll wait for you upstairs then." This evening was turning out so different than what Lanni had hoped. In her mind she'd pictured a loving husband carrying her up the stairs. Her teeth bit into the sensitive flesh of her inner cheek to hold back her disappointment. "Do you want me to wait up for you?"

Without turning to face her, Judd shook his head. "It may be a while. I'll wake you."

With a heavy heart, Lanni trudged up the stairs. Pacing the inside of her room, she felt the urge to stamp her feet in a childish display of temper. They were both trying so hard to make everything between them work that they had become their own worst enemies. Judd wanted to clear the air with his father and all Lanni wanted was her husband at her side.

She sat on the edge of the bed for what seemed like hours. Lethargy took hold and, feeling depressed, she slowly moved down the hall to shower. A half hour later, she listlessly climbed into bed.

Sleep didn't come easily. The last time she looked at the clock on the nightstand beside the bed, it was nearly midnight. Judd still hadn't come upstairs.

The next thing Lanni heard was a soft whimper. The sound activated a maternal instinct she couldn't question and she woke up.

Throwing back the covers, she climbed out of bed and hurried down the hall, not stopping for either her slippers or her bathrobe. Jenny was quietly weeping in Judd's arms.

He glanced at her and whispered, "She had a bad dream."

"Poor sweetheart," Lanni whispered, lowering herself onto the bed beside Jenny and Judd. Gently she patted the little girl's back until she'd calmed down and stopped sniffing. A few minutes later Jenny's even breathing assured Lanni her daughter had returned to sleep.

"How'd it go with Stuart?" Lanni asked.

"Not good." It was like he was eighteen all over again. Judd couldn't make his father understand that he didn't want the old man interfering again. What happened between Judd and Lanni was none of Stuart's business. Stuart had told Judd that he should thank God he'd been around that morning. Steve had phoned again and had demanded to speak to Lanni. He'd been able to put the other man off, but he doubted if he could another time.

"Did you argue?" Lanni asked next.

"Not exactly. He refused to listen to me."

"He has his pride."

"Don't I know it," Judd concurred.

Gently he placed Jenny back inside the bed and led Lanni into the hallway. "I'm surprised you heard her. She barely made a sound."

"I have mother's ears." She paused in front of her door. He looked unbearably weary. His hair was rumpled as if he'd stroked his fingers through it countless times.

Judd hesitated at her side, trying not to stare at her upturned face. She was so incredibly lovely in the moonlight that he felt his body tense just standing beside her. "More than anything I wanted to be with you." He didn't move. His feet felt rooted to the spot and his tongue was thick and uncooperative. He wanted her to sleep with him, tonight and for the rest of their lives. They were good together, and not only in bed. There was so much they could give each other.

Lanni watched the weariness evaporate from his eyes. Now they were keen and sharp, commanding her to come to him.

Slowly, as if sleepwalking, Lanni moved to him and, without a word, her arms crept up his solid chest to encircle his neck and urge his mouth down to hers. As his head descended, she arched closer. Their lips met in a fiery union of unleashed passion. The kiss continued until Lanni was both dizzy and weak. They broke apart panting and breathless.

Smiling, she took Judd by the hand and led him into the room. "I can't believe it took you this long," she whispered.

He brought her into his arms and nuzzled her throat. "All day I've been crazy to get home to you and it seemed like everything stood in our way." With infinite patience, he unfastened the top button of her bodice to slip the material free. Her arms stretched over her head as Judd pulled the gown free. Every part of her body throbbed with need for him. They were man and wife. Lovers. Friends.

"Judd," she pleaded.

Just when her knees were about to give out on her and she was going to collapse onto the bed, he raised his head and gently laid her down on the mattress. In seconds he was free of his clothes.

Lanni had waited all evening for him and wouldn't be denied any longer. As they made love their hearts sang out in joyful celebration. Their cries echoed each other's. The pleasure went on and on until Lanni was convinced it was endless.

Judd wrapped her in his arms, kissing the tears of joy from her face. "Oh, my love," he whispered, his voice trembling with emotion. "Was it always this good?"

"Always," she murmured, not remembering anything ever being less exciting between them. Together they were magic. During the long, lonely months of their separation, Lanni had been only half alive. She recognized that now more than ever. Her life with Jenny had been clouded with a constant sense of expectation, waiting. An unconscious part of her had been seeking a reconciliation with Judd; without him she was incomplete—spiritually handicapped. She was destined to belong to him and only him.

"Don't leave me," she pleaded, wrapping her arms around him and burying her face in his neck.

"No," he promised. "Never again." Love for her flowed through him like floodwaters after a heavy spring rain. She was all that was important to him. The ranch could fall down at his feet tomorrow and he'd survive. He could lose all his personal possessions and never notice their loss. But he wouldn't last another minute without Lanni.

The tension fled from her limbs and Lanni relaxed, cuddling him. He reached for the sheets and covered them. Within minutes they were both asleep.

Judd woke first. Even in their sleep they'd continued to hold each other—neither seemed willing to release the other. He smiled gently and stared at the ceiling. It was later than he'd slept since arriving on the ranch. But he didn't care—Lanni was his and he was whole again.

He closed his mind to the unpleasant scene he'd faced with Stuart before climbing the stairs to bed. He didn't want to argue with his father; he'd hoped they'd come to an understanding, but apparently Judd was wrong. He'd told Stuart if Steve phoned again that he should give Lanni the phone. She would be angry when she learned they'd been hiding the calls from her, but they'd deal with that at the time.

Lanni stirred, content, satisfied. Judd's arms were securely wrapped around her. "Morning," she whispered, stretching. "What time is it?"

Judd kissed the crown of her head and moved his wrist up so he could read his watch. "Later than it should be."

"I feel wonderful," Lanni announced, turning to kiss the hollow of his throat.

"So do I," Judd answered. "It felt so good holding you that I couldn't slip out of bed. Now I'll have to face Jim's wrath for being lazy and sleeping in."

"I'm pleased you didn't leave," Lanni whispered, remembering how disappointed she'd been the day before.

"Mommy." Jenny knocked softly against the closed door, her sweet voice meek and timid.

Lanni jumped up from the bed and after pulling on

her robe, she opened the door. Jenny was standing there, her doll clenched to her breast. Lanni noted that the little girl looked unnaturally pale.

"What's the matter, Cupcake? Aren't you feeling well?" Judd asked. Before Lanni had opened the door, he'd pulled on his jeans.

"I'm not sick," Jenny answered.

"Do you want breakfast?" Lanni inquired.

The little girl adamantly shook her head. "Nope."

"Aren't you hungry?" Breakfast was Jenny's favorite meal, especially when there was Captain Crunch cereal around.

"Grandpa was mean to me. He told me to go away."

Judd felt anger shoot through him. "I don't think he meant that."

"He said it real, real mean."

"Maybe Grandpa isn't feeling well today," Lanni suggested, surprised that Stuart would do or say anything to upset Jenny.

"And you know what else he said?"

"What?" Judd brushed the curls from her cheek and kissed her gently to ease the hurt feelings.

"He said I shouldn't ever answer the phone again."

"He has this thing about the phone," Lanni said, shaking her head in wonder at Judd's father's actions. "It rang yesterday and you would have thought the FBI was on the other end. He nearly wrestled me to the ground to stop me from answering. Then he raced into the other room to get it."

Judd stiffened. "I'm sure there's some explanation."

"You know what, Mommy?"

"What, honey?"

"I know who was on the phone."

"Who was that?" Lanni asked, unconcerned.

"Mr. Delaney, and he was real mad, too. He said that he wants to talk to you and that Daddy didn't have the right to keep you from talking on the phone."

Eleven

"Judd," Lanni murmured, her voice betraying her shock. "Is that true?"

"Jenny, do I hear your doll crying? Maybe you should let her take a nap." Judd turned to his daughter, ignoring Lanni's question. The last thing he needed was to deal with this Steve issue now. One look told him how furious Lanni was.

"Betsy's not crying, Daddy."

"Yes, she is," Lanni said sternly.

Jenny's lower lip began to tremble as she battled back ready tears. "Nobody wants Jenny this morning," she said, her voice wobbling. She paused and glanced from her mother to her father.

"Now look what you've done," Lanni whispered between clenched teeth, reaching for her daughter. She wrapped her arms around the four-year-old. "We're sorry, honey."

"I don't want you and Daddy to fight."

"We won't argue, will we, Mommy?" Judd challenged, raising his eyes to Lanni.

Jenny broke free of Lanni's arms. "But Mommy

looks that way when she gets mad at Aunt Jade. Her face scrunches up and her eyes get small. Like now."

"I think she has something there," Judd commented lightly.

Lanni reached for her clothes, cursing under her breath. "Now I understand why Stuart didn't want me answering the phone. How many times has Steve called?"

"I have no idea."

"I'll just bet you don't."

"Mommy."

"Not now, Jenny. This is serious business."

Jenny sighed expressively. "Business, business, business, that's all you talk about. When are you going to be a Mommy again?"

Lanni stared open-mouthed at her daughter. "That's unfair, Jennifer Lydia Matthiessen. I've always been your mother." Lanni did her best to ignore an attack of guilt for all the times Jade had picked up Jenny from the day-care center and just as many occasions that Jenny had been left with Jade or her parents because Lanni had to work late for a hundred different reasons.

"All you did was business, business, business until Daddy came. I don't want you to talk to Mr. Delaney. He sounded mad just like you and Grandpa."

"She's smarter than you give her credit," Judd tossed in and was almost seared by Lanni's scalding glower.

"I'm calling Steve to find out what's been going on around here."

Judd crossed his arms. "Be my guest." Although he strove to appear as nonchalant as possible, he was worried.

Lanni stormed out of the bedroom and got dressed

in the bathroom. Two minutes later, she raced downstairs. Judd followed her.

Stuart met him at the foot of the stairway. "You got to stop her, boy."

"Why?"

"She's going to contact that city slicker."

"Judd, do something," Lanni cried, her patience long since gone. "Your father's disconnected the phone."

"Dad. It's fine."

"Did you think to inform him that Steve could be contacting me for business reasons?" Lanni flared, her hands placed defiantly on her hips.

"No." Judd's own self-control was weakening. "You and I both know what Steve wants."

"You're jealous!"

"You're darn right I am. I don't like having that milquetoast anywhere near you."

"You tell her, son," Stuart shouted.

"Stay out of this." Judd turned to his father, pointing a finger in his direction. "This is between Lanni and me."

Chuckling, Stuart took Jenny by the hand and led her toward the kitchen. "Got to leave those young lovers to settle this themselves," he whispered gleefully to the little girl.

"Are you still mad at me, Grandpa?" Jenny wanted to know first.

Stuart looked shocked. "I was never angry with my Jenny-girl."

"Good. Betsy cried when you got cross."

"You tell Betsy how sorry your grandpa is."

"It's all right, she told me that she forgives you."

The kitchen door closed and Judd turned to Lanni. "You were saying?"

"You have a lot of nerve keeping those calls from me."

"You're absolutely right."

"If I had any sense, I'd walk out that door."

"You won't," he stated confidently. "You always were crazy about me."

"Judd," she cried. "I'm serious."

"I am, too."

"Don't try to sweet-talk me."

"Come on, Lanni, this is no snow job. I was jealous. I'll admit it if it makes you feel any better. Stuart told me about the calls the other night and I realized how serious this guy is. He isn't going to lose you without a fight and if that's what he wants, I'll give him one."

"You're being ridiculous."

"I don't think so. Apparently Delaney's been trying to reach you since we arrived. I guess I should be grateful there's no cell coverage here."

"And it never occurred to you that it could be something to do with the office?"

"Quite frankly, no. Stuart knew after talking to him only one time and he's right on target. Delaney's after one thing and that one thing happens to involve you. I recognized it the minute I met the man."

"You're imagining things."

"I wasn't seeing things when I saw him gawking at you. Don't be so naive, my sweet innocent."

"I'm not an innocent!"

"Thanks to me." One side of his mouth quirked upward.

"Stop it, Judd Matthiessen, you're only making me madder." She crossed her arms, refusing to relent to his cajoling good mood. He seemed to think this was all some big joke. "Get me the phone," she demanded.

"All right, all right; don't get testy." He went into the kitchen and returned a moment later with the telephone. He handed it to her, crossed his arms and waited.

"Well?"

"Well what?"

"I want you to leave," she hissed, "this is a private conversation."

Judd didn't budge and from the look about him, he wasn't going to. Rather than force the issue, Lanni traipsed into the small office off the living room and inserted the phone jack into place. It was doubtful that Judd would hear much of the conversation anyway.

She punched out the numbers and waited. The phone rang only once. "Steve, it's Lanni."

"Lanni, thank goodness you phoned," he said, his relief obvious in his tone. "What been going on there? I've been trying to contact you for days!"

"I didn't know. Jenny mentioned this morning that you'd phoned, but it's the first I heard of it."

"I don't know what kind of situation you're in there, but I've been tempted to contact the authorities. I think your father-in-law is off his rocker."

"He is a bit eccentric."

"Eccentric. I'd say he was closer to being stark raving mad."

"Steve, I'm sure you didn't contact me to discuss Stuart."

"You're right, I didn't. Lanni," he said her name slowly, in a hurt, self-righteous tone, "you didn't even let me know you were leaving."

"There…there wasn't time. I tried." But admittedly not very hard. She'd left a message for him at the office, but hadn't contacted his cell. Her relationship or non-relationship with her fellow worker embarrassed Lanni now that she and Judd had reconciled. It was true that their dates were innocent enough, but Lanni had seen the handwriting on the wall as far as Steve was concerned and Judd was right. Steve wanted her and was courting her with seemingly limitless patience.

"Lanni," Steve continued, his voice serious. "I'm worried about you."

"There's no need; Jenny and I are perfectly fine."

"Are you there of your own free will?"

"Of course!" The question was ludicrous. "I haven't been kidnapped, if that's what you mean."

"Your father-in-law has told me a number of times that Judd would never let you go."

"He didn't mean it like that."

"Perhaps not, but he also told me that Judd would go to great lengths to keep you married to him."

"I'm sure you're mistaken." Her fingers tightened around the receiver as she remembered the expression in Judd's eyes when he'd told her he needed her. He'd been desperate and just now he'd admitted that he'd known about Steve's phone calls a couple of nights ago.

"What made you leave Seattle with the man? Lanni, he deserted you—left you and Jenny. He's treated you like dirt. What possible reason could there be for you to trust a man like that?"

"Judd claimed that his father was seriously ill and had asked to see Jenny before he died."

"That old man sounds in perfect health to me."

"He apparently made a miraculous recovery when we arrived." Steve almost had her believing his craziness and she paused a moment to recount the details of her coming.

"Lanni," Steve said, and breathed heavily. "I want you to do something for me."

"What?"

"I'm very serious about this, Lanni, so don't scoff. I want you to try to leave and see what happens. I'm willing to bet that Judd and his father are holding you and Jenny captive and you just don't realize it yet."

"Steve, that's loony."

"It's not. Tell them something serious has come up and you have to return to Seattle."

"Steve!"

"Do it. If I haven't heard from you by the end of the day, I'm contacting the police."

Lanni lifted the hair from her forehead and closed her eyes. "I can't believe I'm hearing this."

"Tell me you'll do it."

"All right, but you're wrong. I know you're wrong."

"Prove it to me."

"I can't believe I'm agreeing to this." She shook her head in wonder, but then Steve had always been persuasive.

"You'll phone me back?"

His plan wouldn't work, Lanni realized. "What am I supposed to say after I've got my bags in the car and am ready to leave? They're going to think I've lost my senses if I suddenly announce that this is all a test to see if they'd actually let me go."

"You'll think of something," Steve said confidently.

"Great." Lanni felt none of his assurance.

"I'll be waiting to hear from you."

"I'm only doing this to prove to you once and for all that Jenny and I are perfectly safe."

"Fine. Just do it."

Lanni didn't bother with any goodbyes. She replaced the receiver and sat down, burying her face in her hands, assimilating her troubled thoughts.

"Did you tell him?" Judd asked, standing behind her.

Frightened by the unexpected sound of his voice, Lanni jumped and jerked her head around. "Tell him what?"

Judd's mouth thinned with displeasure. "That you and I are back together and that there will be no divorce."

"No, I didn't tell him."

"Why not?"

Lanni studied him, feeling the overbearing weight of newfound suspicions. Not for a minute did she believe she and Jenny were being kidnapped by Judd and his father. Steve was overreacting because he was naturally suspicious of the circumstances of her leaving Seattle. The whole idea that such a drama was taking place was so farfetched that it was inconceivable. But something else, something far more profound, had captured her attention.

"When did you learn Steve had been trying to contact me?" she asked, surprised at how steady her voice remained when her emotions were in such tumult.

Judd inserted two fingers into the small pocket near the waist of his jeans. "I already told you, Stuart mentioned it the other night."

"What night?"

Judd cursed under his breath. She knew—she'd figured it out. Explaining to Lanni wasn't going to be easy. He sat down across from her. "The night you suspect."

"Then the only reason you came to me—"

"No," he cut in sharply. "That night, for the first time in my life, I realized how right my father was. If I lost you there would be nothing left for me. Nothing. Oh,

I'd stick around the ranch for a while, maybe several years, I don't know, but there would be no contentment, no peace. You give me that, Lanni, only you."

"It didn't work in Seattle. What makes you believe it will here? Aren't you asking a lot of me to abandon everything I know and love on the off chance you'll stick around here? You *think* you'll be content on the Circle M, but you don't know that."

"I do know it. I left the ranch eighteen years ago and now I'm home."

"Maybe."

"I'm home, Lanni. Home. But it doesn't mean a whole lot if you're not here to share it with me. I've loved you from the moment we met; believe me, I've fought that over the last couple of years. There are plenty of things I'd like to change about the both of us. But the underlying fact is that I refuse to give up on our marriage. It's too important to both of us."

"You were jealous of Steve?"

"You're darn right I am," he admitted freely, then added, "but you should know what that feels like."

After her experience in Coeur d'Alene when she'd believed Judd had slept with another woman, Lanni had experienced a mouthful of the green-eyed monster. Enough to make her gag on her own stupidity.

"I have to leave."

Judd shook his head to clear his thoughts. He couldn't believe she meant what she was saying. "What do you mean leave?"

"There's a problem in Seattle—a big one and I've got to be there to handle it. There are people counting on me, and I can't let them down."

"What about letting me down?"

"This is different."

"It isn't," he said hotly. "What kind of problem could be so important that you'd so willingly walk away from me?" He battled down the overwhelming sensation that if he allowed her to drive away from the Circle M, it would be all over for them.

"A house transaction."

"That's a flimsy excuse," he said darkly. "What is Steve holding over you?"

"Nothing. Don't be ridiculous—this is strictly business."

"Obviously that's not true. You were on the phone for a good fifteen minutes. You must have discussed something other than a real estate transaction. I want to know what he said," Judd demanded.

"And I already told you. I need to return to Seattle." She pushed herself away from the desk and stood. "I have to pack my things."

"Lanni," he whispered, his hand stopping her. "Look me in the eye and tell me you're coming back."

"I'm coming back." He had yet to learn she had no intention of leaving. Not really. This was a stupid game and she was furious that she'd agreed to do this. But Steve had been so insistent, so sure she was caught in some trap. She walked past Judd and into the living room.

Her father-in-law was standing in the middle of the room when Lanni came out of the office. His face was pale and pinched and his gaze skidded past Lanni to his son. Questions burned in his faded brown eyes.

"Lanni needs to make a quick trip to Seattle," Judd explained, doing his best to disguise his worries. "There's some problem at the office that only she can handle."

"You letting her go?"

"He has no other option," Lanni cut in sharply.

Stuart ignored her and narrowed his eyes on his son. "Are you going to let her go to that no-good city slicker? He's going to steal her away."

"I have no intention of letting Steve do any such thing," Lanni informed him stiffly. "Judd and I are married and we plan to stay that way for a very long time."

Stuart continued to pretend she wasn't there. "I let Lydia leave once and after she came back things were never the same."

"I'm not Lydia."

"Mommy's name is Lanni," Jenny informed them softly, clenching Judd's hand and staring wide eyed at the three adults.

"Go ahead and pack," Judd spoke softly, resigned. He wouldn't stop Lanni—this was her decision. Unlike his father, Judd was willing to let her go. Sorrow stabbed through him as he thought of the night the roles had been reversed—she'd let him go. But he had begged her to go with him. "I'll call the airlines and find out the time of the next flight. I'll drive you into Billings."

"Boy," Stuart shouted angrily. "What's the matter with you? If Lanni goes it will ruin everything." His hand gripped his stomach. "Don't let her go. Don't make the same mistake as me. You'll be sorry. All your life you'll regret it." His hand reached out and gripped the corner of the large overstuffed chair as he swayed.

"Dad?" Judd placed his hand on his father's shoulder. "What's wrong?"

"Pain," he said through clenched teeth. "Most of yesterday and through the night."

Judd had never seen a man more pale. "Here, let me get you into the bedroom." With his arm around his father's waist, Judd guided the older man into his bedroom and helped him onto the bed. "I'll contact Doc Simpson."

Lanni was so furious that she couldn't stand in one place. She paced the small area in front of the outdated black-and-white television set, knotting and unknotting her fists.

"He's not sick," she hissed in a low whisper the minute Judd reappeared. "This is all a ploy to keep me on the ranch."

"Why don't we let the doctor decide that?"

"Do you honestly believe this sudden attack of ill health?"

Judd's eyes bored into hers. "As a matter of fact, I do." He returned to the tiny cubicle of an office and reached for the phone. He'd experienced enough pain in his life to recognize when it was genuine.

"What wrong with Grandpa?" Jenny asked, tugging at the hem of Lanni's blouse.

"He's not feeling well, sweetheart."

"He didn't eat any Captain Crunch cereal this morning."

Lanni recalled that Stuart hadn't eaten much of anything in the last twenty-four hours.

Judd reappeared, looking toward his father's bedroom door.

"Well?" Lanni was curious to what Stuart's physician had to say.

"I repeated what Dad told me and Doc Simpson thinks it would be best if we drove into Miles City for a complete examination at the hospital."

"Miles City," Lanni cried. "That's over a hundred miles."

"It's the closest hospital."

"Judd, don't you recognize this for what it is? Stuart

isn't sick. This is all part of some crazy ploy to keep me on the ranch."

"You're free to go, Lanni. Jim can drive you into Billings to catch the next flight for Seattle or you can come with me and we'll get you on a private plane to connect with the airlines in Billings."

Lanni crossed her arms over her chest and shook her head. "I can't believe this is happening."

"I don't have time to discuss the options with you now. Make up your mind."

"I'll go with you." And have the extreme pleasure of watching Judd's expression when the doctors in Miles City announce that Stuart was in perfect health.

"Can I come, too?" Jenny wanted to know.

"It would be better if you and Betsy stayed here with Betty. Can you be a good girl and help Betty?"

Jenny nodded eagerly. "I like her."

Judd had apparently already thought to leave the little girl with the housekeeper because Betty arrived a minute later. Jenny was whisked away and Lanni heard the older woman reassuring Jenny that everything was going to be just fine. A smile touched Lanni's lips when she heard Jenny respond by telling the woman that she wasn't afraid, but Betsy was just a little.

While Judd brought the SUV to the front of the house, Lanni took out some blankets and a pillow.

Judd got his father into the back seat of the car and Lanni lined his lap with blankets. For the first time Lanni noted how terribly pale the older man had become. He gritted his teeth at the pain, but offered Lanni a reassuring grin.

"You leaving for Seattle?"

"You're a wicked old man."

"Agreed," Stuart said with a faint smile. "Stay with my son, girl. Fill his life with children and happiness."

"Would you stop being so dramatic. We're going to get you to Miles City and the doctors are going to tell us you've got stomach gas so stop talking as if the back seat of this car is going to be your deathbed. You got a lot of good years left in you."

"Ha. I'll be lucky to make it there alive."

Judd climbed into the front seat and started the engine. "Ready?" he asked, trying to hide his nervousness.

"Ready, boy," Stuart said and lay back, pressing his weathered face against the feather pillow.

The ride seemed to last an eternity. With every mile Lanni came to believe that whatever was wrong with Stuart was indeed very real.

They hit a rut in the road thirty miles out of Miles City and Stuart groaned. Judd's hands tightened around the steering wheel until his knuckles were stark white. Lanni dared not look at the speedometer. The car whipped past the prairie grass at an unbelievable speed, making the scenery along the side of the road seem blurred.

The only sound in the car was that of the revved engine. Lanni's breathing was short and choppy. It wasn't until they reached the outskirts of Miles City that she realized her breathing echoed Stuart's shallow gasps. Only his were punctuated with a sigh now and again to disguise his pain.

Judd drove directly to Holy Rosary Hospital on Clark Street, running two red lights in his urgency to get his father to a medical team as quickly as possible.

After Stuart had been taken into the emergency entrance, Judd and Lanni were directed to a small reception area. The waiting, not knowing what was happening, was by far the worst.

"When did he say he started feeling so terribly ill?" Lanni asked, reaching for Judd's hand, their fingers entwined, gripping each other for reassurance.

"Apparently he hasn't been up to par all week. He saw Doc Simpson yesterday afternoon and the doctor was concerned then. Dad's ulcer is apparently peptic."

"English, please."

"It's commonly referred to as a bleeding ulcer. They're bad, Lanni, painful."

"I feel like an idiot." She hung her head, ashamed at her behavior and how she'd accused Stuart of staging the entire attack so she'd remain in Montana.

"Don't," Judd said, giving her fingers a reassuring squeeze. "Given an identical set of circumstances, I might have believed the same thing. Dad has a way about him that sometimes even I don't trust."

"Why didn't he say something earlier?"

Judd recalled the argument they'd had the night before when he'd confronted Stuart about the bracelet, building the house and fending off Steve's calls. Stuart had been quick tempered and unreasonable, and Judd had attributed it to his stubborn nature. Now he understood that Stuart had been in a great deal of pain even then.

"Judd?" Lanni coaxed.

"Sorry. What were you saying?"

"I wanted to know why Stuart didn't tell us something was wrong earlier."

Judd's smile was off center. "Pride, I suspect. Telling anyone would be admitting to a weakness. In case you haven't noticed, the Matthiessen men refuse to appear weak no matter what it cost."

"Never," Lanni confirmed, doing her best to disguise a smile. "They're not stubborn, either, and hardly ever proud."

When the doctor approached them, Judd rose quickly to his feet. Lanni stood with him, trying to read the doctor's expression and failing.

"Mr. and Mrs. Matthiessen?"

"Yes. How's my father?"

"He's resting comfortably now. We'd like to keep him overnight for observation and a few tests, but he should be able to leave the hospital tomorrow."

Judd sighed with relief. "Thank you, Doctor." The minute the physician turned away, Judd brought Lanni into his arms and buried his face in the curve of her neck.

"I don't mind telling you I was frightened," he whispered.

"I was, too. He's a crotchety old man, but I've grown fond of him."

"It's funny," Judd said with a short laugh. "I'm relieved that he's going to be fine and in the same breath I'd like to shake him silly for worrying us so much."

"I feel the same way."

Judd slid his arm around her shoulder. "Let's go see him for a minute and then we'll drive on out to the airport and see about getting you a plane to Seattle."

Twelve

"Yes, well." Lanni shifted her feet. Her mind went blank for a plausible excuse to cancel the trip. "I may have reacted hastily. I'm sure if I make a couple of phone calls I'll be able to work out the problem from this end of things."

"What do you mean?" Judd's eyes looked capable of boring holes straight through her. "Three hours ago it was imperative that you reach Seattle. You made it sound like a Biblical-style catastrophe would befall the realty if you weren't there to see to it."

"I could have exaggerated a teensy bit." Lanni swallowed uncomfortably, feeling incredibly guilty.

"Lanni?"

"All right, all right," she admitted, hating herself more by the minute. "I made the entire thing up."

"What!" Judd was furious; it showed in every feature of his chiseled masculine face. His eyes narrowed, his nostrils flared and his mouth thinned dangerously.

She couldn't very well admit that Steve had this senseless, idiotic notion that she was being held against her wishes. "Steve seemed to think I was needed in Seattle." Even to her own ears that excuse sounded lame.

"I'll just bet he wanted you back, and I'm smart enough to know the reason why even if you aren't."

"It wasn't like that," she flared.

"You had time to discuss this scheme with Steve, but not enough to tell him we'd reconciled."

"I'll tell him."

"You're darn right you will." His grip on her elbow as he led her into the hospital parking lot was just short of being painful.

"I can't believe you. You're behaving like Steve Delaney is a threat to us. Judd, I swear to you, he isn't," Lanni muttered, slipping inside the front seat of the station wagon. "I'm yours, Judd Matthiessen, and the only thing that could ever come between us again is of your own making."

"And what's that?"

Her unflinching gaze met his. "If you were to leave me again, it'd be over in a minute. Judd, I mean that. My love is strong enough to withstand just about anything, but not that."

"It isn't going to happen."

Lanni leaned her head against the headrest and closed her eyes. Judd started the car and pulled onto the street. His assurances rang shockingly familiar. It seemed every time he returned from a trip in the beginning, she'd made him promise he wouldn't leave her again. To his credit, he'd taken a job in Seattle and a month, maybe two, would pass before he'd find some excuse to be free of her and travel again.

"I'll never leave you, Lanni. I swear to it by everything I hold sacred."

"What happens when money gets tight?" In her mind Lanni had listed the excuses Judd had conveniently used in the past.

"Simple. We'll sell off a few head of cattle and cut down expenses."

"What happens if Jenny gets sickly again?"

"We'll get her to a doctor."

Lanni shook her head and crossed her arms over her chest. "Doctors cost money." He'd used that excuse the first time. Lanni recognized that she sounded like an insecure little girl, but she refused to live in a dream world no matter how comfortable it was. Too much was at stake and she needed to know that this reconciliation with Judd was concrete.

"Montana is a bit different from Seattle. Doc Simpson's a patient man. He'll wait."

"What if…"

"I'm home, Lanni. We all are."

She squeezed her eyes shut. It would be so incredibly easy to give in to her desire to bury the unpleasantness of the last years and start fresh. She wanted it so badly, perhaps too badly.

Judd apparently had a few questions of his own. "What about your family?"

"What about them?"

"They aren't going to be pleased we're back together. Nor are they going to like the idea of you moving to Montana."

Lanni knew what he said was true. It could cause an ugly scene, but Lanni prayed that it wouldn't come to that. "They may not fully understand, but in time, they'll accept it. They'll have to."

"I know how close you are to your mother. I don't want to take you away from her."

"I realize that, and I believe she does as well, but I'm twenty-seven. It's time I left my security blanket behind, don't you think?"

"Yes," he admitted starkly. He reached for her hand, which rested on the seat between them, and brought it to his lips. "We have a lot of time to make up for, Lanni. There've been too many wasted years for us. I'm not going to kid you and say everything's going to be easy. We have some rough roads to travel yet with the ranch. The amount of work that needs to be done is overwhelming."

She nodded. She knew little about ranching, but if the run-down condition of the house was indicative of everything on the Circle M, then she could put it into perspective.

"It's going to require every penny I own to restock the herd. Jim wants me to fly down to Texas on Thursday and look over some stock he read about there. I'm going to do it and put several thousand dollars on the line. It's a gamble, but a calculated one. Are you with me, love?"

"One thousand percent."

Briefly their eyes met and it took all Judd's control not to pull the car to the side of the road, turn off the engine and haul her into his arms.

Jim was pacing the yard restlessly by the time Judd returned. As soon as Judd parked the wagon, the two men were off in the pickup for what Jim called some ranchers' meeting. Feeling better than she had in some time, Lanni moved across the yard to the Petermans' house to get Jenny.

Betty stood at the back door and opened the screen when she approached. "What did the doctors have to say about Stuart?"

"He'll be fine. They're keeping him overnight for

tests and observation. Judd will pick him up in the morning."

Betty poured them each a cup of coffee, stirred hers and focused her gaze on the plain stem of the spoon. "Knowing Stuart, he's going to be a handful once he's back on the ranch, wanting to do more than he should."

"We'll manage him." But Lanni had her own doubts. Stuart Matthiessen could be as stubborn and strong-willed as his son. "It's likely I'll need your help."

"You've got it," Betty said, showing her pleasure that Lanni had asked. "The neighbor down the road, Sally Moore, phoned this morning," Betty told Lanni. "She wanted me to extend an invitation to you for the Twin Deer Women's Luncheon on Friday of this week."

"I'd enjoy that."

Betty's cheeks formed deeply grooved dimples as she grinned.

"I don't suppose you had anything to do with this invitation?"

Chuckling, Betty shook her head. "It's about time you met some of the other young wives in the community. They're anxious to get to know you."

"I'm looking forward to meeting them."

"Most of them are curious to meet the woman who tamed Judd Matthiessen," Betty teased affectionately.

"Then I'm sure to disappoint them."

"Ha!" Betty sputtered. "You've got half the town talking as it is. You're going to fit in nicely in Twin Deer." Betty added emphasis to her statement by nodding. "It does my heart good to see Judd home after all these years. It's where he belongs."

And because Judd belonged on the Circle M, Lanni and Jenny did as well. She'd make Montana their home, with the assurance that Judd would never walk away from her here.

Early on, Lanni had discovered that she loved the wide blue skies of Montana as much as Judd did. She'd always been the homey type and although it didn't look like she would be able to continue in her career as a real estate agent, she'd already picked up on the information that the local grade school needed a third grade teacher. Of course she'd need to renew her teaching certificate, but that shouldn't be so difficult.

After coffee and conversation, Lanni headed back to the house with Jenny and tucked the little girl upstairs for her afternoon nap. She delayed making the call to Steve as long as she dared. Finally she called him from the kitchen phone, leaning her hip against the wall as she spoke.

"Hello, Steve, it's Lanni."

"Thank goodness you phoned. I've been worried sick."

"I'm fine."

"Well don't keep me in suspense for heaven's sake—what happened?" He sounded agitated, his usually calm voice raised and jerky.

"Nothing much. I announced I had to get back to Seattle and it created a lot of heated discussion, but Judd agreed to take me to the airport. However, Stuart had this stomach attack and we ended up having to take him to the hospital first."

"He was playing on your sympathy. Couldn't you see through that ploy, Lanni? With your solid gold heart, you fell for it."

Lanni was furious with her coworker for even suggesting such a thing until she realized her first reaction had been to doubt the authenticity of Stuart's ailment.

"No, it was real enough, although to be honest, I had my doubts at first."

"Stuart wants you to stay on the ranch." Steve didn't sound pleased at the prospect. "You are coming home soon, aren't you?"

"Eventually, I'll be back." Lanni heard the soft gasp over the wire and experienced a nip of regret. Steve had been a good friend and she hated to hurt or disappoint him.

"You don't mean what I think you do? Please, Lanni, tell me you're not seriously considering going back to your husband and moving into that godforsaken piece of tumbleweed?"

"Actually, Steve, that's exactly what I'm going to do." Her fellow worker was silent for so long that Lanni wondered if he were still on the line. "Steve, are you there?"

"I'm here," he mumbled, his voice thick with disappointment. "I remember the first time I met you," he said softly. "You were like this emotionally wounded combat soldier, and I was intrigued. In the beginning you were just another challenge, but it soon became more than that. It took me months to gain your confidence and each and every day I made an effort to show you that I cared."

"Steve, please, don't, I—"

"Let me finish," he cut in sharply. "First you became my friend. You'll never know how excited I was when you agreed to attend that baseball game with me. Later when we went out to dinner, I felt as excited as a schoolboy. I love you, Lanni. I've loved you for months."

Lanni closed her eyes to the waves of regret that washed over her. "I thank you for being such a good friend."

"But I want to be so much more than that."

"It's impossible. You know how much I love Judd; I always have. Even if things hadn't turned out this way, you would have always gotten second best from me. You're too good a man to accept that."

"It would have been enough—with you."

"Oh Steve, please don't say that. This is hard enough. Let's part as friends and remember that what we shared was a special kind of friendship. I'll never forget you."

Another long silence followed. "Be happy, Lanni."

"You, too, partner."

"Keep in touch?" He made the statement a question.

"If you like." For her part she preferred to make a clean break of it.

Again Steve hesitated. "You're sure going back to your husband is what you want?"

"I'm sure. Very sure." Lanni had no doubts now. She had sealed her commitment to Judd the minute she'd let him into her bed.

"Goodbye then, Lanni."

"Yes, goodbye, Steve."

Lanni discovered when she replaced the receiver that her hands were trembling. She'd hurt Steve and that hadn't ever been her intention. He was a good man; a kind man who had cared a great deal for her. He'd been patient and gentle when she'd needed it most. She'd meant what she said about remembering him fondly. In the future, she wanted only the best for him.

The sound of the front screen door slamming brought her thoughts up short.

"Lanni." It was Judd.

"In here," she said somewhat breathlessly, doing her best to appear nonchalant. "What are you doing here? I thought you and Jim had gone to some ranchers' meeting?"

Judd looped his arms around her waist and lowered his voice to a husky whisper. "I came back," he said, looking at Lanni. He wanted to talk to his wife. From the time he'd gotten in the pickup with Jim, Judd had let his conversation with Lanni fill his mind. She was willing to give up everything for him. Her home. Her career. Her family. Her love had given him the most priceless gift of his life—their daughter. His heart swelled with such love that there weren't words with which to express it. His large hands circled her waist and brought her back inside his arms.

His ardent kiss caught Lanni by surprise. While his mouth continued to cover hers, his fingers worked her blouse loose from her waistband and lifted the shirttail enough to allow his hand entry. They sighed in unison when his fingers caressed her breast.

"What about work?" Lanni whispered.

"Not interested." He worked the zipper of her jeans open, kissing away any protest.

"Judd?" Between deep, soul-drugged kisses, Lanni managed to get out his name.

Judd lifted her into his arms, and headed for the stairway.

"Judd," she groaned in weak protest. "It's the middle of the day."

A crooked grin slashed his sensuous mouth. "I know."

Stuart arrived home early the following afternoon, looking chipper and exceedingly pleased with himself. Lanni brought him his dinner on a tray and set it in front of the television.

"I see you're still around," he grumbled.

"No thanks to you."

"You belong here. A city slicker isn't ever going to make you happy."

"I think you may be right." His head came up so fast that Lanni laughed outright. "I have no intention of leaving the Circle M."

Stuart's grin was the closest Lanni had ever seen to a Cheshire cat's smug expression. "This land will be good to you. Mark my words."

With time Lanni would come to appreciate this unorthodox man, she mused. She'd viewed the transformation between father and son. Judd and Stuart could talk now without arguing and that was a good beginning. The icy facade Stuart wore like a Halloween mask the first days after their arrival had all but vanished now. They were all making progress—slow, but sure. Lanni had also come to realize that once Judd accepted that he deeply cared for his father, he'd experienced a sense of release. A freedom. Stuart had lived a hard life. The only real love he'd ever known had been taken from him. Stuart had never forgiven himself for Lydia's death, Lanni believed, and had only recently come to grips with the pain of her loss. He didn't want to see his only son make the same mistakes.

Lanni was mature enough to realize that living on the Circle M in close proximity to Stuart was bound to create certain problems, but ones they could work together toward solving.

For the first time in his life, Stuart accepted Judd for who he was. It didn't matter that Judd hadn't become the attorney or doctor the way Stuart had always planned. Stuart cared about his son and together they would build a solid relationship.

Judd woke Lanni early Thursday morning. The room was still dark, cloaked in the darkest part of the night that comes just before dawn. He knelt above her, fully dressed.

"I'll be leaving in a few minutes."

"Already?" Lanni struggled up onto one elbow in a half-sitting, half-lying position.

"Jim's going to stay here in case there's any problem on the ranch."

Lanni nodded and brushed the wisps of blond hair from her face. "We'll be fine—don't worry about anything here."

Judd's hand eased around the base of her neck. "I'll miss you."

"It's only two nights." After all the weeks and months without him, she could withstand two lonesome nights.

He bent his mouth to hers and kissed her fervently. "I wished I didn't have to go."

Lanni giggled—she couldn't help it.

"What's so all-fired funny?"

"You. For years I couldn't keep you home and now I can't get you to leave. May I be so bold as to remind you that this little jaunt is an important mission for the Circle M ranch? You're going to bring back a sturdy bull to service all our female cattle so that we can have lots of little bulls and little cows and whatever else bulls and cows produce."

"You know why I find it so difficult to leave, don't you?" His hot gaze rained down on her face in the moonlight—his eyes were smoky with desire.

Lanni gave no thought to resisting him as she parted her moist lips, inviting his kiss. She moaned at the sensual pleasure he gave her and her fingers stroked his hair, holding his head to her.

He broke away from her just long enough to unhitch his pants, his gaze holding hers while his fingers worked at his belt.

"Your plane?" she whispered, welcoming him. She pulled him closer, and arched her hips wantonly against his as their mouths feasted on each other.

"The plane can wait," he moaned, sliding into her until they were united completely.

Lanni let out a deep sigh of pleasure and bit her bottom lip to keep from crying out.

"But I can't," Judd finished.

Their lovemaking was long and lusty and Judd held her, their bodies still connected long after they'd finished.

Jim honked the car horn from the yard below, and Judd pulled away reluctantly. "I don't think that I can do without you for two nights." He paused and kissed her hungrily. "Be ready for me when I arrive home."

"Aye, aye, Captain. Just bring back that famous bull."

"I'll do that, love," he told her, already on his way out the bedroom door.

Lanni nestled back against her pillow and sighed her contentment. Not even the first weeks of the marriage had been this lusty. She didn't know how long this honeymoon period would last, but she suspected it would be a very long time and she welcomed it just as she had her husband. There was little she could refuse him, her love was so great.

Although she'd made light of the nights he'd be away, Lanni realized that they would be difficult for her as well. She was becoming accustomed to being well loved. At this rate, Jenny would be a big sister within the year.

Stuart was waiting for her when Lanni came down the stairs an hour later.

"Judd get off okay?"

She nodded, pouring herself a cup of coffee. "This bull must be pretty darn special for him to travel all the way to Texas."

"Heard tell he is. Good bloodlines are important."

Lanni pulled out a chair and joined her father-in-law at the table. "You look like you slept well."

Stuart snorted, then glared at her with a twinkle in his faded eyes. "It ain't me who's got rosy cheeks this morning, girl."

Lanni blushed and reached for a section of the morning paper, doing her best to ignore Stuart's low chuckle.

As she suspected they would, the days passed at a snail's pace. The mornings and afternoons were long, but the nights were worse yet. She didn't hear from Judd, but then Lanni hadn't expected that she would. After all, he was only scheduled to be away three days and two nights.

Saturday afternoon, Stuart, Jenny, Jim and Betty all decided to take the drive into Billings to meet Judd's plane. They made an outing of it, stopping along the way at a restaurant to eat dinner. Stuart kept Jenny occupied in the car with tales of his boyhood on the range.

They arrived at the airport an hour before Judd's scheduled flight and Lanni bought a magazine to help fill the time. Betty took Jenny on a walking tour while Stuart and Jim swapped ranching stories.

When Judd's flight landed, Lanni stood and watched the plane taxi to the building and viewed the jetway fold out to meet the arriving passengers. Lanni was eager to feel her husband's arms and stepped back, surveying each face as the people disembarked.

"Where's Daddy?" Jenny wanted to know when Judd hadn't appeared.

"I don't know, sweetheart." The plane had been empty five minutes.

Jim asked one of the flight attendants to check the roster and learned Judd had never been on board the flight.

"Must have missed his connecting flight," Stuart grumbled when Jim appeared.

"You'd think he'd phone," Betty said, carefully studying Lanni.

Lanni gave the worried housekeeper a bright smile as synthetic as acrylic and murmured, "I'm sure there's a logical explanation. There's no need to fret."

"Right," Betty confirmed. "I'm sure there's no reason to worry; there's a perfectly good reason why Judd wasn't on that plane."

They waited around the airport several more hours until Jenny became fussy and overtired. What had been excited expectation on the long drive to Billings became eerie silence on the ride home.

Lanni didn't sleep that night. It seemed as if the walls were closing in around her. The disappointed tears she was trying to hold back felt like a weight pressing against her breast.

Each time the phone rang the following day, Lanni's heart shot to her throat. They were all on edge. Stuart turned taciturn. Jenny complained continually that Betsy needed her daddy back until Lanni broke into tears and held her daughter to her, giving way to her emotion.

"I could just shake that boy," Betty announced, bringing in a freshly baked apple pie. "I take it no one's heard anything."

"Not a word."

"He checked out of his hotel room just when he was supposed to," Jim said, following his wife inside the kitchen. "I can't understand it."

"I can," Lanni said softly.

All four faces turned to her, wide eyed and curious.

"It's happening again."

"What are you talking about?" Stuart grumbled.

"He's done it before and although he promised he'd never leave me again, he has."

"I don't understand what you're saying," Jim barked.

"Judd will be back when he's good and ready to come home. He's gone."

"Gone? You're not making any sense, girl," Stuart shouted. "Of course he's gone. He went to buy that bull from the Francos."

"No, he's left us—all of us this time and not just me. But I told him and I meant it. When he leaves, I do." She lifted Jenny into her arms. "Jenny and I will be returning to Seattle the first thing in the morning."

Thirteen

"**Y**ou can't leave," Stuart argued, looking lost and defeated. "Judd's coming back. I feel it in my bones."

"Oh, he'll be back," Lanni countered softly. "He always does that, usually bearing fancy gifts as though that is supposed to wipe away all the pain and worry." Jenny wiggled and Lanni placed the little girl back on the floor.

"You mean to tell me Judd's done this sort of thing before?"

"Not exactly like this," Lanni explained, her voice low and incredibly sad. "Usually when he left I realized he'd be gone a good long while. I imagine it'll take him a month to find his way home, but who knows, it could be six."

"I don't believe he'd do a thing like that," Jim said, defiantly crossing his arms over his chest. "There's too much at stake."

Silently Lanni agreed to that. Their lives together. Their reconciliation. Their marriage. Everything was on the line. Lanni had trouble believing he'd do something like this herself. Surely he could find some way to get to a phone no matter where he was. Although Jim had mentioned contacting the hotel, Lanni had already done that herself, in addition to every hospital within a fifty-mile radius of Laredo. Judd had disappeared. Oh, he'd show up again, Lanni was confident of that. In his own time and in his own way. But this time she wouldn't be waiting for him.

"Lanni, don't do something you'll regret," Betty said, patting the back of her hand.

"I won't," she concurred.

The phone pealed and everyone turned and looked at it as if it were a miracle come to save them from themselves. It rang a second time before Lanni stood and reached for it.

"Hello." She tried to hide the expectancy in her voice.

"Lanni, it's Steve."

"Could you hold the line a minute?"

"Sure." Steve hesitated. "Is something wrong?"

"No, of course not."

Lanni placed her hand over the earpiece. "It's the real estate company where I work in Seattle." There wasn't any reason to irritate Stuart with the news it was Steve. "Apparently there's a problem. I'll take it in the other room."

Disappointment darkened the three adults' faces as they turned back to their coffee. Gently Lanni set the receiver aside and hurried into Stuart's office. She waited until the other phone had been reconnected before she spoke.

"Okay, I'm here now."

"I called to let you know the deal on the Rudicelli house closed. Your commission is here if you'd like me to mail it to you."

"Yes, please do," Lanni said, forcing some enthusiasm into her lifeless voice.

"Something's wrong," Steve said with such tender concern that Lanni felt the tears sting the back of her eyes. "I can hear it in your voice. Won't you tell me, Lanni?"

"It's nothing."

"You're crying."

"Yes," she sniffled. "I can't help it."

"What's happened? If that no-good husband of yours has hurt you, I swear I'll punch him out."

The thought of Steve tangling with Judd, who was superior in both height and weight, produced such a comical picture in her mind that she swallowed a hysterical giggle.

"As soon as the check arrives, I'm leaving. I told him I would and I meant it..." She paused and reached for a tissue, blowing her nose again.

"Oh, Lanni."

"I know, I know. I'm such a bloody fool."

"You're a warm, loving tender woman. I wouldn't change a hair on your head."

"Stop it, Steve. I'm an idiot; I haven't got the good sense I was born with—all I want to do now is get back to Seattle. I swear I'll never leave home again." The longer she spoke the faster the tears came.

"Poor sweetheart."

"Do you think," she said and sniffled, striving to find some humor in the situation, "that if I closed my eyes and clicked my heels together three times the magic would work and I'd be home in a flash? Seattle's known as the Emerald City, you know."

"Problem is, Lanni—you could end up in Kansas instead."

"The way my luck's been, that's exactly what would happen and I'd end up there with a house on my head."

"Lanni, I wish I could do something for you."

"No, I'm fine, but do me a small favor, will you? Call Jade and let her know Jenny and I are coming home as quickly as we can."

"Consider it done. What are…friends for?"

They finished speaking a couple of minutes later and feeling both mentally fatigued and physically exhausted, Lanni trudged up the stairs. It took her only a half hour to empty the chests of drawers and neatly fold their clothes inside the suitcases.

The following morning Stuart was sitting at the kitchen table when Lanni came down the stairs. She'd spent another sleepless night tossing, turning and worrying. She could scratch Judd's eyes out for doing this to all of them.

"He'll be here soon," Stuart spoke into the paper.

Lanni's fingers dug into the edge of the counter so hard, she cracked three nails. "Will you stop saying that?" she asked him. "Every morning you make this announcement like you've been given some divine insight. Well in case you haven't noticed, he isn't back yet." She knew she was being unreasonable, but she couldn't stop herself. "I've got to get out of here—I told him I'd leave. I told him." To her horror, Lanni started to cry. Scalding tears seared red paths down her cheeks. She jerked around and covered her face with her hands, not wanting Stuart to view her as an emotional wreck.

The weathered hand that patted her shoulder astonished Lanni. "Cry it out, girl; you'll feel better." It surprised her even more when she turned into Stuart's arms and briefly hugged the old man. "I don't know what any of us would do without you," she told him, drying her eyes by rubbing her index fingers across the bridge of her nose and over her cheeks.

By evening there was nothing left to occupy her time. She'd done so much housework that the place gleamed. Dinner dishes dried on the counter and the sun was setting in a pink sky. Betty wandered outside to weed the small garden she'd planted and Lanni ventured out to help.

Dust flying up along the driveway caused both women to sit up on their knees. Few visitors came out this far. Lanni's heart went stock-still as she settled back on her haunches afraid to hope. Each day she faced a hundred discouragements.

A flashy red sedan pulled into the yard and Lanni's hope died another cruel death. As soon as the dust had settled down, the driver's side opened and Steve Delaney stepped out.

"Steve." Lanni flew to her feet, racing across the yard. She stopped in front of him, suddenly conscious of the mud-caked knees of her jeans and the fact she was without makeup and her hair was tied back in a bandanna.

"Lanni?" Steve looked stunned. "Is that peasant woman inside those rags really you?"

If she didn't realize he was teasing, she would have been offended. Steve's humor was often subtle. "I don't exactly look like a young business executive, do I?"

"Not quite the Lanni I remember."

"Well," she said, so happy to see him that she had to restrain herself from throwing her arms around him, "what are you doing here? How'd you ever find this place?"

"It's a long story to both, let me suffice by saying that I'm delivering the commission check in person and have booked three airplane seats for early tomorrow morning out of Billings. We're headed back to God's country—Seattle."

"Hello, Mr. Delaney." Jenny joined Lanni, clenching her doll to her breast.

"Could this sweet young thing be Jenny?"

"Yup," the four-year-old answered. "My daddy went away."

Steve squatted down so that they could meet eye-to-eye. "I've come to take you home, Jenny, so you won't have to worry about your daddy anymore. Are you ready?"

"Nope," Jenny announced. "I want to wait for my daddy."

"That could be a very long time, Jenny, and Mommy needs you with her." Lanni did her best to explain it to the child. She directed her attention back to Steve. "Give me five minutes to clean up. Do you want to come inside? I can get you something cool to drink while you wait."

Stuart appeared on the top step of the porch, glaring at Steve with a furious frown.

"No thanks," Steve said and ran a finger along the inside of his shirt collar for effect. "If you don't mind, I think I'll be more comfortable standing here in the setting sun."

"Stuart won't do anything," Lanni sought to reassure him.

"Nonetheless I'd rather remain here. But hurry, would you, Lanni? I don't like the looks that old man is giving me. I have a suspicion Custer's men had much the same feeling riding onto the Little Big Horn as I did pulling into this driveway."

"Nobody's going to scalp you."

"Don't be so sure."

Lanni was halfway to the porch when the sound of a truck coming into the driveway caused her to whip around. Judd. She knew it immediately. He honked several times and stuck his hand out the side window waving frantically.

He pulled to a stop and didn't appear to notice Steve or the red sedan. The door flew open and he jumped down from the cab, sending dust swirls flying in his rush to reach Lanni. Without pausing to explain, he grabbed her by the waist and kissed her with such a hunger that she was bent over his forearm by the pressure of his kiss.

Lanni was too stunned to react. For days she'd been worried half out of her mind. "You bastard," she cried, twisting her mouth free of his, then wiping her lips with the back of her hand.

"Lanni, don't be angry. I did what I could."

With both hands flat on his chest, she shoved against him with all her might until Judd freed her voluntarily. "How dare you waltz in here like a returning hero," she cried, hurling the words at him, growing more furious by the moment.

"Has she been this unreasonable the whole time I was away?" Judd directed the question to his father.

Stuart answered with a nod in the direction of Steve.

"What's he doing here?" The humor drained from Judd's gaze as reality hit him between the eyes.

"I'm leaving you, Judd Matthiessen."

"You've got to be kidding!" His happy excitement rushed out of him like air from a freed balloon.

"This is no joke." She pushed past him and into the house and took the stairs two at a time until she reached the top floor. Marching into her room, she located her luggage, and hauled all three suitcases down the stairs with her. Judd met her halfway down the stairway.

"Will you kindly tell me what's going on here?" His eyes revealed his shocked dismay.

"Two nights, remember? You were supposed to be gone two nights. Well in case you can't add, it's been considerably more time than that."

"I know."

"Your nerve galls me. You come back here without a word of explanation and expect me to fall gratefully at your feet. I'm leaving you, Judd, and this time it's for good."

"You can't do that."

"Just watch me. I told you if you ever left me again, it was over. You agreed to that."

"But there were extenuating circumstances. I—"

"Aren't there always extenuating circumstances?" Lanni cut in woodenly.

Judd sagged against the wall, and wiped a hand over his tired face. This was like a horror movie. He'd been driving for fifteen hours straight with a fifteen-thousand-dollar bull in the back of his truck and he was greeted with this?

Lanni pushed past him and out of the house, handing Steve her luggage. "He couldn't have waited fifteen minutes before showing up?" Steve grumbled as he placed the suitcases in the trunk. "Oh, no. Here comes trouble."

"Just what the hell are you doing with my wife, Delaney?"

"Hello, Matthiessen," Steve said, straightening. "I'm taking Lanni home."

"She *is* home."

"You might want to ask her that."

"You left me," Lanni shouted. "I told you that if it happened again, it was over between us."

"What is going on here?" Judd turned to Stuart, his eyes wide and perplexed.

"Where were you, boy?" Stuart asked.

"You don't know?" Now Judd looked utterly shocked. "I got arrested in Mexico."

"Arrested!" Both Lanni and Stuart shouted together.

"It's a long story. Brutus, the bull, got loose and wandered across the border. The Mexican authorities and I had a minor disagreement and I ended up in the local jail, but I paid a king's ransom for—" He stopped abruptly, his fists slowly knotting. "You weren't notified of my whereabouts?"

"No one contacted us, son."

Judd closed his eyes as the pounding waves of frustration swamped over him. "You must have been sick with worry."

"Oh no, we sat around drinking tea and nibbling on crumpets," Lanni informed him primly.

"Lanni, oh love, I thought I'd go crazy before I got home to you. Don't let this minor misunderstanding ruin our lives."

"Minor misunderstanding?" she shouted. "This is a major one, Judd Matthiessen."

"He needs you," Stuart said starkly, his eyes pleading with Lanni to reconsider.

"Then he should have thought of that before he went traipsing halfway across the country."

"Lanni," Judd pleaded.

"Be quiet," she cried, pointing her index finger at him. He was always leaving her, asking her to wait, and for the first time she was giving him a sample of his own medicine. "It's more than a matter of not knowing where you were—I don't know if I can trust you anymore."

"Lanni," he said and raised his arm to reach for her. When she stepped away to avoid his embrace, Judd dropped his hands to his sides. "I swear by everything I hold dear that I'm not going to leave you again."

"And what exactly do you consider so valuable. Me? Jenny? Your father? The Circle M?" The tears rained freely down her face.

"None of it means anything without you," he said, his voice husky with need. Overcome with emotion, Judd turned to Steve. "I'm sorry you went through all the trouble of coming here, Delaney, but Lanni won't be going back with you." He reached inside the trunk to take out her luggage.

"If you don't mind, I'll make that decision myself."

"Lanni?" Judd's eyes looked murderous. "I haven't come this far to lose you over a stupid bull. You don't trust me now, but you will in time because I'll never give you cause to doubt again. I need you," he coaxed. "We're home where we belong and I'm not going to allow you to walk away from that."

"I…" She wavered, caught in a battle that raged between her head and her heart. But the love that shone in his eyes convinced her she had no choice but to cast her fate with him. Her heart demanded as much. "For all the money you spent on him, you would do well not to insult the animal by calling him stupid." She crossed her arms over her chest; she hadn't come this far to lose Judd, either.

"You can't deprive Jenny of a family," Judd murmured, his gaze holding hers tenderly.

"On the next business trip you take, will I get to go along?" Lanni offered the compromise.

"As long as it isn't Mexico."

"Agreed."

"Does that mean she'll stay?" Stuart wanted to know, directing the question at both men, uncertain of what was happening.

"She's staying," Judd answered, wrapping his arms around her waist. "Is that right, heart of mine?"

"If you say the magic word."

"Please?"

Lanni shook her head.

"Thank you?"

"Nope." Her arms circled his neck as he lifted her off the ground so that her eyes were level with his own.

"I'm sorry?"

"Not that, either." She placed a hand on both sides of his face and kissed him square on the mouth.

"You'd better hurry and decide, love; I'm running out of vocabulary."

"How about a simple I love you."

"You know that already."

"But I like to hear it every now and then."

"I love you," Judd said tenderly and then set Lanni on her feet.

"Now that that's settled," Stuart said and stepped forward, extending his hand to Steve. "Would you like something cool to drink before you head back to Seattle?"

"Mommy, Mommy, can I hug Daddy too?"

Judd squatted down so that he could enfold Jenny in his arms. The little girl planted a juicy kiss on his cheek. "I like the bull."

"Good thing, darling, because Daddy isn't about to take him back." Judd chuckled and hugged her to his massive chest. Lanni knelt and hugged both of them.

"I have to go tell Betsy that you're home. She was worried." With that, Jenny ran into the house after her grandfather and Steve.

Still kneeling on the ground, Judd's arms circled Lanni. "No more bridges. No more wanderings. Everything I want is right here."

"Oh, Judd, I love you so."

"I know, love, I know," he said, looking out around him at the Circle M. This was their future. Here they would build their lives. Here they would raise their family. This land would heal them both. Love and trust would blossom, nourished by contentment and commitment.

Helping Lanni to her feet, Judd wrapped his arm around her and paused to glance at the pink sky. It was filled with beauty and promise.

* * * * *

ALMOST PARADISE

One

"Mirror, mirror on the wall—who's the fairest of us all?" Sherry White propped one eye open and gazed into the small bathroom mirror. She grimaced and quickly squeezed both eyes shut. "Not me," she answered and blindly reached for her toothbrush.

Morning had never been her favorite time of day. She agreed with the old adage claiming that if God had intended people to see the sun rise, He would have caused it to happen later in the day. Unfortunately, Jeff Roarke, the director of Camp Gitche Gumee, didn't agree. He demanded his staff meet early each morning. No excuses. No reprieves. No pardons.

Fine, Sherry mused. Then he'd have to take what he got, and heaven knew she wasn't her best at this ungodly hour.

After running a brush through her long, dark curls, Sherry wrapped a scarf around her head to keep the hair away from her face and returned to her room where she reached for a sweater to ward off a chill. Then she hurried across the lush green grass of the campgrounds to the staff meeting room. Once there, a hasty glance around told her she was already late.

"Good morning, Miss White," Jeff Roarke called, when she took the last available seat.

"Morning," she mumbled under her breath, crossing her arms to disguise her embarrassment. He'd purposely called attention to her, letting the others know she was tardy.

His sober gaze had followed her as she'd maneuvered herself between the narrow row of chairs. Now his intense eyes remained on her until her heart hammered and indignation caused heat to color her cheeks. She experienced a perverse desire to shatter Jeff Roarke's pompous attitude, but the feeling died a quiet death as she raised her gaze to meet his. It almost seemed that she saw a hint of amusement lurking there. At any rate, he was regarding her with a speculative gleam that was distinctly unsettling. Evidently satisfied that he'd unnerved her, he began to speak again.

Although she knew she should be taking notes, Sherry was having trouble tearing her gaze away from the camp director, now that his attention was off her. Jeff Roarke was tall, easily over six feet, and superbly fit. His jaw was lean and well defined—okay, he was absurdly good-looking, she'd grant him that. But to Sherry's way of thinking he was arrogant, uncompromising and pompous. She'd known a month earlier when she'd met Mr. Almighty Roarke for the job interview that they weren't going to get along. She'd flown to Sacramento from Seattle for a meeting in his office, praying she hadn't made the long trip in vain. She'd wanted this job so badly...and then she'd blown it.

"I think it's a marvelous idea to name the camp after a cute children's song," she'd said cheerfully.

Roarke looked shocked. "Song? What song? The

camp's name is taken from the poem 'Song of Hiawatha' by Henry Wadsworth Longfellow."

"Oh—uh, I mean, of course," Sherry said, her face flaming.

From there the interview seemed shaky, and Sherry was convinced she'd ruined her chances as Roarke continued to ask what seemed like a hundred unrelated questions. Although he didn't appear overly impressed with her qualifications, he handed her several forms to complete.

"You mean I'm hired?" she asked, confused. "I…I have the job?"

"I'd hardly have you fill out the paperwork if you weren't," he returned.

"Right." Sherry's heart had raced with excitement. She was going to escape her wacky stepmother, Phyliss. For one glorious summer no one need know where she was. But as Sherry began to complete the myriad forms her enthusiasm for her plan dwindled. She couldn't possibly put down references—anyone she'd list would be someone who'd have contact with her father and stepmother. The instant her family discovered where Sherry was hiding, it would be over.

Roarke seemed to note Sherry's hesitancy as she studied the forms. "Is there something you disagree with, Miss White?"

"No," she said, hurriedly filling out the names and addresses of family friends and former employers, but doing her best to make them unreadable, running the letters together and transposing numbers.

Nibbling anxiously on her bottom lip, Sherry finished and handed over the completed paperwork.

From that first meeting with Jeff Roarke, things had gone swiftly downhill. Sherry found him…she searched for the right word. Dictatorial, she decided. He'd let it be known as director of Camp Gitche Gumee that he expected her to abide by all the rules and regulations—which was only fair—but then he'd proceeded to give her a Michener-length manual of rules and regulations, with the understanding that she would have it read by the time camp opened. Good grief! She'd been hired as a counselor for seven little girls, not as a brain surgeon.

"Are there any questions?"

Jeff Roarke's words to the early-morning assembly broke into her consciousness, startling Sherry into the present. Worried, she glanced around her, hoping no one had noticed that she'd casually slipped into her memories.

"Most of the children will arrive today," Roarke was saying.

He'd gotten her up at this time of day to tell her that? They'd have to be a bunch of numskulls not to know when the children were coming. The entire staff had been working all week to prepare the cottages and campgrounds for the children's arrival. Sherry glared at him for all she was worth, then squirmed when he paused and stared back at her.

"Is there a problem, Miss White?"

Sherry froze as the others directed their attention to her. "N-no."

"Good—then I'll continue."

The man never smiled, Sherry mused. Not once in the past week had she seen him joke or laugh or kid around. He was like a man driven, but for what cause she could only speculate. The camp was important to him, that much she'd gleaned immediately, but why a university professor would find such purpose in a children's camp was beyond Sherry's understanding. There seemed to be an underlying sadness in Jeff Roarke, too, one that robbed his life of joy, stole the pleasure of simple things from his perception.

But none of the counselors seemed to think of Jeff Roarke the same way she did. Oh, the other female staff members certainly noticed him, Sherry admitted grudgingly. From the goo-goo eyes some of the women counselors were giving him, they too were impressed with his dark good looks. But he was so stiff, so dry, so serious that Sherry considered him a lost cause. And she had enough on her mind without complicating her life worrying about someone like the camp director.

Sherry expected to have fun this summer. She needed it. The last year of graduate school, living near home, had left her mentally drained and physically exhausted. School was only partly to blame for her condition. Phyliss was responsible for the rest. Phyliss and her father had married when Sherry was a college freshman and Phyliss, bless her heart, had never had children. Seeing Sherry as her one and only opportunity to be a mother, she'd attacked the project with such gusto that Sherry was still reeling from the effects three years later. Phyliss worried that Sherry wasn't eating well enough. Phyliss worried about the hours she kept. Phyliss worried that she studied too hard. To state the problem simply—Phyliss worried.

As a dedicated health nut, her stepmother made certain that Sherry ate correctly. There were days Sherry would have killed for a pizza or a hot dog, but Phyliss wouldn't hear of it. Then there was the matter of clothes. Phyliss loved bright colors—and so did Sherry, in moderation. Unfortunately, her stepmother considered it her duty to shop with Sherry and "help" her choose the proper clothes for college. As a result, her closet was full of purples, army greens, sunshine yellows and hot, sizzling pinks.

So Sherry planned this summer as an escape from her wonderful but wacky stepmother. Sherry wasn't exactly proud of the way she'd slipped away in the middle of the night, but she'd thought it best to avoid the multitude of questions Phyliss would ply her with had she known Sherry was leaving. She'd managed to escape with a text sent from the airport that stated in vague terms that she was going to camp for the summer. She hated to be so underhanded, but knowing Phyliss, the woman would arrive with a new wardrobe of coordinated shades of chartreuse—and order Sherry's meals catered when she learned that her beloved stepdaughter was eating camp food.

Sherry had chosen Camp Gitche Gumee because it had intrigued her. Being counselor to a group of intellectually gifted children in the heart of the majestic California redwoods sounded like the perfect escape. And Phyliss would never think to search California.

"Within the next few hours, fifty children will be arriving from all around the country," Roarke continued.

Sherry childishly rolled her eyes toward the ceiling. He could just as well have given them this information at seven—the birds weren't even awake yet! Expecting her to retain vital information at this unreasonable hour was going beyond the call of duty.

"Each cottage will house seven children; Fred Spencer's cabin will house eight. Counselors, see me following the meeting for the names of your charges. Wherever possible, I've attempted to match the child with a friend in an effort to cut down on homesickness."

That made sense to Sherry, but little else did.

As Roarke continued speaking, Sherry's thoughts

drifted again. In addition to Jeff Roarke, their fearless leader, Sherry knew she was going to have problems getting along with Fred Spencer, who was counselor for the nine- and ten-year-old boys. Fred had been a counselor at Camp Gitche Gumee for several summers and was solidly set in the way he handled his charges.

Sherry had come up with some ideas she'd wanted to talk over in the first few days following her arrival. Since Fred was the counselor for the same age group as hers, it had seemed natural to go to him. But Fred had found a reason to reject every suggestion. Five minutes with him and Sherry discovered that he didn't possess a creative bone in his body and frowned dutifully upon anyone who deviated from the norm.

More than disagreeing with her, Sherry had gotten the distinct impression that Fred highly disapproved of her and her ideas. She wasn't sure what she'd done to invoke his ire, but his resentment was strong enough to cause her to feel uneasy whenever they were in the room together.

With a sigh, Sherry forced her attention back to Roarke. He continued speaking for several minutes, but most of what he had to say was directed to the housekeepers, cooks and groundskeepers. The classroom teachers had been briefed the day before.

A half hour later the staff was dismissed for breakfast—and not a minute too soon, Sherry mused as she walked toward the large dining hall. Blindly she headed for the coffeepot. If Jeff Roarke was going to call staff meetings when the moon was still out, the least he could do was provide coffee.

"Miss White," Roarke called, stopping her.

Sherry glanced longingly toward the coffeepot. "Yes?"

"Could I speak to you a minute?"

"Sure." She headed toward the back of the dining hall, where he was waiting for her.

Roarke watched the newest staff member of Camp Gitche Gumee make her way toward him, walking between the long tables, and he smiled inwardly. That Sherry White wasn't a morning person was obvious. During the staff meeting, her eyes had drooped half-closed and she'd stifled more than one yawn. For part of that time her features had been frozen into a faraway look, as though she were caught in some daydream.

Thinking about her, Roarke felt his brow crease into a slight frown. He'd hired her on impulse, something he rarely acted upon. He'd liked her smile and her spirit and had gotten a chuckle out of her misunderstanding about the name of the camp. He found her appealing, yet she made him nervous, too, in a way he couldn't explain even to himself. All he knew was that she'd shown up for the interview, and before he'd realized what he was doing, he'd hired her. In analyzing his actions later, Roarke had been astonished. Liking the way she smiled and the way her eyes softened when she spoke of children were not good enough reasons to hire her as a counselor. Yet he felt he hadn't made a bad choice. In spite of her apparent dislike of his methods, Roarke felt she would do an excellent job with the children, and more than a good personality match with him, the youngsters were what was most important.

"Yes?" Sherry asked, joining him. Her gaze remained a little too obviously on the coffeepot on the other side of the room.

Opening his briefcase, Roarke withdrew a camp reference sheet and handed it to her. "I'm sorry to bother you, but your application form must have gotten smeared across the top—I wasn't able to read the names of your references."

Sherry swallowed uncomfortably. She should have known scribbled letters and numbers wouldn't work.

"Could you fill this out and have it back to me later this afternoon?"

"Sure—no problem," she said, her smile forced.

"Good," he said, puzzled by the frown that worried her brow. "I'll see you later, then."

"Later," she agreed distractedly. Her gaze fell to the form. If worst came to worst she could always give him false telephone numbers and phony addresses. But that could lead to future problems. Of course if she didn't, it could lead to problems right now!

Depressed, Sherry folded the form, then made a beeline for the coffee. Claiming her seat, she propped her elbows on the table and held the thick ceramic mug with both hands, letting the aroma stir her senses to life. She might not function well in the mornings, but she'd manage for this one summer. She'd have to if Roarke intended to keep holding these merciless 5:00 a.m. staff meetings.

"Morning," Lynn Duffy called out as she approached. Lynn, who had been assigned as housekeeper to Sherry's cabin, claimed the chair next to Sherry's. She set her tray on the table and unloaded her plate, which was heaped with scrambled eggs, bacon and toast. "Aren't you eating?"

Sherry shook her head. "Not this morning."

"Hey, this camp has a reputation for wonderful food."

"I'm not hungry. Thanks anyway." Sherry rested her chin in her hands, worrying about the references and what she could put down that would satisfy Jeff Roarke.

"I wonder what kind of stupid rule he's going to come up with next," she muttered, setting the paper beside her mug.

"Jeff Roarke?"

"Yes, Roarke." Somehow Sherry couldn't think of the camp director as "Jeff." She associated that name with someone who was kind and considerate, like Lassie's owner or an affectionate uncle.

"You have to admit he's got a grip on matters."

"Sure," Sherry admitted reluctantly. Roarke ran this camp with the efficiency of a Marine boot camp. "But I have yet to see a hint of originality. For instance, I can't imagine children's cottages named Cabin One, Cabin Two and so on."

"It's less confusing that way."

"These kids are supposed to be geniuses, I strongly suspect they could keep track of a real name as easily as a boring, unadorned number."

"Maybe so," Lynn said and shook her head. "No one's ever said anything before."

"But surely the other counselors have offered suggestions."

"Not that I've heard."

Sherry raised her eyebrows. "I'd have thought the staff would want something more creative than numbers for their cabins."

"I'm sure Mr. Roarke thought the kids would be more comfortable with numbers. Several of the children are said to be mathematical wizards."

"I suppose," Sherry agreed. Roarke was totally committed to the children and the camp—Sherry didn't question that—but to her way of thinking his intentions were misdirected. Every part of camp life was geared toward academia, with little emphasis, from what she could see, on fun and games.

Lynn's deep blue eyes took on a dreamy look. She shook her head. "I think the whole idea of a special camp like this is such a good one. From what I understand, Mr. Roarke is solely responsible for organizing it. He worked years setting up these summer sessions. For the past four summers, he hasn't taken a penny for his efforts. He does it for the kids."

The news surprised Sherry, and she found herself revising her opinion of the camp director once again. The man intrigued her, she had to admit. He angered and confused her, but he fascinated her, too. Sherry didn't know what to think anymore. If only he weren't such a stick-in-the mud. She remembered that Lynn was one of those who had been making sheep's eyes at Roarke earlier, "I have the feeling you think Jeff Roarke is wonderful," she suggested.

Lynn nodded and released a heavy sigh. "Does it show that much?"

"Not really."

"He's so handsome," Lynn continued. "Surely you've noticed?"

Sherry took another sip of her coffee to delay answering. "I suppose."

"And so successful. Rumors flew around here last summer when Mr. Roarke became the head of the economics department for Cal Tech."

Again Sherry paid close attention to her coffee. "I'm impressed."

"From what I understand he's written a book."

A smile touched the corners of Sherry's mouth. She could well imagine what dry reading anything Roarke had written would be.

"Apparently his book caused quite a stir in Washington. The director of the Federal Reserve recommended it to the President."

"Wow!" Now Sherry really was impressed.

"And he's handsome to boot."

"That much is fairly obvious," Sherry allowed. All right, Jeff Roarke was lean and muscular with eyes that could make a woman go all soft inside, but she wasn't the only one to have noticed that, and she certainly wasn't interested in becoming a groupie.

"He really gets to me," Lynn said with a sigh.

"He does have nice eyes," Sherry admitted reluctantly.

Lynn nodded and continued. "They're so unusual. Yesterday when we were talking I would have sworn they were green, but when I first met him they were an incredible hazel color."

"I guess I hadn't noticed," Sherry commented. Okay, so she lied!

Carefully Lynn set her fork beside her plate, her look thoughtful. "You don't like him much, do you?"

"Oh, I like him—it's just that I figured a camp for children would be fun. This place is going to be about as lively as a prison. There are classes scheduled day and night. From the look of things, all the kids are going to do is study. There isn't any time left for fun."

Evidently Lynn found her observations humorous. A smile created twin dimples in her smooth cheeks. "Just wait until the kids get here. Then you'll be grateful for Mr. Roarke's high sense of order."

Maybe so, Sherry thought, but that remained to be seen. "You worked here last summer?"

Lynn nodded as she swallowed a mouthful of eggs. "I was a housekeeper then, too. Several of us are back for a second go-round, but Mr. Roarke's the real reason I came back." She hesitated. "How old do you think he is?"

"Roarke? I don't know. Close to thirty-five or -six, I'd guess."

"Oh dear, that's probably much too old for someone nineteen."

Lynn's look of abject misery caused Sherry to laugh outright. "I've heard of greater age differences."

"How old are you?"

"Twenty-three," Sherry answered.

Lynn wrinkled her nose, as though she envied Sherry those years. "Don't get me wrong. There's no chance of a romance developing between Mr. Roarke and me, or me and anyone else for that matter—at least not until camp is dismissed."

"Why not?"

"Mr. Roarke is death on camp romances," Lynn explained. "Last year two of the counselors fell in love, and when Mr. Roarke found them kissing he threatened to dismiss them both." Lynn sighed expressively and a dreamy look came over her. "You know what I think?"

Sherry could only speculate. "What?"

"I think Mr. Roarke's been burned. His tender heart was shattered by a careless affair that left him bleeding and raw. And now—years later—he's afraid to love again, afraid to offer his heart to another woman." Dramatically, Lynn placed her hand over her own heart as though to protect it from the fate of love turned sour. She gazed somberly into the distance.

The strains of a love ballad hummed softly in the distance, and it was all Sherry could do to swallow down a laugh. "You know this for a fact?"

"Heavens, no. That's just what I think must have happened to him. It makes sense, doesn't it?"

"Ah—I'm not sure," Sherry hedged.

"Mr. Roarke is really against camp romances. You should have been here last year. I don't think I've ever seen him more upset. He claimed romance and camp just don't mix."

"He's right about that." To find herself agreeing with Roarke was a surprise, but Sherry could see the pitfalls of a group of counselors more interested in one another than in their charges.

Lynn shrugged again. "I don't think there's anything wrong with a light flirtation, but Mr. Roarke has other ideas. There are even rules and regulations on how male and female counselors should behave in each other's company. But I suppose you've already read that."

When Sherry didn't respond, Lynn eyed her speculatively. "You did read the manual, didn't you?"

Sherry dropped her gaze to the tabletop. "Sort of."

"You'd better, because if he catches you going against the rules, your neck will be on the chopping block."

A lump developed in Sherry's throat as she remembered the problem with her references. She'd need to keep a low profile. And from the sound of things, she had best be a good little counselor and keep her opinions to herself. What Lynn had said about studying the manual made sense. Sherry vowed inwardly to read it all the way through and do her utmost to follow the rules, no matter what she thought.

"You'll do fine," Lynn said confidently. "And the kids are going to really like you."

"I hope so." Unexpected doubts were jumping up and down inside Sherry like youngsters on pogo sticks. She had thought she'd be a natural for this position. Her major was education, and with her flair for originality, she hoped to be a good teacher.

The kids she'd come here to counsel weren't everyday run-of-the-mill nine- and ten-year-olds, they were bona fide geniuses. Each child had an IQ in the ninety-eight percentile. She lifted her chin in sudden determination. She'd always appreciated a challenge. She'd been looking forward to this summer, and she wasn't about to let Jeff Roarke and his rules and regulations ruin it for her.

"The only time you need to worry is if Mr. Roarke calls you to his office after breakfast," Lynn said, interrupting Sherry's thoughts.

Sherry digested this information. "Why then?"

Lynn paused long enough to peel back the aluminum tab on a small container of strawberry jam. "The only time anyone is ever fired is in the morning. The couple I mentioned earlier, who fell in love last summer—their names were Sue and Mark—they talked to Mr. Roarke on three separate occasions. Each time in the afternoon. Every time Sue heard her name read from the daily bulletin she became a nervous wreck until she heard the time of the scheduled meeting. Mark didn't fare much better. They both expected to get the ax at any minute."

"Roarke didn't fire them?"

"No, but he threatened to. They weren't even allowed to hold hands."

"I bet they were miserable." Sherry could sympathize with both sides. She was young enough to appreciate the temptations of wanting to be with a boy at camp but old enough to recognize the pitfalls of such a romance.

"But worse than a camp romance, Mr. Roarke is a stickler for honesty. He won't tolerate anyone who so much as stretches the truth."

"Really?" Sherry murmured. Suddenly swallowing became difficult.

"Last year a guy came to camp who fibbed about his age. He was one of three Mr. Roarke fired. It's true Danny had lied, but only by a few months. He was out of here so fast it made my head spin. Of course, he got called in to Roarke's office in the morning," she added.

"My goodness." Sherry's mouth had gone dry. If Roarke decided to check her references her days at Camp Gitche Gumee were surely numbered.

"Well, I'd best go plug in my vacuum."

"Yeah—" Sherry raised her hand "—I'll talk to you later."

The other girl stood and scooted her chair back into position. "Good luck."

Sherry watched the lanky teenager leave the mess hall, and for the first time she considered that maybe escaping Phyliss at summer camp hadn't been such a brilliant idea after all.

Two

Three hours later the first busload of children pulled into Camp Gitche Gumee. The bus was from nearby Sacramento and the surrounding area, but Roarke had announced at their morning get-together that there were children traveling from as far away as Maine and Vermont. The sum these parents paid for two months of camp had shocked Sherry, but who was she to quibble? She had a summer job, and in spite of her misgivings about the camp director, she was pleased to be here.

Standing inside her cabin, Sherry breathed in the clean scent of the forest and waited anxiously for her charges to be escorted to her cabin. When she chanced a peek out the door, she noted Peter Towne, the camp lifeguard, leading a forlorn-looking girl with long, dark braids toward her.

Sherry stepped onto the porch to meet the pair. She tried to get the girl to meet her gaze so she could smile at her, but the youngster seemed determined to study the grass.

"Miss White, this is Pamela Reynolds."

"Hello, Pamela."

"Hi."

Peter handed Sherry Pamela's suitcase.

Thanking him with a smile, Sherry placed her free hand on the shy girl's shoulder and led her into the cabin.

The youngster's eyes narrowed suspiciously as she sat on the nearest bunk. "You're not scared of animals, are you?"

"Nope." That wasn't entirely true, but Sherry didn't consider it a good idea to let any of her charges know she wasn't especially fond of snakes. Not when the woods were ripe for the picking.

"Good."

"Good?" Sherry repeated suspiciously.

With a nervous movement, Pamela nodded, placed her suitcase on the thin mattress and opened it. From inside, she lifted a shoe box with holes punched in the top. "I brought along my hamster. I can keep him, can't I?" Blue eyes pleaded with her.

Sherry didn't know what to say. According to the camp manual, pets weren't allowed. But a hamster wasn't like a dog or a cat or a horse, for heaven's sake. Sherry hedged. "What's his name?"

"Ralph."

"That's a nice name." Her brain was frantically working.

"He won't make any noise and he barely eats anything and I couldn't leave him at home because my parents are going to Europe and I know we aren't supposed to bring along animals, but Ralph is the very best friend I have and I'd miss him too much if he had to stay with Mrs. Murphy like my little brother."

Appealing tears glistened in the little girl's eyes and Sherry felt herself weaken. It shouldn't be that difficult to keep one tiny hamster from Roarke's attention.

"But will Ralph be happy living in a cabin full of girls?"

"Oh, sure," Pam said, the words rushing out, "he likes girls, and he's really a wonderful hamster. Do you want to hold him?"

"No thanks," Sherry answered brightly. The manual might have a full page dedicated to pets, but it didn't say anything about adopting a mascot. "If the others agree, I feel we can keep Ralph as our mascot as long as we don't let any of the other cabins find out about him." Sherry cringed inwardly at the thought of Jeff Roarke's reaction to her decision. The thought of his finding a pet, even something as unobtrusive as a hamster, wasn't a pleasant one, but from the looks of it the little girl was strongly attached to the rodent. Housing Ralph seemed such a little thing to keep a child happy. Surely what Ironjaw didn't know wouldn't hurt him....

Three ten-year-olds, Sally, Wendy and Diane, were escorted to the cabin when the next busload arrived. Although they were different in looks and size, the three shared a serious, somber nature. Sherry had expected rambunctious children. Instead, she had been assigned miniature adults.

Sally had brought along her microscope and several specimens she planned to examine before dinner. Sherry didn't ask to see them, but from the contents of the jars that lined Sally's headboard, she didn't want to know what the child planned to study. Sherry's social circle didn't include many nine- and ten-year-olds, but she wasn't acquainted with a single child who kept pig embryos in jars of formaldehyde as companions.

Wendy, at least, appeared to be a halfway normal preteen. She collected dolls and had brought along an assortment of her prize Barbies and Kens, including designer outfits for each. She arranged them across the head of her bed and introduced Sherry to Barbie-Samantha, Barbie-Jana and Barbie-Brenda. The Kens were also distinguished with their own names, and by the time Wendy had finished, Sherry's head was swimming.

Sherry didn't know what to make of Diane. The ten-year-old barely said a word. She chose her bunk, unpacked and then immediately started to read. Sherry noted that Diane's suitcases contained a bare minimum of clothes and were filled to capacity with books. Scanning the academic titles caused Sherry to grimace; she didn't see a single Nancy Drew.

Twins Jan and Jill were the next to make their entrance. They were blond replicas of each other and impossible to tell apart until they smiled. Jan was lacking both upper front teeth. Jill was lacking only one. Sherry felt a little smug until she discovered Jill wiggling her lone front tooth back and forth in an effort to extract it. Before the day was over, Sherry realized, she would be at their mercy. Fine, she decided, the two knew who they were—she'd let them sort it out.

The last child assigned to Cabin Four was Gretchen. Sherry recognized the minute the ten-year-old showed up that this child was trouble.

"This camp gets dumpier every summer," Gretchen grumbled, folding her arms around her middle as she surveyed the cabin. She paused and glanced at the last remaining cot. "I refuse to sleep near the window. I'll get a nosebleed and a headache if I'm near a breeze."

"Okay," Sherry said. "Is there anyone here who would like to trade with Gretchen?"

Pam suddenly found it necessary to feed Ralph.

Sally brought out her microscope.

Wendy twisted Barbie-Brenda into Ken-Brian's arms and placed them in a position Sherry preferred not to question. Soon, no fewer than three Barbies and an equal number of Kens were in a tangled mess of arms and legs.

Jan and Jill sat on the end of their bunks staring blindly into space while Jill worked furiously on extracting her front tooth.

Diane kept a book of mathematical brainteasers propped open in front of her face and didn't give any indication that she'd heard the request.

"It doesn't look like anyone wants to trade," Sherry told the youngster, whose mouth was twisted with a sour look. "Since you've been to camp before, you knew that the first to arrive claim the beds they want. I saw you lingering outside earlier this afternoon. You should have checked in here first."

"I refuse to sleep near the window," Gretchen announced for the second time.

"In that case, I'll place the mattress on the floor in my room and you can bunk there, although I feel you should know, I sometimes sleep with my window open."

"I sincerely hope you're teasing," Gretchen returned, eyes wide and incredulous. "There are things crawling around down there." She studiously pointed to the wood floor.

"Where?" Sally cried, immediately interested. Her hand curled around the base of her microscope.

"I believe she was speaking hypothetically," Sherry mumbled.

"Oh."

"All right, I'll sleep by the window and ignore the medical risk," Gretchen muttered. She carelessly tossed her suitcase on top of the mattress. "But I'm writing my mother and telling her about this. She's paying good money for me to attend this camp and she expects me to receive the very best of care. There's no excuse for me to be mistreated in this manner."

"Let's see how it goes, shall we?" Sherry suggested, biting her tongue. This kid was a medical risk all right, but the only thing in danger was Sherry's mental health. Already she could feel a pounding headache coming on. By sheer force of will, she managed to keep her fingers from massaging her temples. First Roarke and now Gretchen. No doubt they were related.

"My uncle is a congressman," Gretchen said, to no one in particular. "I may write him instead."

The entire cabin pretended not to hear, which only seemed to infuriate Gretchen. She paused smugly. "Is Mr. Roarke the camp director again this year?"

"Yes," Sherry answered cheerfully. She knew it! Roarke was most likely another of this pest's uncles. "Would you like me to make an appointment for you to speak to him?"

"Yes. I'll let him handle this unfortunate situation." Gretchen removed her suitcase from the bunk and gingerly set it aside, seemingly assured that the camp director would assign her a cot anywhere she wanted.

"I'll see if I can arrange it when you're in the computer class," Sherry said.

By afternoon Camp Gitche Gumee was in full swing. Cabins were filled to capacity and the clamor of children sounded throughout the compound.

After the girls had unpacked and stored their luggage, Sherry led them into the dining hall. Counselors were expected to eat their meals with their charges, but after lunch Sherry's time was basically free. On occasion she would be given the opportunity to schedule outdoor activities such as canoeing and hiking expeditions, but those were left for her to organize. Most of the camp was centered around challenging academic pursuits. Sessions were offered in biochemistry, computer skills and propositional calculus. Sherry wondered what ever happened to stringing beads and basket weaving!

When the girls were dismissed for their afternoon activities, Sherry made her way to the director's office, which was on the other side of the campgrounds, far from the maddening crowd, she noted. It was all too apparent that Roarke liked his privacy.

Tall redwoods outlined the camp outskirts. Wildflowers grew in abundance. Goldthreads, red baneberry and the northern inside-out flower were just a few that Sherry recognized readily. She had a passion for wildflowers and could name those most common to the West Coast. Some flowers were unknown to her, but she had a sneaky suspicion that if she picked a few, either Sally or Diane would be able to tell her the species and Latin title.

When she could delay the inevitable no longer, Sherry approached Roarke's office. She knocked politely twice and waited.

"Come in," came the gruff voice.

Squaring her shoulders, preparing to face the lion in his den, Sherry entered the office. As she expected, his room was meticulously neat. Bookshelves lined the walls, and where there weren't books the space was covered with certificates. His desk was an oversize mahogany one that rested in the center of the large room. The leather high-backed chair was one Sherry would have expected to find a bank president using—not a camp director.

"Miss White."

"Mr. Roarke."

They greeted each other stiffly.

"Sit down." He motioned toward the two low-backed upholstered chairs.

Sherry sat and briefly studied the man behind the desk. He looked to be a young thirty-five although there were lines faintly etched around his eyes and on both sides of his mouth. But instead of detracting from his good looks, the lines added another dimension to his appeal. Lynn's words about Roarke suffering from a lost love played back in Sherry's mind. Like her friend she sensed an underlying sadness in him, but nothing that could readily be seen in the square, determined lines of his jaw. And again it was his piercing gaze that captured her.

"You brought back the reference sheet?" Roarke prompted.

"Yes." Sherry sat at the edge of her seat as though she expected to blurt out what she had to say and make a mad dash for the door. She'd reprinted the names and addresses more clearly this time, transposing the numbers and hoping that it would look unintentional when the responses were delayed.

"I have it with me," she answered, and set the form on his desk. "But there's something else I'd like to discuss. I've been assigned Gretchen Hamburg."

"Ah, yes, Gretchen."

Apparently the girl was known to him. "I'm afraid I'm having a small problem with her," Sherry said, carefully choosing her words. "It seems Gretchen prefers to sleep away from the window, but she dawdled around outside while the others chose bunks, and now she's complaining. She's asked that I make an appointment for her to plead her case with you. She...insinuated that you'd correct this unfortunate situation."

"I'm—"

Sherry didn't allow him to finish. "It's my opinion that giving in to Gretchen's demands would set a precedent that would cause problems among the other girls later."

His wide brow furrowed. "I can understand your concerns."

Sherry relaxed, scooting back in her chair.

"However, Gretchen's family is an influential one."

Sherry bolted forward. "That's favoritism."

"Won't any of the other girls trade with her?"

"I've already suggested that. But the others shouldn't be forced into giving up their beds simply because Gretchen Hamburg—"

"Have you sought a compromise?" he interrupted.

Sherry's hands were clenched in such tight fists that her punch would have challenged Muhammad Ali's powerful right hand. "I suggested that we place the mattress on the floor in my room, but I did mention that I sometimes sleep with my window open."

"And?"

"And Gretchen insisted on speaking to you personally."

Roarke drummed his fingers on the desktop. "If you haven't already noticed, Gretchen is a complainer."

"No!" Sherry feigned wide-eyed shock.

Roarke studied the fiery flash in Sherry's dark brown eyes and again experienced an unfamiliar tug on his emotions. She made him want to laugh at the most inappropriate times. And when he wasn't amused by her, she infuriated him. There didn't seem to be any in-

between in the emotions he felt. Sherry White could be
a problem, Roarke mused, although he was convinced
she'd be a terrific counselor. The trouble was within
himself. He was attracted to her—strongly attracted.
He would have been better off not to have hired her than
to wage battle with his emotions all summer. He'd need
to keep a cool head with her—keep his distance, avoid
her whenever possible, bury whatever it was in her that
he found appealing.

Sherry was convinced she saw a brief smile touch
Roarke's mouth, so faint that it was gone before it completely registered with her. If only he'd really smile or
joke or kid, she would find it infinitely more pleasant to
meet with him. A lock of hair fell across his brow and
he brushed it back only to have it immediately return
to its former position. Sherry found her gaze mesmerized by that single lock. Except for those few strands of
cocky hair Roarke was impeccable in every way. She
sincerely doubted that as a child his jeans had ever been
torn or grass stained.

"Well?" Sherry prompted. "Should I send Gretchen
in to see you?"

"No."

"No?"

"That's what I said, Miss White. I can't be bothered
with these minor details. Handle the situation as you
see fit."

Using the arms of the chair for leverage, Sherry rose.
She was pleased because she didn't want Ms. Miserable to use Roarke to manipulate her and the other girls
in the cabin. Sherry was halfway out the door when
Roarke spoke next.

"However, if this matter isn't settled promptly, I'll

be forced to handle the situation myself. Dorothy Hamburg has been a faithful supporter of this camp for several years."

Well, she might as well jerk Pamela and Ralph from the center cot, Sherry thought irritably. One way or another Gretchen was bound to have her own way.

Three

Dressed in their pajamas, the seven preteens sat Indian fashion on their cots, listening wide-eyed and intent as Sherry read.

"And they lived happily ever after," Sherry murmured, slowly closing the large book.

"You don't really believe that garbage, do you?" Gretchen demanded.

Sherry smiled softly. Gretchen found fault with everything, she'd discovered over the course of the first week of camp. Even when the girl enjoyed something, it was her nature to complain, quibble and frown. During the fairy tale, Gretchen had been the one most enraptured, yet she seemed to feel it was her duty to nitpick.

"How do you mean?" Sherry asked, deciding to play innocent. The proud tilt of Gretchen's chin tore at her heart.

"It's only a stupid fairy tale."

"But it was so lovely," Wendy chimed in softly.

"And the Prince…"

"…was so handsome," Jan and Jill added in unison.

"But none of it is true." Gretchen crossed her arms and pressed her lips tightly together. "My mother claims that she's suffering from the Cinderella syndrome, and here you are telling us the same goofy story and expecting us to believe it."

"Oh no," Sherry whispered, bending forward as though to share a special secret. "Fairy tales don't have to be true; but it's romantic to pretend. That's what makes them so special."

"But fairy tales couldn't possibly be real."

"All fiction is make-believe," Sherry softly assured her chronic complainer.

"I don't care if it's true or not, I like it when you read us stories," Diane volunteered. The child had set aside Proust in favor of listening to the bedtime story. Sherry felt a sense of pride that she'd been able to interest Diane in something beyond the heavy reading material she devoured at all hours of the night and day.

"Tell us another one," Wendy begged. Her Barbie and Ken dolls sat in a circle in front of her, their arms twisting around one another.

Sherry closed the book. "I will tomorrow night."

"Another fairy tale, okay?" Pamela insisted. "Even though he's a boy, Ralph liked it." She petted the hamster and reverently kissed him good-night before placing him back inside his shoe-box home.

Sherry had serious doubts about Ralph's environment, but Pamela had repeatedly assured her that the box was the only home Ralph had ever known and that he'd never run away. All the time the child spent grooming and training him lent Sherry confidence. But then, she hadn't known that many trick hamsters in her time.

"Will you read *Snow White and the Seven Dwarfs* next?" Sally wanted to know. She climbed into her cot and tucked the microscope underneath her pillow.

"Snow White it is."

"You're sort of like Snow White, aren't you?" Diane asked. "I mean, your name is White and you live in a cottage in the forest with seven dwarfs."

"Yeah!" Jan and Jill chimed together.

"I, for one, resent being referred to as a dwarf," Gretchen muttered.

"Wizards then," Wendy offered. "We're all smart."

"Snow White and the Seven Wizards," Sally commented, obviously pleased with herself. "Hey, we all live in Snow White's cottage."

"Right!" Jan and Jill said, with identical nods.

"But who's Prince Charming?"

"I don't think that this particular Snow White has a Prince Charming," Sherry said, feigning a sad sigh. "But—" she pointed her index finger toward the ceiling "—some day my prince will come."

"Mr. Roarke," Gretchen piped in excitedly. "He's the handsomest, noblest, nicest man I know. He'll be your prince."

Sherry nearly swallowed her tongue in her rush to disagree. Jeff Roarke! Impossible! He was more like the evil huntsman intent on doing away with the unsuspecting Snow White. If he ever checked her references, doing away with her would be exactly what happened! In the past week, Sherry had done her utmost to be the most accommodating counselor at camp. She hadn't given Roarke a single reason to notice or disapprove of her. Other than an occasional gruff hello, she'd been able to avoid speaking to him.

"Lights out, everyone," Sherry said, determined to kill the conversation before it got out of hand. The less said about Roarke as Prince Charming, the better.

The girls were much too young to understand that to be called princely a man must possess certain character traits. Sherry hesitated and drew in a shaky breath. All right, she'd admit it—Jeff Roarke's character was sterling. He was dedicated, hardworking and seemed to genuinely love the children. And then there were those incredible eyes of his. Sherry sharply shook herself back into reality. A single week with her charges and already she was going bongos. Roarke was much too dictatorial and inflexible to be a prince. At least to be *her* Prince Charming.

With a flip of the switch the room went dark. The only illumination was a shallow path of golden moonlight across the polished wood of the cabin floor.

Sherry moved into her own room and left the door ajar in order to hear her seven wizards in case of bad dreams or nighttime troubles. The girls never ceased to surprise her. It was as though they didn't realize they were children. When Sherry suggested reading a fairy tale, they'd moaned and claimed that was *kids'* stuff! Sherry had persisted, and now she was exceptionally pleased that she had. They'd loved *Cinderella* and eaten up *Little Red Riding Hood*. Diane, the reader, who had teethed on Ibsen, Maupassant and Emerson, wasn't sure who the Brothers Grimm were. But she sat night after night, her hands cupping her face as she listened to a different type of classic—and loved it.

Sally, at ten, knew more about biochemistry than Sherry ever hoped to understand in her lifetime. Yet Sally couldn't name a single record in the top ten and hadn't thought to bring a radio to camp. Her microscope was far more important!

These little geniuses were still children, and if no one else was going to remind them of that fact, Sherry was! If she could, she would have liked to remind Jeff Roarke of that. He had to realize there was more to life than academia; yet the entire camp seemed centered around challenging the mind and in her humble opinion, leaving the heart empty.

Sitting on the edge of her cot, Sherry's gaze fell on the seven girls in the room outside her own. She had been given charge of these little ones for the next two months, and by golly she was going to teach these children to have fun if it killed her!

"Ralph!"

The shrill cry pierced Sherry's peaceful slumber. She managed to open one eye and peek toward the clock radio. Four-thirteen. She had a full seventeen minutes before her alarm was set to ring.

"Miss White," Pamela cried, frantically stumbling into Sherry's room. "Ralph is gone!"

"What!" Holding a sheet to her breast, Sherry jerked upright, eyes wide. "Gone? What do you mean, gone?"

"He's run away," the little girl sobbed. "I woke up and found the lid from the shoe box off-kilter, and when I looked he was…m-missing." She burst into tears and threw her arms around Sherry's neck, weeping pathetically.

"He didn't run away," Sherry said, thinking fast as she hugged the thin child.

"He didn't?" Pamela raised her tear-streaked face and battled down a fresh wave of emotion. "Then where is he?"

"He's exploring. Remember what I said about Ralph getting tired of his shoe-box home? He just went on an adventure into the woods to find some friends."

Pamela nodded, her dark braids bouncing.

"I suppose he woke up in the middle of the night and decided that he'd like to see who else was living around the cabin." The thought was a chilling one to Sherry. She squelched it quickly.

"But where is he?"

"I…I'm not exactly sure. He may need some guidance finding his way home."

"Then we should help him."

"Right." Stretching across the bed, Sherry turned on the bedside lamp. "Ralph," she called softly. "Allie, allie oxen free." It wouldn't be that easy, but it was worth a shot.

"There he is," Sally cried, sitting up in her cot. She pointed to the dresser on the far side of the outer room. "He ran under there."

"Get him," Pamela screamed and raced out of Sherry's quarters.

Soon all seven girls were crawling around the floor in their long flannel nightgowns looking for Ralph. He was still at large when Sherry's alarm clock buzzed.

"Damn," she muttered under her breath. She looked up to find seven pairs of eyes accusing her. "I mean darn," she muttered back. The search party returned to their rescue mission.

"I've got to get to the staff meeting," Sherry announced dejectedly five minutes later when Ginny, the high-school girl who was working in hopes of being hired as a counselor next summer, arrived to replace her. "Listen, don't say a word to anyone about Ralph. I'll be back as quickly as I can."

"Okay," Jan and Jill answered for the group.

Because she knew what Roarke would say once she asked him about the hamster, Sherry had yet to mention Ralph's presence in their happy little cabin. To be honest, she hadn't figured on doing so. However, having the entire cabin turned upside down in an effort to locate the Dr. Livingstone of the animal kingdom was another matter.

Dressing as quickly as possible, Sherry hopped around on one foot in an effort to tie her shoelace, then switched legs and continued hopping across her pine floor.

"That's working," Diane cried, glancing in Sherry's direction. "Keep doing it."

"I see him. I see him. Ralph, come home. Ralph, come home," Pamela begged, charging in the flannel nightgown over the cold floor.

A minute later, Sherry was out the door, leaving her charges to the mercy of one fickle-hearted hamster. By the time she reached the staff meeting she was panting and breathless. Roarke had already opened the meeting, and when Sherry entered, he paused and waited for her to take a seat.

"I'm pleased you saw fit to join us, Miss White," Roarke commented coolly.

"Sorry. I overslept," she mumbled as she claimed the last available chair in the front row. Rich color blossomed in her already flushed cheeks, reminding her once again why she'd come to dislike Jeff Roarke. The man went out of his way to cause her embarrassment— he actually seemed to thrive on it.

Roarke read the list of activities for the day, listing possible educational ventures for each cabin's nightly get-togethers. Then, by turn, he had the counselors tell the others how they'd chosen to close another camping day.

"We discussed how to split an atom," the first counselor, a college freshman, told the group.

This appeared to please Roarke. "Excellent," he said, nodding his head approvingly.

"We dissected a frog," the second counselor added.

As each spoke, Sherry grew more uncomfortable. The neckline of her thin sweater felt exceptionally tight, and when it was her turn, her voice came out sounding thin and low. "I read them the Cinderella story," she said.

"Excuse me." Roarke took a step closer. "Would you kindly repeat that?"

"Yes, of course." Sherry paused and cleared her throat. "I read my girls 'Cinderella.'"

A needle dropping against the floor would have sounded like a sonic boom in the thick silence that followed.

"'Cinderella,'" Roarke repeated, as though he was convinced he hadn't heard her correctly.

"That's right."

"Perhaps she could explain why anyone would choose to read a useless fairy tale over a worthwhile learning experience?"

The voice behind Sherry was familiar. She turned to find Fred Spencer glaring at her with undisguised disapproval. Since their first disagreement over Sherry's ideas, they hadn't exchanged more than a few words.

Sherry turned her head around and tucked her hands under her thighs, shifting her weight back and forth over her knuckles. "I consider fairy tales a valuable learning tool."

"You do?" This time it was Roarke who questioned her.

From the way he was looking at her, Sherry could tell that he was having a difficult time accepting her reasoning.

"And what particular lesson did you hope to convey in the reading of this tale?"

"Hope."

"Hope?"

The other counselors were all still staring at her as though she was an apple in a barrel full of oranges. "You see, sometimes life can seem so bleak that we don't see all the good things around us. In addition, the story is a romantic, fun one."

Roarke couldn't believe what he was hearing. Sherry was making a mockery of the goals he'd set for this year's camp session. Romance! She wanted to teach her girls about some fickle female notion. The word alone was enough to make his blood run cold.

"Unfortunately, I disagree," Roarke said. "In the rational world there's no need for romantic nonsense." Although he tried to avoid looking at Sherry, his gaze refused to leave her. She looked flustered and embarrassed, and a fetching shade of pink had invaded her cheeks. Her gaze darted nervously to those around her, as if hoping to find someone who would agree with her. None would, Roarke could have told her that. His gaze fell to her lips, which were slightly moist and parted. Roarke's stomach muscles tightened and he hurriedly looked away. Love clouded the brain, he reminded himself sternly. The important things in life were found in education. Learning was the challenge. He should know. By age twelve, he'd been a college student, graduating with full honors three years later. There'd been no time or need for trivial romance.

Sherry had seen Roarke's lips compress at the mention of romance, as though he associated the word with sucking lemons. "People need love in their lives,"

Sherry asserted boldly, although she was shaking on the inside.

"I see," he said, when it was obvious that he didn't.

The meeting continued then, and the staff was dismissed fifteen minutes later. Sherry was the first one to vacate her chair, popping up like hot bread out of a toaster the second the meeting was adjourned. She had to get back to the cabin to see if Ralph had been caught and peace had once again been restored to the seven wizards' cabin.

"Miss White." Roarke stopped her.

"Yes." Sherry's heart bounded to her throat. She'd hoped to make a clean getaway.

"Would it be possible for you to drop by my office later this afternoon?" The references—she knew it; he'd discovered they'd been falsified.

Their eyes met. Sherry's own befuddled brown clashed with Roarke's tawny-hazel. His open challenge stared down her hint of defiance, and Sherry dropped her gaze first. "This afternoon? S-sure," she answered finally, with false cheerfulness. At least he'd said afternoon rather than morning, so if Lynn was right she didn't need to start packing her bags yet. She released a grateful sigh and smiled. "I'll be there directly after lunch."

"Good."

He turned and Sherry charged from the meeting room and sprinted across the grounds with the skill of an Olympic runner. Oh heavens, she prayed Ralph had returned to his home. Life wouldn't be so cruel as to break Pamela's heart—or would it?

Back at the cabin, Sherry discovered Pamela sitting on her bunk, crying softly.

"No Ralph?"

All seven children shook their heads simultaneously. Sherry's heart constricted. "Please don't worry."

"I want Ralph," Pamela chanted, holding the pillow to her stomach and rocking back and forth. "Ralph's the only friend I ever had."

Sherry glanced around, hoping for a miracle. Where was Sherlock Holmes when she really needed him?

"He popped his head up between the floorboards a while ago," Sally explained, doubling over to peek underneath her bunk on the off chance he was there now.

"He's afraid of her microscope," Gretchen said accusingly. "I'm convinced that sweet hamster was worried sick that he'd end up in a jar like those…those pigs."

"He knows I wouldn't do that," Sally shouted, placing her hands defiantly on her hips, her eyes a scant inch from Gretchen's.

"Girls, please," Sherry pleaded. "We're due in the mess hall in five minutes."

A shriek arose as they scrambled for their clothes. Only Pamela remained on her bed, unmoved by the thought of being late for breakfast.

Sherry joined the little girl and folded her arm across the small shoulders. "We'll find him."

Tears glistened in the bright blue eyes. "Do you promise?"

Sherry didn't know what to say. She couldn't guarantee something like that. Pamela was a mathematical genius, so Sherry explained in terms the child would understand. "I can't make it a hundred percent. Let's say seventy-five/twenty-five." For heaven's sake, just how far could one hamster get? "Now, get dressed and go into the dining room with dry eyes."

Pamela nodded and climbed off her cot.

"Girls!" Sherry raised her hand to gain their attention. The loud chatter died to a low hum. "Remember, Ralph is our little secret!" The campers knew the rules better than Sherry. Each one was well aware that keeping Ralph was an infraction against camp policy.

"Our lips are sealed." Jan and Jill pantomimed zipping their mouths closed.

"After breakfast, when you've gone to your first class, I'll come back here and look for Ralph. In the meantime I think we'd best pretend nothing's unusual." Her questioning eyes met Pamela's, and Sherry gave her a reassuring hug.

With a gallant effort, Pamela sniffed and nodded. "I just want my Ralphie to come home."

After the frenzied search that had resulted from his disappearance, Sherry couldn't have agreed with the little girl more.

Before they left the cabin for the dining room, Sherry set the open shoe box in the middle of the cabin floor in the desperate hope that the runaway would find his own way home. She paused to close the door behind her charges and glanced over her shoulder with the fervent wish: *Ralph, please come home!*

In the dining hall, seated around the large circular table for eight, Sherry noted that none of her girls showed much of an appetite. French toast should have been a popular breakfast, but for all the interest her group showed, the cook could have served mush!

As the meal was wearing down, Mr. Roarke stepped forward.

"Isn't he handsome?" Gretchen said, looking toward Sherry. "My mother could really go for a man like him."

After what had happened that morning, Sherry was more than willing to let Gretchen's mother take Jeff

Roarke. Good luck to her. With his views on romance she'd be lucky if she made it to first base.

"He does sort of look like a Prince Charming," Sally agreed.

"Mr. Roarke?" Sherry squinted, narrowing her gaze, wondering what kind of magic Roarke used on women. Young and old seemed to find him overwhelmingly attractive.

"Oh, yes," Sally repeated with a dreamy look clouding her eyes. "He's just like the prince you read about in the story last night."

Sherry squinted her eyes again in an effort to convince the girls she couldn't possibly be interested in him as a romantic lead in her life.

Standing in front of the room, his voice loud and clear without a microphone, Roarke made the announcements for the day. The highlight of the first week of camp was a special guest speaker who would be giving a talk on the subject of fungus and mold. Roarke was sure the campers would all enjoy hearing Dr. Waldorf speak. From the eager nods around the room, Sherry knew he was right.

Fungus? Mold? Sally looked as excited as if he'd announced a tour of a candy factory that would be handing out free samples. Maybe Sherry was wrong. Maybe her charges weren't really children. Perhaps they really were dwarfs. Because if they were children, they certainly didn't act like any she'd ever known.

Following breakfast, all fifty wizards emptied the dining room and headed for their assigned classes. Sherry wasted little time in returning to her cottage.

The shoe box stood forlornly in the middle of the room. Empty. No Ralph.

Kneeling beside the box, Sherry took a piece of

squished French toast from her jeans pocket and ripped it into tiny pieces, piling them around the shoe box. "Ralph," she called out softly. "You love Pamela, don't you? Surely you don't want to break the sweet little girl's heart."

An eerie sensation ran down her spine, as though someone were watching her. Slowly Sherry turned to find a large calico cat sitting on the ledge of the open window. His almond eyes narrowed into thin slits as he surveyed the room.

A cat!

"Shoo!" Sherry screamed, shooting to her feet. She whipped out her hands in an effort to chase the monster away. She didn't know where in the devil he'd come from, but he certainly wasn't welcome around here. Not with Ralph on the loose. When the cat ran off, and with her heart pounding, Sherry shut and latched the window.

By noon, she was tired of looking for Ralph—tired of trying to find a hole or a crack large enough to hide a hamster. An expedition into the deepest, darkest jungles of Africa would have been preferable to this. She joined the girls in the dining room and sadly shook her head when seven pairs of hope-filled eyes silently questioned her on the fate of the hamster. Pamela's bottom lip trembled and tears brimmed in her clear blue eyes, but she didn't say anything.

The luncheon menu didn't fare much better than breakfast. The girls barely ate. Sherry knew she'd made a terrible mistake in allowing Pamela to keep the hamster. She'd gone against camp policy and now was paying the price. Rules were rules. She should have known better.

After lunch, the girls once again went their separate ways. With a heavy heart, Sherry headed for Roarke's office. He answered her knock and motioned for her to sit down. Sherry moistened her dry lips as the girls' comment about Roarke being a prince came to mind. At the time, she'd staunchly denied any attraction she felt for him. To the girls and to herself.

Now, alone with him in his office, Sherry's reaction to him was decidedly positive. If she were looking for someone to fill the role of Prince Charming in her life, only one man need apply. She found it amusing, even touching, that somehow even in glasses, this man was devastating. He apparently wore them for reading, but he hadn't allowed the staff to see him in them before now.

"Before I forget, how did you settle the problem with Gretchen Hamburg?"

"Ah yes, Gretchen." Proud of herself, Sherry leaned back in the chair and crossed her legs. "It was simple actually. I repositioned her cot away from the wall. That was all she really wanted."

"And she's satisfied with that?"

"Relatively. The mattress is too flat, the pillow's too soft and the blanket's too thin, but other than that, the bed is fine."

"You handled that well."

Sherry considered that high praise coming from her fearless director. He, too, leaned back in his chair. He hesitated and seemed to be considering his words as he rolled a pencil between his palms. "I feel that I may have misled you when you applied for the position at Camp Gitche Gumee," he said after a long pause.

"Oh?" Her heart was thundering at an alarming rate.

"We're not a Camp Fire Girl camp."

Sherry didn't breathe, fearing what was coming next. "I beg your pardon?"

"This isn't the usual summer camp."

Sherry couldn't argue with that—canoeing and hiking were offered, but there was little else in the way of fun camping experiences.

"Camp Gitche Gumee aspires to academic excellence," he explained, with a thoughtful frown. "We take the brightest young minds in this country and challenge them to excel in a wide variety of subjects. As you probably noted from the announcements made this morning, we strive toward bringing in top educators to lecture on stimulating subjects."

"Like *fungus and mold*?"

"Yes. Dr. Waldorf is a world-renowned lecturer. Fascinating subject." Roarke tried to ignore her sarcastic tone. From the way she was staring back at him, he realized she strongly disapproved, and he was surprised at how much her puckered frown affected him. Strangely he discovered the desire to please her, to draw the light of her smile back into her eyes, to be bathed in the glow of her approval. The thought froze him. Something was drastically wrong. With barely restrained irritation, he pushed his glasses up the bridge of his nose.

Her lack of appreciation for the goals he'd set for this summer put him in an uncomfortable position. She saw him as a stuffed shirt, that much was obvious, but he couldn't allow Sherry's feelings to cloud his better judgment. He didn't want to destroy her enthusiasm, but he found it necessary to guide it into the proper channels. He liked Sherry's spirit, even though she'd made it obvious she didn't agree with his methods. He hesitated once more. He didn't often talk about his youth, saw no reason to do so, but it was important to him that Sherry understand.

"I would have loved a camp such as this when I was ten," he said thoughtfully.

"You?"

"It might astonish you to know that I was once considered a child prodigy."

It didn't surprise her, now that she thought about it.

"I was attending high-school classes when most boys my age were trying out for Little League. I was in college at twelve and had my master's by the time I was sixteen."

Sherry didn't know how to comment. The stark loneliness in his voice said it all. He'd probably had few friends and little or no contact with other children like himself. The pressures on him would have crumpled anyone else. Jeff Roarke's empty childhood had led him to establish Camp Gitche Gumee. His own bleak experiences were what made the camp so important to him. A surge of compassion rose within Sherry and she gripped her hands together.

"Learning can be fun," she suggested softly, after a long moment. "What about an exploration into the forests in search of such exotic animals as the salamander and tree frog?"

"Yes, well, that is something to consider."

"And how about camp songs?"

"We sing."

"In Latin!"

"Languages are considered a worthy pursuit."

"Okay, games," Sherry challenged next. Her voice was slightly raised as she warmed to her subject. She knew she wouldn't be able to hold her tongue long. It was better to get her feelings into the open than to try to bury them. "And I don't mean Camp Gitche Gumee's afternoon quiz teams, either."

"There are plenty of scheduled free times."

"But not organized fun ones," Sherry cried. "As you said, these children are some of the brightest in the country, but they have one major problem." She was all the way to the edge of her cushion by now, liberally using her hands for emphasis. "They have never been allowed to be children."

Once again, Roarke shoved his glasses up the bridge of his nose, strangely unsettled by her comments. She did make a strong case, but there simply wasn't enough time in a day to do all that she suggested. "Learning in and of itself should offer plenty of fun."

"But—"

Sherry wasn't allowed to finish.

"But you consider fairy tales of value?" he asked, recalling the reason he'd called her into his office.

"You're darn right I do. The girls loved them. Do you know Diane Miller? She's read Milton and Wilde and hasn't a clue who Dr. Seuss is."

"Who?" He blinked.

"Dr. Seuss." It wasn't until then that Sherry realized that Roarke knew nothing of Horton and the Grinch. He'd probably never tasted green eggs with ham or known about Sam.

Roarke struggled to disguise his ignorance. "I'm convinced your intentions are excellent, Miss White, but these parents have paid good money for their children to attend this camp with the express understanding that the children would learn. Unfortunately, fairy tales weren't listed as an elective on our brochure."

* * *

"Maybe they should have been," Sherry said firmly. "From everything I've seen, this camp is so academically minded that the entire purpose of sending a child away for the summer has been lost."

Roarke's mouth compressed and his eyes glinted coldly. Sherry could see she'd overstepped her bounds.

"After one week you consider yourself an expert on the subject?"

"I know children."

His hands shuffled the papers on his desk. "It was my understanding that you were a graduate student."

"In education."

"And a minor in partying?"

"That's not true," Sherry cried, coming to her feet.

Roarke rose as well, planted his hands on the desktop, and leaned forward. "Fairy tales are out, Miss White. In the evening you will prepare a study plan and have it approved by me. Is that understood?"

Sherry could feel color filling her face. "Yes, sir," she responded crisply, and mocked him with a salute. If he was going to act like a marine sergeant then she'd respond like a lowly recruit.

"That was unnecessary!"

Sherry opened her mouth to argue with him when the calico cat she'd witnessed earlier in her cabin window suddenly appeared. A gasp rose in her throat at the tiny figure dangling from the cat's mouth.

"Ralph!" she cried, near hysteria.

Four

"Ralph?" Roarke demanded. "Who in the love of heaven is Ralph?"

"Pamela's hamster. For heaven's sake, do something!" Sherry cried. "He's still alive."

Slowly, Roarke advanced toward the cat. "Buttercup," he said softly. "Nice Buttercup. Put down…" He paused, twisting his head to look at Sherry.

"Ralph," Sherry supplied.

Roarke turned back to the cat. "I thought you said the name was Pamela."

"No, Ralph is Pamela's hamster."

"Right." He wiped a hand across his brow and momentarily closed his eyes. This just wasn't his day. Cautiously, he lowered himself to his knees.

Sherry followed suit, shaking with anxiety. Poor Ralph! Trapped in the jaws of death.

"Buttercup," Roarke encouraged softly. "Put down Ralph."

The absurdity of Roarke's naming a cat "Buttercup" unexpectedly struck Sherry, and a laugh oddly mingled with hysteria worked its way up her throat and escaped with the words, "The cat's name is Buttercup?"

This wasn't the time to explain that his mother had named the cat. "Buttercup isn't any more unusual than a hamster named Ralph!" Roarke said through gritted teeth.

Sherry snickered. "Wanna bet?"

Proud of her catch, Buttercup sat with the squirming rodent in her mouth, seeming to wait for the praise due her. Roarke, down on all fours, slowly advanced toward the feline.

"Will she eat him?" That was Sherry's worst fear. In her mind she could see herself as a helpless witness to the slaughter.

"I don't know what she'll do to him," Roarke whispered impatiently.

By now they were both down on all fours, in front of the sleek calico.

"I'll try to take him out of her mouth."

"What if she won't give him up?" Sherry was about an inch away from pressing the panic button.

Lifting his hand so slowly that it was difficult to tell that Roarke was moving, he gently patted the top of Buttercup's head.

"For heaven's sake, don't praise her," Sherry hissed. "That's Pamela's hamster your cat is torturing."

"Here, Buttercup," he said soothingly, "give me Ralph."

The cat didn't so much as blink.

"I see she's well trained." Sherry couldn't resist the remark.

Roarke flashed her an irritated glance.

Just then the phone rang. Startled, Sherry bolted upright and her hand slapped her heart. A gasp died on her lips as Buttercup dropped Ralph who immediately shot across the room. Roarke dived for the hamster, falling forward so that his elbow hit the floor with a solid thud. His glasses went flying.

"Got him," Roarke shouted triumphantly.

The phone pealed a second time.

"Here."

Without warning or option, Roarke handed Sherry the hamster. Her heart was hammering in her throat as the furry critter burrowed deep into her cupped hands. "Poor baby," she murmured, holding him against her chest.

"Camp Gitche Gumee," Roarke spoke crisply into the telephone receiver. "Just one moment and I'll transfer your call to the kitchen."

Sherry heard him punch a couple of buttons and hang up. In a sitting position on the floor, she released a long, ragged breath and slumped against the side of the desk, needing its support. At the rate her heart was pumping, she felt as if she had just completed the hundred-yard dash.

Roarke moved away from her and she saw him reach down and retrieve his eye-glasses.

"How is he?" he asked, concerned.

"Other than being frightened half to death, he appears to be unscathed."

Silence.

"I...I suppose I should get Ralph back to the cabin," she said, feeling self-conscious and silly.

"Here, let me help you up." He gave her his hand, firmly clasping her elbow, and hauled her to her feet. Sherry found his touch secure and warm. And surprisingly pleasant. Very pleasant. As she stood she discovered that they were separated by only a few inches. "Yes...well," she said and swallowed awkwardly. "Thank you for your help."

His eyes held hers. Lynn was right, Sherry noted. They weren't hazel but green, a deep cool shade of green that she associated with emeralds. Another surprise was how dark and expressive his eyes were. But the signals he was sending were strong and conflicting. Sherry read confusion and a touch of shock, as though she'd unexpectedly thrown him off balance.

Roarke's gaze dropped from her eyes to her mouth and Sherry's breath seemed to jam in her lungs.

She knew what Roarke wanted. The muscles of her stomach tightened and a sinking sensation attacked her with the knowledge that she would like it if he kissed her. The thought of his mouth fitting over hers was strongly appealing. His lips would be like his hand, warm and firm. Sherry pulled herself up short. She was flabbergasted to be entertaining such thoughts. Jeff Roarke. Dictator! Marine sergeant! Stuffed shirt!

"Thank you for your help," she muttered in a voice hardly like her own. Hurriedly, she took a step in retreat, unable to escape fast enough.

Roarke stood stunned as Sherry backed away from him. He was shaking from the inside out. He'd nearly kissed her! And in the process gone against his own policy, and worse, his better judgment. Fortunately, whatever had been happening to him hadn't seemed to affect her. She'd jumped away from him as though she'd been burned, as if the thought of them kissing was repugnant. Even then, it had taken all the strength of his will not to reach out and bring her into his arms.

Sherry watched as Roarke's mouth twisted into a mocking smile. "When you return to your cottage, Miss White, I suggest you read page 36 of the camp manual."

Without looking, Sherry already knew what it said: no pets! Well, anyone with half a brain in his head would recognize that Ralph wasn't a pet—he was a mascot. In her opinion every cabin should have one, but Sherry already knew what Roarke thought of her ideas.

"Miss White." He stopped her at the office door.

The softness in his accusing voice filled her with dread. "Yes?"

"I'd like to review your lesson plans for the evening sessions for the next week at your earliest convenience."

"I'll...I'll have them to you by tomorrow morning."

"Thank you."

"N-no," she stammered. "Thank you. I thought we'd lost Ralph for sure."

Sherry didn't remember walking across the campgrounds. The next thing she knew, she was inside the cabin and Ralph was safely tucked inside his shoe-box home.

Her heart continued to pound frantically and she sank onto the closest available bunk, grateful that Ralph had been found unscathed. And even more grateful that the issue of her application form and the references had been pushed to the side.

As much as she'd like to attribute her shaky knees and battering heart to Buttercup's merciless attack on Ralph, Sherry knew otherwise. It was Roarke. Like every other female in this camp, she had fallen under his magical spell. For one timeless moment she'd seen him as the others did. Attractive. Compelling. Dynamic. Jeff Roarke! There in his office, with Ralph in her hand, they'd gazed at each other and Sherry had been stunned into breathlessness. She wiped a hand over her eyes to shake the vivid image of the man from her mind. Her tongue moistened her lips as she imagined Roarke's mouth over hers. She felt herself melting inside and closed her eyes. It would have been good. Very, very good.

It took Sherry at least ten minutes to gather her composure, and she was grateful she'd kept her wits about her. It wasn't so unusual to be physically attracted to a man, she reassured herself. She had been plenty of times before; this wasn't really something new, and it was only an isolated incident. As a mature adult, she was surely capable of keeping her hormones under control. For the remainder of the summer she would respond to Roarke with cool politeness, she decided. If he were to guess her feelings, she would be at his mercy.

Somehow, Sherry got through the rest of the day. Peace reigned in the cabin, and when the evening session came, Sherry read her young charges the story of Snow White and the Seven Dwarfs. She'd promised them she would, and she wouldn't go back on her word. But to be on the safe side, she also decided to teach them a song.

"Okay, everyone stand," she instructed, when she'd finished the story.

Simultaneously, seven pajama-clad nine- and ten-year-olds rose to their feet.

"What are we going to do now?" Gretchen cried. "I want to talk about Snow White."

"We'll discuss the story later." Sherry put off the youngster, and extended her hands. "Okay, everyone, this is a fun song, so listen up."

When she had their attention, she swayed her hips and pointed to her feet, singing at the top of her lungs how the anklebone was connected to the legbone and the legbone was connected to the hipbone. Seven small hips did an imitation of Sherry's gyrating action. Then the girls dissolved into helpless giggles. Soon the entire cabin was filled with the sounds of joy and laughter.

To satisfy her young charges, Sherry was forced into repeating the silly song no less than three times. At least if she were asked to report tomorrow on their evening activity, Sherry would honestly be able to say that they'd studied the human skeleton. It felt good to have outsmarted Roarke.

"Five minutes until lights-out," Sherry called, making a show of checking her watch. From the corner of her eye, she saw the girls scurry across the room and back to their cots.

"I still want to talk about Snow White," Gretchen cried, above the chaos. "You told me we'd have time to discuss the story."

"I'm sorry," Sherry admitted contritely, sitting on the edge of the young girl's mattress. "We really don't— not tonight."

"But when the lights go out, that doesn't mean we have to go to sleep."

"Yeah," another voice shouted out. Sherry thought it came from Diane, the reader.

"Someone—anyone, turn out the lights," Sally cried. "Then we can talk."

The room went dark.

Gretchen's bed was closest to the cabin entrance. The room felt stuffy, so Sherry opened the door to allow in the cool evening breeze. A soft ribbon of golden light from the full moon followed the whispering wind inside the cabin.

"Did any of you know that Camp Gitche Gumee is haunted?" Sherry whispered. The girls' attention was instant and rapt.

"There's no such thing as ghosts," Gretchen countered, but her tone lacked conviction.

"Oh, but there are," Sherry whispered, her own voice dipping to an eerie low. "The one who roams around here is named Longfellow."

"Oh, I get it," Diane said with a short laugh. "He was the author of the poem—"

"Shh." Sherry placed her index finger over her lips. Dramatically, she cupped her hands over her ears. "I think I hear him now."

The cabin went still.

"I hear something," Wendy whispered. In the moonlight, Sherry could see the ten-year-old had all ten of her Barbies and Kens in bed with her.

"You needn't worry." Sherry was quick to assure the girls. "Longfellow is a friendly ghost. He only does fun, good things."

"What kind of things?"

"Hmm, let me think."

"I bet Longfellow brought Ralph back."

Sherry hadn't told Pamela how Buttercup had captured the hamster. Her pet's narrow escape from the jaws of death would only terrorize the softhearted little girl.

"Now that I think about it, Pamela, you're right. Longfellow must have had a hand in finding Ralph."

"What other kinds of things does Longfellow do?" Jan and Jill wanted to know. As always, they spoke in unison. Jill's front tooth was still intact, but it wouldn't last much longer with the furious way she worked at extracting it.

"He finds missing items like socks and hair clips. And sometimes, late at night when it's stone quiet, if you listen real, real hard, you can hear him sing."

"You can?"

"Actually, he whistles," Sherry improvised.

The still room went even quieter as seven pairs of ears strained to listen to the wind whisper through the forest of redwoods outside their door.

"I hear him," Diane said excitedly. "He's real close."

"When I was a little kid," Sally told the group excitedly, "I used to be afraid of ghosts, but Longfellow sounds like a good ghost."

"Oh, he is."

"Can you tell us another story?" Gretchen pleaded. "They're fun."

For the chronic grumbler to ask for a fairy tale and admit anything was fun was almost more than Sherry could absorb. "I think one more story wouldn't hurt," she said. "But that has to be all." Remembering the conversation with Roarke earlier that afternoon, Sherry felt a fleeting sadness. After tonight, her stories would have to come from more acceptable classics. She thought her girls were missing a wonderful part of their heritage as children by skipping fairy tales. If she didn't want this job so badly, Sherry would have battled Roarke more strenuously.

Leaning back against the wall, she brought her knees up to her chin, sighed audibly while she chose the tale, and started. "Once upon a time in a land far, far away…"

By the time she announced that "they lived happily ever after" the cabin was filled with the even, measured breathing of sleeping children. If the girls weren't all asleep they were close to it.

Gretchen snored softly, and taking care not to wake the slumbering child, Sherry climbed off her cot and checked on the others. She pulled a blanket around Jan's and Jill's shoulders and removed inanimate objects from the cots, placing Sally's microscope on the headboard and rescuing the Barbies and Kens from being crushed during the night. Ralph was firmly secured in his weathered home, and Sherry gently slid the shoe box from underneath Pamela's arm.

"Sleep tight," she whispered to the much-loved rodent. "Or else I'll call Buttercup back."

As she moved to close the cabin door, Sherry was struck by how peaceful the evening was. Drawn outside, she sat on the top step of the large front porch and gazed at the stars. They were out in brilliant display this evening, scattered diamonds tossed on thick folds of black velvet. How close they seemed. Sparkling. Radiant.

Sherry's hands cupped her chin as she rested her elbows on her knees and studied the heavens.

"Good evening, Miss White." Roarke had heard their singing earlier, had come to investigate and had been amused by her efforts to outwit him.

The sound of Roarke's voice broke into Sherry's thoughts. "Good evening, Mr. Roarke," she responded crisply, and straightened. "What brings you out tonight?" Good grief , she hoped he hadn't been around to hear the last fairy tale, or worse, her mention of Longfellow.

He paused, braced one foot against the bottom step and looked over the grounds. "I like to give the camp a final check before turning in for the night."

"Oh." For the life of her, she couldn't think of a single thing more to say. Her reaction to him was immediate. Her heart pounded like a jackhammer and the blood shot through her veins. She'd like to fool herself into believing the cause was the unexpectedness of his arrival, but she knew better.

"How's Ralph?" Roarke questioned.

"Fully recovered. How's Buttercup?"

"Exceptionally proud." The soft laugh that followed was so pleasant sounding that it caused Sherry to smile just listening to him.

"You have a nice laugh." She hadn't meant to tell him that, but it slipped out before she could stop herself. As often was the case when she spoke to Jeff Roarke, the filter between her brain and her mouth malfunctioned and whatever she was thinking slid out without forethought.

"I was about to tell you how effervescent *your* laugh sounds."

Sherry couldn't remember a time she'd ever given him the opportunity to hear her laugh. The circumstances in which they were together prohibited it. Staff meetings were intensely serious. No one dared show any amusement.

"When—"

"Tonight. I suppose you plan to tell me that the legbone connected to the hipbone is a study of the human skeleton?"

Words ran together and tripped over the tip of her tongue. "Of course not…well, yes, but…"

He laughed again. "The girls thoroughly enjoyed it, didn't they?"

"Yes."

"That sort of education wasn't exactly what I had in mind, but anything is better than those blasted fairy tales."

Sherry was forced into sitting on her hands to keep from elbowing him. Fairy tales weren't silly or senseless. They served a purpose! But she managed to keep her thoughts to herself—with some effort.

Silence again.

"I have my lesson plan if you'd like to see it," she said, and started to get up, but his hand on her forearm stopped her.

"Tomorrow morning is soon enough."

He surprised her even more by climbing the three steps and taking a seat beside her. He paused and raised his eyes to the sky.

"Lovely, isn't it?" he asked.

"Yes." The one word seemed to strangle in her throat. Roarke was close enough to touch. All Sherry would have had to do was shift her weight for her shoulder to gently graze his. Less than an inch separated their thighs. Although she strove to keep from experiencing the physical impact of brushing against him, there was little she could do about the soft scent of the aftershave Roarke wore, which was so masculinely appealing. Every breath she drew in was more tantalizing than the one before. Spice and man—a lethal combination.

It was the night, Sherry decided, not the man. Oh, please, not the man, she begged. She didn't want to be so strongly attracted to Jeff Roarke. She didn't want to be like all the others. The two of them were so different. They couldn't agree on anything. Not him. Not her.

Neither spoke, but the silence wasn't a serene one. The darkness seemed charged with static electricity. Twice Sherry opened her mouth, ready to start some banal conversation simply to break the silence. Both times she found herself incapable of speaking. When she chanced a look in his direction she discovered his thick eyebrows arched bewilderedly over a storm cloud of sea-green eyes.

Naturally, neither one of them had the courage to introduce the phenomenon occurring between them into casual conversation. But Sherry was convinced Roarke felt the tug of physical attraction as strongly and powerfully as she did. And from the look of him, he was as baffled as she.

"Well, I suppose I should turn in," she said, after the longest minute of her life.

"I suppose I should, too."

But neither of them moved.

"It really is a lovely night," Sherry said, looking to the heavens, struck once again by the simple beauty of the starlit sky.

"Yes, lovely," Roarke repeated softly, but he wasn't gazing at the heavens, he was looking at Sherry. He'd believed everything he'd said to her about romance being nonsense, but now the words came back to haunt him. Right now, this moment with her seemed more important than life itself. He felt trapped in awareness. The sensations that churned inside him were lethal to his mental health and he wouldn't alter a one. This woman had completely thrown him off balance with the unexpected need he felt to hold her. Slipping his arm around her shoulders seemed the most natural act in the world...and strictly against his own camp policy. The urge to do so was so strong that he crossed his arms over his chest in an effort to keep them still. He was stunned at how close he'd come to giving in to temptation. Stunned and appalled.

Whatever caused Sherry to turn to meet his gaze, she didn't know. Fate, possibly. But she did rotate her head so that her eyes were caught by his as effectively as if trapped in a vise. Mesmerized, their gazes locked in the faint light of the glorious moon. It was as though Sherry were looking at him for the first time—through a love-struck teen's adoring eyes. He was devastatingly handsome. Dark, and compellingly masculine.

Unable to stop herself, she raised her hand, prepared to outline his thick eyebrows with her fingertips, and paused halfway to his face. His troubled eyes were a mirror of her own doubtful expression, Sherry realized. Yet his were charged with curiosity. He seemed to want to hold her in his arms as much as she yearned to let him. His mouth appeared to hunger for the taste of hers just as she longed to sample his. His shallow breath mingled with her labored one. Deep grooves formed at the sides of his mouth, and when his lips parted, Sherry noted that his breathing was hesitant.

Driven by something stronger than her own common sense, Sherry slowly, inch by inch, lowered her lashes, silently bending to his unspoken demand. Her own lips parted in welcome as her pulse fluttered wildly at the base of her throat.

Roarke lowered his mouth to a scant inch above hers.

Sherry was never sure what happened. A sound perhaps. A tree branch scraping against the roof of the cabin—perhaps an owl's screeching cry as it flew overhead. Whatever it was instantly brought her to her senses, and she was eternally grateful. She jerked her head back and willfully checked her watch.

"My goodness," she cried in a wobbly, weak voice, "will you look at the time?"

"Time?" he rasped.

"It's nearly eleven. I really must get inside." Already she was on her feet, rushing toward the front door as though being chased by a mad dog.

Not waiting for a response from Roarke, Sherry closed the door and weakly leaned against it. Her heart was thumping like a locomotive gone out of control. Her mouth felt dry and scratchy. Filled with purpose, she walked over to the small sink and turned on the cold water faucet. She gulped down the first glass in huge swallows and automatically poured herself a second. In different circumstances, she would have taken her temperature. There was something in the air. Sherry almost wished it was a virus.

The next morning, Sherry was on time for the staff meeting. She hadn't slept well and was awake even before the alarm sounded. At least when she was a few minutes early she could choose her own seat. The back of the room all but invited her and she claimed a seat there.

Lynn Duffy scooted in beside her.

"Morning," Sherry greeted her.

"Hi. How's it going?"

Sherry pushed the cuticle back on her longest fingernail. "Just fine. The kids are great."

"You got Gretchen Hamburg—don't tell me everything's fine. I know better."

"She's a cute kid!"

"Gretchen?" Lynn grumbled. "You've got to be teasing. The kid's a royal pain in the rear end!"

Two days ago, Sherry would have agreed with her, but from the minute Gretchen had announced that fairy tales were "fun" she'd won Sherry's heart.

Roarke stepped to the podium, and the small gathering of staff went silent. Sherry noted that he took pains not to glance in her direction, which was fine by her. She preferred that he didn't. This morning the memory of those few stolen moments alone under the stars was nothing short of embarrassing. She'd rather forget the entire episode. Chalk it up to the decreased layer of ozone in outer space. Or the way the planets were aligned. The moon was in its seventh house. Aquarius and Mars. A fluke certainly. She could look at him this morning and feel nothing…well, that wasn't exactly true. The irritation was gone, replaced by a lingering fascination.

After only a minimum of announcements, the staff were dismissed. Sherry stood, eager to make her escape.

"Sherry," Lynn said, following her out of the meeting room, "do you have some free time later?"

"After breakfast."

Her friend looked a bit chagrined. "I have to run into town. Would you like to come along?"

"Sure, I'll come over to your cabin after I get my wizards off to their first class."

Lynn brightened. "I'll look for you around eight, then."

Her friend took off in the opposite direction and Sherry's gaze followed the younger girl. Now that she thought about it, Lynn didn't seem to be her normal, cheerful self. Sherry had the impression that this jaunt into town was an excuse to talk.

It was.

The minute Sherry got into Lynn's car she could feel the other girl's coiled tension. Sherry was uncertain. She didn't know if she should wait until Lynn mentioned what was troubling her, or if she should say something to start Lynn talking. She chose the latter.

"Are you enjoying the camp this summer?" Sherry asked.

Lynn shrugged. "It's different."

"How's that?"

Again her shoulders went up and down in a dismissive gesture. The long country road that led to the small city of Arrow Flats twisted and turned as it came down off the rugged hillside.

"Have you noticed Peter Towne?" Lynn said quietly.

"The lifeguard?"

"Yeah…it's his second year here, too. Last summer we were good friends. We even managed a few emails since then. I wished him a Merry Christmas, and he said hi at Easter and asked if I'd be coming back to camp. That sort of thing."

As Sherry recalled Peter was a handsome sun-bleached blond who patrolled the beaches during the afternoons and worked in the kitchen after dinner. "How old is he?"

"Nineteen—the same age as me."

Whatever was troubling Lynn obviously had to do with Peter. "He seems to be nice enough," Sherry prodded.

"Peter is more than nice," Lynn said dreamily. "He's wonderful."

Sherry wouldn't have gone quite that far to describe him. "So you two worked together last year?"

"Right."

The teenager focused her attention on the roadway, which was just as well since it looked treacherous enough to Sherry.

"What makes you bring up his name?" Sherry ventured.

"Peter's?"

"Yes, Peter's."

"Did I bring him up?"

"Lynn, honestly, you know you did."

The other girl bit the corner of her bottom lip. "Yeah, I suppose his name did casually pop into the conversation."

It seemed to Sherry that Lynn regretted having said anything so she let the matter drop. "I had my first run-in with ol' Ironjaw."

"You mean Mr. Roarke?"

"He and I had a difference of opinion about the evening sessions. He'd prefer for me to discuss the intricacies of U.S. foreign policy. I'd rather tell ghost stories. I imagine we'll agree on a subject somewhere in between."

"I saw you put something on the podium for him this morning."

"Lesson plans."

"He's making you do that?"

"As a precaution."

"Oh."

Lynn eased the car to a stop at the crossroads before turning onto the main thoroughfare. Arrow Flats was about ten miles north of the camp. Sherry noticed the way Lynn's hands tightened around the steering wheel at the intersection.

"Two nights ago, I couldn't sleep," she said in a strained, soft voice. "I decided to take a walk down to the lake. There was an old piece of driftwood there so I sat down. Peter…couldn't sleep, either. He happened to come by, and we sat and talked."

"From everything I've seen, Peter's got a good head on his shoulders."

"It was nearly one before we went back to camp. He kissed me, Sherry. I never wanted anyone to kiss me more than Peter that night in the moonlight. It was so romantic and…I don't know…I've never felt this strongly about any boy before."

Sherry could identify with that from her own surprising experience with Roarke, the night before on the porch. Maybe there really was something in the air, she thought hopefully.

"Now every time I look at Peter I see the same longing in his eyes. We want to be together. I…I think we might be falling in love."

Sherry thought it was wonderful that the friendship between the two had blossomed into something more, but she understood her friend's dilemma. The camp was no place for a romance.

"Oh, Sherry, what am I going to do?" Lynn cried. "If Mr. Roarke finds out, both Peter and I will be fired."

Five

"Good morning, Miss White."

Roarke's voice rose to greet her when Sherry slipped into the back row of chairs in the staff room. She muttered something appropriate, embarrassed once again to be caught coming in tardy for yet another early-morning session. On this particular day, her only excuse was laziness. The alarm had gone off and she simply hadn't been able to force herself out of bed.

As always, Roarke waited until she'd settled in her seat before continuing.

Sherry tried her best to listen to the day's announcements, but her mind drifted to Lynn and Peter and their predicament. It felt peculiar to side with Roarke, but Sherry agreed that a romance at camp could be a source of problems for the teenagers and everyone else. Lynn's attraction to Peter was a natural response for a nineteen-year-old girl, and Peter was a fine boy, but camp simply wasn't the place for their courtship. Sherry had advised her friend to "cool it" as much as possible. In a couple of months, once camp had been dismissed, the two could freely date each other.

Sherry's gaze skidded from the tall blond youth back

to Lynn. They were doing their best to hide their growing affection for each other, but from the not-so-secret glances they shared, their feelings were all too obvious to Sherry. And if she could see how they felt, then it probably wouldn't be long before Roarke did, too.

A chill ran up Sherry's arms, and she bundled her sweater more tightly around her. She yawned and rubbed the sleep from her eyes, forcing herself to pay attention to what Roarke was saying.

The others were beginning to stand and move about before she realized that the session had come to a close. Still she didn't move. Standing, walking about, thinking, seemed almost more than she could manage, especially without coffee. What she needed was some kind soul to intravenously feed her coffee a half hour before the alarm went off.

"Is there a problem, Miss White?"

Sherry glanced up to find Roarke looming above her.

"No," she mumbled and shook her head for emphasis.

"Then shouldn't you be getting back to your cabin?"

She nodded, although that, too, required some effort. A giant yawn escaped, and she cupped her hand over her mouth. "I suppose."

"You really aren't a morning person, are you?"

Her smile was weak. "It just takes a while for my heart to start working."

Roarke straddled a seat in the row in front of her and looped his arm over the chair back as he studied her. She looked as though she could curl up right there and without much effort go back to sleep. The urge to wrap her in his arms and press her head against his shoulder was a powerful one. He could almost feel her softness yield against his muscled strength. Forcibly, he shook the image from his mind. His gaze softened as he studied her. "Did you hear anything of what I said?"

"A…little," she admitted sheepishly. He grinned at that, and she discovered that his smile completely disarmed her. Speaking of getting her heart revved up! One smile from Jeff Roarke worked wonders. No man had the right to look that good this early in the day. Her mind had come up with a list of concrete arguments for him to postpone these sessions to a more decent time of day, but one charming look shot them down like darts tossed at fat balloons. "I don't know what it is about mornings, but I think I may be allergic to them."

"Perhaps if you tried going to bed earlier."

"It doesn't work," she said, and yawned again. "I wish I could, but at about ten every night, I come alive. My best work is done then."

Roarke glanced at his watch, nodded and stood. "Your cabin is due in the mess hall in fifteen minutes."

Sherry groaned and dropped her feet. Her hand crisply touched her forehead. "Aye, aye, Commandant, we'll be there."

Roarke chuckled and returned her mock salute.

When Sherry entered the cabin, she discovered the girls in a frenzy. Pamela had climbed to the top of the dresser and was huddled into a tight ball clutching Ralph, her knees drawn up against her chest. Gretchen faced the open door, a broom raised above her head, prepared for attack, while Jan and Jill were nearby, holding their shoes in their fists like lethal weapons.

Ginny, the high-school girl who had been assigned to stay in the cabin while Sherry was at the morning meeting, was in as much of a tizzy as the girls.

"What happened?" Sherry demanded.

"He tried to kill Ralph," Pamela screamed hysterically.

"Who?"

"I read about things like this," Diane inserted calmly. "It's a natural instinct."

"What is?" Sherry cried, hurriedly glancing from girl to girl.

"The cat," Jan and Jill said together.

"Ralph was nearly eaten," Pamela cried.

Sherry sagged with relief. "That's only Buttercup."

"Buttercup!"

"He belongs to Mr. Roarke."

"Mr. Roarke has a cat named Buttercup?" Gretchen said, lowering her broom to the floor. A look of astonishment relaxed her mouth into a giant O.

"Apparently so."

"But he tried to get Ralph." Pamela opened her hands and the rodent squirmed his head out between two fingers and looked around anxiously.

"We need a cage," Sherry said decisively. "That shoe box is an open invitation to Buttercup."

"Can't Mr. Roarke keep his cat chained up or something?" Wendy suggested. The Barbies and Kens were scattered freely across the top of her mattress.

"I thought we weren't supposed to have pets," Gretchen complained. "I find Mr. Roarke's actions highly contradictory."

"Since we're keeping Ralph, mentioning Buttercup to Mr. Roarke wouldn't be wise," Sherry informed them all with a tight upper lip.

"But we've got to do something."

"Agreed." One glance at her watch confirmed that her troop was already late for breakfast. "Hurry now, girls. I'll take care of everything."

"Everything?" Pam's bold eyes studied her counselor.

"Everything," Sherry promised.

By the time Sherry and her cabin arrived at the mess hall, the meal was already half over. The stacks of pancakes had cooled and the butter wouldn't melt on them properly. Gretchen complained loudly enough for the cooks in the kitchen to hear.

In the middle of breakfast, Sally produced a huge tannish-gold hawk moth she'd trapped the night before and passed it around the table for the others to admire, momentarily distracting Sherry.

"Girls, manners. Please," she cried, when Wendy stuffed a whole pancake into her mouth. Sticky syrup oozed down the preteen's chin.

"But we have to hurry," Diane complained.

"You'll talk to Mr. Roarke about his cat, won't you?" Pam wanted to know as she climbed out of her chair, her meal untouched.

"I'll see what I can do."

When the last girl had left the dining room, rushing to her class, Sherry sighed with relief. She hadn't so much as had her first cup of coffee and already the morning was a disaster.

"Problems, Miss White?" Again Roarke joined her. He handed her a steaming mug of coffee.

She cupped it in her hands and savored the first sip. "Bless you."

Roarke pulled out a chair and sat down across the table from her.

"Buttercup paid us another visit," she said after a long moment.

"Ralph?"

"Is fine...."

His jaw tightened. "May I remind you, Miss White, that it is against camp policy to have a pet?"

"Ralph is a mascot, not a pet."

"He's a nuisance."

"You're a fine one to talk," she returned heatedly and took another sip of coffee in an effort to fortify her courage. "As for camp policy—what do you call Buttercup?"

"The camp cat."

"She's not a pet?"

"Definitely not."

"My foot!"

"If there are problems with Ralph, then the solution is simple—get rid of him."

"No way! Pamela's strongly attached to that animal." Surely Roarke wasn't heartless enough to take away a child's only friend. "This is the first time Pamela's spent more than a few days away from home and family. That hamster's helping her through the long separation from her brother and parents."

"If I allow Ralph to stay, then next year someone is likely to bring a boa constrictor and claim it's not a pet, either."

Sherry twisted her head from side to side, glancing around her. Lowering her voice, she leaned forward and whispered, "No one knows about Ralph. I'm not telling, the girls aren't telling. That only leaves you."

"Buttercup knows."

"She's the problem," Sherry gritted between clenched teeth.

"No," Roarke countered heatedly. "Ralph is."

From the hard set of the director's mouth, Sherry could see that discussing this matter would solve nothing. She held up both palms in a gesture of defeat. "Fine."

"Fine what? You'll get rid of Ralph?"

"No! I'll take care of the problem."

"How?" He eyed her dubiously.

"I haven't figured that out yet, but I will."

"That I don't doubt. Just make sure I don't know a thing about it."

"Right." Playfully, she winked at him, stood, reached for a small pancake, popped it into her mouth and left the dining hall. She understood Roarke's concerns, but occasional exceptions to rules had to be made. Life was filled with too many variables for him to be so hard-nosed and stringent. Ralph had to be kept a secret, and more than that, the rodent couldn't continue to rule the lives of her seven charges. A cage was one solution, but knowing Buttercup, that wouldn't be enough to distract the cat from her daily raids.

She found the answer in town. That night after the evening meal, Sherry carried in the solution for the girls to examine.

"What's it for?" Sally wanted to know when Sherry held the weapon up for their inspection.

Bracing her feet like a trained commando, Sherry looped the strap over her shoulder and positioned the machine gun between her side and her elbow. "One shot from this and Buttercup won't be troubling Ralph again."

"You aren't going to…" Jan began.

"…shoot him?" Jill finished her twin's worried query.

The girls' eyes widened as Sherry's mouth twisted into a dark scowl. "You bet. I'm going to shoot him— right between the eyes."

A startled gasp rose.

"Miss White," Pamela pleaded, "I don't want you to hurt Buttercup."

Sherry relaxed and lowered the machine gun, grinning. "Oh, I wouldn't do that. This is a battery-operated water gun."

"Really?"

"A water gun?" Diane asked, lowering her book long enough to examine Sherry's weapon.

"I knew that all along," Gretchen said.

"I'll show you how it works." Sherry aimed it at her bedroom door and fingered the trigger. Instantly, a piercing blast of water slammed against the pine door ten feet away.

"Hey, not bad," Diane said excitedly.

"It's as accurate as a real gun," Sherry explained further. "After a shot or two from this beauty, Buttercup won't come within fifty feet of this cabin."

The spontaneous applause gladdened Sherry's heart. She accepted the praise of her charges with a deep bow and placed the weapon in her bedroom. Returning a moment later, she entered the room with a dark visor pulled down low over her eyes. She held out a deck of cards toward them.

"Okay, girls, gather 'round," she called. "Tonight's lesson is about statistics." Grinning, she playfully shuffled the cards from one hand to the other. "Anyone here ever played gin rummy?"

If Sherry had thought her charges enjoyed the fairy tales, they were even more ecstatic about cards. Their ability to pick up the rules and the theory behind the games astonished her. It shouldn't, she mused. After all, they were real live wizards!

After she'd taught them the finer points of gin rummy, the seven had eagerly learned hearts and canasta. At nine-thirty, their scheduled bedtime, the girls didn't want to quit. Cards were fun, and there was precious little time for that commodity at Camp Gitche Gumee.

When the lights were out, Sherry lay in her own bed, wishing she could convince Jeff Roarke that camp, no matter what its specialty, was meant to be fun.

No longer did Sherry think of Roarke in negative terms. They still disagreed on most subjects, but the wall of annoyance and frustration she'd felt toward him had been a means of hiding the sensual awareness she experienced the minute he walked into the room. It pricked her pride to admit that she was like every other female over the age of ten at Camp Gitche Gumee. Jeff Roarke was as sexy as the day was long. And since this was June, the days were lengthy enough to weave into the nights.

Sherry expelled her breath and sat upright in the darkened room. It wasn't only thoughts of Roarke that were keeping her awake. Guilt played a hand in her troubled musings. Her father and Phyliss were probably worried sick about her. Leaving the way she had hadn't been one of her most brilliant schemes. By this time, no doubt, her stepmother had hired a detective agency to track her down.

Contrite feelings about her evening sessions with the girls also played a role in her sleeplessness. She'd handed in the lesson plans to Roarke knowing that she'd misled him a little. It was stretching even her vivid imagination to link canasta and gin rummy with statistics.

This summer had been meant to be carefree and fun, and Sherry was discovering that it was neither. Tossing aside the blankets, she reached for her jeans. Because her cell was in a dead zone, she searched for a pay phone and found one situated on the campgrounds, directly across from her cabin. If she talked to her father, she'd feel better and so would he. There wasn't any need to let Phyliss know where she was, but it couldn't hurt to keep in touch.

Pulling her sweatshirt over her head, Sherry tiptoed between the bunks and quietly slipped out the front door. The night was filled with stars. A light breeze hummed across the treetops, their melody singing in the wind. Cotton-puff clouds roamed across the full moon, and the sweet scent of virgin forest filled the air. Tucking the tips of her fingers in her hip pockets, Sherry paused to examine the beauty of the world around her. It was lovely enough to take her breath away.

The pay phone was well lit, and Sherry slipped her quarters into the appropriate slot. Her father's groggy voice greeted her on the fourth ring.

"Hello?"

"Hi, Dad."

"Sherry?"

"How many other girls call you Dad?"

Virgil White chuckled. "You give me as much trouble as ten daughters."

"Honestly, Dad!"

"Sherry, where —"

Her father's voice was interrupted by a frenzied, eager one. "Oh, thank God," a female voice came over the line. "Sherry, darling, is that you?"

"Hello, Phyliss. Listen, I'm in a pay phone and I've only got a few quarters—"

"Virgil, do something…. Sherry's nearly penniless."

"Phyliss, I've got money, it's just quarters I'm short of at the moment. Please listen, I wanted you to know I'm fine."

"Are you eating properly?"

"Three meals a day," Sherry assured her.

"Liver once a week? Fresh fruit and vegetables?"

"Every day, scout's honor."

The sound of her father's muffled laugh came over the wire. "You were never a Girl Scout."

Phyliss gasped and started to weep silently.

"Dad, now look what you've done. Phyliss, I'm eating better than ever, and I have all the clothes I could possibly need."

"Money?"

"I'm doing just great. Wonderful, in fact. I don't need anything."

"Are you happy, baby?"

"Very happy," Sherry assured them both.

"Where are you—at least tell me where you are," her stepmother cried.

Before she could answer, the operator came back on the line. "It will be another $1.25 for the next three minutes."

"I've got to go."

"Sherry," Phyliss pleaded. "Remember to eat your garlic."

"I'll remember," she promised. "Goodbye, Dad. Goodbye, Phyliss." At age twenty-five she didn't require a babysitter, although Phyliss seemed convinced otherwise. As the good daughter, Sherry had done her duty.

Gently she replaced the telephone receiver, feeling much relieved. Looking up she discovered Roarke advancing toward her across the lawn in long, angry strides. Just the way he moved alerted her to his mood. She stiffened with apprehension and waited.

"Miss White." His gaze traveled from the telephone

to her and then back again. "Who's staying with the girls?"

"I...they're all asleep. I didn't think it would matter if I slipped out for a couple of minutes. I'd be able to hear them if there was a problem," she went on hurriedly, trying to cover her guilty conscience. She really hadn't been gone more than a few minutes.

The anger left Roarke as quickly as it came. He knew he was being unreasonable. The source of his irritation wasn't that Sherry had stepped outside her cabin. It was the fact that she'd made a phone call, and he strongly suspected she'd contacted a male friend.

Self-consciously, Sherry lowered her head. "You're right, I shouldn't have left the girls. I'll make sure it doesn't happen again."

"It's a pleasure to have you agree to something I say," Roarke said, his face relaxing into a lazy smile.

Sherry's heart lifted in a strange, weightless way. She'd been tense, conscious once more that she'd done something to irritate him.

"I'll walk you back to your cabin," he suggested softly.

"Thank you." It wasn't necessary, for the cabin was within sight, but she was pleased Roarke chose to keep her company.

"I saw you on the phone," he commented, without emotion, a few minutes later. "I suppose you were talking to one of your boyfriends."

"No," she corrected, "that was my family."

Roarke cleared his throat and straightened. "Is there a boyfriend waiting for you back...where was it again?"

"Seattle, and no, not anyone I'm serious about." Sherry went still, her heart thundering against her breast. "And you? Do y-you have someone waiting in Berkeley?"

Roarke shook his head. There was Fiona, another professor whom he saw socially. They'd seen each other in a friendly sort of way for a couple of years, but he hadn't experienced any of the physical response with Fiona that he did with Sherry. Come to think of it, Fiona's views on romance were much like his own. "There's no one special," he said after a moment.

"I see." From the length of time that it took him to tell her that, Sherry suspected that there was someone. Her spirits dipped a little. Good grief, did she think he lived like a hermit? He couldn't! He was too good-looking.

Roarke's gaze studied her then, and in the veiled shadows of the moon, Sherry noted that it was impossible to make out the exact color of his eyes. Green or tawny, it didn't seem to matter now that they were focused directly on her. Her breathing became shallow and she couldn't draw her gaze away from him. Finally, she dragged her eyes from his and looked up at the stars.

Neither spoke for several minutes, and Sherry found the quiet disarming.

"You seem to have adjusted well to the camp," Roarke commented. "Other than a few problems with mornings, that is."

"Thank you."

"How did the lessons go this evening? Wasn't it statistics you told me you were planning to discuss?"

Sherry swallowed down her apprehension and answered in a small, quiet voice. "Everything went well."

Roarke's eyes narrowed as he watched her struggle to keep the color from invading her cheeks. She might think herself clever, but he wasn't completely ignorant of her creative efforts.

"I may have deviated a little," she admitted finally.

"A little?" Roarke taunted. "Then let me ask you something."

"Sure." She tried to make her voice light and airy, belying her nervousness.

"Who got stuck with the queen of spades?"

"Gretchen," she returned automatically, then slapped her hand over her mouth. "You know?"

"I had a fair idea. A little friendly game of hearts, I take it?"

She nodded, studying him. "And canasta and gin rummy, while I was at it."

He did nothing more than shake his head in a gesture of defeat.

"Are you going to lecture me?"

"Will it do any good?"

Sherry laughed softly. "Probably not."

"That's what I thought."

She relaxed, liking him more by the minute. "Then you don't mind?"

Roarke sighed. "As long as you don't fill their minds with romantic tales, I can live with it. But I'd like to ask about the lesson plans you handed in to me."

"Oh, I was planning to do everything I wrote down… I'm just using kind of…unorthodox methods."

"I figured as much." His face relaxed into a languorous smile. "I'd guess that the night you intend a study on finances is really a game of Monopoly."

"Yes…how'd you know?" He didn't sound irritated, and that lent Sherry confidence.

"I have my ways."

"Do you know everything that goes on in this camp?"

She'd never met anyone like him. Roarke seemed to be aware of every facet of his organization. How he managed to keep tabs on each area, each cabin, was beyond her.

"I don't know everything," he countered, "but I try...."

As his voice trailed off the beauty of the night demanded their attention. Neither spoke for a long moment, but neither was inclined to leave, either.

"I find it surprising that you don't have someone special waiting for you." Roarke's voice was low, slightly bewildered.

"It's not so amazing." A few men had been attracted to her—before Phyliss had drilled them on their intentions, invited them to dinner and driven them crazy with her wackiness. A smile touched the corner of Sherry's mouth. If there was anyone she wished to discourage, all she need do was introduce him to her loony stepmother. "I'm attending Seattle Pacific full-time, and I'm involved in volunteer work. There isn't much opportunity to date."

While she was speaking, Roarke couldn't stop looking at her. Her profile was cast against the moon shadows of the dark violet sky. The light breeze flirted with her hair, picking up the wispy strands at her temple and puffing them out and away from her face. Her dark hair was thick and inviting. He thought about lifting it in his hands, running the silky length through his fingers, burying his face in it and breathing in its fresh, clean scent. From the moment she'd first entered his office he'd thought she was pretty. Now, Roarke studied her and saw much more than the outward loveliness that had first appealed to him. Her spirit was what attracted him, her love of life, her enthusiasm.

He'd never seen a cabin enjoy their counselor more. Sherry was a natural with the children. Inventive. Clever. Fun. A hundred times since she'd arrived at camp, he'd been angered enough to question the wisdom of having hired her. But not tonight, not when he was standing in the moonlight with her at his side. Not now, when he would have given a month's wages to taste her lips and feel her softness pressed against him. She was a counselor and he was the camp director, but tonight that would be so easy to forget. He was a man so strongly attracted to a woman that his heart beat with the energy of a callow youth's.

Sherry turned and her gaze was trapped in Roarke's. At his tender look, her breath wedged in her lungs, tightening her chest. Her heart thudded nervously.

"I guess I should go inside," she said, hardly recognizing her own voice.

Roarke nodded, willing her to leave him while he had the strength to resist her.

Sherry didn't move; her legs felt like mush and she sincerely doubted that they'd support her. If she budged at all, it was to lean closer to Roarke. Never in all her life had she wanted a man to hold her more. His gaze fell to her mouth and she moistened her lips in invitation, yearning for his kiss.

Roarke groaned inwardly and closed his eyes, but that only served to increase his awareness of her. She smelled of flowers, fresh and unbelievably sweet. Warmth radiated from her and he yearned to wrap his arms around her and feel for himself her incredible softness.

"Good night, Sherry," he said forcefully, bounding to his feet. "I'll see you in the morning."

Sherry sagged with relief and watched as Roarke marched away with the purposeful strides of a marine drill sergeant, his hands bunched into tight fists at his sides.

Six

"I demand that we form a search party," Wendy cried, crossing her arms over her chest and glaring at Sherry. "You did when Ralph was missing."

"Wendy, sweetheart," Sherry said, doing her best to keep calm. "Ralph is a living, breathing animal."

"A *rodent hamustro* actually," Sally informed them knowingly.

"Whatever. The thing is—a misplaced Ken doll doesn't take on the urgency of a missing rodent."

"But someone stole him."

Sherry refused to believe that any of the girls would want Ken badly enough to pilfer him from their cabin mate. "We'll keep looking, Wendy, but for now that's the best we can do."

Hands placed on her hips, the youngster surveyed the room, her eyes zeroing in on her peers. "All right, which one of you crooks kidnapped Ken-Richie?"

"Wendy!"

"I refuse to live in a den of thieves!"

"No one stole your doll," Sherry said for the tenth time. "I'm sure you misplaced him."

Wendy gave her a look of utter disgust. "No one in

their right mind would misplace the one and only love of Barbie-Brenda's life."

"Oh, brother," Sherry muttered under her breath.

"I think Longfellow might have done it," Pamela inserted cautiously. "It's just the kind of thing a ghost would do."

"Longfellow?"

"Right," Jan and Jill chimed in eagerly. "Longfellow."

Wendy considered that for a moment, then agreed with an abrupt nod of her head and appeared to relax somewhat. "You know, I bet that's exactly what did happen."

Over the next two days the standard response to any problem was that Longfellow was responsible. Soon the entire camp was buzzing with tales of the make-believe ghost Sherry had invented.

"My mattress has more bumps than a camel," Gretchen claimed one morning.

Six preteens glanced at the chronic complainer and shouted in unison, "Longfellow did it!"

Ralph's cage door was left open to Pamela's dismay. "Longfellow," the girls informed her.

At breakfast, the Cream of Wheat had lumps. The girls looked at one another across the table, nodded once and cried, "Longfellow."

Every time Sherry heard Longfellow's name, she cringed inwardly. That Roarke hadn't heard about the friendly ghost was a miracle in itself. Sherry had already decided that when he did, she would give an Academy Award performance of innocence. By now, news of the spirit had infiltrated most of the cabins, although Sherry couldn't be certain which counselors had heard about him and who hadn't. She did notice, however, that the boys from Fred Spencer's cabin were unusually quiet about the ghost.

Since the night she'd met Roarke at the pay phone, their relationship had gone from a rocky, rut-filled road to a smooth-surfaced freeway. He'd shocked her by ordering coffee served at their early-morning meetings. Although he hadn't specifically said it was for her benefit, Sherry realized it was.

"I don't think I ever thanked you," she told him one morning early in the week, when the staff had been dismissed from their dawn session.

"Thanked me?" He looked up from reading over his notes.

"For the coffee." She gestured with the foam cup, her gaze holding his.

Roarke grinned and his smile alone had the power to set sail to her heart.

"If you'll notice, I haven't been late for a single meeting since the coffee arrived. Fact is, I don't even need to open my eyes. The alarm goes off, I dress in the dark and follow my nose to the staff room."

"I thought that would induce you to get here on time," he said, his gaze holding hers.

Actually, the coffee hadn't a single thing to do with it. She came because it was the only time of day she could count on seeing Roarke. Generally, they didn't have much cause to spend time with each other, because Roarke was busy with the running of the camp and Sherry had her hands full with her seven charges. That he'd become so important to her was something of a quandary for Sherry. The minute he discovered she'd falsified her references, she'd be discharged from Camp Gitche Gumee. More than once Lynn had specifically told her that Mr. Roarke could forgive anything but dishonesty. Sherry had trouble being truthful with herself about her feelings for Roarke for fear of what she'd discover.

"I'm pleased the coffee helped." Dragging his eyes away from her, Roarke closed his notebook and walked out of the building with her. "Have you spent much time stargazing lately?"

She shook her head and yawned. "Too tired."

"Pity," he mumbled softly.

It would have been so easy for Sherry to forget where they were and who they were. She hadn't ever felt so strongly attracted to a man. It was crazy! Sometimes she wasn't completely sure she even liked him. Yet at all hours of the day and night, she found herself fantasizing about him. She imagined him taking her in his arms and kissing her, and how firm and warm his mouth would feel over her own. She dreamed about how good it would be to press her head against his shoulder and lean on him, letting his strength support her. She entertained fleeting fantasies even while she was doing everything in her power to battle the unreasonable desires.

"By the way," Roarke said, clearing his throat, "one of the references you gave me came back marked 'no such address.'"

"It did?" Sherry's heart pounded, stone-cold. She'd prayed he wouldn't check, but knowing how thorough Roarke was made that wish nothing short of stupid. She was going to have to think of something, and quick.

"You must have listed the wrong address."

"Yes…I must have."

"When you've got a minute, stop off at the office and you can check it over. I'll mail it out later."

"Okay."

They parted at the pay phone, Sherry heading toward her cabin and Roarke toward the mess hall.

The cabin was buzzing with activity when Sherry stepped inside, but when the girls spied their counselor the noise level dropped to a fading hum and the seven returned to their tasks much too smoothly.

Suspicious, Sherry paused and looked around, not knowing exactly what she expected to find. The girls maintained a look of innocence until Sherry demanded, "What's going on here?"

"Nothing," Sally said, but she was smiling gleefully.

Sherry didn't believe it for a moment. "I don't trust you girls. What are you up to?" Her gaze swept the room. Never in her life had she seen more innocent-looking faces. "Ginny?" Sherry turned her questions to the teenager who replaced her in the early mornings when she attended the staff meetings.

"Don't look at me." The teenager slapped her sides, looking as blameless as the girls.

"Something's going on." Sherry didn't need to be a psychic to feel the vibrations in the air. The seven wizards were up to something, and whatever it was seemed to have drawn them together. All through breakfast they were congenial and friendly, leaning over to whisper secrets to one another. Not a single girl found fault with another. Not even Gretchen! Their eyes fairly sparkled with mischief.

Sherry studied them as they left the mess hall for their classes. Her group stayed together, looking at one another and giggling with impish delight without provocation.

"Hi." Lynn pulled out a bench and sat across the table from Sherry.

Sherry pulled her gaze away from her wizards. "How's it going?"

Lynn shrugged. "I'm not sure."

"Have you been seeing Peter?"

"Are you kidding?" Lynn asked and snorted softly. "We know better. Oh, we see each other all the time, but never alone."

"That's wise."

"Maybe, but it sure is boring." Lynn lifted her mug to her lips and downed her hot chocolate. "It's getting so bad that the eighth-grade boys are beginning to look good to me."

Despite the seriousness of her friend's expression, Sherry chuckled. "Now that's desperate."

"Peter and I know the minute we sneak off, we'll get caught—besides we aren't that stupid." She sagged against the back of her chair. "I don't know what it is, but Mr. Roarke has this sixth sense about these things. He always seems to know what's happening. Peter's convinced that Mr. Roarke is aware of everything that goes on between us."

"How could he be?"

Lynn shrugged. "Who knows? I swear that man is clairvoyant."

"I'm sure you're exaggerating." Sherry's stomach reacted with dread. She was living with a time bomb ticking away—she'd been a fool to have tried to slip something as important as references past Roarke.

"Since Peter and I haven't seen a lot of each other," Lynn continued, "we've been writing notes. It's not the same as being alone with each other, but it's been…I don't know…kind of neat to have his thoughts there to read over and over again."

Sherry's nod was absent.

"Well, I suppose I'd best get to work." Lynn swung her leg over the bench and stood.

"Right," Sherry returned, "work."

"By the way, I think the signs are cute."

Sherry's head shot up. "Signs? What signs?"

"The ones posted outside the cabins. How'd you ever get Mr. Roarke to agree to it? Knowing the way he feels about fairy tales, it's a wonder—"

Rarely had Sherry moved more quickly. She'd known her girls were up to something. Signs. Oh, good heavens! By the time she was outside the mess hall, she was able to view exactly what Lynn had been talking about. In front of each cabin a large picket had been driven into the ground that gave the cabin a name. The older boys' quarters was dubbed Pinocchio's Parlor, the younger Captain Hook's Hangout, Cinderella's Castle was saved for the older girls. But by far the largest and most ornate sign was in front of her own quarters. It read: The Home of Sherry White and the Seven Wizards.

The quality of the workmanship amazed Sherry. Each letter was perfectly shaped and printed in bright, bold colors. There wasn't any question that her girls were responsible, but she hadn't a clue as to when they'd had the time. It came to her then—they hadn't painted the markers themselves, but ordered them. Gretchen had claimed more than once that her father had given her her own American Express card. She'd flashed it a couple of times, wanting to impress the others. Of all the girls, Gretchen had taken hold of the tales of fantasy with rare enthusiasm. She loved them, and had devoured all the books Sherry had given her.

"Miss White," Roarke's voice boomed from across the lawn.

Her blood ran cold, but she did her best not to show her apprehension. "Yes?"

He pointed in the direction of his headquarters. "In my office. Now!"

The sharp tone of his voice stiffened Sherry's spine. If she'd been in a less vulnerable position, she would have clicked her heels, saluted crisply and marched toward him with her arms stiffly swinging at her sides. Now, however, was not the time to display any signs of resistance. She could recognize hot water when she saw it!

It seemed the entire camp came to a halt. Several children lingered outside the classrooms, gazing her way anxiously. Teachers found excuses to wander around the grounds, a few were in a cluster, pointing in Sherry's direction. Fred Spencer, the counselor who had made his opinion of Sherry's ideas well-known, looked on with a sardonic grin. Each group paused to view the unfolding scene with keen interest.

Before Sherry had a chance to move, Roarke was at her side. Over the past few weeks, she'd provoked the stubborn camp director more times than she could count, but never anything like what he suspected she'd done this time. A muscle worked its way along the side of Roarke's jaw, tightening his features.

"M-maybe it would be best to talk about this after you've had the opportunity to cool down and think matters through. I realize it looks bad, but—"

"We'll discuss it *now*."

"Roarke, I know you're going to have trouble believing this, but I honestly didn't have anything to do with those signs."

His lip curled sardonically. "Then who did?"

Sally and Gretchen hurried up behind the couple.

"Don't be angry with Miss White," Gretchen called out righteously. "She told you the truth. In fact, the signs are a surprise to her, too."

"Then just who is responsible?" Roarke demanded.

The two youngsters looked at each other, grinned and shouted their announcement. "Longfellow!"

"Who?"

Sherry wished the ground would open so she could dive out of sight and escape before anyone noticed. If Roarke had frowned upon her filling the girls' heads with fairy tales as "romantic nonsense," then he was sure to disapprove of her creating a friendly spook.

"Longfellow's our ghost," Sally explained, looking surprised that the camp director wouldn't know about him. "Longfellow, you know—he lives here."

"Your what? Who lives where?" Roarke managed to keep his voice even, but the look he gave Sherry could have forced the world into another ice age.

"The ghost who lives at Camp Gitche Gumee," Sally continued patiently. "You mean, no one's ever told you about Longfellow?"

"Apparently not," Roarke returned calmly. "Who told *you* about him?"

"Miss White," the girls answered in unison, sealing Sherry's fate.

"I see."

Sherry winced at the sharpness in his voice, but the girls appeared undaunted—or else they hadn't noticed.

"You aren't upset with Miss White, are you?" Sally asked, her young voice laced with concern. "She's the best counselor we ever had."

"The signs really were Longfellow's idea," Gretchen added dryly.

Roarke made a show of looking at his watch. "Isn't

it about time for your first class? Miss White and I will discuss this matter in private."

The children scurried off to their class, leaving Sherry to face Roarke alone. Having two of her charges defend her gave her ego a boost. Roarke was so tall and overpowering that she realized, not for the first time, how easily he could intimidate her. Sherry squared her shoulders, thrust out her chin and faced him head-on.

She turned to squarely face him, hands on her hips, feet braced. "I have other plans this morning. If you'll excuse me, I would—"

"The only place you're going is my office."

"So you can shout at me?"

"So we can discuss this senselessness," he said through gritted teeth.

It wouldn't do any good to argue. He turned and left her to follow him, and because she had no choice, she did as he requested, dreading the coming confrontation. For the past few days at camp, Sherry had come to hope that things would be better between her and Roarke. The night he'd walked her back from the pay phone had blinded her to the truth. They simply didn't view these children in the same way. Roarke saw them as miniature adults and preferred to treat them as such. Sherry wanted them to be children. The clash was instinctive and intense.

Roarke held the office door open for her and motioned with his hand for her to precede him. Sherry remembered what Lynn had said about Roarke firing people in the mornings. Well here she was, but she wasn't going down without an argument. Of all the things she had expected to be dismissed over—falsified references, misleading lesson plans, ghost stories—now it looked as if she was going to get the shaft for something she hadn't even done.

"I already told you I had nothing to do with the signs," she spoke first.

"Directly, that may be true, but indirectly there's no one more to blame."

Sherry couldn't argue with him there. She was the one who had introduced the subject to her seven wizards.

"If you recall, I specifically requested that you stop filling the children's heads with flights of fancy."

"I did," she cried.

"It's all too obvious that you didn't." His shoulders stiff, he marched around the desk and faced her. Leaning forward, he placed his hands on the desktop and glared in her direction. "You're one of those people who request an inch and take a mile."

"I…"

"In an effort to compromise, I've given you a free hand with the nine- and ten-year-old girls. Against my better judgment, I turned my head and ignored gin rummy taught in place of statistics classes. I looked the other way while you claimed to be studying frozen molecules when in reality you were sampling homemade ice cream."

"Don't you think I know that? Don't you think I appreciate it?"

"Obviously, you don't," he insisted, his voice gaining volume with each word. "Not if you stir up more problems by conjuring up a…a ghost. Of all the insane ideas you've come up with, this one takes the cake."

"Longfellow's not that kind of spook."

His eyes narrowed with a dark, furious frown. "I suppose you're going to tell me—"

"He's a friendly spirit."

Roarke muttered something she couldn't hear and raked a hand through his hair. "I can't believe I'm listening to this."

"The girls have a hundred complaints a day. Wendy's Ken-Richie doll is missing—one of the ten she brought to camp."

"Ken who?"

"Her Ken doll that she named Ken-Richie."

"What the devil is a Ken doll?"

"Never mind, that's not important."

"Anything you do is important because it leads to disaster."

"All right," Sherry cried, losing patience. "You want to know. Fine. Ken-Richie is the mate for Barbie-Brenda. Understand that?"

Roarke was growing more frustrated by the minute. There had been a time when he felt he had a grip on what was happening at camp, but from the minute Sherry had arrived with her loony ideas, everything had slid downhill.

"Anyway," Sherry continued, "it's so much easier to blame Longfellow for stealing Ken-Richie than to have a showdown among the girls."

"Who actually took the…doll?"

"Oh, I don't know—no one does. That's the point. But I'm sure he'll turn up sooner or later."

"Do you actually believe this…Longfellow will bring him back?" Roarke taunted.

"Exactly."

"That's pure nonsense."

"To you, maybe, but you're not a kid and you're not a counselor."

"No, I'm the director of this camp, and I want this stupidity stopped. Now."

Sherry clamped her mouth closed.

"Is that understood, Miss White?"

"I can't."

"What do you mean you can't? You have my direct order."

She lifted her palms and shrugged her shoulders. "It's gone too far. Almost everyone in the entire camp knows about Longfellow now. I can't put a stop to the children talking about him."

Roarke momentarily closed his eyes. "Do you realize what you've done?"

"It was all in fun."

He ignored that. "This camp has a reputation for academic excellence."

"How can a make-believe ghost ruin that?"

"If you have to ask, then we're in worse trouble than I thought."

Sherry threw up her hands in disgust. "Oh, honestly!"

"This is serious."

Now it was Sherry's turn to close her eyes and gain control of her temper. She released a drawn-out sigh. "What is it you want me to do?" she asked, keeping her voice as unemotional as possible. "I realize that within a few weeks, I've managed to ruin the reputation for excellence of this camp—"

"I didn't say that," he countered sharply.

"By all rights I should be tossed out of here on my ear...."

Roarke raised both hands to stop her. They glared at

each other, each daring the other to speak first. "Before this conversation heats up any more, I think we should both take time to cool down," Roarke said stiffly.

Sherry met his gaze defiantly, her heart slamming against her breast with dread. "Do you want me to leave?"

He hesitated, then nodded. "Maybe that would be best."

Tears burned the backs of her eyes and her throat grew tight with emotion. "I'll...pick up my check this afternoon."

Roarke frowned. "I want us to cool our tempers— I'm not firing you."

Sherry's head snapped up and her heart soared with hopeful expectation. Roarke wasn't letting her go! She felt like a prisoner who'd been granted a death row pardon by the governor at the last minute. "But it's morning—you mean, you don't want me to leave Camp Gitche Gumee?"

Roarke looked confused. "Of course not. What are you talking about?"

The flood of relief that washed over her submerged her in happiness. It took everything within Sherry not to toss her arms around his neck and thank him.

With as much aplomb as she could muster, she nodded, turned around and walked across the floor, but paused when she reached the door. "Thank you," she whispered, sincerely grateful.

It seemed the entire camp was waiting for her. A hush fell across the campus when she appeared. Faces turned in her direction and Lynn gestured with her hands, wanting to know the outcome.

Sherry smiled in response, and it seemed that everyone around released an elongated sigh. All except

Fred Spencer, who Sherry suspected would be glad to see her leave. Until that moment, Sherry hadn't realized how many friends she'd made in her short stay at Camp Gitche Gumee. Her legs felt weak, her arms heavy. Although she'd been fortunate enough to hold on to her job, Roarke remained furious with her. More than anything she wanted to stay for the entire camp session. And not because she was running away from Phyliss, either.

She'd left Seattle because of her crazy, wonderful stepmother, seeking a respite from the woman she loved and didn't wish to offend. But Sherry wanted to stay in California for entirely different reasons. Some of which she sensed she didn't fully understand herself.

At break time, Sally, Gretchen and two other girls came storming into the cabin.

"Hi," Sherry said cheerfully. "What are you guys doing here?"

The girls exchanged meaningful glances. "Nothing," Wendy said, swinging her arms and taking small steps backward.

"We just wanted to be sure everything was okay."

Sherry's answering grin was wide. She winked and whispered, "Things couldn't be better."

"Good!" A breathless Jan and Jill arrived to chime in unison.

Producing a stern look was difficult, but Sherry managed. She pinched her lips together and frowned at her young charges. The last thing she needed was to do something else to irritate Roarke. "Aren't you girls supposed to be in class?"

"Yes, but..."

"But we wanted to see what happened to you."

"It's too hot to sit inside a classroom, anyway," Gretchen grumbled.

"Gretchen's right," Sally added, looking surprised to agree with the complainer.

"Scat," Sherry cried, "before I reach for my machine gun."

The girls let loose with a shriek of mock terror and ran from the cabin, down the steps and across the lawn. Sherry grinned as she watched them scatter like field mice before a prowling cat.

It was then that she noticed the signs in front of each cabin had been removed. She crossed her arms, leaned against the doorjamb and experienced a twinge of regret. Cinderella's Castle was far more original than Cabin Three, even Roarke had to admit that.

After such shaky beginnings, the morning progressed smoothly. Sherry dressed to work out in the exercise room, then ate lunch with the girls, who chatted easily. Sherry took a couple of minutes to joke about the signs, hoping to reassure them that everything was fine. But she didn't mention Longfellow, although the name of the make-believe ghost could be heard now and again from various tables around the mess hall.

Throughout the meal, Sherry had only a fleeting look at Roarke. He came in, made his announcements and joined the teachers at their table for the noontime meal. He spoke to several counselors, but went out of his way to avoid Sherry, she noted. She hadn't expected him to seek her out for conversation, but she didn't appreciate being ignored, either.

Following lunch, Sherry slipped into the exercise room. Ginny was already there working out with the weights.

"Hi," the young assistant greeted, revealing her pleasure at seeing Sherry.

"Hi," Sherry returned, climbing onto the stationary bicycle and inserting her feet into the stirrups. Pedaling helped minimize the effects of all the fattening food she was consuming at camp.

Ginny, strapping a five-pound belt around her own waist, studied Sherry. "You should wear weights if you expect the biking to do any good."

"No thanks," Sherry said with a grin. "I double-knot my shoelaces; that's good enough."

The teenager laughed. "I heard you had a run-in with Mr. Roarke this morning. How'd you make out?"

"All right, I suppose." Sherry would rather let the subject drop with that. The events of the morning were best forgotten.

"From what I heard, he's been on the warpath all day."

"Oh?" She didn't want to encourage the teenager to gossip, but on the other hand, she was curious to discover what had been happening.

"Apparently one of the kids got caught doing something and was sent into Mr. Roarke's office. When Mr. Roarke questioned him, the boy said Longfellow made him do it. Isn't that the ghost you told the girls about not so long ago?"

Sherry's feet went lax while the wheel continued spinning. Oh dear, this just wasn't going to be her day.

"Something else must have happened, too, because he looked as mad as a hornet right before lunch."

Sherry had barely had time to assimilate that when Lynn appeared in the doorway, her young face streaked with tears.

"Lynn, what happened?"

Sherry's friend glanced at Ginny and wiped the tears from her pale cheeks. "Can we talk alone?"

"Sure." Sherry immediately stopped pedaling and climbed off the bike. She placed her arm around the younger girl's shoulders. "Tell me what's upset you so much."

"I-it's Mr. Roarke."

"Yes," she coaxed.

"He found some of the notes I'd written to Peter. He wants to talk to us first thing in the morning…the morning—we both know what that means. I…I think we're both going to be fired."

Seven

Sherry woke at the sound of the alarm and lay with her eyes open, savoring the dream. She'd been in a rowboat with Roarke in the middle of the lake. The oars had skimmed the water as he lazily paddled over the silver water. Everything was different between them. Everything was right. All their disagreements had long since been settled. The pros and cons of a friendly ghost named Longfellow were immaterial. All that mattered was the two of them together.

The looks they'd shared as the water lapped gently against the side of the small boat reminded Sherry of the evening they'd sat on the porch and gazed into the brilliant night sky. Stars were in Sherry's eyes in her dream, too, but Jeff Roarke had put them there.

With a melancholy sigh, she tossed aside the covers and sat on the edge of the mattress. It was silly to be so affected by a mere dream, but it had been so real and so wonderful. However, morning brought with it the chill of reality, and Sherry was concerned for Lynn and Peter. She had to think of some way to help them.

After dressing, she held in a yawn and walked across the thick lawn to the staff room. Her arms were crisscrossed over her ribs, but Sherry couldn't decide if it was to ward off a morning chill or the truth that awaited her outside her dream world. Birds chirped playfully in the background and the sun glimmered through the tall timbers, casting a pathway of shimmering light across the dewy grass, giving Sherry hope.

At the staff room, Sherry discovered that only a couple of the other counselors had arrived. Roarke was there, standing at the podium in the front, flipping through his notes.

With the warm sensations of the dream lingering in her mind, Sherry approached him, noted his frown and waited for him to acknowledge her before she spoke. Uncomfortable seconds passed and still Roarke didn't raise his head. When he did happen to look up, his gaze met hers, revealing little. Sherry realized that he hadn't forgotten their heated discussion. He'd been the one to suggest that they delay talking because things were getting out of hand. But from the narrowed, sharp appraisal he gave her it was all too apparent that his feelings ran as hot today as they had the day before.

"Miss White." He said her name stiffly.

Sherry grimaced at the chill in his voice. "Good morning."

He returned her greeting with an abrupt nod and waited. There had never been a woman who angered Roarke more than Sherry White. This thing with the ghost she'd invented infuriated him to the boiling point, and he'd been forced to ask her to leave his office yesterday for fear of what more he'd say or do. His anger had been so intense that he'd wanted to shake her. *Wrong,* his mind tossed back—it had taken every ounce of determination he possessed, which was considerable, not to pull her into his arms and kiss some common sense into her.

The power she had to jostle his secure, impenetrable existence baffled him. He'd never wanted a woman with the intensity that he wanted Sherry, and the realization was frightening. A full day had passed since their last encounter, and he still wasn't in complete control of his emotions. Even with all this time to cool his temper, she caused his blood to boil in his veins.

No other counselor had been granted the latitude he'd given her. He'd turned a blind eye to her other schemes, accepting lesson plans that stated she would be teaching a study on centrifugal force when he knew she was planning on cooking popcorn. The evening sessions weren't the only rule he'd stretched on her behalf. The other counselors would question the integrity of his leadership if they knew about Ralph. But the ghost— now that was going too far. The truth about Longfellow had driven him over the edge. She'd abused his willingness to adapt to her creativity and in the process infuriated him.

Although his emotions were muddled, no woman had intrigued him the way Sherry did, either. He couldn't seem to get her out of his mind. He had enough problems organizing this camp without entertaining romantic thoughts about one impertinent counselor.

"You wanted something?" he asked, forcing his voice to remain cool and unemotional.

"Yes…you said yesterday that you thought it'd be best if we continued our discussion later."

Roarke glanced at his watch. "There's hardly time now."

"I didn't mean this minute exactly," Sherry answered. He was making this more difficult than necessary.

"Is there something you'd like to say?"

"Yes."

"Then this afternoon would be convenient," Roarke said coldly. He might be agreeing to another meeting, he told himself, but he couldn't see what they had left to say. He'd been angry, true, but not completely unreasonable. Nothing she could say would further her cause.

Sherry tried to smile, but the effort was too much for her. "I'll be there about one o'clock."

"That would be fine."

By now the small room was filled to capacity, and she walked to the back, looking for a chair. Lynn had saved her a seat, and Sherry sank down beside her friend, disappointed and uncomfortable. Twenty minutes into the day and already her dream was shattered. So much for lingering looks and meaningful gazes. She might as well be made of mud for all the interest Jeff Roarke showed her.

The announcements were dealt with quickly, but before Roarke could continue, Fred Spencer, the counselor for the older boys, raised his hand.

"Fred, you had a question?"

"Yes." Fred stood and loudly cleared his throat. "There's been talk all over camp about Longfellow. Who or what is he?"

Sherry scooted so far down in her chair that she was in danger of slipping right onto the floor. Fred Spencer was a royal pain in the rear end as far as Sherry was concerned.

"Longfellow is a friendly ghost," Roarke explained

wryly. "As I understand it, he derived his name from Henry Wadsworth Longfellow, the poet."

Still Fred remained standing. "A ghost?" he shouted. "And just whose idea was this nonsense?" A hum of raised voices followed, some offended, others amused. "Why, I've heard of nothing else for the past twenty-four hours. It's Longfellow this, Longfellow that. The least bit of confusion with kids can become a major catastrophe. These children come to this camp to learn responsibility. They're not gaining a darn thing by placing the blame on an imaginary spirit."

Unable to endure any more, Sherry sprang to her feet. "I believe you're putting too much emphasis on a trivial matter. The camp is visited by a friendly ghost. It doesn't need to be made into a big deal. Longfellow is for fun. The children aren't frightened by him, and he adds a sense of adventure to the few weeks they're here."

"Trivial," Fred countered, turning to face Sherry with his hands placed defiantly on his hips. "I've had nothing but problems from the moment this...this Longfellow was mentioned."

"Sit down, Fred," Roarke said, taking control.

Fred ignored the request. "I suppose you're responsible for this phantom ghost, Miss White? Just like you were with those ridiculous signs?"

Sherry opened and closed her mouth. "Yes, I invented Longfellow."

"I thought as much," Fred announced with profound righteousness.

Again the conversational hum rose from the other staff members, the group quickly taking sides. From bits and pieces of conversations that Sherry heard, the room appeared equally divided. Some saw no problem with Longfellow while others were uncertain. Several made comments about liking Sherry's style, but others agreed with Fred.

Roarke slammed his fist against the podium. "Mr. Spencer, Miss White, I would greatly appreciate it if you would take your seats."

Fred sat, but he didn't remain silent. "I demand that we put an end to this ghost nonsense."

A muscle in Roarke's jaw twitched convulsively and his gaze lifted to meet and hold Sherry's. "I'm afraid it's too late for that. Word of Longfellow is out now, and any effort to do away with him would only encourage the children."

Grumbling followed, mostly from Fred Spencer and his cronies.

"My advice is to ignore him and hope that everyone will forget the whole thing," Roarke spoke above the chatter.

"What about Miss White?" Fred demanded. "She's been nothing but a worry from the moment she arrived. First those ridiculous signs and now this. Where will it end?"

"That's not true," Lynn shouted, and soared to her feet in an effort to defend her friend. She gripped the back of the chair in front of her and glared at the older man. "Sherry's been great with the kids!"

"Miss Duffy, kindly sit down," Roarke barked, raising his hands to quiet the room. The noise level went down appreciably, although the controversy appeared far from settled. He spoke to Fred Spencer with enough authority to quickly silence the other man. "This is neither the time nor the place to air our differences of opinion regarding another counselor's teaching methods."

Sherry wasn't fooled. Roarke wasn't defending her

so much as protecting the others from criticism should Fred take exception to another's techniques. Fred Spencer's reputation as a complainer was as well-known as Gretchen's.

"If the staff can't speak out, then exactly whose job is it?" Fred shouted.

"Mine!" Roarke declared, and the challenge in his voice was loud and infinitely clear.

"Good, then I'll leave the situation in your hands."

From her position, Sherry could see that Fred wasn't appeased. Nor did she believe he would quietly drop the subject. From the beginning, she'd known he disagreed with her efforts with the children. Whenever he had the chance, he put down her ideas and found reason to criticize her.

The remainder of the meeting passed quickly, but not fast enough as far as Sherry was concerned. She and Lynn walked out of the staff room together.

"I can't believe that man," Lynn grumbled. "His idea of having fun is watching paint dry."

"Miss Duffy."

Roarke's cold voice stopped both women. The teenager cast a pleading glance at Sherry before turning around to face her employer.

"I believe we have an appointment."

"Oh, yes," Lynn said with a wan smile. "I forgot."

"I'm afraid that's part of the problem," Roarke returned with little humor. "You seem to be forgetting several things lately."

Sherry opened her mouth to dilute his sarcasm, but one piercing glare from Roarke silenced her. This wasn't her business. She didn't want to say or do anything to irritate him any more. Her greatest fear was that after the events of the morning, Roarke wasn't in any mood to deal kindly with Lynn and Peter. With a heavy heart, Sherry returned to her cabin.

Ginny had roused the girls and there was the typical mad confusion of morning. As usual there was fighting over the bathroom and how long Jan and Jill hogged the mirror to braid each other's hair.

"My mattress has got more lumps than the Cream of Wheat we had the other day," Gretchen muttered, sitting on the side of the bed and rubbing the small of her back.

Pamela was stroking Ralph's head with one finger inserted between the bars of the cage; both girl and rodent appeared content.

Sally and Wendy were already dressed, eager to start another day, while Diane slumbered, resisting all wake-up notices.

Sherry walked over to the sleeping youngster's bunk and pulled out the Hardy Boys novel and flashlight from beneath her pillow. Once she'd turned the ten-year-old on to Judy Blume, Beverly Cleary and other preteen series books, there had been no stopping her. Diane's favorite had turned out to be John D. Fitzgerald's Great Brain books. The dry textbook material had been replaced by fiction, and a whole new world had opened up to the little girl. Now Sherry had to teach Diane about moderation. "Sleeping Beauty," she coaxed softly, "rise and shine."

"Go away," Diane moaned. "I'm too tired."

"Ken-Richie hasn't shown up yet," Wendy muttered disparagingly. "I wonder if Longfellow's ever going to bring him back." She might have mentioned the ghost, but her narrowed gaze surveyed the room, accusing each one who was unlucky enough to fall prey to her eagle eye.

"Hey, don't look at me," Sally shouted. "I wouldn't

take your stupid Ken-Richie if someone paid me. *Batrachoseps attenuatus* are my thing."

"What?" Gretchen demanded.

"The California Slender Salamander," Wendy informed her primly. "If you were really so smart you'd know that."

"I'm not into creepy crawly things the way you are."

"I noticed."

"If my American Express card can't buy it, I don't want it," Gretchen informed her primly.

"It's nearly breakfast time," Sally encouraged Diane, roughly shaking the other girl's shoulder. "And Wednesday's French toast day."

"I don't want to eat," Diane murmured on the tail end of a yawn. "I'd rather sleep."

"Listen, kiddo," Sherry said, bending low and whispering in the reluctant girl's ear, "either you're up and dressed in ten minutes flat, or I won't loan you the other books in the Hardy Boys series."

Diane's dark brown eyes flew open. "Okay, okay, I'm awake."

"Here." Sally handed her a pair of shorts and matching top and Sherry looked on approvingly. The girls were developing rich friendships this summer. Even Gretchen, with her constant complaining and her outrageous bragging, had mellowed enough to find a friend or two. She still found lots of things that needed to be brought to Sherry's attention, like lumpy mattresses and the dangers of sleeping too close to the window. Her credit card was flashed for show when her self-worth needed a boost, but all in all, Gretchen had turned into a decent kid.

Feeling sentimental, Sherry looked around at the group of girls she'd been assigned and felt her heart compress with affection. These seven little wizards had securely tucked themselves into the pocket of her heart. She would long remember them. The girls weren't all she'd recall about this summer, though. Memories of Roarke would always be with her. Her stay at the camp was nearly half over and already she dreaded leaving, knowing it was doubtful that she'd see Roarke again. The thought brought with it a brooding sense of melancholy. For all their differences, she'd come to appreciate him and his efforts at the camp.

Much to Sherry's surprise, and probably Fred Spencer's too, the occupants of Cabin Four arrived in the dining hall precisely on time without stragglers. French toast was a popular breakfast, and when the girls had finished, Pam slipped Sherry an extra piece of the battered bread and asked if she would feed it to Ralph.

"Sure," Sherry assured the child. "But I'll tell him it's from you."

The blue eyes brightened. "He likes you, too, Miss White."

"And I think he's a great mascot for our cabin," she admitted in a whisper.

Once the mess hall had emptied, Sherry poured herself a steaming cup of coffee and paused to savor the first sip. She had just raised the cup to her lips when Lynn entered the room, paused to look around and, seeing Sherry, hurried across the floor.

"How'd it go?"

Lynn bit her lower lip and dejectedly shook her head. "Not good, but then I didn't expect it would with Mr. Roarke in such a lousy mood."

"He didn't fire you, did he?"

"I'm afraid so."

"But..." Sherry was so outraged she could barely speak. She hadn't believed he'd do something so unfair. True, the two had broken camp rules, but so had she, so had everyone. It wasn't as though Lynn and Peter were overtly carrying on a torrid romance. No one was aware that they cared for each other. If Roarke hadn't found their notes, he wouldn't even have known they were interested in each other.

"I have to pack my bags," Lynn said calmly, but her voice cracked, relaying her unhappiness. "But before I go I just wanted to tell you how much I enjoyed working with you." Tears briefly glistened in the other girl's eyes.

Flustered and angry, Sherry ran her fingers through her hair and sadly shook her head. "I don't believe this."

"He was upset, partly because of what happened this morning, I think, and other problems. There's a lot more to being camp director than meets the eye."

Sherry wasn't convinced she would have been so gracious with Roarke had their circumstances been reversed.

"Listen," Sherry said and braced her hands against her friend's shoulders. "Let me talk to him. I might be able to help."

"It won't do any good," Lynn argued. "I've never known Mr. Roarke to change his mind."

While chewing on her lower lip, a plan of action began to form in Sherry's befuddled mind. Sure, she could storm into Roarke's office and demand an explanation, but they'd just end up in another shouting match. As the camp director, he would no doubt remind her that whom he chose to fire or hire was none of her concern. The risk was too great, since he could just as easily dismiss her. Following the events of the past few days, she would be cooking her own goose to openly challenge him.

Her plan was better. Much better.

"Don't pack yet," Sherry said slowly, thoughtfully.

"What do you mean?"

"Just that. Go to your quarters and wait for me there."

"Sherry—" Lynn's brow creased with a troubled frown "—what do you have in mind? You don't look right. Listen, Mr. Roarke isn't having a good day—I don't think this would be the time to talk to him." Lynn paused, set her teeth to chewing at the corner of her mouth and sighed. "At least tell me what you have in mind."

Sherry shook her head, not wanting to answer in case her scheme flopped. "Don't worry. I'll get back to you as soon as possible."

"Okay," Lynn agreed reluctantly.

Sherry headed directly to Roarke's office, knocking politely.

"Yes."

Sherry let herself inside. "Hello."

He hesitated, then raised his pen from the paper. This morning was quickly going from bad to worse. He'd been angry when he'd talked to Lynn and Peter. Angry and unreasonable. He'd dismissed them both unfairly and had since changed his mind. Already, he'd sent a message to the two to return to his office. He never used to doubt his decisions. Everything had been cut-and-dried. Black or white. Simple, uncomplicated. And then Sherry had tumbled into his peaceful existence with all the agility of a circus clown, and nothing had been the same since. He wanted to blame her for his dark mood.

She occupied his mind night and day. Fiona was insipid tea compared to Sherry's sparkling champagne.

Sherry tempted him to the limit of his control. A simple smile left him weak with the longing to hold her. The energy it required for him to keep his hands off her was driving him crazy and weakening him. The situation between them was impossible, and his anger with Lynn and Peter had been magnified by his own level of frustration. And here she was again.

"Is there something I can do for you, Miss White?"

Her steady gaze held his. "I came to apologize."

"What have you done this time?"

His attitude stung her ego, but Sherry swallowed down her indignation and continued calmly. "Nothing new, let me assure you."

"That's a relief."

Her hand touched the chair. "Would you mind if I sat down?"

Pointedly, he glanced at his watch. "If you insist."

Sherry did, claiming the chair. "Things haven't gone very smoothly between us lately, have they?" she began in an even, controlled voice. "I decided that perhaps it would be best if we cleared the air."

"If it's about Longfellow—"

"No," she interrupted, then sadly shook her head. "It's more than that."

For several moments, he was silent, giving Sherry time to compose her thoughts. She'd come on Lynn and Peter's behalf, yearning to turn circumstances so he would rehire the two teenagers. That had been her original intention, but now that she was in his office, she couldn't go through with it. What she felt for this man was real, and their minor differences were quickly forming a chasm between them that might never be spanned unless she took the first leap. She turned her palms up and noted that his hard-sculpted features had relaxed. "I'm not even sure where to start."

"Miss White—"

"Sherry," she cried in frustration. "My name is Sherry and you know it." Abruptly, she made a move to stand, her hands braced on the chair arms. "And this is exactly what I'm talking about. I don't call you Mr. Roarke, yet you insist upon addressing me formally, as if I were…I don't know, some stiff, starched counselor so unbending that I refuse anyone the privilege of using my name."

Roarke's gaze widened with her outburst. "You came to apologize?" He made the statement a question, confused by her irrational behavior. Sherry was too gutsy to be ambivalent. Whatever it was she had to say was real enough to sincerely trouble her.

"That was my original thought," she said, standing now and facing him. "But I'm not sure anymore. All I know is that I want things to be different between us."

"Different?"

"Yes," she cried, "every day, it seems, there's something that I've done to displease you. You can't even look at me anymore without frowning. I don't want to be a thorn in your side or a constant source of irritation."

"Sherry—"

"Thank you," she murmured, interrupting him with a soft smile. "I feel a thousand times better just having you say my name."

The frown worrying Roarke's brow relaxed, and a slow, sensuous smile transformed his face. "Although I may not have said it, I've always thought of you as Sherry."

"But you called me Miss White."

"The others..."

Briefly, she dropped her eyes, remembering Fred Spencer's dislike of her. "I know."

"I haven't been angry with you; it's just that circumstances have been working against us."

"I realize I haven't exactly made things easier."

Sherry didn't know the half of it, Roarke thought. At least once a day he'd been placed in the uncomfortable position of having to defend her from the jealousy and resentment of some others. But she was by far the most popular counselor in camp, and neither he nor anyone else was in any position to argue her success.

"I know, too," she continued, "that you've turned your head on more than one occasion while I've bent the rules and disrupted this camp."

"Bent the rules," he repeated with a soft laugh. "You've out-and-out pulverized them."

Sherry sighed with relief; she felt a hundred times better to be here with him, talking as they once had in the moonlight. How fragile that truce had been. Now, if possible, she wanted to strengthen that.

"It's important to me, Roarke—no matter what happens at camp—that we always remain friends."

Looking at her now, with the sunlight streaming through her chestnut hair, her dark eyes imploring his, searing their way through the thickest of resolves, it wasn't in Roarke to refuse her anything.

"You can be angry with me," she said. "Heaven knows I've given you plenty of reasons, but I have to feel deep down that as long as we share a foundation of mutual respect it won't matter. You could call me Miss White until the year 2020 and it wouldn't bother me, because inside I'd know."

Roarke was convinced she had no idea how lovely she was. Beautiful. Intelligent. Witty. Fun. He felt like a boy trapped inside on a rainy day. She was laughter and sunshine, and he'd never wanted a woman as badly as he did her at this moment.

He stood and moved to her side. Her gaze narrowed with doubt when he placed his hands on her shoulders and turned her to face him. "Just friends?" he asked softly, wanting so much more. After the first week he'd thought to send her straight back to Seattle, because in a matter of only a few days, she'd managed to disturb his orderly life and that of the entire camp. He hadn't. Her candor and wit had thrown him off balance. But staring at her now, he realized her eyes disturbed him far more. She had beautiful, soulful eyes that could search his face as though she were doing a study of his very heart.

Sherry's palms were flattened against Roarke's hard chest; her head tilted back to question the look in his eyes. Surely she was reading more than was there—yet what she saw caused her heartbeat to soar. "Roarke?" she questioned softly, uncertain.

"I want to be more than friends," he answered her, lowering his mouth to hers. "Much more than friends."

Her lips parted under his, warm and moist, eager and curious. For weeks, she'd hungered to feel Roarke's arms around her and experience the taste of his kiss. Now that she was cradled securely in his embrace, the sensation of supreme rightness burned through her. It was as though she'd waited all her life for exactly this moment, for exactly this man.

His arms tightened around her slender frame as he deepened the kiss, his mouth moving hungrily over hers, insistently shaping her lips with his own. Roarke's spirit soared and his heart sang. She'd challenged him, argued with him, angered him. And he loved her, truly loved her. For the first time in his life, he was head over heels in love. He'd thought himself exempt from the emotion, but meeting Sherry had convinced him otherwise.

"Sherry," he groaned. His hands pushing the hair back from her face, he spread eager kisses over her face.

Sherry's world was spinning and she slid her hands up his chest to circle his neck, clinging to the very thing that caused her world to career out of control. She was lost in a haze of longing.

Roarke groaned as she fit her body snugly to his. His mouth crushed hers, sliding insistently back and forth, seducing her with his moist lips until hers parted.

Sherry thought she'd die with wanting Roarke. He tore his lips from hers and held her as though he planned never to let her go. His arms crushed her, but she experienced no pain. Physical limitation prevented her from being any closer, and still she wasn't content, seeking more. His arms were wrapped around her waist, locked at the small of her back. She rotated her hips once, seeking a way to satisfy this incredible longing.

"Sherry, love," he groaned, "don't."

"Roarke, oh, Roarke, is this real?"

"More real than anything I've ever known," he answered, after a long moment.

She moved once more and he moaned, drew in a deep, audible breath and held it so long that she wondered if he planned ever to breathe again.

Raising her hands, she lovingly stroked his handsome face. "I feel like I could cry." She pressed her forehead to his chest. "I'm probably not making the least bit of sense."

Gently, he kissed the crown of her head. "I've wanted to hold you forever."

"Roarke," she said solemnly, raising her eyes to meet his. Her heart was shining through her gaze. "You can't fire Lynn and Peter. Please reconsider."

The words were like a knife ripping into his serenity. Roarke released Sherry and stepped back with such abruptness that she staggered a step. "Is that what this is all about?"

Her eyes mirrored her bewilderment. "No, of course not," she murmured, but she couldn't meet the accusing doubt in his eyes. "Originally I came because Lynn told me you'd dismissed both her and Peter, but…"

"So you thought that if you could get me to kiss you, I'd change my mind."

That was so close to the truth that Sherry yearned to find a hole, curl up in it and magically disappear. The words to explain how everything had changed once she'd arrived at his office died on her lips. It would do no good to deny the truth; Roarke read her far too easily for her to try to convince him otherwise.

She didn't need to say a word for him to read the truth revealed in her eyes. "I see," he said, his voice heavy with resentment.

Sherry flinched. She had to try to explain or completely lose him. "Roarke, please listen. I may have thought that at first, but…"

The loud knock against the door stopped her.

His face had become as hard as stone and just as implacable. "If you'll excuse me, I have business to attend to."

"No," she cried, "at least give me a chance to explain."

"There's nothing more to say." He walked across the room and opened the door.

Lynn and Peter stood on the other side. Instantly Lynn's gaze flew to Sherry, wide and questioning.

"Come in," Roarke instructed, holding open the door. "Miss White was just leaving."

Arching her back, Sherry moved past Peter. As Sherry neared Lynn, the other girl whispered, "Your plan must have worked."

"It worked all right—even better than she dared hope," Roarke answered for her with a look of such contempt that Sherry longed to weep.

Eight

"Sherry, I'm sorry," Lynn said for the tenth time that day. "I didn't think Mr. Roarke could hear me."

Sherry's feet pedaled the stationary bike all the more vigorously. She'd hoped that taking her frustration out on the exercise bike would lessen the ache in her heart. She should have known better. "Don't worry about it. What's done is done."

"But Mr. Roarke hasn't spoken to you in a week."

"I'll survive." But just barely, she mused. When he was through being angry, they'd talk, but from the look of things it could be some time before he cooled down enough to reason matters through. There was less than a month left of camp as it was. For seven, long, tedious days, Roarke had gone out of his way to avoid her. If she were in the same room, he found something important to distract him. At the staff meetings, he didn't call upon her unless absolutely necessary and said "Miss White" with such cool disdain that he might as well have stabbed a hot needle straight through her.

By the sheer force of her pride, Sherry had managed to hold her head high, but there wasn't a staff member at Camp Gitche Gumee who wasn't aware that Sherry

White had fallen from grace. Fred Spencer was ecstatic and thrived on letting smug remarks drop when he suspected there was no one else around to hear. Without Roarke to support her ideas, Fred was given free rein to ridicule her suggestions. Not a single thing she'd campaigned for all week had made it past the fiery tongue of her most ardent opponent.

When Sherry proposed a sing-along at dusk, Fred argued that such nonsense would cut into the cabin's evening lessons. Roarke neither agreed nor disagreed, and the suggestion was quickly dropped. When she'd proposed organized hikes for the study of wildflowers, there had been some enthusiasm, until Fred and a few others countered that crowding too many activities into the already heavy academic schedule could possibly overextend the counselors and the children. A couple debated the issue on Sherry's behalf, but in the long run the idea was abandoned for lack of interest. Again Roarke remained stoically silent.

"Maybe you'll survive," Lynn said, breathing heavily as she continued her sit-ups, "but I don't know about the rest of us."

"Roarke hasn't been angry or unreasonable." Sherry was quick to defend him, although he probably wouldn't have appreciated it.

"No, it's much worse than that," Lynn said with a tired sigh.

"How do you mean?"

"If you'd been here last year, you'd notice the difference. It's like he's built a wall around himself and is closing everybody off. He used to talk to the kids a lot, spend time with them. I think he's hiding."

"Hiding?" Sherry prompted.

"Right." Lynn sat upright and folded her arms around

her bent knees, resting her chin there. "If you want the truth, I think Mr. Roarke has fallen for you, only he's too proud to admit it."

Sherry's feet pumped harder, causing the wheel to whirl and hiss. A lump thickened in her throat. "I wish that were true."

"Look at the way he's making himself miserable and, consequently, everyone else. He's responsible for the morale of this camp, and for the past week or so there's been a thundercloud hanging over us all."

To disagree would be to lie. Lynn was right; the happy atmosphere of the camp had cooled decidedly. As for Roarke caring, it was more than Sherry dared hope. She wanted to believe it, but she sincerely doubted that he'd allow a misunderstanding to grow to such outrageous proportions if he did.

"Have you tried talking to him?" Lynn said next. "It couldn't hurt, you know."

Maybe not, but Jeff Roarke wasn't the only one with a surplus of pride. Sherry possessed a generous portion of the emotion herself.

"Well?" Lynn demanded when Sherry didn't respond. "Have you even tried to tell him your side of it?"

The door to the exercise room opened, and both women turned their attention to the tall, muscular man who stepped inside the room.

"Roarke," Sherry murmured. Her feet stopped pumping, but the rear wheel continued to spin.

He was dressed in faded gray sweatpants and a T-shirt, a towel draped around his neck. Just inside the door, he paused, looked around and frowned.

"Here's your chance," Lynn whispered, struggling to her feet. "Go for it, girl." She gave Sherry the thumbs-up sign and casually sauntered from the room, whistling a cheery tune as she went.

Sherry groaned inwardly; Lynn couldn't have been any more obvious had she openly announced that she was leaving to give the two time to sort out their myriad differences. Sherry nearly shouted for her to come back. Talking to Roarke in his present frame of mind would do no good.

While continuing to pedal, Sherry cast an anxious look in Roarke's direction. He ignored her almost as completely as she strove to ignore him. Lifting the towel from his neck he tossed it over the abdominal board of the weight gym and turned his back to her. The T-shirt followed the towel and he proceeded to go about bench-pressing a series of weights.

Without meaning to watch him, Sherry unwillingly found her gaze wandering over to him until it was all she could do to keep from staring outright. The muscles across his wide shoulders rippled with each movement, displaying the lean, hard build.

The inside of Sherry's mouth went dry; just watching him was enough to intoxicate her senses. His biceps bulged with each push.

The bike wheel continued to spin, but Sherry had long since given up pedaling. She freed her feet from the stirrups and climbed off. Her legs felt shaky, but whether it was from the hard exercise or from being alone with Roarke, Sherry couldn't tell.

"Hello," she said, in a voice that sounded strange even to her own ears. Nonchalantly, she removed the helmet with the tiny side mirror from her head. "I suppose you're wondering why I'd wear a helmet when I'm pedaling a stationary bike," she said, hoping to make light conversation.

* * *

Sweat broke out across Roarke's brow, but it wasn't from the exertion of lifting the weights. It demanded all his concentration to keep his eyes off Sherry. Ignoring her was the only thing that seemed to work. "What you wear is none of my concern," he returned blandly.

"I—I don't feel like I'm really exercising unless I wear the helmet," she said next, looking for a smile to crack his tight concentration. She rubbed her hand dry against her shorts. The helmet hadn't been her only idea. She'd strapped a horn and side mirror onto the handlebars of the bike and had later added the sheepskin cover to pad the seat.

Roarke didn't comment.

He looked and sounded so infuriatingly disinterested that Sherry had to clear the tears from her throat before she went on.

"Roarke," she pleaded, "I hate this. I know you have good reason to believe I plotted...what happened in your office." She hesitated long enough for him to consider her words. "I'll be honest with you—that had been exactly my intention in the beginning. But once I got there I realized I couldn't do it."

"For someone who found herself incapable of such a devious action, you succeeded extremely well." He paused and studied her impassively.

"I w-want things to be different. I don't think we'll ever be able to settle anything here at camp, so I'm proposing that we meet in town to talk. I'll be in Ellen's Café tomorrow at six...it's my day off. I hope you'll meet me there."

Roarke wanted things settled, too, but not at the expense of his pride and self-respect.

"Answer me, Roarke. At least have the common courtesy to speak to me." His manner was so distant, so unconcerned that Sherry discovered she had to look away from him or lose her composure entirely.

"There's nothing to say," he returned stiffly.

The prolonged silence in the room was as irritating as fingernails on a blackboard. Sherry couldn't stand it any more than she could tolerate his indifference.

"If that's the way you wish to leave matters, then so be it. I tried; I honestly tried," she said, with such dejection that her voice was hardly audible.

Pointedly, Roarke looked in another direction.

With the dignity of visiting royalty, Sherry tucked her helmet under her arm, lifted her chin an extra notch and left the room. Jeff Roarke was a fool!

"Miss White, Miss White!" Diane ran across the campus to her side and stopped abruptly, cocking her head as she studied her counselor. "You're crying."

Sherry nodded and wiped the moisture from her face with the back of her hand.

"Are you hurt?"

"In a manner of speaking." Diane was much too perceptive to fool. "Someone hurt my feelings, but I'll be all right in a minute."

"Who?" Diane demanded, straightening her shoulders. From the little girl's stance, it looked as though she was prepared to single-handedly take on anyone who had hurt her friend and counselor.

"It doesn't matter who. It's over now, and I'll be fine in a minute." Several afternoons a week, Sherry sat on the lawn and the children from the camp gathered at her feet. As a natural-born storyteller, she filled the time with make-believe tales from the classics and history.

The children loved it, and Sherry enjoyed spending time with them. "Now what was it you needed?"

Shyly Diane looked away.

Sherry laughed. "No, let me guess. I bet you're after another book. Am I right?"

The youngster nodded. "Can I borrow the last book in the Great Brain series?"

"One great brain to another," Sherry said, forcing the joke.

"Right. Can I?"

Sherry looped her arm around the child's small shoulders. "Sure. This story is really a good one. Tom contacts the Pope...well, never mind, you'll read about it yourself."

They'd gone about halfway across the thick carpet of grass when a piercing scream rent the air. Startled, Sherry turned around and discovered Sally running toward her, blood streaming down her forehead and into her eyes, nearly blinding her.

"Miss White, Miss White," she cried in terror. "I fell! I fell!"

Sherry's stomach curdled at the sight of oozing blood. "Diane," she instructed quickly, "run to the cabin and get me a towel. Hurry, sweetheart."

With her arms flying, Diane took off like a jet from a crowded runway.

"I saw it happen," Gretchen cried, following close on Sally's heels and looking sickly pale. "Sally slipped and hit her head on the side of a desk."

"It's fine, sweetheart," Sherry reassured the injured youngster. She placed her hand on the side of Sally's head and found the gash. Pressing on it gently in an effort to stop the ready flow of blood, she guided the girl toward the infirmary.

"Gretchen, run ahead and let Nurse Butler know we're coming."

"It hurts so bad," Sally wailed.

"I'm sure it does, but you're being exceptionally brave."

Breathless, Diane returned with the towel. Sherry took it and replaced her hand with the absorbent material.

The buzzer rang in the background, indicating that the next class was about to start.

Gretchen and Diane exchanged glances. "I don't want to leave my friend," Gretchen murmured, her voice cracking.

Both Gretchen and Diane were frightened, and sending them away would only increase their dismay and play upon their imaginations, Sherry reasoned.

"You can stay until we're all sure Sally's going to be fine. Now, go do what I said."

Gretchen took off at a full run toward the nurse's office, with Diane in hot pursuit. By the time Sherry reached the infirmary, Kelly Butler, the wife of the younger boys' counselor, had been alerted and was waiting.

"Miss White, I'm scared," Sally said, and sniffled loudly.

"Everything's going to be fine," Sherry assured her mini-scientist, standing close to her side.

"Will you stay with me?"

"Of course." Sally was her responsibility, and Sherry wouldn't leave the child when she needed her most—no matter how much blood there was.

"This way." Kelly Butler motioned toward the small examination room.

While maintaining the pressure to the gash, Sherry

helped Sally climb onto the table. Gretchen and Diane stood in the doorway, looking on.

"You two will have to stay outside until I'm finished," the nurse informed the girls.

Both girls sent pleading glances in Sherry's direction. "Do as she says," Sherry told them. "I'll be out to tell you how Sally is in a few minutes."

Halfway through the examination Sherry started to feel light-headed. Her knees went rubbery, and she reached for a chair and sat down.

"Are you all right?" Kelly asked her.

"I'm fine," she lied.

"Well, it isn't as bad as it looks," the nurse said. She paused to smile at the youngster. "We aren't going to need to take you into Arrow Flats for stitches, but I'll have to cut away your bangs to put on a bandage."

"Can I look at it in a mirror?" The shock and pain had lessened enough for Sally's natural curiosity to take over. "If I don't become a biochemist, then I might decide to be a doctor," Sally explained haughtily.

Sherry's nauseated feeling continued, and forcing a smile, she stood. "I'll go tell Diane and Gretchen that Sally's going to recover before they start planning her funeral."

"Thanks for staying with me, Miss White," Sally said, gripping the hand mirror.

"No problem, kiddo."

"You're going to make a great mom someday."

The way she was feeling caused Sherry to sincerely doubt that. The sight of blood had always bothered her, but never more than now. Taking deep breaths to dispel the sickly sensation, she stood and let herself out of the examination room.

Her two charges were missing. Sherry blinked, but

Jeff Roarke, who sat in their place, didn't vanish. The light-headed feeling persisted, and she wasn't sure if he was real or a figment of her stressed-out senses.

"How is she?" he asked, coming to his feet.

"Fine." At the moment, Sally was doing better than Sherry. "Head wounds apparently bleed a lot, but it doesn't look like she's going to need stitches."

Roarke nodded somberly. "That's good."

"Where are Diane and Gretchen?"

"I sent them back to class," he told her. "I heard how you took control of the situation."

Sherry bristled. "I suppose you'd prefer to believe that I'd panic when confronted with a bleeding child."

"Of course not," he flared.

Trying desperately to control the attack of dizziness, Sherry reached out and gripped the edge of a table.

"You've got blood on your sweatshirt," Roarke said.

Sherry glanced down and gasped softly as the walls started spinning. She wanted to comment, but before she could the room unexpectedly went black.

Roarke watched in astonishment as Sherry crumpled to the floor. At first he thought she was playing another of her silly games. It would be just like her to pull a crazy stunt like that. Then he noted that her coloring was sickly, almost ashen, and immediately he grew alarmed. This wasn't any trick, she'd actually fainted! He fell to his knees at her side and tossed a desperate look over his shoulder, thinking he should call the nurse. But Kelly was already busy with one patient.

He reached for Sherry's hand and lightly slapped her wrist. He'd seen someone do this in a movie once, but how it was supposed to help, he didn't know. His own heart was hammering out of control. Seeing her helpless this way had the most unusual effect upon him. All week he'd been furious with her, so outraged at her underhandedness that he'd barely been able to look at her and not feel the fire of his anger rekindled. He wasn't particularly proud of his behavior, and he'd chosen to blame Sherry for his ill temper and ugly moods all week. He'd wanted to forget she was around, and completely cast her from his mind once the summer was over.

Seeing her now, he felt as helpless as a wind-tossed leaf, caught in a swirling updraft of emotion. He was falling in love with this woman, and pretending otherwise simply wasn't going to work. She was a schemer, a manipulator…and a joy. She was fresh and alive and unspoiled. The whole camp had been brought to life with her smile. Even though this was her first year as a counselor, she took to it as naturally as someone who had been coming back for several summers. Her mind was active, her wit sharp and she possessed a genuine love for the children. They sensed it and gravitated toward her like bees to a blossoming flower.

She moaned, or he thought she did; the sound was barely audible. Roarke's brows drew together in a heavy frown, and he gently smoothed the hair from her face. He'd never seen anyone faint before and he wasn't sure what to do. He elevated her head slightly and noted evidence of fresh tears. Dealing with Sally's injury hadn't been the source of these. From everything Gretchen and Diane had told him, Sherry had handled the situation without revealing her own alarm. No, he had been the one who'd made her cry by treating her callously in the exercise room.

Roarke's eyes closed as hot daggers of remorse stabbed through him. The urge to kiss her and make up for all the pain he had caused her was more than he could resist. Without giving thought to his actions, he secured his arms beneath her shoulders and raised her. Then tenderly, with only the slightest pressure, he bent to fit his lips over hers.

Nine

Sherry didn't know what was happening, but the most incredible sensation of warmth and love surrounded her. Unless she was dreaming, Roarke was kissing her. If this was some fantasy, then she never wanted to wake up. It was as though the entire week had never happened and she was once again in Roarke's arms, reveling in the gentleness of his kiss. The potent feelings were far too wonderful to ignore, and she parted her lips, wanting this moment to last forever. She sighed with regret when the warmth left her.

"Sherry?"

Her eyes blinked open and she moaned as piercing sunlight momentarily blinded her. She raised her hand to shield her vision and found Roarke bending over her.

"Roarke?" she asked in a hoarse whisper. "What happened?"

"You fainted."

She surged upright, bracing herself on one elbow. "I did what?"

Roarke's smile was smug. "You fainted."

It took a moment for her to clear her head. "I did?"

"That's what I just said."

"Sally…"

"Is fine," he reassured her. "Do you do this type of thing often?"

Sherry rubbed a hand over her face, although she remained slightly disoriented. "No, it feels weird. I've never been fond of the sight of blood, but I certainly didn't pass out because of it."

"When was the last time you had something to eat?"

Sherry had to think. Her appetite had been nil for days. She wasn't in the habit of eating breakfast unless it was something like a quick glass of orange juice and a dry piece of toast. This morning, however, she hadn't bothered with either breakfast or lunch.

"Sherry?" he prompted.

"I don't know when I last ate. Yesterday at dinnertime, I guess." She'd been so miserable that food was the last thing she'd wanted.

Roarke's frown deepened, and his arm tightened around her almost painfully. "Of all the stupid—"

"Oh, stop!" She jerked herself free from his grip and awkwardly rose to her feet. "Go ahead and call me stupid…but why stop with that? You've probably got ten other names you're dying to use on me."

Roarke's mouth thinned, but he didn't rise to the bait. The last thing he'd expected was for her to fight him. This woman astonished him. She was full of surprises and…full of promise. Even when she was semiconscious, she had shyly responded to his kiss. He was embarrassed by the impulse now. Who did he think he was—some kind of legendary lover?

"You're coming with me," he commanded.

"Why? So you can shout at me some more?" she hissed at him like a cat backed into a corner, seeking a means of escape.

"No," he returned softly. "So I can get you something to eat."

"I can take care of myself, thank you very much."

Roarke snickered. "I can tell. Now stop arguing."

Sherry closed her mouth and realized what a fool she was being. For an entire week, she'd wanted to talk to him, spend time alone with him, and now when he'd suggested exactly that, she was making it sound like a capital offense.

Roarke led the way out of the infirmary, and Sherry followed silently behind him. The cooking staff were busy making preparations for the evening meal, and the big kitchen was filled with the hustle and bustle of the day. Roarke approached the cook, who glanced in Sherry's direction and nodded as Roarke said something to him.

Roarke returned to her. "He's going to scramble you some eggs. I suggest you eat them."

"I will," she promised, then watched helplessly as Roarke turned and walked out of the mess hall, leaving her standing alone.

Ellen's Café in Arrow Flats was filled with the week-night dinner crowd. Sherry sat at a table by the window and studied the menu, although she'd read it so many times over the past twenty minutes that she could have recounted it from memory.

"Do you want to order, miss?" the young waitress in the pink uniform asked. "It looks like your friend isn't going to make it."

"No, I think I'll hold off for a few more minutes, if you don't mind."

"No problem. Just give the signal when you're ready."

"I will." Sherry felt terrible. More depressed than she

could remember being in months. She'd really hoped tonight with Roarke would make a difference. She'd put such high hopes in the belief that if they could get away from the camp to meet on neutral ground and talk freely, then maybe they could solve the problems between them.

Just then the café door whirled open. Sherry's gaze flew in that direction, her heart rocketing to her throat as Roarke stepped inside. His gaze did a sweeping inspection of the café, and paused when he found Sherry. He sighed and smiled.

To Sherry it seemed that everyone and everything else in the restaurant faded from view.

"Hi," he said, a bit breathlessly, when he joined her. He pulled out the chair across the table from her and sat. "I apologize for being late. Something came up at the last minute, and I couldn't get away."

"Problems at the camp?"

Forcefully, he expelled his breath and nodded. "I don't want to talk about camp tonight. I'm just a lonely college professor looking for a quiet evening."

"I'm just a sweet young thing looking for a college professor seeking a quiet evening."

"I think we've found each other." Roarke's grin relaxed the tight muscles in his face. He'd convinced himself that Sherry had probably left when he didn't show. They both needed this time away from camp. He'd been miserable and so had she.

He was here at last, Sherry mused silently. Roarke was with her, and the dread of the past pain-filled minutes was wiped out with one Jeff Roarke smile.

"Have you ordered?"

Sherry shook her head and lowered her gaze to the memorized menu. "Not yet."

Roarke's eyes dropped, too, as he studied his own. Choosing quickly, he set the menu beside his plate. "I highly recommend the special."

"Liver and onions? Oh, Roarke, honestly." She laughed because she was so pleased he was there, and because liver and onions sounded exactly like a meal he'd enjoy.

"Doubt me if you will, but when liver hasn't been fried to a crisp, it's good."

Sherry closed her menu and set it aside. "Don't be disappointed, but I think I'll go with the French dip."

Roarke grinned and shook his head. "I never would have believed Miss Sherry White could be so boring."

"Boring!" She nearly choked on a sip of iced tea.

"All right, all right, I'll revise that." Laugh lines formed deep grooves at the corners of his eyes. "I doubt that you'll ever be that. I can see you at a hundred and ten in the middle of a floor learning the latest dance step."

Sherry's hand circled her water glass. "I'll accept that as a compliment." But she didn't want to be on any dance floor if her partner wasn't Jeff Roarke, she added silently.

The amusement drained from his eyes. "What you said yesterday hit home."

Sherry looked up and blinked, uncertain. "About what?"

"That you wanted things to be different between us. I do too, Sherry. If we'd met any place but at camp things would be a lot easier. I have responsibilities—for that matter, so do you. Camp isn't the place for a relationship—now isn't the time."

Nervously, her fingers toyed with the fork stem. She didn't know what to say. Roarke seemed to be telling her that the best thing for them to do was ignore the attraction between them, pretend it wasn't there and go on about their lives as though what they felt toward each other made no difference.

"I see," she said slowly, her high spirits sinking to the depths of despair.

"But obviously, that bit of logic isn't going to work," Roarke added thoughtfully. "I've tried all week, and look what happened. I can't ignore you, Sherry, it's too hard on both of us."

The smile lit up her face. "I can't ignore you, either. As it turns out, I'm here and you're here."

His eyes held hers. "And there's no place else I'd rather be. For tonight, at least, we're two people with different tastes and lifestyles who happened to meet in an obscure café in Arrow Flats, California."

Sherry smiled and nodded eagerly.

The waitress came and took their order, and Sherry and Roarke talked throughout the meal and long after they'd finished. They lingered over coffee, neither wanting the evening to end.

They left the café when *the* Ellen herself appeared from the kitchen and flipped the sign in the window to Closed. She paused to stare pointedly at them.

"I have the feeling she wants us to leave," Roarke muttered, looking around and noting for the first time that they were the only two customers left in the café.

Sherry took one last sip of her coffee and placed her paper napkin on the tabletop.

Roarke grinned and scooted back his chair to stand, and Sherry rose and followed him out of the restaurant.

"Where are you parked?" he asked.

"Around the corner."

He reached for her hand, lacing her fingers with his

own. The action produced a soft smile in Sherry. Something as simple as holding her hand would be out of the question at camp. But tonight it was the most natural thing in the world.

"It's nearly ten," Roarke stated, surprise lifting his husky voice.

It astonished Sherry to realize that they'd sat and talked for more than three and a half hours. Although they hadn't touched until just now, she'd never felt closer to Roarke. When they were at camp it seemed that their differences were magnified a thousandfold by circumstances and duty. Tonight they could be themselves. He'd astonished her. Amused her. Being with Roarke felt amazingly right.

He hesitated in front of the SUV. The camp logo was printed on the side panel.

Roarke opened the driver's side for her, and Sherry tossed her purse inside. They stood with the car door between them.

"Roarke?" she whispered, curious. "This may sound like a crazy question, but yesterday when I fainted... did you kiss me?"

His grin was slightly off center as he answered her with a quick nod. He'd felt like a fool afterward, chagrined by his own actions. He wasn't exactly the model for Prince Charming, waking Sleeping Beauty with a secret kiss.

"I thought you must have," Sherry said softly. She'd felt so warm and secure that she hadn't wanted to wake up. "I was wondering is all," she added, a little flustered when he didn't speak.

Roarke caressed her cheek with his right hand. "Are you worried you'll have to pass out a second time before I do it again?"

She smiled at that. "The thought had crossed my mind."

"No," he said softly, sliding his hand down her face to the gentle slope of her shoulder. "Just move out from behind the car door."

Smiling, she did, deliberately closing it before walking into his arms. Roarke brought her close, breathed in the heady female scent of her and sighed his appreciation. His lips brushed against her temple, savoring the marvelous silken feel of her in his arms and the supreme rightness of holding her close. He kissed her forehead and her cheek, her chin, then closed her eyes with his lips.

His gentleness made Sherry go weak. She slipped her arms up his chest and around his neck, letting his strength absorb her weakness.

Roarke paused to glance with irritation at the streetlight, and suddenly decided he didn't care who saw him with Sherry or any consequences he might suffer as a result. He had to taste her. He kissed her then, deeply, yearning to reveal all the things he couldn't say with words. Urgently, his lips moved over hers with a fierce tenderness, until she moaned and responded, opening her mouth to him with passion and need.

Sherry's husky groan of pleasure throbbed in Roarke's ears and raced through his blood like quicksilver. He kissed her so many times he lost count, and she was weak and clinging to his arms. His own self-restraint was tested to the limit. With every vestige of control he possessed, he broke off the kiss and buried his face in her shoulder. He drew in a long breath and slowly expelled it in an effort to regain his wits and composure. He couldn't believe he was kissing her like this, in the middle of the street, with half the town looking on. Holding her, touching her, had been the only matters of importance.

"I'll follow you back to camp," he said, after a long moment.

Still too befuddled to speak, Sherry nodded.

Roarke dropped his arms and watched reluctantly as she stepped away. It was all he could do not to haul her back into his arms and kiss her senseless. From the first moment that he'd watched her interact with the children, Roarke had known that she was a natural. What he hadn't guessed was that this marvelous woman would hold his heart in the palm of her hand. He couldn't tell Sherry what he felt for her now; to do so would create the very problem he strove to avoid between staff members. Romance and camp were like oil and water, not meant to mix. To leave her doubting was regrettable, but necessary until the time was right. Never, in all the years that he'd been camp director, had Roarke more looked forward to August.

Roarke was busy all the following day. Even if he'd wanted, he wouldn't have been able to talk to Sherry. They passed each other a couple of times but weren't able to exchange anything more than a casual greeting. Now, at the end of another exhausting day, he felt the need to sit with her for a time and talk. For as long as he could, he resisted the temptation. At nine-thirty, Roarke decided no one would question it if they saw him sitting on her porch talking.

As he neared her cabin, he heard the girls clamoring inside.

"I saw Buttercup," one of the girls cried, the alarm in her voice obvious.

Roarke glanced around, and sure enough, there was

his calico, snooping around the cabin, peeking through the window. Naturally, Sherry's girls would be concerned over the feline, since they continued to house the rodent mascot. Every other cabin had welcomed Buttercup, but the cat had made his choice obvious and lingered around Sherry's, spending far more time there than at all the others combined. Roarke wasn't completely convinced it was solely the allure of Ralph, the hamster, either. Like almost everyone else in camp, the feline wanted to be around Sherry. Roarke watched with interest whenever Fred Spencer voiced his objections. It was obvious to Roarke that the man was jealous of Sherry's popularity, and his resentment shone through at each staff meeting.

"I saw him, too!" The commotion inside the cabin continued.

Roarke climbed the three steps that led to the front door and crouched down to pick up his cat.

"Now," Sherry's excited voice came at him from inside the cabin.

Just as he'd squatted down the front door flew open, and he looked up to find Sherry standing directly in front of him, pointing a Thompson submachine gun directly at his chest.

Before he could shout a warning, a piercing blast of water hit him square in the chest.

Ten

The blast of water was powerful enough to knock Roarke off balance. Crouched as he was, the force, coupled with the shock of Sherry aiming a submachine gun at him, hurled him backward.

"Roarke," Sherry screamed and slapped her hand over her mouth, smothering her horror, which soon developed into an out-and-out laugh.

Buttercup meowed loudly and scrambled from Roarke's grip, darting off into the night.

"Who the hell do you think you are?" Roarke yelled. "Rambo?" With as much dignity as he could muster, he stood and brushed the grit from his buttocks and hands.

"Mr. Roarke said the H-word." Righteously, Gretchen turned and whispered to the others.

Six small heads bobbed up and down in unison. Unlike Sherry, they recognized that this wasn't the time to show their amusement. Mr. Roarke didn't seem to find the incident the least bit humorous.

"I'm going to say a whole lot more than the H-word if you don't put that gun away," he shouted, his features tight and impatient.

Doing her utmost to keep from smiling, Sherry low-

ered her weapon, pointing the extended barrel toward
the hardwood floor. "I apologize, Roarke, I wasn't aiming for you. I thought Buttercup was alone."

"That cat happens to be the camp pet," he yelled. He
paused and inhaled a steadying breath before continuing. "Perhaps it would be best if we spoke privately,
Miss White. Girls, if you'd kindly excuse us a moment."

"Oh, sure, go ahead," Gretchen answered for the
group, and the others nodded in agreement.

"Sure," Jill and Jan added.

"Feel free," Sally inserted.

"Why not?" Diane wanted to know.

The amusement drained from Sherry's eyes. So much
for the new wonderful understanding between them and
the evening they'd spent together in town. Roarke knew
how much she hated it when he sarcastically called her
Miss White. No one did it quite the way he did, saying
her name with all the coldness of arctic snow. Snow
White. That's what the girls liked to call her when she
wasn't around, although they didn't think she knew it.

Sherry stepped onto the porch and Roarke closed
the door. "I do apologize, Roarke." Maybe if she said it
enough times he'd believe her.

"I sincerely doubt that," he grumbled, swatting the
moisture from his shirt. "Good grief, woman, don't you
ever do anything like anyone else?"

"I was protecting Ralph," she cried, growing agitated. "What was I supposed to do? Invite Buttercup in
for lunch and break seven little girls' hearts?"

"I certainly don't expect you to drown him."

"Fiddlesticks!" she returned, staring him down.
"You're just mad because I got you wet. Believe me, it
was unintentional. If I'd known you were going to be

on the other side of the door, do you honestly think I would have pulled the trigger?"

"You'll do anything for a laugh," he countered.

Sherry was so angry, she could barely speak. "I might as well have, you're a wet blanket anyway." Following that announcement, she marched into the cabin and slammed the door.

Regret came instantly. What was she doing? Sherry wailed inwardly. She'd behaved like a child when she so much wanted to be a woman. But Roarke always assumed the worst of her, and his lack of trust was what hurt most.

Roarke had half a mind to follow her. He opened his mouth to demand that she come back out or he'd have her job, but the anger drained from him, leaving him flustered and impatient. For a full minute he didn't move. Finally he wiped his hand across his face, shrugged and headed back to his quarters, defeated and discouraged.

That night, Roarke lay in bed thinking. Sherry possessed more spirit than any woman he'd ever known. He would have loved to get a picture of the expression on her face once she realized she'd blasted him with that crazy weapon. But instead of laughing as they should have, the episode had ended in a shouting match. It seemed he did everything wrong with this woman. Maybe if he hadn't kept his nose buried in a book most of his life he'd know more about dealing with the opposite sex. Fiona was so much like him that they'd drifted together for no other reason than that they shared several interests. As he lay in bed, Roarke wasn't sure he could even remember what Fiona looked like.

He'd never been a ladies' man, although he wasn't

so naive as to not realize that the opposite sex found him attractive. The scars of his youth went deep. The bookworm, four-eyes and all the other names he'd been taunted with echoed in the farthest corners of his mind. As an adult he'd avoided women, certain that they would find his intelligence and his dedication to the child genius a dead bore. He was thirty-six, but when it came to this unknown, unsettling realm of romance, he seemed to have all the social grace of a sixteen-year-old.

"Miss White," Pamela called into the dark silence.

"Yes?" Sherry sat upright and glanced at the bedside clock. Although it was well past midnight, she hadn't been able to sleep. "Is something wrong, honey?"

"No."

The direction of the small voice told Sherry that Pamela's head hung low. "Come here, and we can talk without waking the others." Sherry patted the flat space beside her and pulled back the covers so Pam could join her in bed.

The little girl found her way in the dark and climbed onto the bed. Sherry sat upright and leaned against the thick pillows, wrapping her arm around the nine-year-old's shoulders.

"It's Ralph's fault, isn't it?" Pamela said in a tiny, indistinct voice.

"What is?"

"That Mr. Roarke yelled at you."

"Honey," Sherry said with a sigh, "how can you possibly think that? I squirted Mr. Roarke with a submachine gun. He had every right to be upset."

"But you wouldn't have shot him if it hadn't been for Ralph. And then he got mad, and it's all my fault because I smuggled Ralph on the airplane without any-one knowing."

"Mr. Roarke had his feathers ruffled is all. There isn't anything to worry about."

Pamela raised her head and blinked. "Will he send you away?"

Knowing that Roarke could still find out that she'd deceived him on the application form didn't lend her confidence. "I don't think so, and if he does it'd be for something a lot more serious than getting him wet."

Pamela shook her head. "My mom and dad shout at each other the way you and Mr. Roarke do."

"We don't mean to raise our voices," Sherry said, feeling depressed. "It just comes out that way. Things will be better tomorrow." Although she tried to give them confidence, Sherry's words fell decidedly flat.

Throughout the staff meeting the following morning Sherry remained withdrawn and quiet. When Roarke didn't seek her out when the session was dismissed, she returned to her cabin. The girls, too, were quiet, regarding her with anxious stares.

"Well?" Gretchen finally demanded.

"Well, what?" Sherry asked, pulling a sweatshirt over her head, then freeing her hair from the constrict-ing collar. When she finished, she turned to find all seven of the girls studying her.

"How did things go with Mr. Roarke?"

"Is he still angry?"

"Did he yell at you again?"

Sherry raised her hands to stop them. "Everything went fine."

"Fine?" Seven thin voices echoed hers.

"All right, it went great," Sherry sputtered. "Okay, let's move it—it's breakfast time."

A chorus of anxious cries followed her announcement as the girls scrambled for their sweaters, books and assorted necessities.

For most of the day Sherry stayed to herself, wanting to avoid another confrontation with Roarke. However, by late afternoon, she felt as if she was suffering from claustrophobia, avoiding contact with the outside world, ignoring the friends she'd made this summer. There had to be a better way!

Most of the classes had been dismissed, and Sherry sat on the porch steps of her cabin, watching the children chasing one another about, laughing and joking. The sound of their amusement was sweet music to her ears. It hadn't been so long ago that she'd wondered about these mini-geniuses, and she was pleased to discover they were learning to be children and have fun. Several of the youngsters were playing games she'd taught them.

A breathless Gretchen soon joined Sherry, sitting on the step below hers. As was often the case when Sherry was within view of the children, she was soon joined by a handful of others.

"Will you tell me the story about how the star got inside the apple again?" Gretchen asked. "I tried to tell Gloria, but I forgot part of it."

"Sure," Sherry said with a grin and proceeded to do just that. Someone supplied her with an apple and a knife, and she took the fruit and cut it crosswise at the end of the story, holding it up to prove to the growing crowd of children that there was indeed a star in every apple.

Fred Spencer approached as she was speaking, pursing his lips in open disapproval. Sherry did her best to ignore him. She didn't understand what Fred had against her, but she was weary of the undercurrents of animosity she felt whenever he was near.

"Shouldn't these children be elsewhere?" he asked, his voice tight and sightly demanding.

Sherry stood and met the glaring dislike in the other man's eyes. "Okay, children, it's time to return to your cabins."

The small group let out a chorus of groans, loudly voicing their protest. Reluctantly, they left Sherry's side, dragging their feet.

"Oh, Miss White," Gretchen murmured. "I forgot to give you this." She withdrew an envelope from her pocket. The camp logo was stamped on the outside. "Mr. Roarke asked me to give this to you. I'm sorry I forgot."

"No problem, sweetheart." Sherry reached for the letter, her heart clamoring. Although she was dying to read what Roarke had written, Sherry held off, staring at her name, neatly centered on the outside of the business-size envelope. Fleetingly, she wondered if Roarke had decided to fire her. Then she realized that he wouldn't have asked Gretchen to deliver the notice; he had more honor than that.

With trembling fingers and a pounding heart, she tore off the end of the envelope, blew inside to open it and withdrew a single sheet. Carefully unfolding it, she read the neatly typed sentence in the middle of the page: Midnight at Clear Lake. Jeff Roarke.

Sherry read the four-word message over and over again. Midnight at the lake? It didn't make sense. Was he proposing that she meet him there? The two of them, alone? Surely there was some other hidden meaning that she was missing. After the incident with Buttercup, he had her so flustered she couldn't think straight.

During the evening, Sherry flirted with the idea of ignoring the note entirely, but as the sun set and dusk crept across the campgrounds, bathing the lush property in golden hues, she knew in her heart that no matter what happened she'd be at the lake as Jeff Roarke had requested.

At five minutes to midnight, she checked her seven charges to be sure they were sleeping and woke Ginny long enough to tell her she was leaving. As silently as possible, Sherry slipped from the cabin. The moon was three-quarters full and cast a silken glow of light on the pathway that led to the lake's edge.

Hugging her arms, Sherry made her way along the well-defined walkway. Roarke's message hadn't been specific about where she was to meet him, although she'd read the note a hundred times. She pulled the letter from the hip pocket of her jeans and read the four words again.

"Sherry."

Roarke's voice startled her. Alarmed, Sherry slapped a hand over her heart.

"Sorry, I didn't mean to frighten you."

"That's all right," she said, quick to reassure him. "I should have been listening for you." He looked so tall and handsome in the moonlight, and her heart quickened at the sight of him. Loving him felt so right. A thousand times over the past few days she'd had doubts about caring so much for Roarke, but not now. Not tonight.

"Shall we sit down?"

"It's a beautiful night, isn't it?" Sherry asked as she lowered herself onto the sandy beach. They used an old log to lean against and paused to gaze into the heavens. The lake lapped lazily a few yards from their feet, and a fresh cool breeze carried with it the sweet, distinctive scent of summer. The moment was serene, unchallenged by the churning problems that existed between them.

"It's a lovely evening," he answered after a moment. He drew his knees up, crossed his legs and sighed expressively. "I'm pleased you did this, Sherry. I felt badly about the episode with the squirt gun."

"You're pleased I did this?" she returned. "What do you mean?"

"The note."

"What note? I didn't send you any note, but I did receive yours."

"Mine!" He turned then to study her, his gaze wide and challenging.

"I have it right here." Agilely, she raised her hips and slipped the paper from her pocket. It had been folded several times over, and her fingers fumbled with impatience as she opened it to hand to him.

Roarke's gaze quickly scanned the few words. "I didn't write this."

"Of course you did." He couldn't deny it now. The stationery and envelope were both stamped with the Camp Gitche Gumee logo.

"Sherry, I'm telling you I didn't write that note, but I did receive yours."

"And I'm telling you I didn't send you one."

"Then who did?"

She shrugged and gestured with her hand. She had a fair idea who was responsible. Her wizards! All seven of them! They'd plotted this romantic rendezvous down to the last detail, and both Roarke and Sherry had been gullible enough to fall for it. It would have angered Sherry, but for the realization that Roarke had wanted these few stolen moments badly enough to believe even the most improbable circumstances.

Roarke cleared his throat. He could feel Sherry's mounting agitation and sought a way to reassure her. He wasn't so naive as not to recognize that her girls must be responsible for this arrangement. The fact was, he didn't care. She was sitting at his side in the moonlight, and it felt so good to have her with him that he didn't want anything to ruin it.

"It seems to me," he said slowly, measuring his words, "that this is Longfellow's doing."

"Longfellow?" Sherry repeated. Then she relaxed, a smile growing until she felt the relief and amusement surge up within her. "Yes, it must be him."

"Camp Gitche Gumee's own personal ghost—Longfellow," Roarke repeated softly. He paused, lifted his arm and cupped her shoulder, bringing her closer into his embrace.

Sherry let her head rest against the solid strength of his shoulder. Briefly she closed her eyes to the swelling tide of emotion that enveloped her. Roarke beside her, so close she could smell his aftershave and the manly scent that was his alone. He was even closer in spirit, so that it was almost as if the words to communicate were completely unnecessary.

Silence reigned for the moment, a refreshing reprieve from the anger that had so often unexpectedly erupted between them. This was a rare time, and Sherry doubted that either would have allowed anyone or anything to destroy it.

"We do seem to find ways to clash, don't we?" Sherry said, after a long moment. They'd made a point of not talking about life at camp when they'd had dinner, but tonight it was necessary. "Roarke, I want you to know I've never intentionally gone out of my way to irritate you."

"I had to believe that," he said softly, gently riffling his fingers through her soft dark hair. "Otherwise I would have gone a little crazy. But maybe I did anyway," he added as an afterthought.

"It just seems that everything I do—is wrong."

"Not wrong," he corrected, his voice raised slightly. "Just different. Some of your ideas have been excellent, but a few of the other counselors…"

"Fred Spencer." Roarke didn't need to mention names for her to recognize her most outspoken opponent. Almost from the day of her arrival, Fred had criticized her efforts with the children and challenged her ideas.

"Yes, Fred," Roarke admitted.

"Why?"

"He's been with the camp for as long as we've been operating, dedicating his summers to the children. It's been difficult for him to accept your popularity. The kids love you."

"But I don't want to compete with him."

"He'll learn that soon enough. You've shown admirable restraint, Sherry. The others admire you for the way you've dealt with Fred." He turned his head just enough so that his lips grazed her temple as he spoke. "The others nothing; *I've* admired you."

"Oh, Roarke."

His arm around her tightened, and Sherry held her breath. The magic was potent, so very potent. His breath fanned her cheek, searing her flushed skin. Without being aware that she was rotating her head toward him, Sherry turned, silently seeking his kiss.

Roarke's hand touched her chin and tipped her face toward him. Sherry stared up at him, hardly able to believe what she saw in his eyes and felt in her heart. His gaze was full of warmth and tenderness and he was smiling with such sweet understanding. It seemed that Roarke was telling her with his eyes how important she was to him, how much he enjoyed her wit, her creativity. Her.

Slowly he bent his head to her. Sherry slid her hands up his shoulders and tilted her head to meet him halfway. He groaned her name, and his lips came down to caress hers in a long, undemanding, tender kiss that robbed her lungs of breath.

The kiss deepened as Roarke sensually shaped and molded her lips to his. Sherry gave herself over to him, holding back nothing. He kissed her again and again, unable to get enough of the delicious taste of her. She was honey and wine. Unbelievably sweet. Sunshine and love. He kissed her again, then lifted his head to tenderly cup her face between his large hands and gaze into her melting brown eyes.

"Roarke?" she said his name, not knowing herself what she would ask. It was in her to beg him not to stop for fear that something would pull them apart as it had so often in the past.

"You're so sweet," he whispered, unable to look away. His mouth unerringly found hers, the kiss lingering, slow and compelling so that by the time he raised his head Sherry was swimming in a sea of sensual awareness.

"Roarke, why do we argue?" Her hands roamed through his hair, luxuriating in the thick feel of it between her fingers. "I hate it when we do."

"Me, too, love. Me, too." His tongue flickered over

the seam of her lips, teasing them at first, then urging them apart. "Sherry, love," he whispered, and inhaled deeply. "We have to stop."

"I know," she answered and nodded.

But neither loosened the embrace. Neither was willing to forsake the moment or relinquish this special closeness growing between them.

Roarke rubbed his moist mouth sensuously against hers. Back and forth, until Sherry thought she would faint with wanting him. When she could tolerate it no longer, she parted her lips and once again they were tossed into the roiling sea of sensual awareness.

Without warning, Roarke stopped.

Kissed into senselessness, Sherry could do nothing to protest. Breathing had taken on an extraordinary effort, and she pressed her forehead to his chest while she gathered her composure.

"Roarke," she whispered.

"In a minute."

She raised her gaze enough to view the naked turmoil that played so vividly across his contorted features.

"I'm sorry," she told him. "So sorry for what happened with Lynn and Peter that day. Sorry for so many things. I can't have you believing that I'd use you like that. I couldn't...I just couldn't."

His smile was so gentle that Sherry felt stinging tears gather in her eyes.

"I know," he said softly. "That's in the past and best forgotten."

"But, Roarke, I..."

He placed his index finger across her lips, stopping her. "Whatever it is doesn't matter."

Sherry's wide-eyed gaze studied him. She dreaded

the moment he learned the whole truth about her. "But I want to be honest."

"You can't lie," he said as his hands lovingly caressed the sides of her face. "I've noticed that about you."

"But I have—"

"It doesn't matter now, Sherry. Not now." Unable to resist her a moment longer, he bent low and thoroughly kissed her again.

Any argument, any desire for Sherry to tell him about the falsified references was tossed aside as unimportant and inconsequential. Within a few weeks the camp session would be over, and if he hadn't discovered the truth by then, she would simply trust that he never would. Later, much later, she'd tell him, and they could laugh about it, her deception would be a source of amusement.

Roarke stood, offering Sherry his hand to help her to her feet. She took it and pulled herself up, then paused momentarily to brush the sand from her backside and look out over the calm lake. This summer with Roarke would always be remembered as special, but she didn't want it to end. The weeks had flown past, and she couldn't imagine ever being without him now.

With a sigh of regret to be leaving the tranquil scene, Roarke draped his arm over her shoulder and guided her back to the main campgrounds.

"My appreciation to Longfellow," he whispered outside her cabin door.

They shared a secret smile, and with unspoken agreement resisted the urge to kiss good-night.

"I'll tell the girls— Longfellow—you said so," she murmured.

Roarke continued to hold her hand. "Good night, Sherry."

"Good night, Roarke." Reluctantly he released her fingers, moved back and turned away.

"Roarke?" she called, anxiously rising onto her tiptoes.

He turned around. "Yes?"

She stared at him, uncertain; her feet returned to the porch. It was in her mind to ask his forgiveness for everything she'd done that had been so zany and caused him such grief. She yearned to confess everything, clean the slate, but anxiety stopped her. She was afraid that a confession now would ruin everything. She could think of only one thing to say. "Friends?"

"Yes," he answered and nodded for emphasis. Much more than friends, he added silently. Much more.

Things changed after that night. Roarke changed. Sherry changed. Camp Gitche Gumee changed.

It seemed to Sherry that Roarke had relaxed and lowered his guard. Gone was the stiff, unbending camp director. Gone was the tension that stretched between them so taut that Sherry had sometimes felt ill with it. Gone were the days when she'd felt on edge every time they met. Now she eagerly anticipated each meeting.

Roarke spent less time in his office and was often seen talking to the children. The sound of his amusement could frequently be heard drifting across the campgrounds. He joked and smiled, and every once in a while, he shared secret glances with Sherry. These rare moments had the most curious effect upon her. Where she'd always been strong, now she felt weak, yet her weakness was her strength. She'd argued with Roarke, battled for changes, and now she was utterly content. The ideas she'd fought so long and hard to instill at the camp came naturally with her hardly saying a word.

The late afternoons became a special time for Roarke and Sherry with the camp kids. All ages would gather around the couple, and Sherry would lead an impromptu songfest, teaching them songs she'd learned as a youngster at camp. Some were silly songs, while others were more serious, but all were fun, and more than anything, Sherry wanted the children of Camp Gitche Gumee to have fun.

Soon the other counselors and staff members joined Sherry and Roarke on the front lawn, and music became a scheduled event of the day, with two other musically inclined counselors taking turns leading the songs. Within a week, as if by magic, two guitars appeared, and Sherry played one and Lynn the other, accompanying the singers.

Someone suggested a bonfire by the lake, and the entire camp roasted marshmallows as the sky filled with twinkling stars.

When they'd finished the first such event in the history of the camp, Gretchen requested that Sherry tell everyone about Longfellow, and after a tense moment, Sherry stepped forward and kept the group spellbound with her make-believe tales.

To her surprise, Roarke added his own comical version of a trick the friendly spook had once played on him when he'd first arrived at the camp. Even Fred Spencer had been amused, and Sherry had caught him chuckling.

The night was such a success that Sherry was too excited to sleep. Her charges were worn-out from the long week and slept peacefully, curled up in their cots. Sherry sat on top of her bed and tried to read, but her thoughts kept wandering to Roarke and how much had changed between them and how much better it was to be with him than any man she'd ever known.

The pebble against her window caught her attention.

"Sherry?" Her name came on a husky whisper.

Stumbling to her feet, she pushed up the window and leaned out. "Who's there?"

"How many other men do you have pounding on your window?"

"Roarke?" Her eyes searched the night for him, but saw nothing. "I know you're out there."

"Right again," he said, and stepped forward, his hands hidden behind his back.

Sherry sighed her pleasure, propped her elbows against the windowsill and cupped her face with her hands. "What are you doing here?"

He ignored the question. "Did you enjoy tonight?"

Sherry nodded eagerly. "It was wonderful." *He* was wonderful!

"Couldn't you sleep?" he asked, then added, "I saw your light on."

"No, I guess I'm too keyed up. What about you?"

"Too happy."

Sherry studied the curious way he stood, with his hands behind him. "What have you got?"

"What makes you think I have anything?"

"Roarke, honestly."

"All right, all right." He swept his arm around and presented her with a small bouquet of wildflowers.

The gift was so unexpected and so special that Sherry was speechless. For the first time in years she struggled to find the words. She yearned to let him know how pleased she was with his gift.

"Oh, Roarke, thank you," she said after a lengthy moment. "I'm stunned." She cupped the flowers in her hand and brought them to her face to savor the sweet scent.

"I couldn't find any better way to let you know I think you're marvelous."

Their eyes held each other's. "I think you're marvelous, too," she told him.

He wanted to kiss her so much it frightened him—more than the night they'd sat by the lake. More than the first time in his office. But he couldn't. She knew it. He knew it. Yet that didn't make refusing her easy.

"Well, I guess I'd better get back."

Sherry's gaze dropped to the bouquet. "Thank you, Roarke," she said again, with tears in her throat. "For everything."

"No." His eyes grew dark and serious. "It's me who should be thanking you."

He'd been gone a full five minutes before Sherry closed the window. She slumped onto the end of her bed and released a sigh. In her most farfetched dreams, she hadn't believed Jeff Roarke could be so wonderfully romantic. Now she prayed nothing would happen to ruin this bliss.

Eleven

"Sleepy and Grumpy are at it again," Wendy told Sherry early the next morning. "Diane doesn't want to wake up and Gretchen's complaining that she didn't sleep a wink on that lumpy mattress."

With only a week left of camp, the girls seemed all the more prone to complaints and minor disagreements. Sherry and the other counselors had endured more confusion these past seven days than at any other time in the two-month-long session of Camp Gitche Gumee.

"Say, where'd you get the flowers?" Jan and Jill blocked the doorway into Sherry's room. Jill had long since lost her tooth, making it almost impossible to tell one twin from the other.

Sherry's gaze moved from Jan and Jill to the bouquet of wildflowers Roarke had given her. They had withered long before, but she couldn't bear to part with them. Every time she looked at his gift she went all weak inside with the memory of the night he'd stood outside her window. The warm, caressing look in his eyes had remained with her all week. She'd never dreamed Jeff Roarke could be so romantic. Pulling herself up straight, Sherry diverted her attention from the wilted wildflowers and thoughts of Roarke. If she lingered any longer, they'd all be late to the mess hall.

Taking charge, Sherry stepped out of her room and soundly clapped her hands twice. "All right, Sleeping Beauty, out of bed."

"She must mean me," Gretchen announced with a wide yawn and tossed aside her covers.

"I believe Miss White was referring to Diane," Wendy said, wrinkling up her nose in a mocking gesture of superiority.

"I was speaking to whoever was still in bed," Sherry said hurriedly, hoping to forestall an argument before it escalated into a shouting match.

"See," Gretchen muttered and stuck out her tongue at Wendy, who immediately responded in kind.

"Girls, please, you're acting like a bunch of ten-year-olds!" It wasn't until after the words had slipped from her mouth that Sherry realized her wizards *were* ten-year-olds! Like Roarke, she'd fallen into the trap of thinking of them as pint-size adults. When she first arrived at camp, she'd been critical of Roarke and the others for their attitudes toward the children. She realized now that she'd been wrong to be so judgmental. The participants of Camp Gitche Gumee weren't normal children. Nor were they little adults, of course, but something special in between.

Moving at a snail's pace that drove Sherry near the brink of losing her control, the girls dressed, collected their books and headed in an orderly fashion for the dining hall. Sherry sat at the head of the table, and the girls followed obediently into their assigned seats.

"I hate mush," Gretchen said, glaring down at the serving bowl that steamed with a large portion of cooked cereal.

"It's good for you," Sally, the young scientist, inserted.

Diane nodded knowingly. "I read this book about how healthy fiber is in the diet."

Gretchen looked around at the faces staring at her and sighed. "All right, all right. Don't make a big deal over it—I'll eat the mush. But it'll taste like glue, and I'll probably end up at Ms. Butler's office having my stomach pumped."

When Roarke approached the front of the mess hall and the podium, the excited chatter quickly fizzled to a low murmur and then to a hush.

Sherry's gaze rested on the tall director, and even now, after all these weeks, her heart fluttered at the virile sight he made. She honestly loved this man. If anyone had told her the first week after her arrival at camp how she'd feel about Jeff Roarke by the end of the summer, she would have laughed in their face. She recalled the way Roarke had irritated her with his dictatorial ways—but she hadn't known him then, hadn't come to appreciate his quiet strength and subtle wit. She hadn't sat under the stars with him or experienced the thrill of his kisses.

Now, in less than a week, camp would be dismissed and she'd be forced to return to Seattle. Already her mind had devised ways to stay close to Roarke in the next months. A deep inner voice urged her to let him speak first. Most of the times they'd clashed had been when Sherry had proceeded with some brilliant scheme without discussing it with Roarke first. No—as difficult as it would be, she'd wait for him to make the first move. But by heaven that was going to be hard.

When Roarke's announcements for the day were completed, the children were dismissed. With an eager cry, they crowded out of the mess hall door to their first classes.

Sherry remained behind to linger over coffee. Soon Roarke and Lynn joined her.

"Morning," Sherry greeted them both, but her gaze lingered on Roarke. Their eyes met in age-old communication, and all her doubts flew out the window and evaporated into the warm morning air. No man could look at her the way he did and not care. Her tongue felt as if it was stuck to the roof of her mouth and her insides twisted with the potency of his charm.

"The natives are restless," Lynn groaned, cupping her coffee mug with both hands.

"Yes, I noticed that," Roarke commented, but his gaze continued to hold Sherry's. With some effort he pulled his eyes away. Disguising his love for her had become nearly impossible. Another week and he would have the freedom to tell her how much he loved her and to speak of the future, but for now he must bide his time. However, now that camp was drawing to a close, he found that his pulse raced like a locomotive speeding out of control whenever he was around her. His hands felt sweaty, his mouth dry. He'd discovered the woman with whom he could spend the rest of his life and he felt as callow as a boy on his first date.

"The kids need something to keep their minds off the last days of camp," Sherry offered.

"I agree," Lynn added. "I thought your suggestion about a hike to study wildflowers was a good one, Sherry. Whatever became of that?"

Fred Spencer had nixed that plan at a time when Roarke might have approved the idea, had he not been so upset with Sherry. She couldn't remember what had been the problem: Longfellow or their first kiss. Probably both. It seemed she'd continually been in hot water with Roarke in the beginning. How things had changed!

"Now that I think about an organized hike, it sounds like something we might want to investigate," Roarke commented, after mulling over the idea for a couple of minutes.

Sherry paused, uncertain, remembering Fred. "What about...you know who?"

"After a couple more days like this one, Fred Spencer will be more than happy to have you take his group for an afternoon."

"We could scout out the area this morning," Lynn suggested, looking to Sherry for confirmation.

"Sure," Sherry returned enthusiastically. She'd had a passion for wildflowers from the time she was ten and camped at Paradise on Washington state's Mount Rainier with her father; hiking together, they'd stumbled upon a field of blazing yellow and white flowers.

"Then you have my blessing," Roarke told the two women, grinning. "Let me know what you find and we'll go from there."

When Sherry and Lynn returned to camp after their successful exploratory hike of the area surrounding the camp and the lake, there was barely time to wash before lunch. Although Sherry was eager to discuss what she'd found with Roarke, she was forced into joining her girls in the mess hall first.

The wizards chattered incessantly, arguing over a paper napkin and a broken shoelace. Wendy reminded everyone that Ken-Richie was still in the hands of a no-good, lily-livered thief and she wasn't leaving camp until he was returned.

The meal couldn't be over soon enough to suit Sherry. The minute the campers were excused, she eagerly crossed the yard to Roarke's office. He hadn't made an appearance at the meal, which was unusual, but it happened often enough not to alarm Sherry.

When she reached his office, she noted that he was alone and knocked politely.

"Come in." His voice was crisp and businesslike.

He looked up from his desk when Sherry walked into the room, but revealed no emotion.

"Is this a bad time?" she asked, hesitant. She could hardly remember the last time he'd spoken to her in that wry tone. Nor had he smiled, and that puzzled her. Her instincts told her something was wrong. His eyes narrowed when he looked at her, and Sherry swallowed her concern. "Do you want me to come back later?"

"No." He shook his head for emphasis. "What did you find?"

"We discovered the most beautiful flowers," she said, warming to the subject closest to her heart. "Oh, Roarke, the trail is perfect. It shouldn't take any more than an hour for the round trip, and I can show the kids several different types of wildflowers. There are probably hundreds more, but those few were the ones I could identify readily. The kids are going to love this."

Her eyes were fairly sparkling with enthusiasm, Roarke noted. Seeing her as she was at this moment made it almost impossible to be angry. His stomach churned, and he looked away, hardly able to bear the sight of her. The phone call had caught him off guard. He'd had most of the morning to come to grips with himself and had failed. Something had to be done, but he wasn't sure what.

* * *

"When do you think we could start the first hikes? I mean if you think we should, that is." He was so distant—so strange. Sherry didn't know how she should react. When she first entered the office she'd thought he was irritated with her for something, but now she realized it was more than anger. He seemed distressed, and Sherry hadn't a clue if the matter concerned her or some camp issue. Several times over the past couple of months, she'd been an eyewitness to the heavy pressures placed upon Roarke. He did a marvelous job of managing Camp Gitche Gumee and had gained her unfailing loyalty and admiration.

"Roarke?"

"Hmm?" His gaze left the scene outside his window and reluctantly returned to her.

"Is something wrong?"

"Nothing," he lied smoothly, straightening his shoulders. "Nothing at all. Now regarding the hike, let's give it a trial run. Take your girls out this afternoon and we'll see how things go. Then tomorrow morning you can give a report to the other counselors."

Sherry clasped her hands together, too excited to question him further. "Thank you, Roarke, you won't regret this."

His stoic look was all the response he gave her.

As Sherry knew they would, the girls, carrying backpacks, grumbled all the way from the camp to the other side of the small lake. The pathway was well-defined, and they walked single file along the narrow dirt passage.

"Just how long is this going to take?"

"My feet hurt."

"No one said the Presidential Commission on Physical Fitness applied at Camp Gitche Gumee."

Listening to their complaints brought a smile to Sherry's features. "Honestly," she said with a short laugh, "you guys make it sound like we're going to climb Mount Everest."

"This is more like K-2."

"K-what?" Jan and Jill wanted to know.

"That's the highest peak in the Himalayas," Sally announced with a prim look. In response to a blank stare from a couple of the others, she added, "You know? The mountain system of south-central Asia that extends fifteen hundred miles through Kashmir, northern India, southern Tibet, Nepal, Sikkim and Bhutan."

"I remember reading about those," Diane added.

Gretchen paused and wiped her hot, perspiring face with the back of her hand. "You read about everything," she told her friend.

"Well, that's better than complaining about everything."

"Girls, please," Sherry said, hoping to keep the peace. "This is supposed to be fun."

"Do we get to eat anything?" Jan muttered.

"We're starved," Jill added.

The others agreed in a loud plea until Sherry reminded them that they'd left the mess hall only half an hour before.

"But don't worry," she said, "it's against camp policy to leave the grounds without chocolate chips." Sherry did her best to hide a smile.

Pamela laughed, and the others quickly joined in.

For all their bickering, Sherry's wizards were doing well—and even enjoying themselves. With so much time spent in the classroom in academic ventures, there had been little planned exercise for the girls.

"We'll take a break in a little bit," Sherry promised.

"It's a good thing," Gretchen muttered despairingly.

"Really," Sally added.

"Don't listen to them, Miss White," Pamela piped in, then lowered her voice to a thin whisper. "They're wimps."

"Hey! Look who's calling a wimp a wimp!"

In mute consternation, Sherry raised her arms and silenced her young charges. Before matters got out of hand, she found a fallen log and instructed them to sit.

Grumbling, the girls complied.

"Snack time," Sherry told them, gathering her composure. She slipped the bulky backpack from her tired shoulders. "This is a special treat, developed after twenty years of serious research."

"What is it?" Sally wanted to know, immediately interested in anything that had to do with research.

Already Gretchen was frowning with practiced disapproval.

Sherry ignored their questions and pulled a full jar of peanut butter from inside her pack. She screwed off the lid and reached for a plastic knife. "Does everyone have clean hands?"

Seven pairs of eyes scanned seven pairs of hands. This was followed by eager nods.

"Okay," Sherry told them next, "stick out an index finger."

Silently, they complied and shared curious glances as Sherry proceeded down the neat row of girls, spreading peanut butter on seven extended index fingers. A loud chorus of questions followed.

"Yuk. What's it for?"

"Hey, what are we suppose to do with this?"

"Can I lick it off yet?"

Replacing the peanut butter in her knapsack, Sherry took out a large bag of semisweet chocolate chips.

"What are you going to do with that?"

"Is it true what you said about not leaving camp without chocolate chips?"

"Scout's honor!" Dramatically, Sherry crossed her heart with her right hand, then tore open the bag of chocolate pieces, holding it open for the girls. "Okay, dip your finger inside, coat it with chips and enjoy."

Gretchen was the first to stick her finger in her mouth. "Hey, this isn't bad."

"It's delicious, I promise," Sherry told her wizards as she proceeded from one girl to the next.

"It didn't really take twenty years of research for this, did it?" Sally asked, cocking her head at an angle to study her counselor.

Sherry grinned. "Well, I was about twenty when I perfected the technique." She swirled her finger in the air, then claimed it was all in the wrist movement.

The girls giggled, and the sound of their amusement drifted through the tall redwoods that dominated the forest. Sherry found a rock and sat down in front of her wizards, bringing her knees up and crossing her ankles.

"When I was about your age," she began, "my dad and I went for a hike much like we're doing today. And like you, I complained and wanted to know how much farther I was going to have to walk and how long it would be before I could have something to eat and where the closest restroom was."

The girls continued licking the chocolate and peanut butter off their fingers, but their gazes centered on Sherry.

"When we'd been gone about an hour, I was convinced my dad was never going back to the car. He kept telling me there was something he wanted me to see."

"Can you tell us what it was?"

"Did you ever find it?"

"Yes, to both questions," Sherry said, coming to her feet. "In fact, I want to show you girls what my father showed me." She led them away from the water's edge. The girls trooped after her in single file, marching farther into the woods to the lush meadow Sherry had discovered with Lynn earlier in the day.

A sprinkling of flowers tucked their heads between the thick grass, hidden from an untrained eye.

"This is a blue monkshood," Sherry said, crouching down close to a foot-tall flower with lobed, toothed leaves and a thin stalk. Eagerly the girls gathered around the stringy plant that bloomed in blue and violet hues.

"The blue monkshood can grow as tall as seven feet," Sherry added.

"That's even bigger than Mr. Roarke," Diane said in awe.

At the sound of Jeff Roarke's name, Sherry's heart went still. She wished now that she'd taken time to talk to him and learn what he'd found so troubling. His eyes had seemed to avoid hers, and he'd been so distant. The minute they returned to camp, Sherry decided, she was going directly to his office. If she wasn't part of the problem, then she wanted to be part of the solution.

"Miss White?"

"Yes?" Shaking her head to clear her thoughts, Sherry smiled lamely.

"What's this?" Wendy pointed to a dwarf shrub with white blossoms and scalelike leaves that was close by.

"These are known as cassiopes." Sherry pronounced

the name slowly and had the girls repeat it after her. "This is a hearty little flower. Some grow as far north as the arctic."

"How'd you learn so much about wildflowers?" Gretchen asked, her eyes wide and curious.

"Books, I bet," Diane shouted.

"Thank you, Miss White," Gretchen came back sarcastically.

"I did study books, but I learned far more by combining reading with taking hikes just like the one we're on today."

"Are there any other flowers here?"

"Look around you," Sherry answered, sweeping her arm in a wide arc. "They're everywhere."

"I wish Ralph were here," Pamela said with a loud sigh. "He likes the woods."

"What's this?" Sally asked, crouched down beside a yellow blossom.

"The western wallflower."

Gretchen giggled and called out, "Sally found a wallflower."

"It's better than being one," came the other girl's fiery retort.

"Girls, please!" Again Sherry found herself serving as referee to her young charges.

"I don't want camp to end," Wendy said suddenly, slumping to the ground. She shrugged out of her backpack and took out her Barbie and Ken dolls, holding them close. "But I want to go home, too."

"I feel the same way," Sherry admitted.

"You do?" Seven faces turned to study her.

"You bet. I love each one of you, and it's going to be hard to tell you all goodbye, but Camp Gitche Gumee isn't my home, and I miss my friends and my family."

As much as she'd yearned to escape Phyliss, Sherry knew what she was saying was in fact true. She did miss her father and her individualistic stepmother. And although California was beautiful, it wasn't Seattle.

"Are you planning to come back next year, Miss White?" Pam asked timidly.

Sherry nodded. "But only if you and Ralph will be here."

"I come back every summer," Gretchen said. "Next year I'm going to have my mother request you as my counselor."

Sherry tucked her arm around the little girl's shoulders and gently squeezed. "What about the lumpy mattress?"

"I said I was going to request you as my counselor, but I definitely don't want the same bed."

Sherry laughed at that, and so did the others.

The afternoon sped past, and by the time they returned to camp, Pam had gotten stung by a bee, Jan and Jill had suffered twin blisters on their right feet and Sally had happened upon two varieties of skipper moths. With a little help from her friends, she'd captured both and brought them back to camp to examine under her microscope.

The tired group of girls marched back into camp as heroes, as the other kids came running toward them, full of questions.

"Where did you guys go?"

"Will our counselor take us on a search for wildflowers, too?"

"How come you guys get to do all the fun stuff?"

"Miss White."

Jeff Roarke's voice reached Sherry, and with a wide, triumphant grin she turned to face him. The smile quickly faded at the cool reception in his gaze, and his dark, brooding look cut through her like a hot needle.

"You wanted to see me?" Sherry asked.

"That's correct." He motioned with his hand toward his office. "Lynn has agreed to take care of your girls until you return."

Lynn's smile was decidedly weak when Sherry's gaze sought out her friend's. Sherry paused, heaved in a deep breath and wiped the grime off the back of her neck with her hand. Her face felt hot and flushed. So much for her triumphant entry into Camp Gitche Gumee.

"Would you mind if I washed up first?" she asked.

Roarke hesitated.

"All right. A drink of water should do me."

They paused beside the water fountain, and Sherry took a long, slow drink, killing time. She straightened and wiped the clear water from her mouth. Again, Roarke's gaze didn't meet hers.

"I-it's about the references, isn't it?" she asked, trying her best to keep her voice from trembling. "I know I shouldn't have falsified them—I knew it was wrong— but I wanted this job so badly and—"

It didn't seem possible that Roarke's harsh features could tighten any more without hardening into granite. Yet, they did, right before her eyes.

"Roarke," she whispered.

"So you lied on the application, too."

Sherry's mind refused to cooperate. "Too? What do you mean, too? That's the only time I ever have, and I didn't consider it a real lie—I misled you is all."

His look seared her. "I suppose you 'misled' me in more than one area."

"Roarke, no…never." Sherry could see two months of

a promising relationship evaporating into thin, stale air, and she was helpless to change it. She opened her mouth to defend herself and saw how useless it would be.

"Are you finished?" Roarke asked.

Feeling sick to her stomach, Sherry nodded.

"This way. There are people waiting to see you."

"People?"

At precisely that moment the door to Roarke's office opened and Phyliss came down the first step. With a wild, excited cry, she threw her arms in the air and cried, "Sherry, baby, I've found you at last."

Before Sherry had time to blink, she found herself clenched in her stepmother's arms in a grip that would have crushed anyone else. "Oh, darling, let me look at you." Gripping Sherry's shoulders, the older woman stepped back and sighed. "I've had every detective agency from here to San Francisco looking for you." She paused and laughed, the sound high and shrill. "I've got so much to tell you. Do you like my new hairstyle?" She paused and patted the side of her head. "Purple highlights—it drives your father wild."

Despite everything, Sherry laughed and hugged her. Loony, magnificent Phyliss. She'd never change.

"Your father is waiting to talk to you, darling. Do you have any idea what a wild-goose chase you've led us on? Never mind that now...we've had a marvelous time searching for you. This is something you may want to consider doing every summer. Your father and I have had a second honeymoon traveling all over the country trying to find you." She paused and laughed. "Sherry, sweetheart," she whispered, "before we leave, you and I must have a girl-to-girl talk about the camp director, Mr. Roarke. Why, he's handsome enough to stir up the blood of any woman. Now don't try to tell me you haven't noticed. I know better."

Flustered, Sherry looked up to find Roarke watching them both, obviously displeased.

Twelve

"Roarke, please try to understand," Sherry pleaded.

A triumphant Phyliss and Virgil White had left Camp Gitche Gumee only minutes before. Her stepmother had evidently decided to look upon Sherry's disappearance as a fun game and had spent weeks tracking her down. It was as if Phyliss had won this comical version of hide-and-seek and could now return home giddy with jubilation for having outsmarted her stepdaughter.

As if that wasn't enough, Phyliss stayed long enough to inspect the camp kitchen and insist that Sherry tint her dark hair purple the minute she returned to Seattle—it was absolutely the in thing. She also enumerated in embarrassing detail Sherry's "many fine qualities" in front of Roarke, then paused demurely to flutter her lashes and announce that she'd die for a stepson-in-law as handsome as he was.

Sherry was convinced the entire camp sighed with relief the minute Phyliss and her father headed toward the exit in their powder-pink Cadillac. As they drove through the campgrounds, Phyliss leaned over her husband and blasted the horn in sharp toots, waving and generously blowing kisses as they went.

During the uncomfortable two hours that her parents were visiting, Sherry noted that Roarke didn't so much as utter a word to her. He carried on a polite conversation with her father, but Sherry had been too busy keeping Phyliss out of mischief to worry about what her father was telling Roarke.

Now that her parents were on their way back to Seattle, Sherry was free to speak to the somber camp director. She followed him back to his office, holding her tongue until he was seated behind the large desk that dominated his room.

"Now that you've met Phyliss you can understand why I needed to get away. I love her…in fact, I think she's wonderful, but all that mothering was giving me claustrophobia."

Roarke's smile was involuntary. "I must admit she's quite an individual."

Without invitation, Sherry pulled a chair close to Roarke's desk and sat down. She crossed her legs and leaned forward. "I—I'm sorry about the references on the application."

"You lied." His voice was a monotone, offering her little hope.

"I—I prefer to think of it as misleading you, and then only because it was necessary."

"Did you or did you not falsify your references?"

"Well, I did have the good references, I just equivocated a little on the addresses…."

"Then you were dishonest. A lie is a lie, so don't try to pretty it up with excuses."

Sherry swallowed uncomfortably. "Then I lied. But you wouldn't have known," she added quickly, before losing her nerve. "I mean, just now, today, when I mentioned it, you looked shocked. You didn't know until I told you."

"I knew." That wasn't completely true, Roarke thought. He'd suspected when the post office returned the first reference and then two of the others; but rather than investigate, Roarke had chosen to ignore the obvious for fear he'd be forced to fire her. Almost from the first week, he'd been so strongly attracted to her that he'd gone against all his instincts. Now he felt like a fool.

Sherry's hands trembled as she draped a thick strand of hair around her ear. She boldly met his gaze. "There are only a few days of camp left. Are…are you going to fire me?"

Roarke mulled over the question. He should. If any of the other counselors were to discover her deception, he would be made to look like a love-crazed fool.

"No," he answered finally.

In grateful relief Sherry momentarily closed her eyes.

"You understand, of course, that you won't be invited back as a counselor next summer."

His words burned through her like a hot poker. In one flat statement he was saying so much more. In effect, he was cutting her out of his life, severing her from his emotions and his heart. The tight knot that formed in her throat made it difficult to speak. "I understand," she said in a voice that was hardly more than a whisper. "I understand perfectly."

Sherry made her way to her cabin trapped in a haze of emotional pain. Lynn's words at the beginning of the camp session about Roarke's placing high regard on honesty returned to taunt her. The night they'd sat by the lake under the stars and kissed brought with it such a flood of memories that Sherry brushed the moisture from her cheek and sucked in huge breaths to keep from weeping.

"Miss White," Gretchen shouted when Sherry entered the cabin. "I liked your stepmother."

"Me, too," Jan added.

"Me, three," Jill said, and the twins giggled.

Sherry's smile was decidedly flat, although she did make the effort.

"She's so much fun!" Wendy held up her index finger to display a five-carat smoky topaz ring.

Costume jewelry, of course, Sherry mused. Phyliss didn't believe in real jewels, except her wedding ring.

"Phyliss told me I could have the ring," Wendy continued, "because anyone who appreciated Barbie and Ken the way I did deserved something special."

"She gave me a silk scarf," Diane said with a sigh. "She suggested I read Stephen King."

"Is her hair really purple?"

"She's funny."

Sherry sat at the foot of the closest bunk. "She's wonderful and fun and I love her."

"Do you think she'll visit next year?"

"I...I can't say." Another fib, Sherry realized. Phyliss wouldn't be coming to Camp Gitche Gumee because Sherry wouldn't be back.

"She sure is neat."

"Yes," Sherry said, and for the first time since she'd spoken to Roarke, the smile reached her eyes. "Phyliss is some kind of special."

"Miss White, Miss White, give me a hug," Sally cried, her suitcase in her hand. Sally was the first girl from Sherry's cabin to leave the camp. Camp Gitche Gumee had been dismissed at breakfast that morning.

The bus to transport the youngsters to the airport was parked outside the dining room, waiting for the first group.

"Oh, Sally," Sherry said, wrapping her arms around the little girl and squeezing her tight. "I'm going to miss you so much."

"I had a whole lot of fun," she whispered, tears in her eyes. "More than at any other camp ever."

Tenderly, Sherry brushed the hair from Sally's forehead. "I did, too, sweetheart."

Goodbyes were difficult enough, but knowing that it was unlikely she would ever see her young charges again produced an even tighter pain within Sherry. She'd grown to love her girls, and the end of camp was all part of this bittersweet summer.

"Miss White," Gretchen cried, racing out of the cabin. "Miss White, guess what?"

Wendy followed quickly on Gretchen's heels. "I want to tell her," the other girl cried. "Gretchen, let me tell her."

A triumphant Wendy stormed to Sherry's side like an unexpected summer squall. "Look!" she declared breathlessly and held up the missing Ken-Richie.

"Where was he?" Sherry cried. The entire cabin had been searching for Ken-Richie for weeks.

"Guess," Gretchen said, hands placed on her hips. She couldn't hold her stern look long, and quickly dissolved into happy giggles. "I was sleeping on him."

Sherry's eyes rounded with shock. "You were sleeping on him?"

"I kept telling everyone how lumpy my mattress was, but no one would listen."

"Little wonder," Wendy said. "You complain about everything."

"Ever hear the story of the boy who cried wolf?" Sally asked.

"Of course, I know that story. I read it when I was three years old," Gretchen answered heatedly.

"But how'd Ken-Richie get under Gretchen's mattress?" Sherry wanted to know.

Wendy shuffled her feet back and forth and found the thick grass of utmost interest. "Well, actually," she mumbled, "I may have put him there for safekeeping."

"You?" Sherry cried.

"I forgot."

A pregnant pause followed Wendy's words before all four burst into helpless peals of laughter. It felt so good to laugh, Sherry decided. The past few days had been a living nightmare. In all that time, she hadn't spoken to Roarke once. He hadn't come to her. Hadn't so much as glanced in her direction. It was as though she were no longer a part of this camp, and he had effectively divorced her from his life.

Past experience in dealing with Roarke had taught Sherry to be patient and let his anger defuse itself before she approached him. However, time was running out; she was scheduled to leave camp the following day.

"The bus is ready," Sally said, and her voice sagged with regret. She hugged Sherry's middle one last time, then climbed into the van, taking a window seat. "Goodbye, Miss White," she cried, pressing her face against the glass. "Can I write you?"

"I'll answer every letter, I promise."

Sherry stood in the driveway until the van was out of sight, feeling more distressed by the moment. When she turned to go back to her cabin, she found Fred Spencer standing behind her. She stopped just short of colliding with his chest.

He frowned at her in the way she found so irritating.

"One down and six to go," she said, making polite conversation.

"Two down," he murmured, and turned to leave.

"Fred?" She stopped him.

"Yes?"

She held out her hand in the age-old gesture of friendship. "I enjoyed working with you this summer."

He looked astonished, but quickly took her hand and shook it enthusiastically. "You certainly added zip to this year's session."

She smiled, unsure how to take his comment.

"I hope you don't think my objections were anything personal," the older man added self-consciously. "I didn't think a lot of what you suggested would work, but you proved me wrong." His gaze shifted, then returned to her. "I hope you come back next summer, Miss White. I mean that."

Fred Spencer was the last person she'd ever expected to hear that from. "Thank you."

He tipped his hand to his hat and saluted her. "Have a good year."

"You, too."

But without Roarke, nothing would be good.

By three that afternoon, Sherry's cabin was empty. All her wizards were safely on their way back to their families. The log cabin that had only hours before been the focal point of laughter, tears and constant chatter seemed hollow without the sound of the seven little girls.

Aimlessly, Sherry wandered from one bunk to another, experiencing all the symptoms of the empty-nest syndrome. With nothing left to do, she went into her room and pulled out her suitcase. Feeling dejected and depressed, she laid it open on top of her mattress and sighed. She opened her drawer, but left it dangling as she slumped onto the end of the bed and reread the book the girls had written for her as a going-away present. Tenderly, her heart throbbing with love, she flipped through each page of the fairy tale created in her honor.

The girls had titled it *Sherry White and the Seven Wizards*. Each girl had developed a part of the story, drawn the pictures and created such a humorous scenario of life at Camp Gitche Gumee that even after she'd read it no less than ten times, the plot continued to make her laugh. And cry. She was going to miss her darling wizards. But no more than she would miss Roarke.

A polite knock at the front of the cabin caught Sherry by surprise. She set the book aside and stood.

"Yes." Her heart shot to her throat and rebounded against her ribs at the sight of Jeff Roarke framed in the open doorway of the cabin.

"Miss White."

He knew how she detested his saying her name in such a cool, distant voice, she thought. He was saying it as a reminder of how far apart they were now, telling her in two words that she'd committed the unforgivable sin and nothing could be the same between them again.

"Mr. Roarke," she returned, echoing his frigid tone.

Roarke's mouth tightened into a thin, impatient line.

"Listen," she said, trying again. "I understand and fully agree with you."

"You do?" His brows came together in a puzzled frown. "Agree with me about what?"

"Not having me back next year. What I did was stupid and foolish and I'll never regret anything more in my life." Her actions had cost her Roarke's love. Because there was nothing else for her to do, Sherry would leave Camp Gitche Gumee and would wonder all her life if she'd love another man with the same intensity that she loved Jeff Roarke.

"Fred told me the two of you had come to terms."

Sherry rubbed her palms together. Fred had smiled at her for the first time all summer. Sherry could afford to be generous with him.

"He isn't so bad," she murmured softly.

"Funny, that's what he said about you."

Sherry attempted a smile, but the effort was feeble and wobbly at best.

With his hands buried deep within his pockets, Roarke walked into the cabin and strolled around the room. The silence hung heavy between them. Abruptly, he turned to face her. "So you feel I made the right decision not to ask you back."

She didn't know why he insisted on putting her through this. "I understand that I didn't give you much of a choice."

"What if I made another request of you?"

Sherry's gaze held his, daring to hope, daring to believe that he would love her enough to overcome her deception. "Another request?"

"Yes." In an uncustomary display of nervousness, Roarke riffled his fingers through his hair, mussing the well-groomed effect. "It might be better if I elaborate a little."

"Please." Sherry continued to hold herself stiff.

"Camp Gitche Gumee is my brainchild."

Sherry already knew that, but she didn't want to interrupt him.

"As a youngster I was like many of these children. I was too intelligent to fit in comfortably with my peers and too immature to be accepted into the adult community."

Sherry just nodded.

"The camp was born with the desire to offer a summer program for such children. I regretted having hired you the first week of camp, but I quickly changed my mind. Maybe because I've never experienced the kind of fun you introduced to your girls, I tended to be skeptical of your methods." He paused and exhaled sharply. So many things were rummaging around in his head. He didn't know if he was saying too much or not enough.

"I'm not sure I understand," Sherry said.

"I'd like you to come back."

"As a counselor?"

"No." He watched the joy drain from her eyes and tasted her disappointment. "Actually I was hoping that you'd consider becoming my partner."

"Your partner?" Sherry didn't understand.

Silently, Roarke was cursing himself with every swearword he knew. He was fumbling this badly. For all his intelligence he should be able to tell a woman he loved her and wanted her to share his life. He rubbed his hand along the back of his neck and exhaled again. None of the things he longed to tell her were coming out right. "I'm doing this all wrong."

"Doing what? Roarke," she said. "You want me to be your partner—then fine. I'd do anything to come back to Camp Gitche Gumee. Work in the kitchen. Be a housekeeper. Even garden. All I want in the world is here."

"I'm asking you to be my partner for more reasons than you know. The children love you. In a few weeks' time, you've managed to show everyone in the camp, including me and Fred Spencer, that learning can be fun. There wasn't a camper here who doesn't want you back next year."

"As your partner what would be my responsibilities?"

"You'd share the management of the camp with me and plan curriculum and the other activities that you've instigated this summer."

Some of the hope that had been building inside her died a silent death. "I see. I'd consider it an honor to return in any capacity."

"There is one problem, however."

"Yes?"

"The director's quarters is only a small cabin."

"I understand." Naturally, he'd want his quarters.

Roarke closed his eyes to the mounting frustration. He couldn't have done a worse job of this had he tried. Finally he just blurted it out. "Sherry, I'm asking you to marry me."

Joy crowded her features. "Yes," she cried, zooming to her feet. Her acceptance was followed by an instantaneous flood of tears.

"Now I've made you cry."

"Can't you tell when a woman is so overcome with happiness that she can't contain herself?" She wiped the moisture from her cheeks in a furious action. "Why are you standing over there? Why aren't you right here, kissing me and holding me?" She paused and challenged him, almost afraid of his answer. "Jeff Roarke, do you love me?"

"Dear heaven, yes."

They met halfway across the floor. Roarke reached for her and hauled her into his arms, burying his face in the gentle slope of her neck and shoulder while he drew in several calming breaths, feeling physically and mentally exhausted. He'd never messed anything up more in his life. This woman had to love him. She must, to have allowed him to put her through that.

Being crushed against him as she was made speaking impossible. Not that Sherry minded. Her brain was so fuddled and her throat so thick with emotion that she probably wouldn't have made sense anyway.

Roarke tucked his index finger beneath her chin and raised her mouth to meet his. His hungry kiss rocked her to the core of her being. Countless times, his mouth feasted on hers, as though it were impossible to get enough of her. Not touching her all these weeks had been next to impossible, and now, knowing that she felt for him the same things he did for her made the ache of longing all the more intense.

Freely, Sherry's hands roved his back, reveling in the muscular feel of his skin beneath her fingers. All the while, Roarke's mouth made moist forays over her lips, dipping again and again to sample her sweet kiss.

"Oh, love," he whispered, lackadaisically sliding his mouth back and forth over her lips. "I can't believe this is happening." He ground his hips against her softness and sharply sucked in his breath. "Nothing can get more real than this."

"Nothing," she agreed and trapped his head between her two hands in an effort to study him. "Why?"

"Why do I love you?"

Her smile went soft. "No, how can you love me after what I did?"

"I met Phyliss, remember?"

"But…"

"But it took me a few days to remember that you'd tried to tell me about the references."

"I did?"

Resisting her was impossible, and he kissed the tip of her pert nose. "Yes. The night at the lake. Remember? I knew then, or strongly suspected, but I didn't want to hear it, didn't want to face the truth because that would have demanded some response. Yet even when I was forced to look at the truth, I couldn't send you away. Doing that would have been like sentencing my own heart to solitary confinement for life."

"Oh, Roarke." She leaned against him, linking her hands at the base of his spine. "I do love you."

"I know."

Abruptly, her head came up. "What about school?"

"What about it?"

"I've only got one year left."

"I wouldn't dream of having you drop out," he rushed to assure her. "You can transfer your credits and finish here in California."

Sherry pressed her head against his heart and sighed expressively. "I can and I will." Being separated from him would be intolerable. Roarke met the intensity of her gaze with all the deep desire of his own. He wanted Sherry to share his life. She was marvelous with the youngsters, and having her work with him at Camp Gitche Gumee would be an advantage to the camp and the children. But with all of his plans, he hadn't paused to think that one day he would have a child of his own. The love he felt for Sherry swelled within him until he felt weak with it. And strong, so strong that he seemed invincible.

"Someday we'll be sending our own wizards to this camp," Sherry told him.

Roarke's hold on her tightened.

"The girls told me you were my prince," she said, her gaze falling on the book her wizards had created.

"We're going to be so happy, Sherry, my love."

"Forever and ever," she agreed, just as the book said.

* * * * *

If you enjoyed these stories, I think you'll like *What She Wants* by Sheila Roberts. Sheila is both a friend of mine and one of my favorite writers.

This excerpt will introduce you to Jonathan Templar and his poker buddies, who are busy trying to figure out…what women want. Then Jonathan stumbles upon a romance novel at the local library sale. That's when he realizes he's found the love expert he's been looking for. Soon Jonathan and his friends are all reading romance—and when all is *read* and done, they're going to be the kind of men that women want!

What She Wants is one of the stories in Sheila's Life in Icicle Falls series, which—like my Cedar Cove books—is set in small-town Washington state. Prepare to fall in love with this town and these characters. And prepare to laugh!

Debbie Macomber

One

Working in such close quarters with a woman that you could bump knees (thighs, and maybe even other body parts) was probably every man's dream job. Except Dot Morrison's knees were knobby and she was old enough to be Jonathan Templar's grandmother. And she looked like Maxine of greeting card fame. So there was no knee (or anything else) bumping going on today.

"Okay, you're good to go," he said, pushing back from the computer in the office at Breakfast Haus, Dot's restaurant. "But remember what I told you. If you want your computer to run more efficiently, you've got to slick your hard drive once in a while."

"There you go talking dirty to me again," Dot cracked.

A sizzle sneaked onto Jonathan's cheeks, partly because old ladies didn't say things like that (Jonathan's grandma sure didn't), and partly because he'd never talked dirty to a woman in his life. Well, not unless you counted a *Playboy* centerfold. When talking with most real-life women, his tongue had a tendency to tie itself into more knots than a bag of pretzels, especially when a woman was good-looking. This, he told himself, was one reason he was still single at the ripe old age of thirty-three. That and the fact that he wasn't exactly the stuff a woman's dreams were made of. It was a rare woman who dreamed of a skinny, bespectacled guy in a button-down shirt. Those weren't the only reasons, though. Carrying a torch for someone tended to interfere with a guy's love life.

Never certain how to respond to Dot's whacked-out sense of humor, he merely smiled, shook his head and packed up his briefcase.

"Seriously," she said, "I'm glad this didn't turn out to be anything really bad. But if it had, I know I could count on you. You can't ever leave Icicle Falls. What would us old bats do when we have computer problems?"

"You'd manage," Jonathan assured her.

"I doubt it. Computers are instruments of torture to anyone over the age of sixty."

"No worries," he said. "I'm not planning on going anywhere."

"Until you meet Ms. Right. Then you'll be gone like a shot." The look she gave him was virtually a guarantee that something was about to come out of her mouth that would make him squirm. Sure enough. "We'll have to find you a local girl."

Just what he needed—Dot Morrison putting the word out that Jonathan Templar, computer nerd, was in the market for a local girl. He didn't want a local girl. He wanted…

"Tilda's still available."

Tilda Morrison, supercop? She could easily bench-press Jonathan. "Uh, thanks for the offer, but I think she needs someone tougher."

"There's a problem. Nobody's as tough as Tilda.

Damn, I raised that girl wrong. At this rate I'm never going to get grandchildren." Dot shrugged and reached for a cigarette. "Just as well, I suppose. I'd have to spend all my free hours baking cookies for the little rodents."

Sometimes it was hard to know whether or not Dot was serious, but this time Jonathan was sure she didn't mean what she'd said. She was only trying to make the best of motherly frustration. Dot wanted grandkids. Anyone who'd seen her interacting with the families who came into the restaurant could tell that. It was a wonder she made any money with all the free hot chocolate she slipped her younger patrons.

She lit up and took a deep drag on her cigarette. Her little office was about to get downright smoggy. Washington state law prohibited smoking in public places, but Dot maintained that her office wasn't a public place. Jonathan suspected one of these days she and the local health inspector were going to get into it over the cigarettes she sneaked in this room.

"I'd better get going," he said, gathering his things and trying not to inhale the secondhand smoke pluming in his direction.

"You gonna bill me as usual?"

"Yep."

"Don't gouge me," she teased.

"Wouldn't dream of it. And put your glasses on to read your bill this time," he teased back as he walked to the door. He always tried to give Dot a senior's discount and she always overpaid him, claiming she'd misread the bill. Yep, Dot was a great customer.

Heck, all his customers were great, he thought as he made his way to Sweet Dreams Chocolate Company, where Elena, the secretary, was having a nervous breakdown thanks to a new computer that she swore was possessed.

The scent of chocolate floating up from the kitchens below greeted him as he entered the office and Elena looked at him as if he were Saint George come to slay a dragon. "Thank God you're here."

People were always happy to see the owner and sole employee of Geek Gods Computer Services. Once Jonathan arrived on the scene, they knew their troubles would be fixed.

He liked that, liked feeling useful. So he wasn't a mountain of muscle like Luke Goodman, the production manager at Sweet Dreams, or a mover and shaker like Blake Preston, manager of Cascade Mutual. Some men were born to have starring roles and big, juicy parts on the stage of life. Others were meant to build scenery, pull the curtains, work in the background to make sure everything on stage ran well. Jonathan was a backstage kind of guy. Nothing wrong with that, he told himself. Background workers made it possible for the show to go on.

But leading ladies never noticed the guy in the background. Jonathan heaved a sigh. Sometimes he felt like Cyrano de Bergerac. Without the nose.

"This thing is making me loco," Elena said, glaring at the offending piece of technology on her desk.

The company owner, Samantha Sterling—recently married to Blake Preston—had just emerged from her office. "More loco than we make you?"

"More loco than even my mother makes me," Elena replied.

Samantha gave her shoulder a pat. "Jonathan will fix it."

Elena grunted. *"Equipo del infierno."*

"Computer from hell?" Jonathan guessed, remembering some of his high school Spanish.

Elena's frustrated scowl was all the answer he needed.

"Don't worry," Samantha told her. "Jonathan will help you battle the forces of technology evil. When Cecily comes in, tell her I'll be back around one-thirty. Try to keep my favorite assistant from tearing her hair out," she said to Jonathan.

"No worries," he said, then promised Elena, "I'll have this up and running for you in no time."

No time turned out to be about an hour, but since Elena had expected to lose the entire day she was delighted. "You are amazing," she told him just as Samantha's sister Cecily arrived on the scene.

"Has he saved us again?" she asked Elena, smiling at Jonathan.

"Yes, as usual."

Jonathan pushed his glasses back up his nose and tried to look modest. It was hard when people praised him like this.

But then, as he started to pack up his tools, Cecily said something that left him flat as a stingray. "I heard from Tina Swift that you guys have your fifteen-year reunion coming up."

"Uh, yeah."

"Those are so much fun, seeing old friends, people you used to date," she continued.

This was worse than Dot's cigarette smoke. Chatting with Cecily always made him self-conscious. Chatting with Cecily about his high school reunion would make him a nervous wreck, especially if she began asking about women he used to date. Jonathan hit high speed gathering up his tools and his various discs.

"Are you going to the reunion?" she asked him.

"Maybe," he lied, and hoped she'd leave it at that.

She didn't. "I moved back just in time for my ten-year and I'm glad I went. There were some people I wouldn't have had a chance to see otherwise."

There were some people Jonathan wanted to do more than see. Some people with long, blond hair and... He snapped his briefcase shut and bolted for the door. "So, Elena, I'll bill you."

"Okay," she called. The door hadn't quite shut behind him when he heard Elena say to Cecily, "He needs confidence, that one."

It was an embarrassing thing to hear about himself, but true. He needed a lot more than confidence, though. How could a guy be confident when he didn't have anything to be confident *about*?

By now it was time for lunch, so he grabbed some bratwurst and sauerkraut at Big Brats and settled in at one of the café tables in the stone courtyard adjacent to the popular sausage stand. This was a perfect day for outside dining. The sun warmed his back and a mountain breeze worked as a counterbalance to keep him from getting too hot. A cloudless sky provided a blue backdrop for the mountains.

During weekends the eating area was so crowded you had to take a number. Today, however, it was relatively quiet with only a few tables occupied.

Ed York, who owned D'Vine Wines, and Pat Wilder, who owned Mountain Escape Books, sauntered across the street to place an order. They stopped by Jonathan's table to say hello but didn't ask him to join them. No surprise. Pat and Ed had a thing going.

According to Jonathan's mom, Ed had been interested in Pat ever since he moved to Icicle Falls and opened his wine shop. But Pat had been mourning a husband and wasn't remotely interested. It looked like that was changing now. Watching Ed's romantic success kept the small flame of hope alive in Jonathan. Maybe, if a guy hung in there long enough, getting the woman of his dreams could become a reality.

Or maybe the guy was just wasting his life dreaming. Jonathan crumpled his napkin. Time to get back to work.

His next client was Gerhardt Geissel, who owned and ran Gerhardt's Gasthaus with his wife, Ingrid. Gerhardt was a short, husky, fifty-something man with gray hair and a round, florid face. He loved his wife's German cooking, loved his beer and was proud to celebrate his Tyrolean heritage by wearing lederhosen when he played the alpenhorn for his guests first thing every morning.

He played it even when he didn't have guests. Recently he'd gotten carried away celebrating his birthday and had decided to serenade his dinner guests after having one too many beers and had fallen off the ledge of the balcony outside the dining room. He'd fallen about twelve feet but fortunately had broken his arm instead of his back.

"Jonathan, *wie geht's?*" he greeted Jonathan, raising his cast-encased arm as Ingrid showed Jonathan into his office. "I hope you are here to solve all my problems."

"That is an impossible task," said his wife.

Gerhardt made a face. "See how she loves me."

His wife made a face right back at him and left. But she returned a few minutes later with a piece of Black Forest cake for Jonathan. "You're too skinny," she informed him. "You need to eat more."

"You need a wife to cook for you," her husband added.

"My youngest niece, Mary, lives just over in Wenatchee, and she's very pretty," Ingrid said.

"And very stupid." Gerhardt shook his head in disgust. "Jonathan's smart. He needs a smart woman."

"Mary is smart," Ingrid insisted. "She just makes bad choices."

"Well, uh, thanks," Jonathan said. "I appreciate the offer." Sometimes he wondered if everyone in Icicle Falls over the age of fifty wanted to match him up.

Heck, it wasn't only the older people. Even his sister had been known to take a hand, trying to introduce him to the latest someone she'd met and was sure would be perfect for him. Of course, those someones never were.

Gerhardt's computer problem was simple enough. Jonathan reloaded his operating system and he was done.

"You'd better get out of here before my wife comes back with Mary's phone number," Gerhardt advised after he'd written Jonathan a check.

Good idea. Jonathan left by the side door.

After leaving Gerhardt, he fit in two more clients and then headed home.

May's late-afternoon sun beamed its blessing on his three-bedroom log house at the end of Mountain View Road as he drove up. He'd originally planned for two bedrooms, but his folks had talked him into the extra one. "You have to have room for a wife and children," his mother had said. Good old Mom, always hopeful.

Fir and pine trees gave the house its rustic setting, while the pansies and begonias his mother and sister had put in the window boxes and the patch of lawn edged with more flowers added a homey touch. Someone pulling up in front might even think a woman lived there. They'd be wrong. The only female in this house had four legs.

But Jonathan often pictured the house with a wife and kids in it—the wife (a pretty blonde, naturally) cooking dinner while he and the kids played video games. He could see himself as an old man, sitting on the porch, playing chess with a grandson on the set he'd carved himself. The house would've, naturally, passed on to his own son, keeping the property in the family.

His grandpa had purchased this land as an investment when it was nothing more than a mountain meadow. Gramps could have made a tidy profit selling it, but instead he'd let Jonathan have it for a song when Jonathan turned twenty-five.

He'd started building his house when he was twenty-seven. A cousin who worked in construction in nearby Yakima had come over and helped him and Dad. Dad hadn't lived to see it finished. He'd had a heart attack just before the roof went on, leaving Jonathan on his own to finish both his house and his life.

Jonathan had become the man of the family, in charge of helping his mom, his grandmother and his sister cope. He'd been no help to his widowed grandmother, who had tried to outrun her loss by moving to Arizona. He hadn't been much help to his mom, either, beyond setting her up with a computer program so she could manage her finances. He'd tried to help Julia cope but he'd barely been able to cope himself. He should never have let Dad do all that hard physical work.

"Don't be silly," his mother always said. "Your father could just as easily have died on the golf course. He was doing what he wanted to do, helping you."

Helping his son be manly. The house was probably the one endeavor of Jonathan's that his father took pride in. It wasn't hard to figure out what kind of son Dad had really longed for. He'd never missed an Icicle Falls High football game, whether at home or away. How many times had he sat in the stands and wished his scrawny son was out there on the field or at least on the bench instead of playing in the band? Jonathan was glad that he had no idea.

"I love you, son," Dad had said when they were loading him into the ambulance. Those were the last words Jonathan heard and he was thankful for them. But he often found himself wishing his dad had said he was proud of him.

As he pulled up in his yellow Volkswagen with Geek Gods Computer Services printed on the side, his dog, Chica, abandoned her spot on the front porch and raced down the stairs to greet him, barking a welcome. Chica was an animal-shelter find, part shepherd, part Lab and part...whatever kind of dog had a curly tail. She'd been with Jonathan for five years and she thought he was a god (and didn't care if he *was* a geek).

He got out of the car and the dog started jumping like she had springs on her paws. It was nice to have some female go crazy over him. "Hey, girl," he greeted her. "We'll get some dinner and then play fetch."

He exchanged his slacks for the comfort of his old baggy jeans, and his business shirt for a T-shirt sporting a nerdy pun that cautioned Don't Drink and Derive. Then, after a feast of canned spaghetti for Jonathan and some Doggy's Delight for Chica, it was time for a quick game of fetch. It had to be quick because tonight was Friday, poker night, and the guys would be coming over at seven. Poker, another manly pursuit. Dad would have been proud.

* * *

The first to arrive was his pal Kyle Long. Kyle and Jonathan had been friends since high school. They'd both been members of the chess club and had shared an addiction to old sci-fi movies and video games.

Kyle didn't exactly fit his name. He was short. His hair was a lighter shade than Jonathan's dark brown—nothing spectacular, rather like his face.

His ordinary face didn't bug him nearly as much as his lack of stature. "Women don't look at short guys," he often grumbled. And short guys who (like Jonathan) weren't so confident and quick with the flattery—well, they really didn't get noticed, even by girls their own height. This had been a hard cross to bear in high school when it seemed that every girl Kyle liked chose some giant basketball player over him. These days the competition wore a different type of uniform, the one worn to the office, but his frustration level remained the same.

The grumpy expression on his face tonight said it all before he so much as opened his mouth. "What's with chicks, anyway?" he demanded as he set a six-pack of Hale's Ale on Jonathan's counter.

If Jonathan knew that, he'd be married to the woman of his dreams by now. He shrugged.

"Okay, so Darrow looks like friggin' Ryan Reynolds."

Ted Darrow, Kyle's nemesis. "And drives a Jag," Jonathan supplied. Darrow was also Kyle's boss, which put him higher up the ladder of success, always a sexy attribute.

"But he's the world's biggest ass-wipe," Kyle said with a scowl. "I don't know what Jillian sees in him."

Jonathan knew. Like called to like. Beautiful people naturally gravitated to one another. He had seen Jillian when he'd gone to Kyle's company, Safe Hands Insurance, to install their new computer system. As the receptionist, it had been her job to greet him and he'd seen right away why his friend was smitten. She was hot, with supermodel-long legs. Women like that went for the Ted Darrows of the world.

Or the Rand Burwells.

Jonathan shoved that last thought out of his mind. "Hey, you might as well give up. You're not gonna get her." It was hard to say that to his best friend, but friends didn't let friends drive themselves crazy over women who were out of their league. Kyle would do the same for him—if he knew Jonathan had suffered a relapse last Christmas and had once again picked up the torch for his own perfect dream girl. The road to crazy was a clogged thoroughfare these days.

Kyle heaved a discouraged sigh. "Yeah." He pulled an opener out of a kitchen drawer and popped the top off one of the bottles. "It's just that, well, damn. If she looked my way for longer than two seconds, she'd see I'm twice the man Darrow is."

"I hear you," Jonathan said, and opened a bag of corn chips, setting them alongside the beer.

Next in the door was Bernardo Ruiz, who came bearing some of his wife's homemade salsa. Bernardo was happily married and owned a small orchard outside town, in which he took great pride. He wasn't much taller than Kyle, but he swaggered like he was six feet.

"Who died?" he asked, looking from one friend to the other.

"Nobody," Kyle snapped.

Bernardo eyed him suspiciously. "You mooning around over that bimbo at work again?"

"She's not a bimbo," Kyle said irritably.

Bernardo shook his head in disgust. "Little man, you are a fool to chase after a woman who doesn't want you. That kind of a woman, she'll only make you feel small on the inside."

Any reference to being small, either on the inside or outside, never went over well with Kyle, so it was probably a good thing that Adam Edwards arrived with more beer and chips. A sales rep for a pharmaceutical company, he earned more than Jonathan and Kyle put together and had the toys to prove it—a big house on the river, a classic Corvette, a snowmobile and a beach house on the Washington coast. He also had a pretty little wife, which proved Jonathan's theory of like calling to like, since Adam was tall and broad-shouldered and looked as though he belonged in Hollywood instead of Icicle Falls. Some guys had all the luck.

"Vance'll be late," Adam informed them. "He has to finish up something and says to go ahead and start without him."

Vance Fish, the newest member of their group, was somewhere in his fifties, which made him the senior member. He'd built a big house on River Road about a mile down from Adam's place. The two men had bonded over fishing lures, and Adam had invited him to join their poker group.

Although Vance claimed to be semiretired, he was always working. He owned a bookstore in Seattle called Emerald City Books. He'd recently started selling Sweet Dreams Chocolates there, making himself popular with the Sterling family, who owned the company.

He dressed like he was on his last dime, usually in sweats or jeans and an oversize black T-shirt that hung clumsily over his double-XL belly, but his fancy house was proof that Vance was doing okay.

"That means we won't see him for at least an hour," Kyle predicted.

"What kind of project?" Bernardo wondered. "Is he building something over there in that fine house of his? I never seen no tools or workbench in his garage."

"It has to do with the bookstore," Adam said. "I don't know what."

"Well, all the better for me," Kyle said gleefully. "I'll have you guys fleeced by the time he gets here." He rubbed his hands together. "I'm feeling lucky tonight."

He proved it by raking in their money.

"Bernardo, you should just empty your pockets on the table as soon as you get here," Adam joked. "I've never seen anybody so unlucky at cards."

"That's because I'm lucky in love," Bernardo insisted.

His remark wiped the victory smirk right off Kyle's face. "Chicks," he muttered.

"If you're going where I think you're going, don't," Adam said, frowning at him.

"What?" Kyle protested.

Adam pointed his beer bottle at Kyle. "If I hear one more word about Jillian, I'm gonna club you with this."

"Oh, no," said a deep voice. "I thought you clowns would be done talking about women by now."

Jonathan turned to see Vance strolling into the room, stylish as ever in his favorite black T-shirt, baggy jeans and sandals. In honor of the occasion he hadn't shaved. Aside from the extra pounds (well, and that bald spot on the top of his head), he wasn't too bad-looking. His sandy hair was shot with gray but he had the craggy brow and strong jaw women seemed to like even in a big man. They were wasted on Vance; he wasn't interested. "Been there, done that," he often said.

"We're finished talking about women," Adam assured him.

Vance clapped him on the back. "Glad to hear it, 'cause the last thing I want after a hard day's work is to listen to you losers crab about them."

"I wasn't crabbing," Kyle said, looking sullen.

Vance sat down at the table. "It's that babe where you work, isn't it? She got your jockeys tight again?" Kyle glared at him, but Vance waved off his anger with a pudgy paw. "You know, women can sense desperation a mile away. It's a turnoff."

"And I guess you'd be an expert on what turns women off," Adam teased.

"There isn't a man on this planet who's an expert on anything about women. And if you meet one who says he is, he's lying. Now, let's play poker." Vance eyed the pile of chips in front of Kyle. "You need to be relieved of some of those, my friend."

"I think not," Kyle said, and the game began in earnest.

After an hour and a half, Vance announced that he had to tap a kidney.

"I need some chips and salsa," Adam said, and everyone took a break.

"Did you get the announcement in the mail?" Kyle asked Jonathan.

No, not this again.

"What announcement?" Adam asked.

"High school reunion," Kyle said. "Fifteen years."

Jonathan had gotten the cutesy little postcard with the picture of a grizzly bear, the Icicle Falls High mascot, lumbering across one corner. And of course, the first thing he'd thought was, maybe Lissa will come. That had taken his spirits on a hot-air balloon ride. Until he'd had another thought. *You'll still be the Invisible Man.* That had brought the balloon back down.

"Yeah, I got it," he said. "I'm not going." But Rand probably would. Rand and Lissa, together again.

Now his balloon ride was not only over, the balloon was in a swamp infested with alligators. And poker night was a bust.

Just like his love life.

Two

Poker night hadn't ended well for Kyle. Vance, the old buzzard, had picked him clean. And that set the tone for the weekend.

Saturday was nothing but chores and errands. He filled the evening playing *War on Planet X* with a bunch of online gamers, which left him feeling unsatisfied. He was getting too old for this crap. He needed more in his life. It seemed like everybody was getting paired up but him.

He was even more aware of this fact when he went over to his folks' house for Sunday dinner and learned that his baby sister had gotten engaged. Of course he'd seen it coming for months and he was happy for her. But now it was official—he was the last of the three siblings left unattached. And Kerrie was four years younger, which didn't help. Neither did remarks like, "We have to find somebody for Kyle." He didn't need his baby sister finding someone for him.

He'd found someone. All he had to do was make her realize he was the man for her.

Well, the weekend was over and it was a new day. TGIM—Thank God It's Monday. He walked through the glass doors of Safe Hands Insurance Company and into the lobby with its modern paintings, the strategically placed metal sculpture of two giant hands stretched out in a gesture of insurance paternalism, and plants that looked like they'd escaped from an African jungle. He kept his eyes front and center, because there, straight ahead, was the receptionist's desk.

Behind it sat a vision. Jillian. She had long, reddish-blond hair that she tossed over her shoulder when she talked, full, glossy lips he dreamed of kissing, a perfect nose and sky-blue eyes. *Blind* sky-blue eyes. One of these days she was going to see him, really see him. Maybe even this morning.

He sure saw everything about her. Today she was wearing a white blouse that plunged in a V pointing to her breasts—as if a man needed any help finding them—and she'd worn a necklace made up of glass baubles to fill the gap between neck and heaven. She'd tucked her hair behind her ears, showing off dangly earrings that matched the necklace. She had a funny little habit of tapping her pencil on the desk as she talked on the phone, which she was doing now. The call only lasted a moment. She pushed a button and sent the caller on, probably to one of the bosses. Such an efficient woman.

Now she smiled as she caught sight of him walking down the hall in his gray slacks and his white Oxford shirt, his hair slicked into the latest style (at least according to the new barber he'd gone to at Sweeney Todd Barbershop—the one highlight of his weekend). He puffed out his chest and donned his best smile. He did have a good smile; even his sisters said so.

Oh, man, look at the way her eyes lit up at the sight

of him. It was the hair, had to be. He forced his chest to swell to its fullest capacity.

Look at that smile. She had a great smile and she used it a lot. When a woman smiled a lot, it meant she was happy and easygoing. That was exactly the kind of woman Kyle wanted.

He was almost at her desk when he realized they weren't making eye contact. She was looking beyond him.

Then he heard a rich tenor voice behind him say, "Jillian, you're especially beautiful this fine morning."

Ted Darrow, the ass-wipe. Kyle's supervisor. Kyle could feel his smile shrinking even as he shrank inside. He mumbled a hello to Jillian and slunk by her desk.

"IIi," she said absently as he passed. Then for Ted it was a sexy, "Hi, Ted."

"Hi, Ted," Kyle mimicked under his breath as he strode to his cubicle. Jillian shouldn't waste her breath saying hello to that fathead. Men like that, they flirted with women, they used women, but they didn't appreciate women. Kyle flung himself into his chair with a growl.

"Starting the day off well, I see," said a soft voice from the cubicle next door.

Unlike *some people,* Mindy Wright always had the decency to acknowledge his existence. It didn't make him feel any better, though. Mindy was no Jillian.

"Hi, Mindy." His hello probably sounded grudging, so he added, "How was your weekend?"

"Well, it was interesting."

Mindy had been trolling the internet for her perfect match. So far she'd hauled in a truck driver who was ten years older than she was and about forty pounds heavier than he'd looked in his picture on the dating site, a man who claimed to be a churchgoer but hadn't gone in two—okay, make it five—years, a shrink who Mindy said was the most screwed-up person she'd ever had dinner with and someone who'd seemed like a great catch until she learned he had no job. "And he wasn't planning on finding one anytime soon, either," Mindy had confessed. "He's writing a book."

"Oh, well, that's good," Kyle had said, trying to put a positive spin on the latest loser.

"About mushrooms."

"Bound to be a bestseller."

That had made her laugh. Kyle made Mindy laugh a lot. If only he could work up his nerve to ask Jillian out. He was sure he could make her laugh, too. But so far, his attempts to get her attention had all been thwarted.

Shakespeare had it right. The course of true love never did run smooth. For Kyle, it seemed to run into nothing but dead ends.

At least Mindy was getting some action. "So, who'd you go out with this weekend?" he asked.

"No one I want to keep, that's for sure. I think I'm done looking."

"Hey, you can't give up. Your perfect man may be right around the next corner."

"The next internet corner?" She peeked around the cubicle wall, a grin on her face.

It was an okay face, fringed with dark hair and deco-rated with glasses, a turned-up little nose that made him think of Drew Barrymore and a small chin that seemed to sport a zit once a month. (What was with that, any-way?) As for the bod, well, not a ten like Jillian. Still, she was pretty nice. Someone would want her.

"Yeah," he said. "The next internet corner. Or maybe

at the Red Barn." If you wanted cold beer and hot music, that was the place to go.

She shook her head. "I haven't gone there in a long time." Then she disappeared back behind the cubicle wall.

"Why's that?" he asked, booting up his computer.

"Too much competition."

"I know what you mean." Funny how the walls of an office cubicle could make you feel like you were in a confessional, willing to say things you wouldn't share face-to-face. Not that he'd been in the confessional for a while.

Maybe he needed to spend some time there. And maybe he should be talking to God more. God saw him, even if Jillian didn't. Maybe God would consider working a miracle and opening Jillian's eyes. At the rate things were going here at Safe Hands, improving her eyesight was going to *take* a miracle.

It was nine o'clock and time for Jonathan's morning ritual. He grabbed his bowl of cereal with sliced banana and turned on the TV to a station in Oregon. "Barely made it in time," he told Chica, who'd settled on the couch beside him. "We shouldn't have taken such a long walk."

Her only response to that was a big yawn.

"You know, you've got a bad attitude," he said.

She let out a bark.

"And you're jealous," he added, making her whine. He put an arm around her and gave her head a good rub. "But I'll keep you, anyway."

The commercial for laser skin treatment ended and Chica was forgotten as an image of the city of Portland came on the screen, accompanied by perky music. A disembodied voice called out, "Good morning, Oregon!"

Then there she was—trim, blonde and beautiful—seated at a couch in a fake living room next to a gray-haired guy wearing slacks and an expensive shirt.

Scott Lawrence. Jonathan frowned at the sight of him. Media guys, they were just too smooth. *Now who's jealous?*

He was, of course. Talk about stupid. In order to be jealous of other men, you first had to be with the woman. Jonathan was not with Lissa Castle, never had been.

"Well, Lissa, I'm sure your weekend was stellar," Scott said to her.

"Yes, it was." She had such a sweet voice, so full of cheer and kindness. Lissa had always been kind.

"Did you have a hot date?" Scott teased. "What am I saying? Of course you had a hot date."

She neither denied nor confirmed, just sat in her leather chair and smiled like the Mona Lisa in a pink blouse.

Which meant she'd had a hot date, Jonathan deduced miserably.

Her cohost turned to face the camera. "Speaking of dates, some of you out there in our viewing audience might be doing internet dating and finding it frustrating."

"It can be stressful when it comes time to meet that other person off-line," Lissa said. "And that's why I know you're going to appreciate our first guest this morning, who'll be sharing tips with us on how to transition from online to face time."

Sometimes even face time didn't win a girl, Jonathan thought sadly, not when the girl was out of a guy's league.

He'd been in love with Lissa ever since he'd discovered girls. In fact, Lissa had been the first girl he discovered when she moved in next door at the age of nine. They'd become pals, which was great when he was nine. But as they got older and she got even prettier, Jonathan began to look beyond the borders of friendship.

He wasn't the only one. During high school, his friend Rand took a new interest in Lissa once she became a cheerleader. And she was interested right back. Hardly surprising, since Rand was the cool one. When they were kids, everyone had fought over Rand while picking teams for playground softball games. In high school he'd been captain of the football team. The boys all wanted to be his bud and the girls all looked at him like he was a free trip to Disneyland.

As for Jonathan, he was captain of…the chess team, and hardly any girls looked at him at all. Not that he'd wanted any girl but Lissa.

No matter what he'd done, though, he couldn't win her interest. She always thought of him simply as her good friend.

He'd wanted to be more. When they were juniors, in the hopes of getting her to see him in a new way, he'd sneaked into Icicle Falls High early on Valentine's Day and taped a hundred red paper hearts to her locker.

But she'd thought Rand had done it. Rand happily took the credit and took Lissa to the junior prom. And Jonathan took a swing at Rand. And that was the end of their friendship.

But not the end of Rand and Lissa. They were an item clear through senior year.

As for Jonathan, he wasn't an item with anyone. He'd

tried, gone out with a few girls as desperate as he was, but every time he'd closed his eyes and kissed a girl he'd seen Lissa.

After everyone graduated and scattered he still saw her on holidays when she was in town visiting her parents and he was over at his folks' next door. Once in a while they'd talk. He'd say brilliant things like, "How's it going?" and she'd ask him questions like, "Anyone special in your life yet?" He'd never had the guts to say, "There's been someone special in my life since I was nine."

When his dad died, she'd sent him a card telling him how sorry she was. Mostly, though, she just waved to him while hurrying down her front walk to catch up with girlfriends. He'd tried not to see when she left on the arm of the latest local whose attention she'd captured.

A couple of summers ago, he'd seen her when she came home to surprise her mom for her birthday. He'd been at his mom's, up on a ladder painting the side of the house, when she called a cheery hello from next door.

He'd almost lost his balance at the sound of her voice.

"Jonathan Templar, paint specialist. And I thought you were only a computer genius," she'd teased from the other side of the hedge that ran between their houses.

He'd had a perfect view of her from his perch on the ladder and the view was great. She'd looked like a cover girl for a summer issue of some women's magazine in her pink top and white shorts.

"That, too," he'd said, then asked, "Are you in town for long?"

"Only the weekend."

He knew what that meant. This moment was all he'd have with her.

"We've got Mom's big birthday dinner tonight. Then brunch tomorrow and then I've got to get back to Portland. I don't think I'll even have time to bake you any cookies. How sad is that?" Before he could answer, her cell phone had rung. "I know, I'm on my way," she'd said, and ended the call. "I'm late, as usual," she'd said to Jonathan. "I'd better get going. Good to see you, Jonathan. You look great." Then she'd hurried off down her front walk, her long, blond hair swinging.

That hadn't been the only thing swinging. Watching her hips as she walked away had been hypnotic, addictive. And dumb.

Jonathan had leaned over to keep her in view just a little longer and lost his balance. With a startled cry, he'd grabbed for the ladder but only succeeded in bringing the bucket of paint down on himself as he fell, turning him blue from head to toe. A one-man Blue Man Group act.

He'd bruised his hip in the process, but his ego had taken an even bigger hit when Lissa came running to where he'd fallen. "Jonathan, are you okay?"

He'd been far from okay. He'd been mortified, his face probably red under the blue paint. But he'd said, "Oh, yeah. No problem. I'm fine."

Then his mom had come out and started fussing over him and that had been the final humiliation. He'd tried to wash his clothes and turned his underwear baby blue, and it had taken him days to get the last of the paint off. Bits of it stubbornly lingered under his fingernails to remind him of what a dork he was. Well, that and the blue undies. Lissa did find time to bake him cookies. She'd dropped them by his place on her way out of town.

He'd tried to play it cool by leaning one hand against

the door frame but had missed the mark and nearly lost his balance. Again.

She'd pretended not to notice. "I just stopped by to make sure you didn't break anything."

"Naw, I'm fine." His briefs were another story, but he wisely kept that bit of information to himself.

"That's good," she said, handing over the paper plate of goodies. "But if you *had* broken something, I'd have signed your cast."

Would you have kissed it and made it all better? That had been an unusually clever remark. Too bad he hadn't thought of it until she was long gone. But even if he had, he'd have never gotten up the nerve to say it. Instead, he'd said, "Then I'd have to save the cast 'cause your signature will probably be valuable someday."

That had made her smile and making her smile had made his day.

"See you soon," she'd called as she got in her car.

"Yeah, see you," he'd called back.

And he had ever since, every day on TV. He'd liked her on Facebook, too, not that she'd noticed. It wasn't much, but it was all he had and it was better than nothing. Barely.

"I wonder if she's coming to the reunion," he mused.

Next to him Chica whined.

"Yeah, you're right, what does it matter?" Jonathan muttered. These days she was way too busy to hang out with nerdy guys she'd hung with as a kid. And if he went to the reunion, history would repeat itself and the high school hunks would squeeze him out.

He listened as the guest expert talked about how to make a first date with an internet match-up successful. If only there was an expert out there who could help a guy have a successful encounter with a woman he'd known all his life.

"I can't keep just seeing her this way," he said to Chica. "And I can't go on doing nothing. She won't stay single forever."

As if, when she finally walked down the aisle, it would be to him! "You're dreaming," he told himself.

Well, so what if he was? A man needed dreams, needed to think big. *Go big or go home.*

Oh, yeah. He was already home. Forget about it, he advised himself.

The morning show ended and Jonathan turned off the TV, leaving Chica in charge of yard patrol and napping, and then got in his car and drove down the long, gravel road toward town. He passed a few large lots with big houses on them, but mostly here, in his neck of the woods, the land remained dense with trees and brush.

He liked it that way. Jonathan Templar, rugged mountain man. Well, mountain man, anyway.

The town itself looked picturesque on this sunny morning. The window boxes and hanging planters that decorated the quaint Bavarian-style buildings overflowed with red geraniums and pink and white begonias. And with the mountains rising up behind, he could almost believe he was somewhere in the German Alps. A few people were stirring, some running errands, some visiting, others sweeping off the sidewalks in front of their shops.

It sure wasn't New York or Seattle but that was okay with Jonathan. Icicle Falls was perfect the way it was. Who would want to live anywhere else?

Lissa Castle, that was who. Would she ever give up her TV career and move back to Icicle Falls? Probably not. Would he say goodbye to this beautiful place and follow her wherever her career led? In a heartbeat, if only she'd ask him.

Even a man caught in the net of unrequited love had to think about other things once in a while. Jonathan parked his car on Center Street and turned his mind to business.

He had plenty to keep him busy the rest of the morning, so busy in fact that he wound up working clear through lunch. He found himself with twenty minutes to kill before he had to be at Mountain Escape Books to work on Pat Wilder's computer, so he decided to duck into Bavarian Brews for a quick pick-me-up.

The aroma of coffee kissed his taste buds as he walked in. Yes, he was probably going to go a million years without sex, might never connect with the woman of his dreams, but at least he had coffee.

Coffee. Sex. Was there really any comparison? Jonathan frowned at the thought of what he was settling for in life. Cecily Sterling came in right behind him. "Hi, Jonathan. You need a caffeine fix, too?" she asked as they got in line to place their orders.

"Yeah," he said, showing off his suave to the most beautiful woman in Icicle Falls. Jonathan Templar, lady killer.

He was racking his brain to come up with something clever to say when Todd Black, who had just entered the coffee shop, stepped confidently into the conversation. "By this time of day, who doesn't need a hit?"

Cecily rolled her eyes at him. "You make it sound like you've been up for hours."

Todd owned the Man Cave, a tavern on the edge of town. He kept late hours and so was bound to sleep late.

"I was up early this morning doing the books. Not easy after a hard day's night."

"I'm sure you work very hard watching over your kingdom of Kahlua," she sneered.

"It's not a bad kingdom. By the way, Kahlua and chocolate go well together. Bring me some more of yours and I'll prove it."

"I'll take your word for it."

Jonathan had been standing in line behind Cecily, but somehow Todd managed to cut in front of him. He watched with a mixture of irritation and envy as Todd leaned in close to her and said, "One of these days you're going to watch some sappy movie where the couple is dancing real slow and you're going to remember my offer to give you a tango lesson."

She shook her head and moved away a step. He closed the distance.

Oh, this was a master in action. Jonathan eavesdropped shamelessly.

"Or you're going to get an urge to come check out the action on my pinball machine. You said you were good but so far you haven't proved it."

"I don't have to prove anything to you." She turned to look at him and they almost brushed lips.

"You're invading my space," she said, frowning.

"I bet that's not all I'm invading. How you sleeping these days, Cecily? Do you get hot? Throw off the covers?"

Her cheeks went pink. "I sleep fine, thanks." She took two giant steps away and placed her order, leaving Todd with a confident smirk on his face.

Jenni, the barista, whipped up Cecily's coconut mocha latte and set it on the counter, but Cecily chose that moment to send a text on her cell phone. Todd's drink order came up and she put away her phone and picked up her to-go cup. They stood trading words that,

Jonathan suspected, had secret messages attached, then, with her cheeks even pinker, she left the coffee shop. Todd watched her go, smiling like a man who'd just landed a fish and was now contemplating how he'd cook it.

Speaking of cooking, there'd been enough current zipping back and forth between those two to light the giant fir tree in the town square at Christmas and the rest of the town, too. How did guys like Todd manage to stir up a woman's hormones with nothing more than a few well-chosen words? Jonathan wished he knew.

The only way to find out was to ask.

Todd was about to saunter out the door. Jonathan grabbed his drink and hurried after him. "Uh, Todd. Can I ask you something?"

Todd turned, an easy smile on his face, his brows raised. "Sure. What?"

"How do you do that?"

The brows knit. "Do what?"

Okay, maybe he didn't want to have this conversation in the middle of Bavarian Brews. He opened the door and motioned that they should go out on the street. Once outside he wasn't sure how to frame his question.

"What's on your mind, computer man?" Todd prompted him.

"I was watching you with Cecily. You're smooth."

Todd shrugged and took a drink of coffee.

"How do you do it? How do you know what to say?"

"I just say what comes into my head." Todd watched Cecily running across the street toward Sweet Dreams. "She likes being chased. But you know what? She's about ready to let me catch her, and she's going to like getting caught even more." The smile on his face oozed confidence.

Well, Jonathan would have confidence, too, if he looked like Johnny Depp's kid brother. He realized he was frowning. He probably looked like a pitiful loser.

"Woman troubles?" Todd guessed.

"Always."

"Yeah, well, women and trouble go together." He clapped Jonathan on the back. "But you've got to hang in there. Never give up. That's what Winston Churchill said, and he saved England in World War II."

Jonathan nodded and trudged off down the street. Winston Churchill only had to save England. Jonathan wanted to win Lissa Castle. And he didn't look like Todd Black.

He was halfway to the bookstore when he saw Tina Swift coming down the sidewalk from the other direction. Tina was recently divorced and had half the men in town sniffing after her. Hardly surprising, considering how cute she was.

Cute and stuck-up. She'd been in his class, a cheerleader and a member of the top social tier at Icicle Falls High. She'd never paid any attention to Jonathan then or in the twelve years after graduation. It was only once she'd opened a shop that sold imported lace and china three years ago and needed someone to design a website that she'd remembered his existence.

Now she'd spotted him and was smiling as if they were buds, which meant she wanted something. And it sure wasn't a date.

Jonathan pretended not to see and crossed the street.

Undeterred, she called his name and ran after him.

Okay, he gave up. He stopped.

She hardly allowed him time to say a self-conscious hello before asking, "Did you get your reunion invitation?"

"Uh, yeah."

"I hope you put the date on the calendar."

"Well," he began.

She didn't let him finish. "It's going to be even better than the ten-year. We've already heard from a ton of people. Cam Gordon…"

Football fathead and snob. There's someone I want to see.

"Feron Prince…"

The Prince of Darkness. He stuffed me in a locker when we were freshmen.

"Kyle Long. He was a friend of yours, wasn't he?"

"Still is." And Jonathan didn't need to go to the reunion to see him.

"I think Rand is coming."

Which meant Jonathan wouldn't be, for sure.

"Did you know he got married?"

Married? Jonathan smiled. "No." So Rand was out of circulation. Well, well.

"Oh, and we just heard from Lissa Castle, our very own celebrity. She's definitely coming."

Rand was out of circulation and Lissa was coming. Was he imagining it or were the stars aligning? (Whatever that meant.) If he went to the reunion, he'd have a whole weekend of close proximity to Lissa. Maybe he could separate her from her adoring fans long enough to talk with her, impress her, maybe even dance with her. Except he couldn't dance.

"Jonathan?"

Tina was looking at him, eyebrows raised.

He pulled himself back into the present. "What?"

"Like I just said, I was hoping you could help me out with a couple of things. We want a website for the reunion, and I thought maybe you wouldn't mind making one. You do such good work. And you did a wonderful job designing the webpage for the chocolate festival."

But that had been something he *wanted* to do. This, not so much.

"We could put a bunch of pictures from the yearbook up there, along with any current ones we get. Have a place for people to post. You know, that sort of thing."

"You could just do that on Facebook," he said, hoping to dodge this assignment.

"Oh, great idea! Could you do that, too?"

Wait a minute. He hadn't said yes and already she'd doubled his work, and none of it was anything he would get paid for.

But how to say no to a pretty woman? Jonathan didn't have a clue.

"Oh, *please* say yes. I need a tech wizard."

"I guess I could." What the heck. She was going to wear him down, anyway, and they both knew it.

He sighed inwardly. Now he could hear all about how successful his former classmates had been, see pictures of their wives and kids. Yuck.

Meanwhile, here was Tina, gushing away. "Fabulous! Thank you, Jonathan. You are just…"

A sucker.

"…the best."

The best geek. Nothing wrong with being a geek, he reminded himself. It had worked fine for Bill Gates.

"I should get going," Tina said. "I'm late for the committee meeting. But I'm so glad I ran into you."

Yeah, him, too. Before he could say anything, sarcastic or otherwise, she was hurrying off down the sidewalk.

Jonathan continued on toward the bookstore, deep in thought. Lissa would be back for the reunion in August. Now that Rand was married, maybe he stood a chance of at least getting her attention for a few minutes.

Realistically, that was about all he'd get. She'd been way too popular, and practically everyone else would want to hang with her. Still, he and Lissa had known each other for years. Surely she'd want to visit with him, too.

But simply visiting wasn't going to cut it. He had to figure out a way to shake things up, make an impression.

Hmm. Following that line of thought to its logical conclusion... If he wanted to make an impression, he had to come up with a plan.

His earlier conversation with Todd Black returned for a visit. *You've got to hang in there.*

He pulled his smartphone out of his jeans pocket and looked up Winston Churchill's famous quote. *"Never, never, never, never give up."* What chance did he have of winning Lissa's love? About one in a million. If he didn't even try? None.

He squared his shoulders. He was not going to give up. Somehow he was going to find a way to transform himself from zero to hero, find a way to make her see that her truest childhood friend could also be her truest love.

But how?

He needed a love coach.

* * * * *

WHAT SHE WANTS by Sheila Roberts
is available now in print and eBook formats
from MIRA

REQUEST YOUR FREE BOOKS!

2 FREE NOVELS
FROM THE ROMANCE COLLECTION
PLUS 2 FREE GIFTS!

YES! Please send me 2 FREE novels from the Romance Collection and my 2 FREE gifts (gifts are worth about $10). After receiving them, if I don't wish to receive any more books, I can return the shipping statement marked "cancel." If I don't cancel, I will receive 4 brand-new novels every month and be billed just $6.24 per book in the U.S. or $6.74 per book in Canada. That's a savings of at least 22% off the cover price. It's quite a bargain! Shipping and handling is just 50¢ per book in the U.S. and 75¢ per book in Canada.* I understand that accepting the 2 free books and gifts places me under no obligation to buy anything. I can always return a shipment and cancel at any time. Even if I never buy another book, the two free books and gifts are mine to keep forever.

194/394 MDN F4XY

Name _____ (PLEASE PRINT)

Address _____ Apt. #

City _____ State/Prov. _____ Zip/Postal Code

Signature (if under 18, a parent or guardian must sign)

Mail to the **Harlequin® Reader Service:**
IN U.S.A.: P.O. Box 1867, Buffalo, NY 14240-1867
IN CANADA: P.O. Box 609, Fort Erie, Ontario L2A 5X3

Want to try two free books from another line?
Call 1-800-873-8635 or visit www.ReaderService.com.

* Terms and prices subject to change without notice. Prices do not include applicable taxes. Sales tax applicable in N.Y. Canadian residents will be charged applicable taxes. Offer not valid in Quebec. This offer is limited to one order per household. Not valid for current subscribers to the Romance Collection or the Romance/Suspense Collection. All orders subject to credit approval. Credit or debit balances in a customer's account(s) may be offset by any other outstanding balance owed by or to the customer. Please allow 4 to 6 weeks for delivery. Offer available while quantities last.

Your Privacy—The Harlequin® Reader Service is committed to protecting your privacy. Our Privacy Policy is available online at www.ReaderService.com or upon request from the Harlequin Reader Service.

We make a portion of our mailing list available to reputable third parties that offer products we believe may interest you. If you prefer that we not exchange your name with third parties, or if you wish to clarify or modify your communication preferences, please visit us at www.ReaderService.com/consumerschoice or write to us at Harlequin Reader Service Preference Service, P.O. Box 9062, Buffalo, NY 14269. Include your complete name and address.